Praise for
All the Bells on Earth

"**With acrobatic grace,** Blaylock, winner of two World Fantasy Awards, once again walks the dividing line between fantasy and horror. Blaylock's gentle satire on 'capitalism gone rancid' is supported by his authentic rendering of a small town . . . While the author probes the dark side of small town life, he ultimately celebrates the virtues of simple living."

—*Publishers Weekly*

"**Blaylock's blend of the mundane and the macabre** makes for an absolute page-turner, at once reminiscent of C. S. Lewis's *That Hideous Strength* and Clive Barker's urban fantasies."

—*Washington Post Book World*

"**Blaylock is better than anyone else** at showing us the magic that secretly animates our world."

—Tim Powers

"**[Has] a warm-hearted quirkiness** that will particularly delight fans of Blaylock's earlier books."

—*Locus*

"**Blaylock is a true American original.**"

—Bruce Sterling

"**Satisfying** . . . A steady and well-appointed yarn."

—*Kirkus Reviews*

Continued . . .

Night Relics
a ghost story

"**A first-rate atmospheric tale of the supernatural,** with well-drawn characters and plenty of shivery moments. It is thoroughly satisfying, memorable, and the best thing James Blaylock has written."

—Dean Koontz

"**A powerful story** full of creepy moments, made meaningful by a cast of well-drawn characters, living and dead . . . World Fantasy Award–winner James Blaylock explores the power of memory and the influence of the past from a very different perspective."

—*Washington Post Book World*

"**A ghost story with the fever-dream logic of nightmare** . . . Dark currents of sexuality, anger, jealousy, and longing run through this tale, mingling with its potent landscapes to produce something more powerful than anything Blaylock has achieved before."

—*Locus*

"**Quietly creepy events,** an understated element of mystery, and a really twisted villain. The result is a very fine story that will leave a series of haunting images with the reader."

—*Science Fiction Chronicle*

"**Tantalizing** . . . A fresh take on the ghost story which should prove very satisfying to both Blaylock fans and new readers alike."

—*The Scream Factory*

The Last Coin

"**Refreshingly natural lunacy** . . . this is his finest book to date."
—Bruce Sterling

"**Hilarious** . . . *The Last Coin* should confirm Blaylock's position as a trendsetter, breaking new ground rather than just exploring the old."
—*San Francisco Chronicle*

"**A quirkily poetic vision** . . . this book is an achievement that demonstrates Blaylock is well on his way to taking a place among the first rank of American novelists."
—Lucius Shepard

"**A gleeful farce** . . . strange and wonderful."
—*Publishers Weekly*

"**Weird, oddball charm** . . . peopled with the kind of characters usually found in a John Irving novel."
—*Booklist*

"**One of the best books I have ever read.** This is Blaylock at the height of his ability, dazzling us with cosmic mysteries one second, paralyzing us with laughter the next."
—Lewis Shiner

Continued . . .

The Paper Grail

"Delightful and original."
—Publishers Weekly

"A wry celebration of humanity at its quirkiest."
—Locus

"No one should be spared the unique perversity of Jim Blaylock's world view."
—Robin McKinley

"Blaylock allows us to see the mundane world through new eyes, to perceive familiar as strange and therefore fascinating."
—Charles DeLint, *OtherRealms*

"Blaylock is an original author grounded in the quintessential classics, yet ready without notice to astonish."
—Philip K. Dick

"A master of domestic surrealism."
—James Morrow

"A serious talent in contemporary fantasy."
—Roland Green, *Booklist*

"Blaylock is a magician."
—Michael Swanwick

All the Bells on Earth

⊰ ⊱

Ace Books by James P. Blaylock

THE DIGGING LEVIATHAN
HOMUNCULUS
LAND OF DREAMS
THE STONE GIANT
THE LAST COIN
THE PAPER GRAIL
LORD KELVIN'S MACHINE
NIGHT RELICS
ALL THE BELLS ON EARTH
WINTER TIDES

All the Bells
on Earth

James P. Blaylock

ACE BOOKS, NEW YORK

This Ace Book contains the complete text of the original hardcover edition. It has been completely reset in a typeface designed for easy reading, and was printed from new film.

ALL THE BELLS ON EARTH

An Ace Book / published by arrangement with the author

PRINTING HISTORY
Ace hardcover edition / November 1995
Ace mass-market edition / December 1997

All rights reserved.
Copyright © 1995 by James P. Blaylock.
Cover art by John Jude Palencar.
This book may not be reproduced in whole or in part, by mimeograph or any other means, without permission.
For information address: The Berkley Publishing Group, a member of Penguin Putnam Inc., 200 Madison Avenue, New York, New York 10016.

The Putnam Berkley World Wide Web site address is http://www.berkley.com

Make sure to check out *PB Plug*, the science fiction/fantasy newsletter, at http://www.pbplug.com

ISBN: 0-441-00490-3

ACE®
Ace Books are published by The Berkley Publishing Group, a member of Penguin Putnam Inc., 200 Madison Avenue, New York, NY 10016.
ACE and the "A" design are trademarks belonging to Charter Communications, Inc.

PRINTED IN THE UNITED STATES OF AMERICA

10 9 8 7 6 5 4 3 2 1

For Viki, John, and Daniel

And this time,
for the Meyer Family,
Denny, Judy, Anderson, and Amanda

Mahalo
" 'O ke aloha ke kuleana o kahi malihini"

Acknowledgments

As ever, I'd like to thank a number of people for the help they gave me with this book: Tim Powers and Lew Shiner especially, for their friendship and for the right stuff at the right time, and John Accursi, who could make a fortune as a story editor. I'd also like to thank Chris Arena, who not only cheerfully put up with a thousand questions over the phone and over lunch, but who put up with them again when I called back for details. And thanks to Mark Ziesing, the king of Shingletown and the guru of catalogue sales. . . .

For sheer inspiration, energy, joy, and faith in the future, I'm grateful to the kids of the Orange County Children's Theatre, who have added a whole lot of color to my life. "Give a little love to a child, and you get a great deal back." John Ruskin wrote that, and he was right.

All the Bells on Earth

PART ONE

❧ ❧

The Dragon

*Our full energies are to be given to the
soul's work—to the great fight with the
Dragon—the taking of the kingdom of
heaven by force.*

JOHN RUSKIN
PRE-RAPHAELITISM

1

A WET WINTER NIGHT. NEARLY TWO IN THE MORNING AND the spirit of Christmas haunts the ocean wind, sighing through the foil candy canes that sway from lampposts along Chapman Avenue, through the ribs of the illuminated Santa Claus in the distant Plaza, along empty alleys dark with shifting, anxious shadows. Raindrops slant across the misty glass globes of streetlamps, and heavy, broken clouds drift across the face of the moon. For a few moments the terra-cotta roof tiles of St. Anthony's Church glisten in the moonlight. The downtown houses appear out of the darkness: clapboard bungalows with shadowy porches and leafy flowerbeds, curb trees pushing up the sidewalks, the houses dark except for the yellow glow of front porch lamps and here and there strings of Christmas lights left on all night.

The moon slips behind clouds again, and in the deepening gloom a human figure steps out of the shadows onto the peak of the church roof and walks carefully across the rainwashed tiles, bent low and carrying a stiff cloth bag. The bell tower rises before him, above the west wall of the church, its white stucco a pale ghost against the deeper darkness of the roof. Within the open arches of the tower stand the crossmembers and struts of the iron framework that supports a carillon of eleven heavy bells.

He climbs over the cast concrete railing in the east-facing arch and dissappears among the maze of shadows cast by the bells, and suddenly the silent night is broken by a tumult of flapping wings, and the sky above the tower is clouded with circling white doves.

*   *   *

FATHER MAHONEY SAT IN THE SMALL SACRISTY OF HOLY
Spirit Catholic Church and listened to the water dripping from
the eaves outside the windows, which were tilted open to let
in the melody of the rain. The room was pleasantly scented
with the smell of the night air, mingling with the odor of floor
wax and incense blocks. It was early in the morning—he
wasn't sure just what time it was—but he rarely slept later
than four these days, and over the years he had gotten used to
seeing the sunrise as well as the sunset. And anyway, today
he was seventy—he didn't have the leisure to be wasting a
morning of this quality.

He heard a noise from somewhere off in the church, what
sounded like the creaking of wooden joints.

Probably it was just the old church settling in the weather.
He sat for a moment listening to hear it again, but there was
nothing, just the sound of the rainy morning. Something about
the rain improved the silence, something vast and deep that
reminded him of the last notes of a hymn or the silence that
followed the ringing of bells.

On the library table in front of him lay an open cigar box
next to his cup of instant coffee. The box was filled with seashells. He picked out several kelp scallops and paired them
according to size and color, but none of the pairs looked quite
right. There had already been half a dozen Pacific storms this
winter, and the shelling was better than any year he could
remember. He had found two perfect chestnut cowries beneath
the Huntington Beach pier last week—the first he had ever
found. They sat on the table now, neatly arrayed beside the
scallops and a handful of jewel-box shells.

He picked up an issue of *The Nautilus* and began to flip
through the pages, but right then he heard the sound of wood
scraping against wood, as if someone had pushed a pew out
of its place in the church. He stood up and walked to the door,
edging it open and looking out past the altar, seeing no one.
He stepped across the choir and looked down into the nave,
which was empty, the pews sitting square and neat and solid.
After a moment he went back into the sacristy and sat down
again, idly stirring the shells in the box with his index finger
and gazing at the three stained-glass windows in the east wall.

It was in the early morning that he most liked to sit in the
wood-paneled room and simply look at these windows, which

depicted Christ and two angels ascending into heaven. Holly leaves with red berries bordered the windows, and the same color of red tinted the stigmata on Christ's out-turned palms. The windows looked out on a garden of tree ferns and maidenhair, and tonight the ivory light from the garden lamps muted the colors of the rain-washed glass, tinting the holly berries and the bleeding wounds an unearthly shade of deep red that reminded him of the sacrament. He couldn't help making these connections, seeing the spirit of one thing alive in something else; it was evidence of the great design.

There was the sound of car wheels swishing on the wet asphalt of the street, and he was momentarily thankful to be inside, where it was warm and dry and close. Picking up one of the cowries, he ran his finger over the smooth hump of its shell. And then, as he set it back down on the table among the others, the sacristy door creaked open.

A man stepped into the room. He wore an oversized coat and trousers, rubber gloves, and a pair of dirty white loafers with tassels. Covering his head was a rubber mask that resembled the face of a goat, complete with a protruding rubber tongue, curled-back horns, and a tuft of coarse hair.

THE MAN IN THE CHURCH TOWER REELED AGAINST THE RAILing, shocked at the rush of wings around him, at the wheeling birds that had been nesting in the belfry. Dropping the canvas sack full of tools, he held onto the smooth stucco of the tower wall with both hands. Although there was a floor beneath the bells, he felt himself to be standing at the edge of a yawning pit, as if the tower were a deep open well into the darkness.

Birds landed on the peak of the roof and stood in the rain before wheeling away again, disappearing into the deep shadows of a big cypress tree in the lot next door. In a moment the night was quiet, and he felt steady again. He let go of the wall, shoved his tools aside with his foot, and forced himself to attend to the bells. There was just enough light to make out the immense bolts that secured them—three bolts in each of the two biggest bells, which must have been three feet in diameter, their bronze walls some three or four inches thick. He groped in the bag of tools, his heart racing, and found a can of lubricant, then sprayed the heavily rusted nuts that secured the biggest bell.

It would be easier simply to cut the wires attached to the clappers and silence the bells that way, but then it would be equally easy for the bellringer to reattach the wires. He wanted something else to happen, something more permanent.

He took a big wrench from the bag and fit it to the nut, leaning into it hard, throwing his weight behind it. Nothing happened. It was frozen tight. The wind blew a flurry of raindrops through the arch, and he let up on the wrench, picking up the can of spray lube again and spraying the nuts heavily. A car drove past on the street below, its headlights glaring against the wet asphalt, and he cursed the driver under his breath.

Christmas lights winked off and on along the eaves of a house across the street, throwing a faint glow of blue and red and green across the dull metal of the bells. Somehow the colors horrified him, as if they were live things, tiny spirits dancing on the cold bells, mocking him, appearing and disappearing like goblin gold. The bells began to thrum in the wind, as if they had a voice, and for a moment he fancied he could hear a melody in the raindrops plinking against the bronze. The iron framework before him was dizzyingly complicated, and the bells swam in and out of his vision.

He dropped the wrench and reached for a crossbar in order to steady himself, but touched the surface of the bell instead. It was horribly solid, the bronze so cold that for a moment he thought he'd been burned. He jerked his hand away and grabbed for the railing, looking away from the bells and the reflected Christmas lights, out into the night where the palms along the avenue moved slowly in the wind. Like a tide beneath a pier, the shifting palm fronds made the tower seem to sway, and he held on desperately. A dove alighted on the concrete railing, stark white in the moonlight, and in a moment of wild rage and fear he swung his hand at it, lurching forward to grab it by the neck. The dove lifted off again, and the back of his hand struck the stucco corner of the arch.

The pain sobered him. He stood breathing hard, the rain in his face. He had nearly lost his mind there for a moment. It occurred to him abruptly that something was actively working against him, some power, filling his head with confusion—the rain, the colored lights, the doves. . . .

The idea of it appealed to him, giving him a strange sensation of potency. He was filled with the certainty that he was laboring at the heart of an ages-old struggle, that with his bag of tools he might shift something so monumentally heavy that it made the ponderous bell in front of him nothing more than a dust mote.

Full of wild purpose, he picked up the spray lube, and held down the nozzle until all three nuts ran with oil. Then he fumbled in the sack again, pulling out a small propane torch. He lit the torch, adjusted the flame, and held it to the center nut. The oil burst into flame, and the flame ran out across the steel plate, flickering like witch fire, casting a glare on the walls around him. He held the torch to the nut, which had sat there immobile for sixty years, and watched the flaming oil burn itself out. Then, shutting off the torch, he fixed the wrench on the nut again and leaned hard against it. There was a spray of rust flakes and a loud squeak as the nut disengaged, but he didn't let up. He cranked the wrench around in a big circle, forcing it up the rusty threads until the nut fell loose, dropping to the floor. The second nut was easier than the first; there was no need to heat it with the torch. He eased the third nut up the bolt until, with a heart-stopping shriek, the bell twisted away from its steel plate, the bolt itself bending backward from the bell's weight. He stood for a moment, afraid to go on. If the bell came down now . . .

But the bell didn't fall. He counted four threads exposed above the remaining nut. Carefully he turned the wrench, easing the nut upward, the rusty iron groaning. Even when the nut was flush with the top of the bolt, he continued to turn the wrench, picturing the bell dropping, the terrible noise of it crashing through the floors below, slamming into the concrete floor at the bottom of the tower.

The top of the bolt slowly edged its way down into the nut. He counted the revolutions, stopping at the fourth, trusting utterly to instinct: another quarter turn and it would fall. The bell swayed there, defying gravity, thousands of pounds of cast bronze held by a thin curl of iron. One of the doves could dislodge it. The wind could blow it down.

He stepped backward and laughed out loud, picturing it, full of wild confidence now, of boundless exhilaration as he slid the wrench free, slipping it into the bag along with the torch and the spray can. Then he swung his leg over the raiiing,

stepped out onto the roof again, and set out toward the back
of the church. The moon shone now as if someone had turned
on a lamp in the night sky. He hurried. It wouldn't do to be
caught. Not now. Never mind what it would do to his life, to
his career, if he were seen up here. It had quite simply been
vital that the bells be silenced, but the awful compulsion that
had led him out into the rainy night was already draining
away. . . .

A car approached from the west. He stepped down the back
slope of the roof, trying to move out of sight, hunching forward to shrink himself. Suddenly he was off-balance, and he
threw out his free hand, trying to grab the peak of the roof as
his foot slipped on the wet terra-cotta and his leg splayed outward. He dropped the bag, throwing out his arms to catch
himself as he fell forward. His fingernails scraped across the
slick tiles and he skittered downward, scrabbling uselessly,
moaning out loud.

In that instant there flew into his mind an image of himself
lying dead on the ground, his soul sucked out of him, down
through the dirt and rock of the cold earth, fleeing away toward
some infinitely empty place. Terror and remorse surged
through him, and for one appalling moment he thought he
heard the bells themselves begin to toll.

Then his right foot struck the rain gutter that ran along the
eave, and he hugged the terra-cotta tiles to him as he jolted to
a stop right at the roof's edge. For a moment he lay there
simply breathing, his eyes closed, feeling the cold rain against
his back. Then, carefully, he looked behind him, down at the
lawn and at the scattering of tools that had flown out of the
canvas bag.

He hunched forward, crawling up the rusted metal valley
like a bug, hanging onto the edges of the roof tiles and
breathing hard now, desperately careful. The wild elation he
had felt in the tower was utterly gone, all of it replaced by the
terrible need to save himself, to get down off the roof, retrieve
his tools, and make his way to safety without being seen.

When he was well clear of the edge, he stood up and quick-
ened his pace, and within seconds was at the peak again, then
past it, letting himself down the back side of the roof, which
was hidden from the street by a row of trees.

*   *   *

THE WET SIDEWALKS REFLECTED THE GLOW FROM THE OLD cast-concrete streetlamps on the parkway, and water dripped with a slow, hollow plink in the metal downspout at the edge of the porch. The wind was full of the promise of more rain. Walt Stebbins stood on the porch and listened to the night. He wore his pajama shirt tucked into a pair of pants that he'd pulled on hastily. He hadn't bothered with his bedroom slippers. The wisteria vine that climbed the downspout was bare of leaves, and the yellow buglight on the porch threw a tangle of moving shadows out onto the front lawn. There was a gust of wind, and the heavy vines scraped against the eaves of the house.

He noticed then that he'd left the Christmas lights on again—the third time that season. It was amazing how a few colored lights could run up the bill. He stepped down off the porch now and peered around the outside corner of the front bedroom, up the driveway toward the garage. The driveway gate was shut. It was a little section of picket fence hinged to the latticework wall of the carport, supported by a single steel wheel that made a gravelly, metallic sound when it rolled open.

That's what had awakened him, or so he thought—the sound of the gate rasping open across the concrete. A moment later a car had started up somewhere down the block, and, lying there in bed, it had seemed nearly certain to him that someone had been in the backyard, and had made a noise going out. Now he wasn't quite so certain. Ivy, his wife, would no doubt remind him of the time he'd woken up convinced he was in a submarine under the Indian Ocean. . . .

And now that he thought about it, the noise could as easily have been the bare wisteria vines scraping the house. The garage door was locked. He could see the padlock from where he stood. The back doors of the house were dead-bolted. He walked softly down the driveway, listening hard, and slipped the latch on the gate, picking the wheel up off the concrete and swinging it open noiselessly. The backyard was quiet, the lawn pooled with rainwater. The stepping-stone path that led to the sheds behind the garage was wet, so there was no real chance of footprints. All in all, there was no indication of any prowler—nothing stolen, nothing out of order. If anyone had been back there, they were apparently only sightseeing.

Blame it on the wind. He went out through the gate again,

lifting it to shut it and then easing the latch into place. It was too early in the morning to make noise. He stood for a moment on the sidewalk, looking down toward Chapman Avenue and simply taking in the rainy darkness. A car rolled past the end of the block, its tires humming on the wet pavement, speeding up to beat the light at the corner. The neighborhood was dark and silent, and the sky was like something out of a painting, full of clouds illuminated by moonglow. What a morning! He was thankful all of a sudden that the wind had woken him up and lured him outside, as if it had something to show him.

A flock of birds rose into the air from the roof of St. Anthony's Church a block away, and for a moment they glowed impossibly white in the moonlight, flying in a circle around the bell tower before alighting again. Then he saw a movement on the roof—a shadow silhouetted against the darker hedge of trees beyond. In an instant it was gone.

A man on the roof? At this hour? Walt stood watching, waiting to see it again. Except for the birds, the church roof remained empty of movement now.

He seemed to have prowlers on the mind. The neighborhood was apparently alive with them. There was probably some kind of cat-burglar convention over at the Twin Palms Motel. The wind blew straight through the flimsy cotton of his pajama shirt, and he thought about his bed upstairs, about how Ivy would yell at him when he climbed in with frozen feet.

Rain began to fall, and he turned and hurried toward the porch. Then, on a whim, he stopped at the steps, bending over to pinch through a half dozen pansy stems before going in through the door, locking the dead bolt behind him and carrying the little bouquet upstairs.

Back in the bedroom, he watched Ivy sleep for a moment. She lay tucked up in the heap of blankets she'd stolen from him in the night. She was a restless sleeper, and had a sort of tidal effect on blankets, which invariably shifted to her side of the world by morning. His side of the bed was pitifully bare except for the corner of the top sheet. He glanced at the clock: quarter to five, nearly time to get up anyway. He looked around for somewhere to put the pansies so that Ivy would find them when she woke up. An idea came to him, and he turned around and headed into the bathroom, where he dropped a pansy into each of the toothbrush slots in the brass holder on the wall, entwining the handle of Ivy's toothbrush with the flimsy stem of the last flower.

Satisfied, he went quietly back out into the bedroom, took his shirt and sweater off the chair, and found his shoes and a pair of socks. He thought again about what he'd seen on the church roof. Something had startled the birds; he hadn't simply imagined the shadowy figure. Still, what could he do about it? Call the cops? It was raining like in the tropics outside now. There wasn't a chance in hell that they'd be interested in his observations. And it occurred to him that if someone *had* been on the roof, it was good odds that they were simply patching a leak during a lull in the storm—probably the minister himself. Surely it wasn't someone breaking in; you didn't break into a church by burrowing through the tile roof. He pushed the matter out of his mind and slipped downstairs again, anxious to put on a pot of coffee out in the garage.

WHEN HE SAW THE INTRUDER IN THE DOORWAY, FATHER MAhoney stood up, his throat constricting, a rush of fear slamming through him. For a single terrible moment he was certain that the man wasn't wearing a mask at all, that he actually had the face of a goat. He fought to control himself, but he simply couldn't speak, even when the moment passed and he knew he was wrong. There was something odious about the mask, something filthy that he simply couldn't abide, and without thinking he lunged forward, snatching at it, suddenly wanting to jerk it off the man's head. He felt himself struck hard in the chest and he fell heavily back down into the chair. There was a low laugh from within the confines of the mask, and he threw up his hands and ducked his head as the intruder drew a homemade blackjack from inside his coat—a length of pink rubber hose with a bulbous tip wrapped in cloth tape.

The intruder cracked it down on the corner of the table, leaving a dent. Father Mahoney winced backward, pressing himself into the chair as the man walked slowly around the desk, his head bobbing. The man leaned over until the mask nearly brushed the priest's ear. "Fatty," he whispered, his voice pitched weirdly high. He pushed the taped piece of hose into Father Mahoney's cheek and made little clucking sounds. Then he began to giggle, picking up a marking pen off the table and striding to the wall, where he jerked a painting of

Job off its nail and let it drop to the floor. With the marker he wrote a filthy word on the white plaster.

He stopped giggling, turning around as if in alarm. He stood there swaying, his breath rasping within the mask. Abruptly he picked up the cup of coffee from the desktop and drank it through the mouth hole of the mask, half the coffee dribbling out from beneath the rubber chin and down his coat.

He pitched the coffee cup into the wall and slammed the blackjack across the cigar box full of shells, breaking apart the wooden panels of the box and knocking the whole thing to the floor, the shells scattering across the linoleum. He picked up one of the cowries and looked closely at it, making little smacking noises with his lips, as if he wanted to taste it. Carefully, he set it at the corner of the table, and then smashed it flat with a single, quick blow, dusting the fragments onto the floor before smashing the second one the same way. Then, one by one, he hammered the scallops and jewel-box shells into fragments, working methodically, as if smashing the shells was the one great purpose of his visit. He trod through the scattered pieces of seashell on the floor, stomping around on them, crushing them to powder beneath his feet. There was something clearly insane about it, a drooling madness, and yet he moved with a singleness of purpose, as if the seashells were an enemy that had to be utterly destroyed.

"What do you want?" Father Mahoney asked finally. His voice shook. The man stood among the trampled shells, hunched over, his breath wheezing in his throat. "We haven't got much money," the priest said, "not in the church. The offering . . ."

The man pulled a short piece of nylon cord from his coat, made a loop in the end of it, grabbed Mahoney's wrist, and settled the loop over it, drawing it tight, yanking his other hand around and tying them both to the chair. Then he took a cloth bag from his pants pocket and pulled it over Mahoney's head. The bag stank, as if something dead had been stored in it, and Mahoney closed his eyes, the idea of praying only now coming to him through the haze of fear and bewilderment.

For uncounted seconds he listened to the man walking back and forth in the room, as if he were pacing, uttering an odd chanting noise that was almost idiotic, the meaningless de-monic gibbering of a man who had given up all claim to humanity. There was the sound of the blackjack thudding against something wooden, then a loud grunt followed by the crash of heavy furniture toppling—the carved cabinet that held the Host and sacramental wine. Bottles broke against the floor, and Mahoney could smell the spilled wine.

Abruptly he found himself thinking that, thank God, the Host wasn't blessed, but then it struck him that the idea was almost foolish; he was thinking almost like the man in the goat mask—that God, somehow, could be damaged by this kind of pathetic vandalism.

Almost immediately there was another thump and the clank of something metallic falling to the floor. The chalice? It was gold; no doubt he'd steal it. There was a racket of sound: the hand-bells falling, the clanking roll of the censer, then the scrape of hangers on wooden rods—the vestments being yanked out of the wardrobe. A fold of cloth settled over his head—probably an altar boy's gown. He opened his mouth, sucking in air. The layers of cloth made it difficult to breathe, and he wondered suddenly if the man meant to kill him. The idea of suffocation terrified him, and he tore his mind away from the thought, forcing himself to visualize the picture in the stained glass of the windows.

Dimly he heard repeated blows of the blackjack and of glass breaking, and it came to him that the man was destroying the windows too, hammering the leaded joints apart, breaking out the glass. Surely he was making enough noise so that someone on the street would hear. But it was late, and the church and its buildings took up the entire square block. . . .

Father Mahoney stood up, the chair legs coming up off the floor. He hunched away from the desk, bending his head to his chest to dislodge the cloth bag. "Stop!" he yelled. "In the name of God . . . !" He yanked at the ropes that bound his wrists, jerking up and down, full of fury now.

There was a silence, and then the sound of ragged breathing again, coming from somewhere behind him. Father Mahoney tensed, waiting for the blow, for the man to hit him with the blackjack. The hair on his neck crept, and he imagined the intruder standing behind him, the goat mask regarding him now, the blackjack upraised. . . .

And then the sacristy door banged shut. He heard footsteps pounding across the tiles of the nave. The noise faded away, leaving the night silent again but for the sound of the rain.

2

GEORGE NELSON SAT IN HIS LAW OFFICE ON THE PLAZA,
waiting uneasily for the arrival of a business associate—Murray LeRoy. Through the window he could see the Plaza fountain and the small wooden nativity scene next to it. A lamp in the grass cast light on the nativity scene as a discouragement to vandals, but the light apparently hadn't done its job, because the packing-crate manger was kicked to pieces, its palm frond roof scattered into the street, and the plaster of Paris figures knocked over and broken. It was almost ironic: Nelson himself represented a citizens' group opposed to the display of nativity scenes on public property—the suit against the city was still pending—and here someone had come along in the night and done the job single-handedly.

He picked up the phone and dialed LeRoy's number. Nothing. LeRoy was already out, already on his way. There were only a couple of hours left before the arrival of Nelson's secretary, and before then he wanted to be finished with LeRoy. There were a number of reasons for cutting LeRoy loose forever. Mostly it was because LeRoy was a little unsteady these days.

In fact, if his behavior yesterday morning was any indication, the man was positively cracking up, and that was a dangerous thing. He had looked like he'd slept in his clothes, and he hadn't shaved for days. He was half drunk, too, at nine in the morning, and his head shook with some kind of palsy that had made Nelson want to slap him. Six months ago the man didn't drink except at weddings, and then he didn't enjoy it and was always willing to say so in a loud voice. Nelson knew that there had been good reasons for LeRoy to keep his personal life private, but he had the public persona of some kind of scowling Calvinist missionary, and that's what made his downhill slide so strange—he was making it so damned obvious. The thought wasn't comforting.

Nelson had no idea exactly what he'd do about it in the end, but this morning he intended to try to buy the man out. That was the simplest route—something he should have done two or three months ago when LeRoy first started to crack. He wondered suddenly if the business with the nativity scene had been LeRoy's doing. It would certainly fit the pattern. If the man were arrested again, he'd probably babble like the nut he'd become.

He heard a sound then, like the laughter of cartoon devils. "Murray?" He stood up out of his chair, listening. He opened his desk drawer and slipped his hand in, sliding the loaded .38 to the front. Then he saw a glow beyond the window curtains, and he realized that what he heard now no longer sounded like laughter. There was a crackling, almost like fat sizzling on a griddle, and at that moment he smelled the burning. There was something sulphurous about it, something that nearly choked him even though the windows were shut and locked.

Abruptly it dawned on him that the building might be on fire, that LeRoy had torched it. Thank God the man had become an incompetent fool! He slammed shut the desk drawer and hurried out into the foyer, opening the coat closet and pulling out the fire extinguisher. In a second he had unlocked the door and was out on the sidewalk, yanking the little plastic cotter key out of the lever of the extinguisher. The streets were empty. He slowed down, fully expecting to find LeRoy himself squatting in the flowerbed and dressed up like a clown or a little girl. He angled out toward the street and peered into the alley, which was lit up now with flames.

At first it looked like someone must have dumped burning trashbags onto the pavement. The heat was intense and glowing with a corona of white haze that obscured the burning figure, whatever it was. The fire flickered, rising and falling as if something were literally breathing life into it. The effect was almost hallucinatory, and for a moment he seemed to be looking into the mouth of a burning, circular pit. He heard what sounded like voices, like human cries, and a sulphurous reek drifted skyward like a mass of whirling black shadows.

Clearly it wasn't trashbags. A big dog? The burning thing

had a face like an ugly damned goat. He saw then that there were shoes at the other end of it. A man! He pointed the nozzle of the extinguisher in the general direction of the body and squeezed the lever. White dust sputtered out of it, but it was as if a whirlwind encompassed the burning body, and the chemicals blew away uselessly in the air. The flames didn't diminish; shouting at them would do as much good. He tried to get closer, but gave it up; there was no way that he intended to have his hair singed off over this. He pointed the extinguisher into the air and blew the rest of the contents in the direction of the flaming body, knowing it was pointless—no one could live through such a thing anyway—but wanting to make damn well sure that the extinguisher was empty when the investigators had a look at it.

There was something about the shoes. . . . He looked closely at them, recognizing them with a start of surprise—loafers, white, with tasseled laces.

God, it was Murray LeRoy! Someone must have dumped gasoline over him and lit a match. One of the shoes ignited just then, with an audible hiss, and Nelson backed away, turning around and heading up the sidewalk again, hurrying toward the door to the office, swept with relief and fear both.

This certainly solved the problem with LeRoy. He wouldn't be babbling to anyone now. But who had done this? In his mind Nelson ran through his list of enemies. Its being done outside his office, in the early morning like this, that was the bad thing. LeRoy must have talked to someone, said something. God, but to whom? Nelson and his associates were involved in a lot of shaky dealings, but nothing that would warrant something like this.

Inside he locked the door before punching 911 into the phone and reporting the incident. He sat down then at his desk, taking out the .38. If someone wanted LeRoy dead this badly, there was no reason to think they wouldn't want him dead, too. But who, damn it? Argyle? He was capable of it. It dawned on him just then that perhaps there were other explanations. The city didn't have any real gang problems, but there'd been several incidents in the past couple of years of homeless people being mugged, and he seemed to remember something about a man set on fire somewhere—probably Santa Ana. Who could say how long LeRoy had been in the alley?

No doubt he was drunk as a judge and was easy prey for a gang of sadistic skinheads who happened to be out joyriding.

And then there was the possibility that LeRoy had simply gone to Hell.

He pushed the idea out of his mind. There were flashing lights outside the window now—a paramedics truck. He returned the gun to the drawer and went out, carrying the fire extinguisher. The fire was already out except for a weird flickering on the surface of the asphalt itself. The paramedics stood looking at the body, or what was left of it—only a heap of gray ash and charred fragments of bone. One of the shoes sat on the ground, strangely intact, but the other was gone.

"You called this in?"

"What?" Nelson looked up at the paramedic. He realized that he'd been gaping at the shoe with its ridiculous tassel. There was an ankle bone thrust up out of it, charred in half, and he wondered suddenly if there was still flesh on the foot. The idea made him sick, and he turned away and looked across at the Plaza, at the big grinning Santa Claus waving at the traffic coming up Glassell Street.

"Was it you that called, sir?"

He turned back, pulling himself together. "Yes. I tried to put the fire out, but this didn't seem to do any good."

"Probably too much heat," the paramedic said. "If there's enough heat it can blow this stuff right back at you. It's like spraying a hose into the wind. You did what you could."

Another truck pulled up, followed by a squad car, and in a moment the alley was full of investigators taking pictures and searching the ground, talking in undertones, their voices full of disbelief. There was a flurry of raindrops, and in moments the rain was coming down hard. Four firemen unfolded a tarp, trying in vain to keep LeRoy's ashes dry while a plainclothes investigator hastily swept it all into a black metal dustpan that he emptied into a plastic sack. Nelson saw that there was a dime in among the ashes, and something else that might have been a tooth.

Without warning, rainwater sluiced out of the drainpipes on either side of the alley and flooded out onto the asphalt. A fireman attempted to dam it up with a yellow slicker, but it was no use: the water washed the alley clean, and within two minutes there was no trace of Murray LeRoy left in the world except the heap of ashes and teeth and bone that lay with the godawful white shoe in the bottom of the plastic sack.

⊰ 3 ⊱

THERE WAS THE SOUND OF THUNDER SOMEWHERE FAR OFF, like a door closing on the season, and in the direction of the distant ocean the sky was the color of wet slate. The wind gusted now, carrying on it the first deep notes of the bells from the tower at St. Anthony's on Chapman Avenue a block away, and for a moment Walt thought that the sound of the bells was a remnant of the thunder, echoing through remote canyons in the clouds.

Raindrops pattered down onto the concrete walk, and he ducked into the garden shed that stood beneath the canopy of an enormous avocado tree in the back corner of the yard. There was something lonesome in the rain this winter afternoon, in the smell of wet leaves and the low sound of thunder that mingled with the weather-muffled ringing of the bells.

They rang every afternoon during the month of December—something that Walt, happily, had never really gotten used to even though he and Ivy had lived in the neighborhood for upwards of twelve years. Hearing them was always a pleasant surprise, like coming around a corner and suddenly seeing a cherry tree or a hawthorne in blossom.

Abruptly he remembered that Ivy's aunt and uncle were due shortly—maybe even later this afternoon—and thinking about it took some of the magic out of the afternoon. They were on the last leg of their trip from the east. For a couple of weeks they'd been driving out from Michigan in a motor home, fully self-contained—toilet, refrigerator, awning, the whole works. They'd bought it last year with dividends from Uncle Henry's stocks and bonds. The idea was to spend the winter in California—specifically in Walt and Ivy's driveway, which, Walt had to admit, was better than them staying on the foldout couch in the den like last year.

"It's an Ex*e*cutive," Uncle Henry had said to him over the phone, leaning heavily on the second syllable, and it had taken Walt most of the rest of the conversation to figure out what he meant, that it was the brand name of the motor home. He had tried to imagine the kind of vehicle it was, what it must look like, given its name—a desk in the back, maybe, with a Rolodex on it, and a swivel chair and file cabinet—an outfit suitable for a man of business. Last night Aunt Jinx had called from Kingman, from a pay phone in the parking lot of the Alpha Beta Market where they were spending the night.

Happily alone, at least for the moment, Walt looked out through the dripping branches of the avocado tree and knew that right now there was no place in the world he'd rather be. Even the threat of pending houseguests was somehow diminished by the misty weather. Solitude—that was the good thing about working out of the house, especially on a day like this with the rain coming down and with Christmas on the horizon. Ivy was earning pretty good money, thank God, and her income allowed Walt to run his catalogue sales business out of the garage. Once the business was really up and running, the money would roll in, and Ivy could flat-out quit if she wanted to. The Christmas season was already boosting sales, and he was counting on his most recent catalogue to turn things around for him.

"You hope," he said out loud. Money—the subject had gotten increasingly unbearable to him. The truth was that he was past forty and still didn't have a real job. He worked like a pig, but somehow that didn't equate to bringing home the bacon. Ivy never complained, of course. She wasn't the complaining type. But a man had his pride.

Anyway, he wasn't in much of a position to complain about Jinx and Henry, no matter how long they intended to stay. He looked at his watch. It was just past noon.

He noticed now that there were a couple of dark red tomatoes on last summer's vines along the fence. The vines were still green, but it was a gray-green, not the emerald green of high summer, and of course there were no blooms left at all. The two tomatoes were probably fossilized by now. The basil in the adjacent herb garden had gone to seed, and the three

basil plants had maybe six leaves between them, but the rosemary and sage would last out the winter no matter how lousy
the weather got. And during the cool fall months the lemon
tree at the opposite end of the garden had set on so many
lemons that now the wet boughs were bent nearly to the
ground beneath their weight. Avocadoes, lemons, lawns green-
ing up in the rain—that was winter in southern California; no
wonder Henry and Jinx got the hell out of Michigan every
year and drove west. They must miss the hell out of California
since they'd moved away.

Right then a spider, some kind of daddy longlegs, crawled
out of the hole in the bottom of an overturned flowerpot on a
shelf and stood there looking around, as if it had slept late and
the thunder had awakened it. The pot had a sort of door in the
front, a ragged arch where a piece had broken off. It occurred
to Walt that the spider worked out of its house, too, and he
wondered suddenly what kind of furnishings it had inside—a
hammock, a pantry, shelves of books. If Walt had kids he'd
be tempted to load the flowerpot up with doll furniture and
tiny books and then pretend to find it like that, forever changing his children's notions about bugs.

Thinking about children, he wondered uneasily if Ivy would
bring up that subject again tonight. She'd been on a kick lately
about starting a family. Usually the subject came up around
bedtime. He'd managed so far to fend her off with logic, just
like he had in the past. But that couldn't go on forever. Ivy
had a deep suspicion of logic. She said it was a leaky boat.
Last night she had told him that there was nothing logical
anyway about starting a family, and so trying to apply logic
to it was illogical.

Even now the argument looked irrefutable to him, and he
had the vague notion that he'd been defeated. Well, he was
safe for the moment anyway, there among the sacks of planting
mix and tools and clay pots, watching the heavy branches of
the avocado tree shift in the wind, and listening to the swish
of its big green leaves and the sound of the rain pelting down.
A haze of mist rose from the shingles of the garage, and he
could hear the drops pounding on the tin roof of one of the
storage sheds, nearly drowning out the sound of the church
bells. The bellringer was a hell of a dedicated man, out in
weather like this in an open tower, yanking on soggy ropes

whether anyone could hear the bells or not: art for art's sake, or more likely for the glory of God, like the old Renaissance painters.

Walt listened closely. It took him a moment to recognize the melody. It was "In the Bleak Midwinter," one of his favorites, and it really needed a big church choir to do it justice. He recalled the words to his favorite stanza, and was just on the verge of singing along when the bells broke into a clamor that sounded like a train wreck, the discordant echoes finally clanging away into silence.

4

THE KEY TO THE THIRD DRAWER WAS TAPED TO THE BACK side of the old metal desk. There was nothing in the drawer but the red telephone, and it hadn't rung for nearly ten years. Unless the phone rang, the drawer stayed locked. There was a phone jack behind the desk, and the phone cord exited through a hole drilled in the back of the drawer. Most of the time it was unplugged from the wall, the cord shoved back into the drawer. It was only when Flanagan was in the building alone that he plugged it in. And it was only when the phone rang that he called himself Flanagan. He had plugged the phone in religiously for the ten years that the phone hadn't rung at all. It was like walking along a sidewalk: once it occurred to him to avoid stepping on cracks, it became a small obsession. And until he arrived at his destination, he was a careful man.

As far as the phone was concerned, he hadn't arrived at his destination yet, but there was something in the rainy winter air this morning that made him fear that he was close. It was twenty years ago that he had helped send three men off in the general direction of Hell, and by now he understood that the pit he had dug for these other men was deep enough to contain him, too.

So when the phone rang now, inside its drawer, it wasn't really a surprise, despite the ten years. He put down his pen, letting the phone ring four times before he reached behind the desk and pried the key out from under its tape. He unlocked the drawer, still counting the rings, and picked it up on the tenth.

"Flanagan." The name sounded idiotic to him.

There was a silence. Then a voice said, "Is it you?"

"It's me."

"We have to talk."

"We're talking."

"I don't mean over the telephone. This kind of business can't be conducted over the telephone. I think . . . I believe something's happening."

"I'm certain it is."

"What do you mean by that?"

"What do *you* mean?"

There was a silence again, as if the man was forcing himself to be patient. His voice was urgent; something had happened to frighten him. "I mean I want out," he said at last.

Now it was Flanagan's turn to be silent. Was this what he had expected? He looked around at the old paint, the exposed extension cords, the water dripping in the sink that Mrs. Hepplewhite optimistically called her "kitchen." He didn't have to do any calculations now; he had already done them a hundred times—how much hard cash he needed just to keep the church afloat. "I can't help you," he said, and he knew it was only partly right even as he said it. The flesh was weak.

"Name your price."

"I'm not talking about price. I mean to say that I've never helped you. What you've done, you've done alone." This was wrong, too. He himself was as blameworthy as a felon.

"You know, Mr. Flanagan, I don't think so. If I thought so, I wouldn't have called you. What have you taken from me over the years, twenty thousand?"

"I don't keep accounts."

"Of course you do. We both know the truth."

"The truth is, I'm not in that line of work any more, so never mind the past. You might say that I've changed; I've gone over to the other side."

"The other side! And yet you answer to the same name and at the same old number. I wonder if some things haven't changed. How about the color of money? Has that changed, too?"

"I recommend that you ask God for help."

"Let's not drift off the subject," the man said. "I'm willing to pay you a hundred thousand dollars, any way you like—through Obermeyer, cash in a briefcase, trust fund, you name

it. I have a certain naive faith in you. Can you believe that?
You've kept your word to me in the past, and I'm willing to
take a gamble on you again. What do I have to lose? Stay near
the phone while you think it over. I'll call back.''

⇥ 5 ⇤

WHEN ARGYLE HUNG UP THE TELEPHONE HIS HAND WAS shaking. He stood by the desk for a moment, getting a grip on himself, then stepped across and turned up the stereo. The children out on the playground had just come out for their midmorning recess. The sound of them shouting and screaming and laughing gave him a headache, or worse, and he'd found that tapes of special-effects-type noises—train sounds, ocean waves, thunderstorms—served to drown out their voices better than music did. And these days the sound of music was nearly as intolerable as the sound of children. Nothing was free. Everything had its price.

He realized that his phone was ringing, his personal line, and he turned the stereo volume down slightly and picked up the receiver, sitting down at his desk. "Robert Argyle," he said. He listened a moment. It was George Nelson with news about Murray LeRoy—good news; LeRoy was dead.

"When?" Argyle asked. His momentary enthusiasm for LeRoy's death started to wane as Nelson went into detail, and he found himself staring at his desktop, recalling the conversation he'd had a few moments ago. Probably he should have offered Flanagan more money, pushed all his chips into the center of the table. "What did the police say? Did they have any kind of explanation for it?"

"They found the metal parts of a Bic lighter in the alley and the presence of gas from the manhole that's right there. One theory is that the lighter leaked butane gas into LeRoy's pocket, and then when he lit his cigarette the gas followed his hand to his mouth and ignited. Apparently it happens more often than you'd guess. If he was wearing flammable clothes, he could have gone up like a torch. All of this is just conjecture, of course, since there aren't any clothes left to examine except one of those damned white patent leather loafers that he wears, with the tassels. Everything else burned to ash. Even his shirt buttons vaporized. The heat was incredible.''

''And the fire investigators buy this? The butane lighter and all?''

''There was the manhole, too. Apparently gasses might have built up out there in the alley. A spark can set them off. They think it's some kind of combination of this stuff, perhaps aggravated by chemicals like deodorant and cologne. I suggested kids—punks, skinheads, street gang, something like that—but they didn't like the idea. The city doesn't need that kind of talk. There's also a good possibility that it was a suicide, that he doused himself with flammable liquids and lit himself on fire. There was no gas can, though, no more evidence of suicide than anything else.''

''And you were the one that told them who it was, who you thought it was?''

There was a pause, then Nelson said, ''I didn't think I had any choice, and it turns out I was right. It seems that a couple hours before dawn, LeRoy broke into Holy Spirit Church, up on Almond. He roughed up the old priest and smashed some windows. Apparently our man had a *very* busy morning, dragging those white shoes all over town. I've got it on good authority that the priest described them to the police. I'd swear that LeRoy *wanted* to be caught, or at least didn't give a damn if he was recognized. There must be fifty people around town who'd know straight off the shoe was his. I couldn't see any choice but to identify it myself.

''Anyway, what I said is that I was expecting him at the office, that we were supposed to head across the street to Moody's for breakfast at six. I saw the flames through the curtains and ran out with a fire extinguisher, but couldn't do any good. Every part of that was true, including my trying to put out the flames. Of course I didn't know who it was then, but I didn't say so.''

''Who was the investigating officer?''

''Tyler, from Accident Investigations.''

''And he's satisfied?''

''There's no reason he shouldn't be. As I said, it's the truth, lock, stock, and barrel. Oh, and by the way, somebody kicked apart the nativity scene in the Plaza early this morning, too. We know that was LeRoy, don't we? That'll be his footprints in the flowerbeds?''

Argyle wondered suddenly if the question was simply rhetorical, or whether it was full of implication. ''Of *course* it was him, unless there's something you're holding back.''

''*I'm* not holding anything back,'' Nelson said, and then paused again, letting his silences speak volumes. Argyle waited him out. ''One way or another,'' he continued, ''I hinted around that LeRoy had been talking about destroying the creche, which is true again; half a dozen people heard him. You should have seen him last night, crying and swearing. His tears were pure gin. No wonder he burned like that; his cells were saturated with alcohol.''

''Do you believe that?''

''I'm a lawyer. I'm not in the business of believing in things. I simply wanted to make sure you understood the entire affair. As far as the police are concerned, the case is closed, and I can tell you that I'll breathe a little easier now. But I think we ought to get together tonight anyway, just to make sure we've all got the same perspective on things.''

Argyle hung up the phone finally, moderately satisfied. It was certainly convenient to have a dead man to point the finger at, if a finger needed pointing. They could clean out LeRoy's house at the first opportunity. Probably there was nothing there to implicate either of them anyway. There was no reason to think they'd have any trouble with the police. Nelson was thorough and convincing—utterly treacherous.

He listened to the noise on the stereo, thinking about how close he had come last night to destroying himself, and at very nearly the same moment that LeRoy had fallen over the edge! What horrors had been visited upon Murray LeRoy? What urges and fears had driven him into the darkness at last? A surge of disconnected terror swept through him, the knowledge that he was somehow being swept into the same uncharted seas into which LeRoy had sunk, beneath black tides of compulsion and desire. . . .

He picked up the phone and called Flanagan again, but the line was busy now.

⁂ 6 ⁂

THE WIND KICKED UP, SUDDENLY SWEEPING COLD RAIN UNDER the overhanging branches and into the open shed. The spider had disappeared, back inside its home. Walt hunched out into the rain and sprinted across the lawn toward the garage, rounding the corner into the carport, suddenly anxious to be in out of the weather and to crank up the space heater. His shirt was soaked. He reached for the door latch, but then stopped and jerked his hand away.

The garage doors were shut, like he'd left them, but the padlock was gone. He always left it hanging in the hasp, whether it was locked or not. And that's where he'd left it when he'd gone into the house for lunch; he was certain of it. He thought about last night, the noise that had woken him up. Suddenly it was clear to him: someone had come in, found the place locked up, and left again. Then today they'd come back, probably cased the house, waiting for him to go inside before making their move. They were bold sons-of-bitches, he had to give them that.

He listened for the scrape of shoe soles on the concrete floor inside, for the sound of paper rustling or boxes being shifted. All was silent; he could even hear the sound of the wind-up clock ticking on the workbench. He looked around for wet footprints, but there were none—which meant nothing, what with the rain and all. He reached for the latch, took a step backward, and pulled the door open slowly, keeping behind it, out of the way.

The door at the rear of the garage stood open to the rain. They'd gone out the back. Walt strode past piled-up cartons, a couple of which had been dumped out, their contents scattered on the concrete floor along with crumpled Chinese newspaper and clumps of excelsior. He looked around hurriedly. The stuff on the desk hadn't been touched—his cassette player, the Toshiba laptop. A twenty-dollar bill and a couple of singles lay on the blotter, in plain sight, money left over from a trip down to the stationers. The burglar hadn't touched any of it.

Warily, he held onto the doorknob and looked out into the backyard, half expecting to find someone crouched along the wall or sprinting across the wet lawn. But the yard was empty, the rain coming down steadily now. He picked up a claw hammer from the bench top and went out into the weather, angling across to where he could see past the corner of the new storage shed but keeping well away from it so he couldn't be jumped. Nobody. Nothing. Probably they'd gone out fast through the back door when they'd heard him coming around the side of the garage, and had climbed straight over the redwood fence.

He walked back across to the fence, and, sure enough, there were blades of grass on the rain-soaked middle rail. Someone had climbed over after walking across the wet grass. He pulled himself up onto the rail and looked over into the neighbor's backyard, but it was empty. There were two more houses beyond that, and from what he could see their yards were empty, too. Noontime traffic moved along Cambridge Street a half block down. He could see a couple of people hunched beneath the acrylic roof of a bus-stop shelter on the opposite side of the distant street.

On impulse he went back inside the garage and shut and locked the back door. He grabbed the padlock from where it lay on the counter and came out again through the front, sliding the padlock into the ring on the hasp and locking it. It occurred to him that the lock could be dusted for prints, but he saw at once that the idea was ludicrous. It didn't even look as if the thief had stolen anything, although he couldn't be sure without looking around a little at the stuff on the floor, maybe checking it against an invoice.

He rolled down the back window of his old Suburban and yanked out his umbrella, then hurried toward the corner. If the burglar had cut through the backyards, then the fences would have slowed him down. Probably it was a kid, looking for an easy score. But then why leave the radio and the cash? He looked hard along the sides of the houses, which were thick

with shrubbery, wondering suddenly what he would do if he
saw a pair of shoes beneath a bush.

But he didn't see any. Aside from a couple of cats on front
porches, there wasn't a living soul out and about. He might
have been the last man in the world. There was a rumble of
thunder again, closer now, and rain poured down, dripping like
a curtain from the rim of his umbrella. He tilted it into the
wind, keeping the water out of his face and finally reaching
the corner, where the gutter was flooded with water surging
toward the storm drain. A bus pulled in across the street,
blocking his view of the bus stop, which was empty of people
when the bus pulled out again, maybe carrying his burglar.

Abruptly he decided to give it up. All he was getting for
his trouble was wet shoes. He turned around, starting to head
back up the sidewalk, when he saw a man round the distant
corner, coming along down the sidewalk from the east. Walt
changed directions, walking toward the man, who could easily
be the burglar. Perhaps he had gone over the back fence of
one of the houses behind Walt's own and made his way out
to the street that way. The man didn't hesitate, but sloped
along through the rain with his hands in the pockets of his
coat.

⊰ 7 ⊱

THE LUNCH COUNTER AT WATSON'S DRUG STORE WAS
crowded, mostly with local businesspeople ordering hot turkey
sandwiches and meatloaf and burgers. Ivy was supposed to
meet a client for lunch, a woman named Linda Marvel, who
honestly didn't seem to know what a great, sideshow-sounding
name she had. She and her husband wanted to buy a bungalow
on Center Street that was priced a little steep, and Linda had
a moderate dose of buyer's remorse, although it was nothing
she couldn't be talked out of. Right now she was nowhere to
be seen.

Ivy stood near the magazine rack and looked at the people
who occupied the tables. Lots of them wore coats and ties,
and she was suddenly glad she'd worn her wool suit. She hated
to look unprofessional when she was working. Better to overdo
it a little bit than to underdo it. Half of the people gobbling
lunch at the tables qualified as old-timers. That was one of
Walt's great goals in life, to be recognized as an old-timer at
the lunch counter.

Watson's had been there since the 1920s and had gone
largely unchanged through the years—lots of chrome fixtures
and red Naugahyde that was meant to be stylish back around
1945. They made big milkshakes on one of the old Waring
machines, using real ice cream and whole milk and flavored
syrups, and served it in those big stainless-steel buckets that
easily held two full glasses. Walt always acted pettish when
she wanted to share one, but she usually got her way by bringing up the subject of calories and waistlines. Today was strictly
iced tea, though, unless Linda wanted to share one of the
shakes, in which case she'd drink it for the sake of business.
Any sacrifice for a sale.

Right now the Marvels lived out in Mission Viejo, and liked the "personality" of downtown Orange, especially since the suburbs of Mission Viejo and Irvine had almost no personality at all. That's why Watson's Drug Store was perfect for their meeting. It had ambience to spare. It was a place where you saw your postman eating a sandwich and where the druggist knew your name. They still served vanilla Cokes at the fountain.

A couple in a corner booth got up and left, and Ivy pounced on the table before anyone else made a rush for it. She ordered an iced tea from the waitress and relaxed, sliding her purse and attaché case onto the adjacent chair. The house the Marvels wanted to buy was worth every penny of the asking price, even in today's market. It had already been extensively restored, and the tiled kitchen had a walk-in pantry, a Sub-Zero refrigerator, and a Wolf stove with a big copper hood. There was a fireplace in the master bedroom, and adjacent to that was a small room that had already been turned into a nursery, with a frieze around the walls depicting fairy-tale scenes, all of it framed in wood. The Marvels were the perfect owners for the house. Linda was three months pregnant.

Ivy realized she envied the woman—her baby, the house, the fact that her husband made a hundred and fifty thousand a year and they could afford this dream house without thinking about it more than twice. When she had shown it to them for the first time a week ago, Linda had become a sort of happy-faced zombie, drifting from room to room in a trance, until Bill, her husband, had said to her, in a voice that sounded like he'd been practicing in front of the mirror, "Darling, say the word."

That was it. Linda had said the word right there on the spot, like something out of a Doris Day movie circa 1955. She spun around and shouted, "Oh, yes! Darling!" and they'd kissed each other right there in the empty living room. Actually it *had* been fairly wonderful. Ivy had very nearly kissed him, too. She'd been calculating the commission in her head all that afternoon, and what it added up to, from her perspective and Linda's both, was Bill being the hero of the week. He was handsome, too, in a weathered sort of way. Probably he was a creep in some other area: came home late and got drunk in front of the television.

The waitress brought her iced tea and a menu, and she told herself to cut it out. Still, she couldn't help thinking about her and Walt—how devoted he was to their house, their neighborhood. He was stodgy; that was the only word for it. The idea of change gave him heartburn. She had tried him out once—suggested that they move into a house that had just been listed with the agency. It was a steal. They could have moved up by a factor of fifty thousand dollars and not felt it once they refinanced, except for the increase in property taxes. But the very idea of it had left him speechless with dismay. He wasn't interested, he'd said, in the mathematics of investment, only in "the damage" it would do to his soul.

What it boiled down to, she had finally decided, was that he couldn't give up his sheds in the backyard. Sheds were some kind of philosophy to him. Last night he had gone on and on about them, all worked up, about how the best sheds were built out of used materials, old boards and cinderblocks, and about how that made his new tin shed from Sears inferior, except that, he'd said very seriously, there was something "nicely musical" about the sound of a new tin shed in the rain.

That's why he didn't need any children, Ivy figured; he had all these sheds in the backyard, each one with its own personality. Ivy had told him as much last night. She had advised him to go ahead and build one more shed, maybe out of brick this time, in order to organize them into a basketball team. They could play in the shed leagues. Ivy could be a team mom, and the two of them could drive the sheds back and forth to games in the back of the Suburban. Walt had laughed as if he thought it was funny and then had turned over and pretended to go to sleep. That was the end of the conversation.

She looked out the window at the street. It had started to rain. There was only one customer at the outside tables, and when the wind blew the rain under the canvas awning, he grabbed his half-full coffee cup and headed for the door.

Abruptly she recognized him, just at the moment that he saw her through the window. He waved at her and smiled, looking pleased, and although she hated herself for doing it, she smiled back. Probably she couldn't manage to look authentically pleased no matter how hard she tried. Thank heaven she had an excuse not to sit with him; it would simply be too difficult.

He came across to her table, and she stood up, taking his hand when he held it out and trying to hold onto the smile, too, reminding herself to let bygones be bygones, especially with a man like Robert Argyle, who, as much as she hated to say it, had acquired a certain amount of power in the city—multiple businesses, charities, residential and commercial properties. . . . Because of Walt, she couldn't bring herself to refer to him as anything but Argyle. Walt had banished his Christian name and most often turned his last name into a joke, predictably having to do with socks. She and Walt had carefully avoided him over the past couple of years that they'd been neighbors. When it had been absolutely necessary, a nod or a monosyllable had been enough. Three years ago he had run for school board, and Ivy had to stop Walt from driving around the neighborhoods and vandalizing his campaign signs.

But, God, his face had gotten coarse over the years. He looked almost grainy, and his eyes were too active, as if he were afraid of something. Gravity hadn't been kind to him, and he was getting a little jowly. He was tall—taller than Walt, who was nearly six-two—and had always walked with just a slight stoop, as if he'd been timid and withdrawn as a child. His hair was still just as brown as it had been when they had dated in college. Walt's was gray at the temples, but Argyle looked older than Walt despite that.

He put his coffee cup on the next table, which was cluttered with dirty dishes, and then asked, "Can I join you?"

She thought immediately of Walt's stock rejoinder: "What's the matter, do I look like I'm coming apart?" and she nearly giggled out loud, realizing at the same time that she was nervous. There was too much history between them for it to be any other way. Sometimes things broke and you couldn't fix them. It was better to throw them away.

"Only for a moment," she said. "I'm afraid I'm meeting a client."

"Good. That's nothing to be afraid of. In this economy, any business is good business."

He looked searchingly at her, as if he were trying to see if there was anything in her face that he could read, some evidence that she still carried a torch for him, perhaps a candle, a lighted match. . . . Whatever kind of man he had been twenty years ago, he was made of something different now. The years had turned him upside down and shaken all the good things out of his pockets, unless you counted money as a good thing, and in his case it wasn't. Aunt Jinx had called him a "husk" once, when Walt was going on about him, which was the word Jinx used for worthless, empty men. Ivy wondered now if that was fair. The evidence was twenty years old. Maybe there was a statute of limitations on that kind of thing.

Argyle remained standing as he talked, and she realized that she'd tuned him out. ". . . a couple of industrial properties over on Batavia, if you're interested," he said.

She nodded. What was this, a business proposition? "I'm sorry," she said. "I thought I saw my client coming in. What were you saying?"

He looked at her for a moment before speaking. "I was wondering whether you were interested in listing a couple of pieces of property."

The idea struck her as odd. The last time she had spoken to him he'd—what?—propositioned her; there was nothing else to call it. She'd put him off pretty hard. Of course she hadn't told Walt, who would simply have gone out of his mind. So the suggestion that they have dealings of any sort, even business dealings, was a complete surprise. Her first impulse was to turn him down.

But if there was ever a time that she and Walt needed the income from commissions, it was now. Why not take the man's money? Walt was determined to make his business work, and he deserved to. Probably he *would* make it work, given enough time, because as screwball as some of his ideas could be, he had a certain strange genius for seeing the sense in nonsense, and making other people see it too. Not that catalogue sales was nonsense—Argyle apparently had done all right with his own mail-order businesses over the years. . . .

"Perhaps I could drop by the office," she said to him. Breakfast or lunch was out of the question.

"Tomorrow, then?"

"Make it day after tomorrow, can you? I'm going over to my sister's tomorrow."

"That's fine," he said. "Morning? Say ten?"

"Ten's fine." She wondered why she'd mentioned her sister. Her personal life wasn't any business of Argyle's, and hadn't been for a long time.

"How *is* Darla? I haven't seen her in . . ." He shook his head, as if he was unable to remember.

"She's fine," Ivy said.

"What was her husband's name?"

"Jack."

"They're still happy, then?"

"Tolerably. You know—ups and downs, like the rest of the world."

"You're not giving anything away, are you?" He smiled wistfully. "You aren't still hard on me, are you?"

There was no answer to the question; whatever she was, it had little to do with him. The waitress approached just then, carrying the iced tea pitcher. Argyle pulled his lunch check out of his shirt pocket along with a five-dollar bill and waved it at her, smiling broadly and starting to say something.

And at that moment the check and the five-dollar bill burst into flame, flaring up like burning phosphorus with a bright, white glow. He dropped it on the ground, jerking his hand back and shaking it as if he'd been burned. The waitress, without seeming to think twice about it, bent over and poured iced tea on the burning paper, which fizzled out.

She picked it up and looked at the five-dollar bill, which was charred black along one edge. She shrugged. "Looks okay," she said. "No harm done." A busboy appeared and wiped up the floor with a rag, and at that moment Linda Marvel came in through the front door carrying a dripping umbrella. Ivy waved at her and motioned her over, relieved to be saved from Argyle, who seemed to be embarrassed nearly to the point of apoplexy. He stood unblinking, gaping at the waitress, then opened and closed his mouth like a fish.

"I guess the candle . . ." He gestured, not finishing the sentence. He tried to piece his smile back together. Linda slid past him and sat down in the empty seat. "Oh, yes," he said. "I'll just . . . I'll leave you two alone." He rubbed his hands together, looking detached, as if he'd been tapped on the shoulder by a ghost.

"Did you burn yourself?" Ivy asked.

"No. Not at all. Thursday, then?"

"Fine. Ten."

He nodded and fled, going out through the door and into the rain where he hurried away down the sidewalk on foot, pulling his coat shut and angling out into the street.

"Do you want the candle relit?" the waitress asked, pouring what was left of the iced tea into Ivy's glass. "I don't know why it was lit anyway. Usually we don't light them until later. A customer must have lit it."

"I don't think it *was* lit," Ivy said. "Do we need a candle?" She looked at Linda, who shook her head. "I guess we don't care about the candle." She touched the bumpy glass vase that the candle was in. The glass was cool.

The waitress shrugged, and Ivy looked out the window again, distracted now. She could still see Argyle, far down the block, hurrying through the rain in the direction of Maple Street, probably heading home. He cut a very small and sorry figure from this distance, and Ivy was suddenly struck with the notion that whatever power he'd ever had over her had been illusory. Had she changed? *He* certainly had. There was a loud crack of thunder just then, and the rain poured down in a torrent, concealing him altogether behind a gray veil of mist.

❊ 8 ❊

WALT RECOGNIZED THE MAN COMING TOWARD HIM. HELL. IT wasn't the burglar at all; it was worse—a minister, the Reverend Bentley from the storefront church down on Grand Street who had the irritating habit of making door-to-door forays through the neighborhoods, looking for converts, passing out little tracts.

Walt turned around to avoid him, but it was too late. He'd been seen, recognized. Bentley hurried forward, as if he had something urgent to say. He looked rumpled and beat, and his wet jacket was streaked with dirt. The rain let up just then, and for a moment the sun showed through a gap in the clouds. The minister looked up at the clouds and smiled, as if he'd put in a request and God had seen fit to grant it.

"Henry and Jinx on the horizon, then?" Bentley asked, shaking Walt's hand.

Walt nodded. The Reverend Bentley was an old friend of Henry's; they went way back—lodge brothers of some sort. Walt hardly knew Bentley, though, and he was slightly surprised that the man recognized him so easily, looking half drowned and hiding behind the umbrella. "They're due any moment, actually. They were in Needles last night, and were thinking about taking a detour through apple country, but I expect them any time."

"Good," the minister said, looking around. "That's good. I'm going to drag that old sinner in front of the congregation and flush out his soul with a firehose."

"It's high time," Walt said. "What brings you out on a day like this?"

"Trouble in paradise," Bentley said. "How's *your* soul, by

the way? You look like a worried man, like maybe you swallowed some kind of sin."

The question took Walt by surprise. The minister could be a hell of an irritating old interloper when he was on a mission in the neighborhood. He was something of a local joke, in fact, and his church had a congregation you could put into the back of a pickup truck and still have room for the dog. He did good works, though, taking food around to shut-ins and the like. Lord knows how he continued to fund his projects. He had a sort of meals-on-wheels van that Uncle Henry had driven for a few weeks last winter, dropping off hot lunches at the houses of neighborhood widows. Aunt Jinx had put an end to it, though, after talking to one of the widows among the vegetable bins at Satellite Market. Walt himself had donated a hundred bucks to the meals program in a generous moment. That was a few years ago, when money had been a little easier to come by.

"I guess it's still hobbling along," Walt said.

"What is?" The minister was looking vaguely off down the street, not paying attention.

"My soul. You asked how my soul was doing."

"Well . . . good. Keep at it, then. This is Babylon we're living in, make no mistake about that. There's a lot of temptations out there." He looked meaningfully at Walt now, as if this tidbit of information had been hand-selected.

"That's the truth," Walt said.

"I can tell you that a lot of people fall," Bentley said.

"Like ripe fruit." Walt shook his head at the seriousness of it.

"Don't be cocky." The minister narrowed his eyes, convinced that Walt was making fun of him. "Pride goeth, as they say. Here—here's a little something to read."

He handed Walt a pamphlet, maybe three inches square, with a picture of a lion and a lamb on the front, lying down together with such wide, dopey grins on their faces that it looked as if they'd just been hit over the head with a mallet. The title of the booklet was "Marriage as an Obstacle to Sin."

Bentley took Walt's elbow suddenly and steered him toward the corner, pointing across the street, toward St. Anthony's. "What's going on there? My vision's not . . ."

Without waiting for an answer he let go of Walt's arm and

hurried forward. Walt followed him, noticing now that there was a police car in the parking lot. Half a dozen people milled around near the base of the bell tower. It looked like the top of the tower had collapsed. At least one of the bells had fallen, and the bronze edge of it, shiny with rainwater, was shoved out of a gaping hole in the stucco tower. That was the noise he'd heard twenty minutes ago.

Bentley slogged through the water in the gutter, waiting for a gap in the traffic before sprinting across, two steps ahead of Walt. There was the sound of a siren from up the boulevard, and in moments an ambulance pulled up, slamming to a halt, its siren cutting off. The crowd parted, and for a moment Walt got a good look at the man who lay on the concrete floor at the base of the tower. Clearly the heavy bell had gone right through the upper floor, smashing the bellringer on the head and knocking him down the steep wooden stairs. The side of his head was crushed, and his mouth hung open unnaturally. . . .

A couple of kids came around the side of the church, and a woman in the crowd turned and corralled them with her arms. "Stay back," someone else hollered. "One of the bells came down. It's still . . ."

Walt didn't hear the rest of it. He turned away, walking back toward the street. The shadow on the roof early this morning—someone *had* been up there. Someone evidently had sabotaged the bell. Why the hell hadn't he called the police? Now the bellringer was dead.

Without thinking he stepped down into the gutter, heard a horn honk, and jumped back up onto the curb as a car whizzed by, the driver shouting something at him and flipping him off out the window, over the top of the car.

Walt waved. The picture of the dead man—surely he was dead—remained in his mind as he waited to recross the street: in his mind he saw the bell tower, the stairs leading away into the shadows above, a shoe lying on the second step, the bottom step smeared with blood, a woman's face mesmerized with the horror of it, her hand to her mouth as if to stop herself from screaming. . . .

Walt shuddered. He wanted desperately to go home, to change out of his wet clothes and warm up. It was raining again, but he didn't raise the umbrella. He walked a few steps farther, standing in the shelter of a big cypress tree and shielding his eyes from the water dripping through the branches. The two ambulance drivers stepped toward the back of the ambulance, carrying the body on a blanket-covered gurney. Presently the ambulance pulled out into traffic, switching on its siren and accelerating toward the west, probably heading for the emergency room at St. Joseph's. Walt wondered if there was anything hopeful in the sound of the siren. Would they bother with it if the bellringer was dead? Would they cover the man's face if he wasn't?

He realized he was still carrying the tract that Bentley had given him, and suddenly the little folded bit of paper enraged him—a trivial little scrap of holier-than-thou advice in a world where someone had just been crushed to death in a blind instant. And at such a moment! Did the bellringer have a wife, a family? Did his wife consider marriage an obstacle to sin, or something considerably more than that?

Bentley was nowhere to be seen now; otherwise Walt would have thrown the tract in his face. He shoved it into his pocket instead, and then walked toward where two policemen stood talking, up under the roof of the portico at the front of the church.

And even as he stepped toward them he told himself that he could just as easily not say anything at all. It was too damned late now anyway. Speaking up now was nothing but useless humiliation, self-revenge. . . .

But he forced himself forward, refusing to listen. One of the policemen turned and nodded at him, and Walt introduced himself, clearing his throat but still unable to get the gravel out of his voice, suddenly wishing to heaven that Ivy was there with him, holding his hand, that he wasn't standing there wet and alone and empty on this bleak December morning.

9

WALT UNLOCKED THE PADLOCK ON THE GARAGE DOOR AND
pulled it open, taking Bentley's tract out of his pocket and
tossing it into the galvanized bucket he used as a trash can.
His hand shaking, he switched on the space heater and then
filled the coffeemaker at the sink, spooned ground coffee into
the filter, and plugged it in. He found his work sweater and
put it on, only now realizing how cold he was, and for a long
time he stood in front of the heater, letting the warm air blow
across him while he listened to the sounds of the coffeepot
and the rain on the roof.

The two policemen had listened closely to his story, which
had taken all of forty seconds to recount. They nodded, writing
down maybe two sentences along with his name and address.
Neither of them seemed to see anything shameful in any of it.
One of them, though, seeing that somehow this had wrecked
Walt, had tried to make him easier about it. Even if they'd
sent a squad car to the church, he said, they'd have found
nothing. The prowler wouldn't have shown himself—even if
he were still hanging around—and there was no way the officer would have climbed onto the roof in the pouring rain.
And it certainly wouldn't have dawned on anyone that the
bells might have been sabotaged. Sherlock Holmes couldn't
have guessed it.

"Give yourself a break," the cop had said, squeezing Walt's
shoulder. And his being kind about it had turned out to be the
hardest part.

Walt looked around the floor now, thinking suddenly that it
was high time to get to work. Pouring a cup of coffee, he
looked at the boxes on the floor. Random odds and ends had
been hastily unwrapped and set around, as if the burglar had

tried to be neat, and didn't want to break anything. Nothing about it made any sense. If the burglar wasn't after quick cash, then what was he after, one of the plaster-of-Paris tiki god mugs that sat now on the concrete floor? There were sixty or seventy cartons stacked up in the garage, maybe more; had the burglar meant to work his way through every blessed one of them?

He took a long sip of coffee, listening to the rain on the roof and wondering what Ivy would make of the break-in, if you could call it that; more like the walk-in. Then abruptly he saw that he couldn't tell Ivy about it at all. What was the use? They'd never been broken into before. The idea of it would only frighten her—intruders snooping around in the night, then breaking into the garage in midday. Every little noise would set her off. She'd wonder out loud if this was another one of the risks of doing business out of your garage. Walt wasn't making enough money at it yet to justify any kind of risk at all. From now on he'd keep the place locked up, just like you'd lock up any business when you went to lunch. And besides, this wasn't looking much like a real burglary anyway; it was certainly more curious than threatening.

It dawned on him then that the burglar had no idea what he was after; he had apparently opened a couple of boxes, discovered that the stuff wasn't valuable enough to steal, and then, hearing Walt come outside, had gone out through the back door in such a hurry that he didn't even see the stuff on the desk. This was some kind of random incident, the sort of thing that probably happened in dozens of garages every afternoon. . . .

He turned a snow globe over in his hand. Silver glitter cascaded around a washed-out pink flamingo standing on one leg. There was no way the base of the thing was deep enough to be hollow. All of the stuff in the boxes was Chinese—from mainland China, but shipped out of Hong Kong—and somehow that suggested opium to him, heroin, whatever. But what sort of dope smuggler would be so dainty about retrieving his contraband? That theory just didn't figure.

Rewrapping the flamingo, he put it back in the box, then weaved the top of the box shut and scribbled the contents on the side with a felt marker. It was a crude system of organization, but there was no way he had enough space in the garage and in the sheds to unpack any boxes. Someday, when the business was humming, he'd open up in a small industrial building or in one of the old turn-of-the-century houses that were zoned for commercial use along Chapman Avenue. Meanwhile he'd make do with a garage and a couple of sheds.

In the second box there were bags of rhinestone-studded sunglasses, a dozen umbrella hats, and a gross of boxes of Magic Rocks, which were big stocking stuffers at Christmastime. All of the boxes were sealed, the bags were stapled shut. Nothing, apparently, had been tampered with.

One small box had been opened but not emptied; no doubt the burglar hadn't had time for it. It was stuffed tight with some kind of primitive, coarsely cut packing material that looked like the fiber from coconut husks. There was a bag visible at the corner of the box, folded up out of heavily waxed paper, as if someone had melted a candle over unbleached butcher paper. The ends were twisted tight and tied off with strips of the coconut-husk fiber. Puzzled, Walt untied the little parcel and folded it open. There was a bundle of sticks inside—sticks about six inches long, carefully stripped of bark. The glistening wood was a fleshy-looking pink, and the wood and paper both smelled of something—creosote, maybe. He parted the packing material and looked beneath it. There were three little bundles of wax-soaked cloth, tied off with string. He squeezed one, trying to determine what was inside, but it was impossible to say; it felt like a beanbag full of human teeth. The whole box, now that it was opened, smelled vaguely rancid, as if there was a dead mouse inside.

He sure as hell hadn't ordered any twigs, or sacks of teeth either. This was some kind of mistake. He looked at the invoice he'd razored off the cover flap of the first box, but there was nothing on it that sounded even remotely similar to this. He pulled out more of the packing material, exposing a box full of small vials with crimped-on metal lids. Inside each vial was a jumble of small seed pods and quartz crystals and colored beans packed in oil, as well as an inch-long segment of what might have been alabaster, crudely painted with the depiction of an elongated human figure the color of dried blood.

There was something awful about the vials—the discolored oil inside, maybe, or the yellowed alabaster that might as easily have been bone or fossil ivory. There were other boxes of vials in the carton, too—unsymmetrical, hand-blown bottles made of clouded glass and filled with amber-colored liquid, corked and then dipped in wax.

Nearly at the bottom lay a cloth bag with something inside—a small jar, maybe an ounce, sealed with a piece of canvas like a stiff fragment of an old ship's sail, tied off with twine and again dipped in wax. Despite the wax, the jar stank to high heaven, which explained the rancid smell, and Walt could see that ointment of some sort had oozed out from where the layer of wax was cracked. There was writing on the bag— two Chinese ideograms above a short phrase that might have been in English, except that it was so ill-written that Walt could barely make it out. He held it under the light, trying to puzzle through the words letter by letter.

After a moment it struck him, not one word at a time, but the whole phrase at once, and he dropped the bag onto the countertop. "Dead mans grease" was what it said. There was no apostrophe, and the writing was mostly loops and slashes, but once he saw it, the meaning was clear.

Some kind of joke gift? A starter kit for suburban witches? He picked up the jar, slid it back into the bag, and tied the top shut. Then he pulled the rest of the packing fiber out of the carton. At the bottom lay a painted tin box. Stamped on the lid of the box were the words "Gong Hee Fot Choy," and beneath them was the painting of a bluebird on the wing, towing a banner that read "happiness."

Vaguely relieved, Walt pried the lid off the box. Inside lay a tiny folded pamphlet that reminded him immediately of the kind of thing the Reverend Bentley passed out. Under the pamphlet, protected by a ring of corrugated paper, lay a jar, this one smelling weirdly of gin and containing what appeared to be a dead bird. It looked awful, as if it had been dead a week before it was pickled in the gin. Abruptly, as if he had shaken the jar, the bird moved, or seemed to. He set it on the bench and stood back, shivering with a sudden chill. He must have imagined it. The bird floated there, turning slowly in the moving liquid until one of its open eyes seemed to be staring right at him, as if in contemplation.

He picked the jar up again and slid it back into the tin, then opened the pamphlet, which was written on some sort of parchment. It looked like instructions in about ten languages

including Korean, French, Spanish, and German, two or three
lines each, and a couple of other languages that were uniden-
tifiable Arabic-looking swirls and dots. The English was illit-
erate—the kind of thing you'd find on badly translated
directions for assembling a foreign-made toy.

"Best thing come to you," it read. *."Speak any wish."*

It was a good-luck charm, some kind of wish-fulfillment
object that was apparently meant to bring happiness to its
owner—although not, presumably, to the bluebird itself, which
was as unhappy an object as he had ever seen.

He decided suddenly that the whole works disgusted him.
How it had gotten mixed up in his order he couldn't say. There
was something nasty and primitive about it, even without the
jar of "dead mans grease," whatever the hell that was. He
started to shove the stuff back into the box, cramming the
packing fiber back in around it. His first impulse now was to
throw it into the trash can, but then he decided he wanted it
out of there altogether—better to pitch it into the bin behind
the medical buildings on the corner. Probably it would be even
better to incinerate it and bury the ashes.

It dawned on him then—surely this must be the stuff that
the burglar had been after, this box of diabolical trash.

Walt turned the box over and looked for the first time at the
mailing label on the bottom side. He saw at once that it had
been misdelivered. It was addressed to a party named Dilworth
at a residential address a block away. The number was the
same as Walt's own, but the street was wrong. This had happened before. The address numbers on the downtown streets,
both north and south, repeated so often that it was a mailman's
nightmare. What was puzzling about this was that 225 North
Cambridge wasn't owned by anyone named Dilworth; it was
owned by a man named Robert Argyle—the one man in the
world with whom Walt was not on speaking terms.

At one time he and Argyle had been close friends and business partners. And it wasn't just because Argyle had been in
love with Ivy, either, back when they were both just out of
college. Walt couldn't hold that against the man; it was almost
the only thing about him that was sane. Argyle had turned out
to be a corrupt, cheating son-of-a-bitch. Ultimately, he had
ended up with the business, and Walt had ended up with almost nothing, except Ivy, of course, and the rotten realization

that he'd been betrayed by a man whom he had once considered a friend. Hell, who had *been* his friend.

Argyle, gratifyingly, had gone broke after falling into some sort of trouble, and for years Walt had lost track of him. Then he had reappeared, buying the house at 225 North Cambridge—the most ostentatious house in Old Towne. It was built on a half acre—three stories, leaded glass windows, a wrought-iron elevator and detached servants' quarters. With his money Argyle could have moved up Chapman Avenue and bought one of the big homes on Orange Hill, but then he would have been just one more Orange County millionaire among the teeming masses of them. Here in his hometown he could be a tin god, a man who had made something of himself by working like a pig and behaving the same way.

And now fate had misdelivered to Walt a box meant for Argyle. Surely, he thought, there was some way to put this happy coincidence to use. . . .

Clearly the name ''Dilworth'' was a fraud, unless Argyle was renting out the servant's quarters these days. More likely it was some kind of blind—a way of protecting himself from being charged with improbable postal crimes if the contents were discovered.

Was it *Argyle* that had broken into the garage? The idea struck him like a stone. It was almost funny—a millionaire reduced to looting garages.

With his felt pen he crossed out the name ''Dilworth'' and wrote ''Robert Argyle'' above it. He picked up the tape roller and held it over the box. Then he put the tape down, opened the box again, and pulled out the bluebird of happiness, replacing it with wadded-up Chinese newspaper. He would keep the bluebird for a few days; he wasn't quite sure why.

Well, he *was* sure why. He'd keep it in order to make Argyle unhappy, mystified, and irritated. At the end of the week he would throw it down the storm drain at the end of the street.

There was the sound just then of a horn honking, and he looked out through the barely open door. There were Henry and Jinx, pulling into the driveway, right on time. Walt went out through the back door carrying the bluebird tin with him. Hurrying, he crossed the lawn to the garden shed, already having made up his mind. He found the trowel, then stepped across the muddy garden to the tomato vines, where he

scooped a hole in the dirt, shoving the tin into the ground and
covering it nearly to the top. Then he arranged the vines over
it so that unless you looked right at it, from a couple of feet
away, you couldn't see a thing.

"Bring me a decent tomato," he said to the bluebird. Then
he tossed the trowel into the shed and trotted back out toward
the front of the garage. In the driveway, Aunt Jinx and Uncle
Henry were pulling shopping bags full of wrapped Christmas
presents out of the rear end of the motor home, which looked
like a soda-cracker box on wheels.

❧ 10 ❧

HENRY'S HAIR WAS NEARLY PURE WHITE, AND HE KEPT IT trimmed in a brush cut that gave him the look of a retired military man who would be going in for a haircut within the next day or two. He wore a polyester polo shirt, buttoned up, with a sports jacket and Sansabelt slacks and black loafers. He was short—shorter than Jinx—probably five-two or -three, but he made up for this by having the attitude that there was nothing a man couldn't do if he put his mind to it, and Walt always got the notion that Henry had put his mind to a thousand things in his life and had accomplished them all, even though it wasn't really clear what those things were. He was somewhere in his middle seventies, but it seemed as if he'd been retired forever.

He never gave any hint, though, that Walt, or anybody else, should be accomplishing anything in particular, and when Walt had told him, months ago, about the catalogue sales, he had said it sounded "fabulous." He would have said the same thing if Walt were starting up a shoe store or an amphibian import service. Henry seemed to assume that every other man on earth felt the same way that he himself did, and was up to the same things, and that with luck and perseverance they'd all succeed together. Because of that he had a built-in respect for nearly everyone he met, and struck up conversations with sales clerks and gas station attendants. Henry didn't have any enemies, and Walt liked him for that, although the blind trust that Henry had in the world seemed like a dangerous philosophy for a man of business.

Walt had always known that Henry and Jinx had money, largely because of family talk about Henry's investments and business dealings. And so the motor home was no surprise to

him. There was a shower in it as well as a toilet, and a refrigerator that ran off propane or electricity, whichever was handy.
The cabinetry was first-rate—lots of chrome, a twenty-inch
television set with a built-in VCR.

"What do you think?" Henry said to him, waving his hand
at things in general. "Fabulous, isn't it?" Jinx had already
disappeard into the house to see about dinner.

"Nice," Walt said. "Real deluxe." He realized that Henry
thought it *was* fabulous, too. He liked it. Things were right
with the world, and this motor home was proof of it.

The screen door on the house slammed, and in a moment
Aunt Jinx looked in, holding a bottle of salad dressing. "I
found everything I need for muffins and a salad," she said,
"if that suits the two of you."

"Suits me down to the ground," Walt said. "What else will
we have?"

"Oh, that's enough, don't you think? I'll put chickpeas and
tuna in the salad—a meal in itself. Is this what you two dress
salads with?" She held out the bottle, which was nearly empty.

Walt nodded. "Not much there."

"I'll pep it up with a little canola oil. There's less saturated
fat than in bottled dressings. No stabilizers, either, or MSG."
She climbed up the steps into the motor home and pushed past
Walt and Henry in order to open a cupboard, where she found
the oil and a small bottle of dark red vinegar. There wasn't a
lot in the cupboard besides Styrofoam boxes of instant noodles.
"The muffins are made entirely without oil or salt and are
high in bran. They're a first-rate source of roughage."

"Good," Walt said. "That sounds perfect." He hated it
when people advised him to eat "roughage," like he was a
cow or something. He imagined a big plate of chopped-up
shrubbery.

"You'll be surprised how satisfying it is. And with the
Christmas season starting up, we'll all be overeating. Fats,
sugar . . ." She shook her head. "There's no better time to
start a new regimen. I called Ivy at the office, and she's entirely in agreement. So you two quit nodding like fools and
get it into your heads."

"No," Walt insisted. "It sounds fine to me."

There was the sound of drumming on the roof, and Walt
realized that it had started to rain again. Aunt Jinx picked up

a newspaper from the table and held it over her head before going back out.

"She intends to make men out of us," Walt said, smiling at Henry.

"She's a juggernaut. I've lost five pounds." Henry patted himself on the stomach and then pulled open a drawer full of clothes, shifted some socks out of the way, and found a small box of Cheez-Its. Together they ate the crackers, sitting at the table, while Henry fiddled with the television set, trying to improve the reception. "It's got cable hookup," he said. "We'll have to get a roll of coax and a splitter down at Radio Shack."

With the rain falling outside now, the motor home began to feel snug and comfortable, and Walt was disappointed when Jinx came back out and told him he had a phone call in the house. He followed her in, jogging through the rain, and picked up the receiver in the kitchen.

"Hello," he said, listening to the staticky connection. It sounded like somebody rustling paper on the other end. "Sorry, can you speak up?"

The man wanted something. It was a business call, and he was using a phone that was apparently wired into a beehive. "I was wondering about a certain product line having to do with . . . what shall we call it? Third-world religions—voodoo, Santeria. Do you carry anything along those lines?"

"I don't believe so," Walt said. "Anything in particular?"

"Herbals, perhaps?"

He thought about the stuff he'd found in the misdelivered box, and suddenly wondered who this was on the line. Argyle? It didn't sound like him, but of course it wouldn't make any sense that Argyle would call anyway; the call would come from one of his employees. "I guess not," he said. "I've got nun finger puppets and plastic holy water bottles from Lourdes, night lights—that kind of thing."

"Sounds basically like gag gifts. I wanted something more . . . primitive. Authentic."

"Was there some *specific* item you were looking for?" Walt asked.

"Not really, no. Charms, elixirs, primitive religious artifacts, that sort of thing. Do you have a catalogue?"

"A new one, in fact," Walt said. "I'll send it out tomorrow. Where are you located?"

There was a pause. "Costa Mesa," the man said. "Two-twenty-five Fourteenth Street, 93341."

Walt wrote it down and hung up after promising to send the catalogue. Then he went out into the rain and pulled the Thomas Bros. mapbook out of the Suburban, climbing onto the front seat and pulling the door shut. He was virtually certain that the zip was a fake, made up on the spot. He flipped to the index and scanned the addresses. Just as he thought, there was no 200 block of Fourteenth Street in Costa Mesa.

⪪ 11 ⪫

WALT FLIPPED ON THE GARAGE LIGHT AT SIX IN THE EVENING, leaving Ivy to wash up the dishes with Aunt Jinx. Henry was watching the news in the living room, drinking a cup of coffee laced with Half and Half and about a pound of sugar as an antidote to the chickpeas and shrubbery. Actually, there hadn't been anything wrong with the food at dinner—nothing that a double cheeseburger from Wimpy's wouldn't cure. Of course, Jinx was probably right about what they needed, dietetically speaking. And probably she'd tire out soon.

It was pitch dark out and raining in flurries, but he decided he wouldn't bother with an umbrella. He picked up Argyle's cardboard carton and went down the carport toward the street, where the dim yellow circles of light from the streetlamps seemed, if anything, to make the night a little darker. The wind was blowing out of the east, and the sky overhead was heavy with clouds barely illuminated by a hidden moon. A car passed as he hurried toward the corner, but otherwise the streets were deserted. The bad weather kept everyone indoors.

He turned the corner and walked up toward Sycamore, and even from a distance he could see that Argyle's house was lit up. There were a couple of cars parked along the street and smoke coming out of the chimney, and for a moment Walt thought about turning around and heading back home. But there was no sign of anyone outside, and the porch light was off.

He decided to risk it. He crossed the street, angling toward Argyle's front porch, prepared to walk straight on past if anyone came out. Quickly he cut across the lawn, slid the box beneath the porch railings and gave it a good shove. It slid beneath a wicker chair where it lay hidden in the shadows.

The box was nearly invisible; when Argyle found it he'd have to wonder whether it hadn't been lying there for a week.

Just then the porch light blinked on, and Walt ducked, sliding around the side of the porch toward a couple of big hydrangea bushes against the side of the house. Immediately he knew he'd made a mistake. He should simply have headed for the street—just another pedestrian hurrying home in the rain. Now it was too late. He felt like a kid, out marauding through the neighborhood at night. There was the rattling of a latch, and then the door swung open, casting light from the entryway out onto the lawn. Walt crammed himself in behind the bush, pressing himself into the shadows.

It started to rain harder, and he pulled his coat shut, waiting for them to leave, listening to shoe soles scraping on the wooden floorboards of the porch. Then there was silence for a moment, followed by low conversation. Somebody laughed, and a voice said, "*I'll* say." Then there was silence again, as if they were standing there watching the rain fall, hoping that it would let up so they could make a dash for their cars.

"I hate this damned rain," someone finally said.

"It's the season," someone else said.

"Well, I hate the season, too."

"Too commercialized. I agree with you."

"That isn't what I mean. God, I hate it when people say that. To my mind it isn't half commercial enough, not this year. Profit—that's the only thing about Christmas that does me any good, and here we are in the middle of it and nobody's spending any money."

A third voice spoke, Argyle this time. "Call me after someone's had a look at LeRoy's. Don't worry about waking me up. We want those jars."

"Yes, *we* do." It was the second man now, the one who didn't like Christmas. "I'm still not clear on something. I understand that we've got a green light over there tonight, but if we can't—what shall I say—*clean it out*, are we absolutely certain . . . ?"

"And it rained fire and brimstone out of heaven and destroyed them all," Argyle said, interrupting him.

"That's just your style, Bob, to dismiss something like this with an irrelevant quote. It's easier than thinking, isn't it?"

Argyle laughed then. "Relax, George. You're making a

mountain out of a molehill. Just have your people take care of
things over at LeRoy's and let me know. They won't be bothered over there tonight. When we've got what we want, we
can *all* dismiss it. It'll *be* an irrelevancy. And have them look
around good—crawl spaces, secret panels, throw rugs. Don't
rush it. LeRoy had his own way with things, if you follow me.
He went in for all the trappings. Leave the place clean.''

The rain let up abruptly, and Walt watched through the
branches, hearing them descend the porch steps now, their
shadows jutting out across the lawn. Something told him that
he didn't want to know anything more than he already knew—
which was virtually nothing—but he couldn't stop himself
from wondering who the two men were. One of the cars was
visible from where he was hidden, and when the door swung
open the driver was illuminated for a moment by the dome
light. Walt recognized him, from downtown. He was one of
the Watson's morning regulars, which meant he probably
worked in one of the buildings around the Plaza. He usually
wore a suit, too; so he was likely a professional of some sort—
lawyer, maybe, or chiropractor.

The engines started up and the cars moved off. He heard
footsteps crossing the porch, and then a moment later the
house door shut and the light went out. Walt peeked past the
edge of the house, making sure the porch was empty. He saw
immediately that there was no carton beneath the wicker chair;
Argyle had retrieved it, probably wondering right now how
long it had lain there, gathering dust. He hurried out to the
sidewalk and headed home, his jacket soaked and his hair plas-
tered to his forehead with rainwater.

⚜ 12 ⚜

UNCLE HENRY STOOD IN THE GARAGE, EATING A DOUGHNUT out of the box on the bench. He held out the box. "I helped myself. Hope you don't mind."

"They're probably a little dry by now." There was only one left, so Henry must have eaten two of them. That didn't surprise Walt any; last winter Henry had developed a habit, and he was probably anxious to take it up again.

"They're just right," Henry said. "Dryness improves the roughage." He winked.

Walt took the last doughnut, realizing that he was famished.

"Been out for a walk?"

"Yes," Walt replied. "I had to run something over to a neighbor's house, and the rain started up on me. Caught me on the way home." He noticed that the sleeve of his jacket was streaked with dirt from leaning against the wet wall of Argyle's house. He'd leave it in the garage when he went in. There was no use trying to explain it to Ivy.

"Quite a setup you've got here," Henry said, looking around.

"It's cramped," Walt said, "but it'll have to do till I can find a bigger place."

Henry shrugged. "There's a lot of overhead in a bigger place. You can deduct overhead from your profits. Pretty soon you're hiring help, buying trucks. Insurance goes through the roof. What's wrong with this?"

"Nothing," Walt said. "It's a little small-time, that's all. And I'm not zoned commercial either. I get away with it because there's no customers coming around—just UPS trucks, and they come through the neighborhood twice a day anyway."

Henry nodded, looking around at the stacked cartons, ordered and numbered, their contents listed on the sides in felt pen—rubber chickens, false noses, glow-in-the-dark fish, garden elves. . . . "Quite an inventory."

"Yeah, I'm cramped for storage. I just bought a jumbo tin shed from Sears and Roebuck for overflow. It's all set up, but I don't think I'll get around to shifting stock till after the Christmas rush." There was nothing in Henry's attitude to suggest that he found any of this stuff laughable, as if to him it was merchandise to be bought and sold, and might as well have been shoes or automobile parts. Well, that was all right. Walt was content to let the customers do the laughing. The world needed more laughing.

"To tell you the truth," Henry said, "I came out here tonight because I've got a small proposition for you. I've been thinking along a different line altogether—a way to make this business of yours fly without leaving home. No trucks. No warehouse. You hire all that out to someone else and take a profit right off the top."

"Well, I hadn't thought . . ."

"That's the future, you know—electronics, the information highway. Everything out of your house with the push of a button. Are you willing to listen?" He squinted his eyes a little bit, as if Walt was going to have to make an effort here, but that it would be worth it.

This was exactly what Walt had feared—that Henry was going to try to rope him in on some kind of business deal. Last winter it had been asphalt and roof paint, sold door-to-door, but somehow it had never quite got going because the company had gone broke at the last moment, and Henry's sample kits and sales-pitch brochures were suddenly worthless. To Henry it made no difference; you win some and you lose some. Walt couldn't afford to lose any. He hadn't ever leveled with Henry about it, though. Walt and Henry got along on a level of gentlemanly good humor and mutual support, and there wasn't much room for truth in it, not any kind of practical truth, anyway.

"Has it occurred to you that the real money might be in design?" Henry asked. "Right now you're on the distribution end, the narrow end of the funnel. Have you read any of Dr. Hefernin's books? Aaron Hefernin?"

Walt shook his head. He could hear the rain coming down. Out toward the street, the motor home was nearly invisible through the downpour. He switched on the space heater, listening doubtfully as Henry talked and wondering what the sales pitch would finally amount to.

"The man's a genius," Henry said. "He developed what he calls the 'Funnel Analogy' to explain business from the inside out. Look here."

Henry picked up a manila envelope that lay on the bench and carefully shook out four or five stapled pamphlets. There was an illustration on the first one of a funnel, upside down, like the Tin Man's hat. Arrows went in one way and came out another, along with words and sentences and phrases. Below it was a paragraph that began, "Welcome to the world of money, *real* money."

"Eh?" Henry said, slapping the pamphlet. "What do you think?"

Walt nodded.

"It's fascinating. Rock solid. I read this introductory pamphlet and subscribed to the entire series—nearly ten volumes so far. Each one clarifies another aspect of what Dr. Hefernin calls 'the business of business.' Remember that phrase, because it's the key to this entire method. You see, most people fail for a simple reason: they don't understand the business of business. They understand food, let's say, so they open a restaurant. In six weeks it's kaput. Why?"

"Because they don't understand the business of business?" Walt said.

"Bingo! That's it! There's a dynamic that they don't see. They don't see the *big picture*."

"Aah," Walt said, nodding as if he were only now seeing the big picture himself. He picked up the pamphlet and looked at it closely, making out the words "profit margin" alongside the arrow that moved up the funnel toward the top of the page. The word "overhead" was contained within the loops of a spiral that looked almost like a snail crawling toward the margin. The caption at the bottom of the page read, "When opportunity knocks, answer the door dressed to go out!"

"This is . . . something," Walt said. "Where do you get these?"

"Subscription. The first pamphlet doesn't cost one red cent.

It lays everything out on the page, take it or leave it. If you want to take it, the second pamphlet is fourteen dollars, but the information is priceless.''

"What does Dr. Hefernin do, exactly? Is he a publisher?''

"Oh, my goodness, no. Publishing is only one of his ventures, but I'd warrant he's made a fortune on it.''

"I guess so,'' Walt said. "That's good money for a six-page pamphlet.''

"And worth every cent. How do you put a price on that kind of knowledge? Apply it, and it'll return a thousandfold. Here.'' He held out another pamphlet entitled "The Thousandfold Return,'' this one illustrated with a picture of hundred-dollar bills, fanned out like a hand of cards. "Think about this,'' Henry said, nodding profoundly. "Dr. Hefernin is a wealthy man.''

"I don't doubt it,'' Walt said.

"He's gotten a lot of *my* money, hasn't he?''

"Sure.'' Walt gestured at the pamphlets. Nearly a hundred and fifty bucks for a few scraps of paper. You could shove all of them into your back pocket and not feel them when you sat down.

"Try this on for size: the more of my money he takes, *the more I ought to send him.* Do you know why?''

Walt shook his head. "You've lost me.''

"Because *you can't argue with success.* Hefernin calls it 'the miracle of the self-fulfilling prophecy.' ''

"Gosh,'' Walt said. "That . . . *is* hard to argue with.''

"I mean to say that the proof is in the pudding. Put your faith in a man who warrants your faith.''

"Makes sense,'' Walt said. He looked into the doughnut box, but of course it was empty. He'd already eaten the last one. He wondered suddenly if Henry was soliciting subscriptions for Dr. Hefernin, if that was his "small proposition.''

"I just want you to read these,'' he said. "That's all for now. They're brief, but I think they're convincing.''

"All right,'' Walt said, taking the pamphlets and laying them on the bench. Things were working out pretty much like he had feared: first a salad full of garbanzo beans and carrot coins, now an envelope full of "advice'' that was actually part of an infinite come-on for more advice. And the come-on worked, which was proof that the amazing Dr. Hefernin understood the business of business, and so you sent him more money to provide further evidence. It was like a school for pickpockets where they pick your pocket going in the door and then convince you that they'd done it to illustrate a point, and that you ought to pay them for it. Maybe the man *was* a genius.

"I'd like your opinion tomorrow," Henry said.

"You'll have it."

"Good, because there's more to it than I can tell you right now. I'm going to turn in. Driving wears me out. Jinx thinks I'm already in bed." He started toward the door, then turned and said, "There's no need to talk to the ladies about any of this, is there?"

"No," Walt said. "Not at all. Whatever you say."

"They don't have much of a head for business sometimes."

Walt thought about Ivy's last commission check, which had actually been very nice. In fact, along with everything else it was financing Christmas. He nodded shamelessly. "I've never believed in operating by committee anyway," he said, shifting things around to something he was comfortable with, but realizing when he said it that he was already entering into some kind of agreement with Henry. And it occurred to him at the same time that Aunt Jinx probably wasn't as crazy about all these Hefernin pamphlets as Henry was—if she even knew about them.

Uncle Henry went off down the carport, carrying his envelope. He heard the back door open, and then Ivy's voice: "Are you staying out there all night?"

"No!" he shouted. "Just locking up." There was the sound of the back door shutting. He took off his jacket and hung it over the chair, then switched off the heater and the lights. He thought about the bird in the jar, buried out in the garden, and suddenly felt a little foolish about it—more than foolish. Apprehensive was the word. It was probably a bad idea to antagonize a man like Argyle, especially over something like a grudge that was nearly twenty years old.

The conversation he'd overheard an hour ago returned to him. There was something sinister in all that guarded talk, and for a moment he thought about retrieving the jar and running it over there. It wouldn't take half a minute, and he could be rid of Argyle for good and all.

"You out there in the dark?" Ivy shouted through the open door again.

To hell with the jar. He stepped out of the garage and started to close up. Ivy stood inside the back door, already dressed for bed despite it being early. She was wearing her kimono, loosely tied, the one he'd bought her in the Japanese antiques store in Seattle, and the red and black silk against her fair skin suggested something exotic to him tonight, something he didn't need to define. Her dark hair was pulled back loosely, into some kind of knot fixed with two glittery chopsticks.

He hunched through the rain, and Ivy kissed him as he came through the door. He could see that she was carrying two glasses and a bottle of champagne. The rest of the house was dark. Jinx must already have gone out to the motor home.

"Congratulate me," Ivy said as they moved together toward the stairs. "We've got a lot to celebrate."

‡ 13 ‡

"AN EMERGENCY MARRIAGE ENCOUNTER?" WALT ASKED, pouring himself another glass of champagne. "I like that—sounds like emergency car repair or something. They probably use duct tape and baling wire and cans of that tire inflator."

Ivy gave him a dark look, so he cut the joke off short. "A church counselor suggested it to Darla," she said. "And whether it sounds silly or not, it's the only thing anybody's come up with that's positive."

"Except me," Walt said. "What I said was that Darla needs a lawyer and Jack needs a subpoena. I've been positive about that for years. Why does she hang around?"

"Because she's desperate. She loves him, I guess."

"She's crazy about him is what you mean. Like in out of her mind."

"It's easy to say that from a distance."

"What makes it easy is knowing Jack, and she ought to know him better than I do. She's had to live with him all these years."

"That's the purpose of the marriage encounter, isn't it? So you can get to know each other better. People are married for years and they don't have a clue about some of the things that matter most to their wives."

"Or their husbands," Walt said, but he knew it was the wrong thing to say as soon as it was out of his mouth. He put down his champagne glass.

Ivy was silent for a moment. He knew where the conversation was leading. And he knew that he was going to have to be careful. Saying the first damned thing that came into his mind wasn't going to help unless he wanted a fight, which he didn't. He looked at Ivy, who had put on her kimono, but hadn't tied it. She pulled it shut now, as if closing a door, and he turned his eyes away, looking instead at the fire in the fireplace. It was mostly burned down now, but it was too near bedtime to throw another log on. He sipped the champagne and waited her out.

"Please don't go on at me about the size of the car tonight, okay? We've got to get past all that."

Right like that she dropped into the middle of it. There was no way out except to get through it. "All I meant by that was that children are expensive," Walt said. "That's all. I read somewhere that the average kid costs about five grand a year as a child. Then it goes up."

"I don't plan on having average kids."

"I don't either," he said, ignoring her tone. "When it comes to raising kids, it's a mistake to do things halfway. And that's my point, that's what I was saying about the car. A family needs room. Kids need *stuff*. This commission today is great, but it's only one commission. Things are tight, what with the economy and all. In a couple of years . . ." He listened to himself, chattering like some kind of preprogrammed Walt robot, and suddenly he hated the sound of his own voice.

"Next year I'm forty," Ivy said. "And besides, we both know that this has nothing to do with money. Money's not the issue."

"What is the issue, then?" Walt asked.

"You're afraid of raising children," Ivy said. "That's the issue—self-doubt. And you're self-centered. When a person's afraid of the world like you are, it's easier to be self-centered. It's safer, only worrying about yourself."

He shrugged. It didn't seem worth denying. "Bringing a child into a world like this . . ."

"That's not what I meant. The world's better off than it has any right to be. I mean you're the one that's full of fear. Change scares the hell out of you."

"No, it doesn't."

"Yes, it does. You can't imagine having kids, and do you know why?"

"Why?"

"Because you don't have any. If you had a child, you could imagine it easily. It would all become clear to you. It would seem right. You're afraid of it now because you can't see it.

It's the unknown. And I don't think you like the unknown.''

"That's not fair. Having kids doesn't *scare* me. I'm just practical about it, that's all. I don't get all hormonal about it.''

"Is that right?''

"Yeah. And you know what I mean. Don't pretend to be insulted on behalf of women.''

"You were pretty hormonal a half hour ago.''

"That's different. That was . . .''

"Sex. I know. Someday maybe it'll be more than that.''

He gaped at her, not believing she'd say such a thing.

"And you know what *I* mean. Don't go looking for an excuse to explode. You've got all these dreams and desires, and I've supported all of them, haven't I?''

He nodded. Here it came.

"I'm happy about it, too, because you're the man I married. I did it on purpose. It wasn't a mistake.''

"I wonder . . .'' he muttered, but thank God she went right on.

"And what I want you to think about is who *you* married, because there's things that I want, too, and I've always wanted them, and . . .''

She stopped. He could see that she was on the verge of tears, and he suddenly felt like a jerk. "Maybe you're right,'' he said after a moment. "Maybe I'm afraid of not making it and of dragging my family down with me—finding myself a middle-aged failure.''

"I don't think that's going to happen,'' she said. "Why can't we make it together? You know, the Marvels' signing the papers today wasn't the only thing good that happened.''

"What else?'' He acted surprised and happy, trying to cheer her up. Maybe they'd gotten through the storm.

"You wouldn't guess who I ran into at Watson's.''

He shook his head. "Jimmy Carter?''

"Bob Argyle.''

"What do you mean, 'ran into'? Did you hit him with the car? I hope you killed him, because otherwise he'll sue us.''

"He wanted to talk business.''

"What kind of business?''

"He's got a couple of properties he wants to sell, commercial properties from what I could make out. There might be money in it. A lot.''

"We don't want his money." Walt caught himself. "Do we?"

"It's not *his* money, really, is it? All kinds of people profit from a sale of property. Why shouldn't I? Too many scruples? Scruples about what, exactly?"

"Well," Walt said, "all I can say is that I don't like it. I think he's still a damned criminal. It's a bad idea to get involved with him."

"Who said anything about getting involved with him? We're not going into some kind of partnership. All I'm going to do is sell a couple of pieces of property. And that's why there's escrow companies and legal documents—to keep everything aboveboard. What can be criminal about it? And how do you know he's a criminal anyway?"

"I don't know what kind of depths he's sunk to, but it's probably deeper than we can guess."

"How would you know? You've avoided him for years."

"Let's just say I have my hunches. A leopard doesn't change his spots."

"Let's just say that you're not a disinterested party. You've got a conflict of interest the size of an elephant. I've gotten the man out of my life, and I'd suggest you try to do the same."

"If you mean that my interests are different from his, then you win the prize. What I want to do is *keep* him out of my life. So why don't you just tell him to go to Hell? No, wait a minute—he probably owns real estate there, too."

Ivy stared at the ceiling, as if she were counting to ten. "I don't know anything for sure yet," she said, getting up out of bed. "I'm going to talk to him Thursday morning. So there's no use fighting this one out right now. We might as well go to sleep and pick it up again tomorrow night. God knows we don't want to get into the habit of going to bed happy."

She disappeared into the bathroom, and Walt reached over to the nightstand to shut off his light. It was a good thing no one was keeping score; he knew vaguely that she'd mopped up the floor with him tonight, forced him into corners. Christ, he wished she wouldn't cry in the middle of an argument. That always got him. He knew that he was in great shape when it came to throwing words around. He could go on all night, beating her up with words till she couldn't take it any more.

That was his strategy, wasn't it? He just didn't like to admit it. And so what if he was right? Was that enough to justify it?

Argyle! He'd been rid of the man for years, and now the dirty pig had polluted the whole day, popping up everywhere like some kind of damned jack-in-the-box.

Ivy came out of the bathroom wearing her nightshirt. She got into bed and turned out her light.

"Goodnight," Walt said, bending over to kiss her on the cheek.

"Goodnight."

"Sorry I'm so difficult sometimes."

"So am I," she said.

He didn't take the bait. Hell, it wasn't bait, it was a statement of fact. "Give me time to think about all of it," he said.

"Fine," she said. "Think."

"I will." He laid his head on the pillow and stared at the ceiling, knowing he wouldn't fall asleep easily, thinking about Argyle and what he was up to, his "dead mans grease." There was the sound of rain running in the gutters outside, and somewhere in the distance the sound of sirens—fire engines pulling out of the station house down on Center.

It was a hell of a night for putting out a fire, he thought, raining like this. . . . The idea amused him, and for a moment he considered waking Ivy up and telling her, but probably she wouldn't think it was all that funny anyway.

❧ 14 ❧

IT WASN'T YET DAWN WHEN WALT GOT OUT OF BED. MOON-light shone through the blinds, and the morning was quiet out-side, with no sound of rain. It was his routine to put on a pot of coffee in the garage and read the newspaper for a half hour before starting to work, but he didn't like to waste any real daylight on it. It was better to read while the rest of the world slept. For a moment, before going downstairs, he watched Ivy lying tucked up in the heap of blankets she'd stolen from him in the night.

After pulling his sweater on, he went downstairs and out through the back door. Except for a couple of big, swiftly moving clouds, the sky was full of stars, washed clean by the storm. In the east, toward the Santa Ana Mountains, the sky was gray with the dawn, and the twin peaks of old Saddleback stood out solid black against it. Everything smelled wet—the concrete, the soggy leaves in the flowerbeds, the morning wind that blew in off the ocean.

He stepped across the soaked lawn and in among the inter-twined tomato vines in the garden. In the early dawn the vines looked black-green, dense with shadow, more lush than they had appeared to be yesterday afternoon. There was no sign of the tin box. It had sunk, probably, in the soft soil. Pulling up a tomato stake, he poked around in the dirt, wishing he had more light. Yesterday he really hadn't paid any attention to where he was planting the damned thing; he'd been in too much of a rush.

He bent down and parted the vines, soaking the sleeves of his sweater. His elbow bumped one of the two leftover to-matoes, which was heavy, nearly the size of his fist. He hadn't remembered them being as healthy as that, but then he hadn't really looked closely at them, either. Forgetting about the blue-bird of happiness for a moment, he found the other tomato, which hung beside a cluster of about half a dozen green ones, unseasonably late. The green ones would never ripen, not this time of year. He picked the pair of ripe ones, realizing sud-denly why he couldn't find the tin—a tangle of vines covered the ground over it now: the rain or something must have weighted them down, and they'd fallen across the mud.

He pushed them out of the way and scrabbled around with his fingers. There it was—the lid of the box, nearly sunk be-neath the mire. He wiggled it free and stood up, stepping past the herb garden toward the lawn again, carrying the tin and the two tomatoes. Then he paused for a moment, surprised at what he saw: the herbs looked bad this morning, wilted and pale. The sage and the rosemary had collapsed like old mush-rooms, and in the dim moonlight they were white, as if blighted with some kind of fungus. The basil was just a couple of wet brown sticks now. Two weeks of nearly constant rain must finally have rotted the roots. . . .

He carried the tin back to the garage, suddenly unsure what to do with it. It was still dark enough outside to run it over to Argyle's, where he could simply push it under the railing and come home again. Argyle could think anything he wanted to think.

He closed the garage doors before turning on the lights, then washed the tin in the sink and dried it off with paper towels. He set it on the bench and put the coffee on, then opened the tin and looked again at the bird, which floated in its slightly milky bath. The jar had leaked, and it smelled of gin, the whole thing reminding him suddenly of the worm in the bottom of a mescal bottle. The bird wasn't quite as badly decomposed as he remembered.

What on earth did Argyle want with such a thing? That was the twenty-five-cent question. Anything good? Walt couldn't imagine what. If it was for resale, then the man should be ashamed of himself, trafficking in rubbish. Walt had half a mind to show it to Ivy, just to illustrate what sort of a monster she was having business dealings with. But clearly he couldn't, unless he made up some kind of elaborate lie to explain what he was doing with the tin in the first place.

The two tomatoes sat on the bench, as nice as any he'd

picked last summer. The rain was hell on the herb garden, but the tomatoes apparently loved it . . .

. . . which was nonsense, of course. It rained every winter, but it had never made any difference at all to his tomatoes. There was no explaining them away so easily. But making a wish on a dead bird—wasn't that about twice as loony? He wouldn't allow himself to believe it.

What if Argyle believed it? How badly would he want the thing back? The thought stunned him, and the tin looked suddenly different to him, perhaps more repulsive than it had, but mysterious at the same time, attractive in some dark and primitive way.

He looked out through the door. There was a light on in the motor home, and the day was brightening. Whatever he meant to do, he should simply do it, before Henry figured out he was awake and wanted to talk about Dr. Hefernin and the pamphlets.

Abruptly deciding against returning the tin, he put it inside a drawer in the bench, then almost at once took it out and looked around for a better hiding place, just in case Argyle sent someone after it again. Climbing up onto the stepladder, he pushed aside the dusty junk piled in the rafters on a couple of sheets of plywood. He spotted his tackle box, opened the lid, and put the tin in the bottom, in among jars of salmon eggs and cheese bait and bobbers. Then he shut the box and wedged it in between his lashed-together fishing poles and a clothes-drying rack made out of wooden dowels.

He got down and looked. The tackle box was perfectly hidden from the ground, and it didn't seem likely that anyone would pull junk out of the rafters looking for the damned tin anyway. There were a thousand more likely places for it to be hidden—dozens of boxes lying right there on the floor. He'd leave the back door to the garage locked, and the same with the shed doors. The motor home in the driveway, with Henry and Jinx going in and out, would discourage anyone from coming in through the front.

Quietly, he went out through the door and down the drive, past the motor home to the sidewalk. The coffee was ready. All he needed was the newspaper—which, in fact, was nowhere to be seen. Usually it lay near the sidewalk, wrapped in plastic in weather like this. He stooped and looked under the motor home, but the paper wasn't there, either. Doubtful, he checked the front porch, then looked into the shrubbery. The last thing he wanted to do was call the paperboy on a morning like this, make him come all the way back out here with a single paper. . . .

He saw Henry's silhouette on the window curtain of the motor home. He was sitting at the table—no doubt reading the paper himself. Walt considered knocking on the door, but he stopped himself. It would look like he was miffed, which he was, but there was no use carrying on like that with Henry, who deserved an early-morning newspaper as much as anybody else. Henry tended to read the hell out of a paper, though, taking it apart like a cadaver so that what was left was a scattering of wrecked parts.

Giving up on the paper, Walt returned to the garage and poured himself a cup of coffee, then idly turned the pages of one of Dr. Hefernin's pamphlets, trying to memorize a few phrases for Henry's benefit. But his thoughts wandered to the jar, and it struck him suddenly that he ought to make another test of the thing. He thrust the idea out of his mind. There was something about toying with it that repelled him, that was almost obscene.

Immediately he saw that he was being silly. What harm could it do? And if he wasn't going to use it—whatever that meant—then there was no point in keeping it, in stirring up a man as potentially dangerous as Argyle. Probably he should haul it down and throw it into the trash bin at the end of the street like he'd threatened to do yesterday.

Very well, then, he would try it:

"Throw the newspaper into the bushes tomorrow morning so that Henry can't find it," he said out loud, then immediately regretted it. His own voice sounded unnatural to him, hollow, like a voice out of a machine, and he wondered whom, exactly, he was talking to.

The question was vaguely disturbing, and he focused on the Hefernin pamphlets, chasing all thoughts of the bluebird out of his mind. "Water Seeks Its Own Level," one of the pamphlets was titled. It was full of advice on "taking the plunge" but not "getting in over your head. Don't thrash around," Hefernin warned, and there was actually a sketch of a toothy-looking shark swimming along, the words "insufficient capi-

tal'' written across its back. Walt skimmed the article, searching for something concrete, something that wasn't all clichés
and ready-made phrases—something that would warrant
spending fourteen dollars and would make an intelligent man
order another one. But there was nothing, only a few testimonials at the end regarding the huge sums of money that
people had made by putting Hefernin's ''philosophy'' into
practice. The Reverend Bentley's tracts looked positively useful by comparison. Bentley nearly always promised you
something final and discernible, an actual destination. It was
generally always Hell, but at least he was decisive about it.

Walt turned the pamphlet over finally and looked at the
business address. It took him a moment to make sense out of
it, for it to sink in that the address was local—a post office
box in Santa Ana. Why that was so startling he couldn't say;
southern California was no doubt the capital of mail fraud,
probably of every sort of fraud.

The door opened and Uncle Henry looked in, carrying the
newspaper, which was so completely taken apart that it looked
like it had thirty or forty sections to it.

''I stepped out for some air and noticed the light was on in
here.''

''Good,'' Walt said. ''I just put on some coffee. Sleep
okay?''

''Well, not badly, anyway. It gets a little cramped in there
after a few weeks. And the toilet . . .'' He waved his hand,
dismissing the toilet with a gesture. ''I see you've been reading
Dr. Hefernin.'' He poured himself a cup of coffee out of the
pot, widening his eyes at Walt, who nodded.

''Very interesting material in these pamphlets,'' Walt said.

''That there is. We've established quite a correspondence,
Aaron and I—first-name basis. And I can guarantee you that
if you query the man you'll get a prompt response. That's
another one of Hefernin's requirements—promptitude.''

''I read about that,'' Walt lied, gesturing toward the bench.
''I'm in agreement with the man there.'' He shoved the pamphlets back into their envelope. There was the bare chance that
if they were out of sight, they'd be out of mind, at least for
the moment. ''I see you've brought the newspaper. Anything
earthshaking in the headlines?''

''Local interest story, actually.'' Henry laid the paper on the bench. On the front page was a two-column article about the death of Murray LeRoy and the coincidental fire a few hours later that destroyed his house. . . .

"Say," Henry said, "I'm about starved."

There was a photo of an alley downtown, nearly flooded with rainwater, people standing around, a man holding out a single white shoe hung with tassels. Walt read it through, hardly able to believe what he saw, remembering the way that Argyle had emphasized the second syllable of LeRoy's name when he'd stood talking to his cronies on the front porch last night.

Walt looked at Henry, finally making sense out of his words. "Sure," he said, skimming the rest of the article. LeRoy's house had burned when a gas leak was ignited by a pilot light. The man had apparently stored kerosene in his cellar, and the whole place had gone up so fast and hot that there'd been no saving it, although the fire department had prevented the nearby houses from burning.

"What about a couple of sinkers?" Henry asked. "After that dinner last night . . ." He shook his head. "Oh, it was good, mind you. Nothing wrong with it. Jinx is dead right— penny saved, penny earned, as they say. There's no reason the same thing shouldn't go for calories, in a way." He widened his eyes, as if he knew he was lying through his teeth. "I've been eating like that for weeks now."

"Boyd's All-Niter?" Walt asked, reaching for the lights.

"Just what I was thinking. We'll spend a few of those calories we saved last night."

At the last moment Walt decided to leave the lights on, just for safety. If there was going to be another break-in, it would probably come soon. He snapped the padlock shut, and the two of them walked down the drive without speaking, past the now darkened motor home toward where the Suburban sat parked on the street. Just then a car rounded the corner, its headlights swinging around toward Walt as he opened the door and slid in onto the seat. He glanced at the car as it swept past, gunning toward Chapman Avenue.

"Slow down," Walt said out loud. It was an old red Toyota with a dented fender and bent bumper. The Reverend Bentley sat hunched behind the wheel, looking straight ahead, his face hidden by shadow.

❧ 15 ❧

IN HIS NIGHTMARE ARGYLE FLED ALONG A STONE CORRIDOR deep in the earth. The shadows of insects twitched on the walls, and there was a metallic rasping and clicking like beetles in a can. Orange firelight glowed from vast rooms hidden behind half-closed doors, and from all around him there came the sound of moaning and shrieking and knocking, as if from something that had once been human but was human no longer, shrieks cut off sharp only to be taken up again in a monotony of pain.

There came into his mind the terrible certainty that he was running headlong *toward* something, not away from it now, running, perhaps, to embrace that pain. Soon the shrieks and howls would be his own. Inevitably there hovered before him, far away down the dim corridor, a disembodied head, its mouth working spasmodically, its face half turned away so that its eyes were hidden by an iron-dark shadow. There was the smell of sulphur and the corruption of rotten things, of death and hot metal. The face swiveled slowly toward him, and a voice whispered unintelligibly, like a sand-laden wind off the desert. He held his ears against it.

He woke up trying to scream. He heard his own voice rasp in his throat, and he launched himself forward, scrambling off the end of the bed, falling to the floor, his legs tangled in the sheets, his eyes adjusting to the moonlight in the dim bedroom. There was a slow and steady knocking, like someone beating on the pipes beneath the house, and a creaking sound like loose floorboards. Distantly, like ghost voices over a telephone, there sounded the echo of the shrieking and moaning that he'd heard in his nightmare, and he pressed his hands over his ears as he staggered to his feet, yanking open the top drawer of his dresser.

Inside lay two jars—common pint-size peanut butter jars, seemingly empty. He drew one out and shakily unscrewed the lid, and there was the faint, brief sound of a human cry in the closed air of the room. And at that moment the knocking ceased, the moaning and shrieking evaporated. The air was still heavy with sulphur and the smell of hot metal lingering like smoke, but that, too, was dwindling.

He was safe. For the moment he was safe.

He pulled himself free and pushed up onto his hands and knees. Although the window was open to the wind and rain, he was sweating hot. This wasn't the first time that he had fought to wake up from the dream. Each time it was more real, more solid, and even now the walls of his bedroom looked insubstantial to him, barely opaque, as if they were film projections on black basalt. There was a noise like the rustling of insect wings in the depths of his mind, and staticky, disembodied voices muttering obscenities—infantile idiot gibberish.

He picked up the jar and twisted the lid back on tight. What had been in it was used up, and what remained was a useless leathery shaving of human flesh. He dropped the jar and its contents into the trash can next to the dresser, then walked across to the window, where he leaned out into the morning darkness. Soon, it seemed to him, there would come a night when the dream would take him with it, just as some similar tentacle of Hell had reached out to clutch at Murray LeRoy.

Stop it. He squeezed his eyes shut. This was nonsense. He would still beat it.

There weren't many jars left. He needed something else to offer—more spirit jars. Something. And soon it would demand something more solid than the dying exhalations in the spirit jars. But when? Each night was worse than the last: the shadows more dense, the sounds more anxious, closer. Yesterday morning the bedsheets had burst into flame—spontaneous combustion, just like the five-dollar bill at Watson's, just like Murray LeRoy.

He noticed suddenly that there were a couple of limbs broken off the hydrangea beneath the window, hanging by strips of bark. The dirt of the flowerbed was stomped down, the outlines of shoe soles in the wet soil clearly visible even in the moonlight. It took a moment to work it out: somebody had been there snooping around. And not the gardener, either; he hadn't been on the property since Thursday.

Argyle thought suddenly about the parcel he'd found last night on the porch. He hadn't looked closely at it, at the box itself; he'd been too anxious to get at the contents, and had simply slit the thing open and dumped it out, only to find that the item he wanted, that he had been waiting for, was missing.

It hadn't occurred to him that it might have been stolen. Now he was certain it had.

Someone had meddled with the address on the box. They'd crossed out the name *Dilworth* and written in *Argyle*. Why? Who would have done such a thing? The man in China who gathered these things for him knew him only as Dilworth. The post office? It didn't seem likely that they'd mark up the outside of the box like this. They never had before. He switched on the lamp on the dresser and peered closely at it. It was easy to see, now that he looked, that the box had been opened and then re-taped.

He looked closely at the handwriting in the rewritten name—the vertical, elongated letters, the way the *G* looked like a pulled-apart number eight, the way the *A* was crossed with a line about twice as long as necessary. It was Walt Stebbins's handwriting. Stebbins had got hold of the box, opened it, ditched the invoice, and stolen the only thing of real value in it.

How could he have known what it was?

Probably he didn't; he was just being a meddlesome hick, and this was some kind of pathetic joke.

Of course Stebbins could be compelled to return it. The thought came to him that perhaps he should spare Walt for Ivy's sake.

Ivy . . . He stood for a moment, thinking about her, about them, him and Ivy—about the way things had been only a few short years ago—and suddenly he knew he was wrong: Walt Stebbins wasn't any kind of asset to her, and the world would be a happier place if he fell off the edge of it and disappeared.

He pulled on his bathrobe and walked out of the room, up the hall, and across a broad living room heavy with oak moldings and built-in cabinets. Another narrow hall led off the living room, and he followed it to a locked door at the end, switching on the hallway lamp and taking a key from his pocket. He opened the door and stepped into a room furnished with an easy chair and bookcases. On the floor lay a coffin-sized packing crate, the wooden lid covered with Chinese ideographs. He leaned over and opened the lid, tilting it back on recessed hinges. Within lay a body. It might have been his identical twin. Did it look dead, or merely asleep?

Without the item that Stebbins had taken from the carton, the thing in the box might as well be dead. What if he never recovered it? What if that fool Stebbins had destroyed it out of common stupidity?

Full of a sudden fear, he closed the box, locked the room, and went into his study, where he picked up the phone and punched in Flanagan's number. Of course the bastard wouldn't be in. He was never in. He kept you waiting and wondering. . . .

"Flanagan."

The voice startled him. "It's me," he said breathlessly.

"I know who it is."

"Can you help me? Have you considered my offer?"

"It would be better if you helped yourself."

"So what? Do you want more? Is that it?"

"It's quite likely that you can't buy your way out of this, that you're wasting your money."

Argyle laughed out loud. "*Wasting* it? That's rich. How much was Murray LeRoy worth when he went down that alley?"

There was a silence for a time. Argyle could hear Flanagan breathing. "You haven't forgotten Obermeyer's address?"

"Of course not," Argyle started to say, but Flanagan hung up on him.

❧ 16 ❧

HENRY AND WALT DROVE EAST ON CHAPMAN AVENUE AS THE
sun rose over the dark shadow of the mountains, which stood
out now like an etching against the rain-scoured sky. Queen
palms along the parkways stirred in the freshening wind, and
big gray clouds sailed past overhead. Walt turned into the
small parking lot of Boyd's All-Niter, a doughnut shop that
sat at the edge of the several old neighborhoods that made up
Old Towne—the downtown square mile of the city. The
doughnut shop had been there for something like thirty years,
and for a sign it had an enormous doughnut on a pole that
stood at the curb, lit up all night long with neon. When he had
climbed up onto his roof a few days ago to string up Christmas
lights, Walt had seen the illuminated doughnut hovering in the
sky above the housetops like a strange religious icon.

There were no other customers in the All-Niter, but the
racks under the glass and chrome counter were half empty,
which was strange at this time of the morning. Lyle Boyd was
an old-school doughnut man who made no concessions to fashion or health. He served his doughnuts in pink, blue, and yellow plastic baskets, and although Walt couldn't quite define
his feelings about these baskets, he had always found that they
added something extra to the quality of the doughnuts—something that even a china plate, say, wouldn't confer. The baskets
and the big doughnut in the sky added up to something large
and almost mystical that compensated for Boyd's high prices—
fifty cents apiece or four bucks a dozen. And also, Lyle Boyd
didn't hold with Styrofoam cups for the coffee, but used heavy
old white mugs that he'd bought at auction when Hosmer's
coffee shop had folded up years ago in town.

They ordered doughnuts, a half dozen glazed, and Walt

filled the mugs from a fresh pot—Boyd's coffee policy was strictly serve-yourself—and they sat down to eat, both of them disappointed to discover that the glazed doughnuts were a little off this morning, a little papery. Clearly they'd been sitting in the display case for a few hours. Generally there were hot glazed doughnuts by six, but the three cooking vats at the back of the shop were shut off and Lyle Boyd himself was nowhere to be seen. The woman behind the counter was new to the shop; Walt had never seen her before. She was at least sixty-something, and was probably retired, earning a few bucks on the side. She was pleasant-looking, jolly, with a full figure and what must be a red wig, and she wore a garish Hawaiian muu-muu with a hibiscus flower print.

Henry had looked at her hard when she'd handed back their change, and he watched her now, over the top of his coffee cup. He had mentioned the "business proposition" again, but then had eaten his doughnuts in silence, the woman apparently having distracted him. Another of his manila envelopes lay on the table, clamped shut with its clip and then sealed with a strip of tape, as if the contents were top secret. Walt was in no particular hurry to look inside.

"Excuse me for a moment," Henry said, and he got up from the table and headed for the rest room door.

Walt nodded, turning back to the newspaper account of LeRoy's death: a one-time member of the city council and a highly respected local businessman, LeRoy had been "troubled" in the last months and had been questioned by police in regard to several cases of church vandalism, the nature of which made it sound to Walt as if "troubled" was too small a word; LeRoy had pretty clearly gone off his chump. He was suspected, the article said, of having loosened the bolts holding the bells at St. Anthony's and causing the death of Mr. Simms, the bellringer. . . .

Mr. Simms . . . The dead man he'd seen yesterday suddenly had a name, and Walt almost wished he hadn't learned it. He recalled the interrupted melody of the bells, how he'd felt standing under the roof of the garden shed while the rain fell, the words that had formed in his mind in anticipation of the next few notes: "What can I give him, poor as I am?" The lyric almost sounded fateful now, and it occurred to Walt unhappily that there wouldn't be any church bells today at noon.

Why that should particularly bother him he couldn't say, but he had a wild, momentary urge to volunteer to carry on for poor Mr. Simms, take a few minutes out of every afternoon just to do his part to provide a little solace in a world that didn't have nearly enough. But of course he didn't know the first thing about church bells except for what he'd seen in *The Hunchback of Notre Dame*.

The article went on to speculate that LeRoy might have committed suicide, immolating himself in the alley near the Continental Cafe after a night of rabid vandalism. A lawyer named Nelson had made a heroic effort to save him, but failed.

Walt heard laughter, and he turned around to look back at the woman behind the counter, who stood talking now to Henry. Henry nodded slowly, said something else that made her laugh again, and she put her hand on top of his hand for a moment and then took it away.

Walt coughed and got up, making a noisy issue out of pouring another cup of coffee. Henry looked at him and winked, and Walt smiled weakly. Probably there was no harm in it—just another one of Henry's flirtations—but Walt had the uncomfortable feeling that Jinx would take a dim view of it, especially after the lunch wagon fiasco last year. He picked up the envelope and waved it, then looked at his watch. It was just six-thirty, and he was in no great rush, but Henry didn't know that. The old man bowed gallantly, and for a moment Walt thought he was going to kiss her hand, but just then the door swung open and two men came in, and the woman turned away to help them.

"She's in from Hawaii," Henry explained, sitting down again and taking the envelope from Walt. He pried the tape up with his thumb and straightened out the clip. "Lived in Honolulu since thirty-six and ran a restaurant called the Eastern Paradise out on King Street—best damned Taiwan noodles you've ever eaten—red chili sauce, kimchee on the side. Jinx and I spent some time out there ourselves in the fifties."

"I remember," Walt said. "Couple of years, wasn't it?"

"Three and a half. I wish we'd held onto that little bungalow on Kahala Boulevard." Henry shook his head, regretting the past for a moment. "Right on the water—coconut palms, sand. You couldn't touch it today for two million. We took twelve thousand for it and felt lucky. Anyway, we used to eat at the Eastern Paradise every Tuesday night—bowl of Taiwan noodles and a cold beer. Pure heaven. I *thought* I recognized that woman when we came in. The years haven't touched her. Maggie Biggs, right here in Orange. It's like fate, isn't it?'' He shook his head wonderingly, waving toward the counter with his fingers, tilting his head a little bit and smiling.

"Aunt Jinx will be amazed," Walt said.

"Oh, I wouldn't mention it to Jinx," Henry said hastily. He frowned, remembering again. "I'm afraid there's skeletons from those years that we'd better just leave salted away, if you follow me. They'd just make a hell of a stink if we dug them up now." He looked around slowly then, as if something had come into his mind.

The two other customers sat two tables back, eating doughnuts and talking in undertones. One of them was a big man, immense. There were a half dozen doughnuts in his basket, and he took one out and bit it nearly in half. He seemed to know Mrs. Biggs, and he wore a flowered shirt, as if he'd just blown in from the Islands, too. Suddenly Henry stood up, nodded at Walt, and gestured toward the table in the far back corner. Walt shrugged, getting up and grabbing the two coffee mugs and following him over.

"As soon as we apply for the patents I won't care," Henry whispered, gesturing at the envelope. "But for now . . ." He widened his eyes meaningfully.

"Of course," Walt said. "Keep it between us. What do you have?"

Henry slid a paper out of the envelope—some sort of drawing, apparently of a space alien. Then Walt saw that it was meant to be a dignitary of the Catholic Church, maybe the Pope himself, or some pope, but badly compressed, as if he'd lived on the sea bottom all his life or on a planet with heavy gravity. There was a dotted line across his throat and a thing coming out of the back of his hat, which was pretty clearly on fire.

"What do you think?"

"It's . . . It's good. What . . . ?" He motioned helplessly with his hands. This was going to be worse than he'd feared.

Henry winked, took a pen out of his pocket, and wrote the words "Corn Cob Pope" across a napkin, let it lie on the table long enough for Walt to take it in, then wadded up the napkin and threw it into a nearby trash can. He sat there silently again, waiting for a response, casting an anxious glance toward the other two doughnut eaters, as if he feared that at any moment they'd leap up and rush the trash can.

It struck Walt all at once. "It's a smoking pipe?"

Henry nodded. In a low voice he said, "Simple corncob pipe, really, carved to look like the pope. Novelty item." He bent forward, pointing at the picture with the end of the pen. "The stem fits into a hole in his neck, body's the bowl, smoke comes out here, through the fedora." He indicated the pope's hat.

"Fedora? Are you sure about that? I thought his hat was something else—a miter or something?"

"Isn't the miter that stick thing he carries around? I couldn't see any way to work that in. It has something to do with holy water, maybe, but either way, it doesn't concern us here."

"You must mean the smiter," Walt said. "That's what Catholics call the stick they used to beat the Protestants with. What's this line across his throat?"

"It's a tip from Dr. Hefernin, believe it or not."

"Hefernin's in on this?" Walt's appreciation for Dr. Hefernin soared suddenly. Apparently Hefernin was simply a world-class nut, which excused all kinds of sins.

Henry shook his head. "I applied one of Hefernin's rules— 'diversify your market.' "

"Ah." Walt nodded slowly.

Henry pointed with the pen again. "Look here. Stem's detachable, and there's a hinge at the back of the neck. Cock the head back and load it with candy. It doubles as a Pez dispenser. We grab the youth market that way."

"Shrewd," Walt said, suppressing the desire to laugh out loud. "I don't suppose you'd load it with candy once it's been smoked."

"Absolutely not," Henry said. "That would limit your market again. My idea is that you'll indicate whether you want the Pez Pope or the Smoke Pope. A good share of the families will buy two—at *least* two. *We've* only got to have one model, though, with interchangeable parts. Overhead takes a nosedive."

Walt was silenced. This made last winter's asphalt paint look reasonable.

"Speak your mind," Henry said to him. Then without waiting he said, "It's a dandy, isn't it?"

Suddenly, out of nowhere, Walt remembered last night's argument with Ivy, about the way he'd lain awake for who knows how long wrangling with it, with what had gone wrong. His wasn't the only point of view. That was the lesson he'd learned last night—the lesson he'd been learning over and over again, but couldn't quite remember whenever it was really *necessary* to remember. He forced himself to consider the fabulous popes from this new angle: what *would* people think about it? They'd gone crazy over gimmicks far more mundane. He looked at the drawing again, trying to picture someone smoking the thing in public.

"I'm virtually certain of one thing," Henry said, sitting back in his chair and sliding the drawing back into the envelope.

Walt nodded for him to go on.

"The Japanese will buy it. The Pope's scheduled his first Japanese visit summer after next—part of a goodwill tour, a big powwow with the Buddhists. The Japanese are crazy for this kind of thing. They have a word for it—I can't remember what it is—gomi-something. Have a look. . . ."

He slipped several more sheets of paper out of the envelope, shuffling through drawings with carefully lettered subscripts and explanations. All of it was there: Pope Corn; Pope-sicles; Pope-on-a-Rope; something called Pope-in-a-Blanket, which was apparently a breaded hot dog; and Pope-pourri, a mixture of hyssop and myrrh and other biblical herbs that you put in a decorative Pope-shaped jar in the bathroom.

"All we need is seed money," Henry said, speaking with utter confidence. He poured the rest of his coffee down his throat and clanked the mug down on the Formica tabletop. "The sky's the limit."

❧ 17 ❧

Ivy pulled onto Capricorn Avenue, the street where her sister lived in Irvine, a "planned community." The houses were all a uniform color—some variety of beige—and were landscaped with railroad ties and olive trees and junipers. Twenty years ago neighborhoods like this were going to be the future, but time hadn't been kind to them, and the aluminum windows and Spanish lace stucco and rough-cut wood had deteriorated at about the same rate that the houses had gone out of style. The neighborhood didn't have any air of financial poverty about it, just a poverty of imagination that was depressing, and for the hundredth time Ivy reminded herself that she couldn't live happily here, no matter how close she was to the supermarket and the mall. Darla hadn't exactly thrived here either.

A truck sat in Darla's driveway with a magnetic sign on the side that read "Mow and Blow." Ivy parked on the street and headed toward the house, past the three gardeners who worked furiously on the front lawn. There was the terrible racket of the mower, edger, and blower all going at once, the three men racing against the potential rain. The sky had gotten dark again, full of heavy clouds. All the blinds were drawn in the front of the house, as if no one were home, but that was just Darla's style—the house dark and the TV constantly on for background noise or distraction or companionship. Darla rarely paid any attention to it.

Ivy rang the bell, and her sister opened the door, saw who it was, and burst into tears. Ivy walked in, putting her arm around Darla's shoulder. The house smelled of dirty ashtrays and cooking odors, and on the television screen two soap opera people accused each other of treachery. Ivy shut it off and yanked on the drapes cord, trying to brighten the place up. The two-story house to the rear loomed above the fence, though, shading the sliding glass door. Rain began to patter down onto the concrete patio slab just then, and Ivy nearly slid the door open in order to pull the kids' big wheels and bikes under cover. It was hopeless, though; the backyard, a narrow strip of patchy brown Bermuda grass lined with weedy brick planters, was strewn with toys and knocked-over lawn chairs and an expensive-looking propane barbecue that had clearly been rained on all winter anyway.

"How are you holding up?" Ivy asked.

Darla sobbed out loud, wiping her eyes with the back of her hand. "Jack's gone."

"For good?"

Darla shrugged.

"Has he been drinking?"

She nodded. "He agreed to go to the marriage encounter, like I told you, but then he started going out after dinner. And last night he didn't come home at all."

"He's a dirty shit."

"He's seeing somebody, some barfly. I know he is. I'm all packed." She gestured in the general direction of the bedroom, then let her hand fall to her lap.

Darla looked pale, and she'd gained a couple of pounds since Ivy had seen her last, which was when? Last month some time, Ivy realized guiltily. Her hair needed some work, too, and she had yesterday's makeup on.

"You slept on the couch last night?"

Darla nodded. "I waited up for Jack, but . . ."

Ivy tried to think of something to say to her, but realized she'd said it before. The junk-strewn backyard and darkened house was some kind of reflection of Darla's fate, something that had crept up on her over the years. Walt was right about Jack. Drunk or sober the man was a creep. It was no secret to anybody else; how could it be a secret to Darla? How could any of this be a secret to Darla? "Where's Eddie and Nora?"

"At daycare."

"You want me to pick them up still? It's your call. I said we'd take them, and I meant it."

"Thanks." Darla shook her head tiredly. "What I decided . . . I decided to go home for a while."

Ivy looked at her. "Home?"

"Ann Arbor."

"With Mom and Dad?" Their parents had retired to a two-bedroom house on a rural lane. It was idyllic, all hardwood trees and gardens and pastures, but there was hardly any room for the children, for Eddie and Nora.

"I've got an interview back there," Darla said. "Receptionist at this doctor's office." She started crying again. "I just have to get out," she said. "Anywhere. Away from this. Goddamn Jack can have it if he wants it." She waved her hand again, taking it all in.

"What about the kids?" Ivy asked. Suddenly it wasn't just a week-long marriage encounter; it was what?—indefinite? "Are you thinking of taking Eddie and Nora back to live with Mom and Dad?"

"Jesus, Ivy, I don't know what to do. I booked a flight this morning with Jack's Mastercard. You said you'd take care of the kids for a while, so . . . I guess I just need some space."

Space. Ivy hated that word. Darla needed considerably more than space. What she was doing was running, but she had no idea from what, aside from Jack, who she should have run from years ago. Darla hadn't had a job in ten years. She didn't need to; Jack brought home the bacon along with the grief, and Darla had always been satisfied with that, or was supposed to be.

"It's okay with Walt, isn't it?" Darla asked. "About Nora and Eddie? He's such a goddamn hero. How did you marry someone like him and I married something I scraped out of a garbage can?"

"Luck," Ivy said.

"Men are such shits."

"Some of them."

"I didn't mean Walt. I just thank God Jack isn't their real father, the lying shit." She shook her head. "It killed me when Bill walked out on me and the kids, but at least he wasn't the kind of weak . . . asshole that Jack is."

"I talked it over with Walt last night," Ivy lied. "He's all for taking the kids."

"You sure, sis? Because if you're not sure . . ."

What? You'll what? Ivy thought it but didn't say it. She *should* have told Walt last night, but he was being such a—

well, such a shit. Now he'd just have to be surprised. "Sure I'm sure," she said. "What will Jack say about our taking the kids? He'll think that's his territory."

"He can't have them," Darla said heatedly. "He . . . I'm afraid he'll hurt Eddie."

"Why?"

"He has before, when he's drunk."

"Okay then, to hell with Jack."

⊰ 18 ⊱

ARGYLE SAT IN TRAFFIC, THE CARS CRAWLING SLOWLY ALONG the streets in the cloudy afternoon twilight, as if the air itself was thick and heavy. He had the wild desire to accelerate, to drive like a madman, to flee from the spinning darkness that seemed always to hover right outside his vision. The car in front of him stopped at an intersection, and Argyle braked again, closing his eyes, imagining himself mired forever in the winter gloom, his car immovable, the doors rusted shut, the engine frozen, his own withered visage staring out at the world from within the glass and iron cage. The thought came to him that he wouldn't make it to Obermeyer's at all, that he wouldn't be allowed to make the transaction.

He glanced into the car in the next lane, and for a split second saw the burned corpse of Murray LeRoy, wearing the goat mask, sitting in the passenger seat and staring back at him. . . .

He blinked hard, inclining his head toward the window. A woman returned his stare. She looked irritated and turned to say something to the man driving. He realized what she must have seen in his own face: the demented fear, the horror. He glanced quickly away, an afterimage of her bright yellow scarf burned onto his retinas. The colors of the world were too bright suddenly, too sharp and brittle, sharp enough to cut him, and the car seemed to close in around him like shrink-wrap, smelling of upholstery and paper and dust. The whir and rumble of the car engine filled the interior of the car with noise, vague and distant from beyond the firewall, almost like the sound of breathing, of whispering.

Something moved in the periphery of his vision, dark and vague and quick, like the shadow of a hand snatching a fly out of the air. He focused on the traffic light, at the cars swinging around out of the left-hand turn lane. There was a soft rustling, moth wings fluttering in a paper sack. He set his teeth, ignoring it, and glanced at the dashboard clock. The second hand was still. Nothing moved outside the windows. Again he heard the sound of some small dry thing, an insect sound, the *tick-tick-tick* of a fingernail on glass.

He turned his head slowly, his breath shallow, and looked into the back seat, ready to throw open the door, to abandon the car and run. Something *was* there!—a vague shape like a dark memory, the shadowy, larval form of something struggling to be born; or worse, of something bound and dying. The air was thick, hot, full of insistent whispering, smelling of scorched bone. . . .

And then he was aware of a horn honking, and he realized that his mouth hung open and his breath was whimpering out of his throat, and he was staring at his briefcase on the back seat.

The driver of the car behind him gestured impatiently, honking again, and two cars farther back pulled out into the adjacent lane, gunning past him. Argyle pulled forward, both hands on the steering wheel now, and drove south on Grand Street into Santa Ana. He turned on the radio, finding an all-news station, cranked up the volume, and then lowered all the windows to let the wind blow through the car, as if the rush of moving air could carry away the thing that he'd seen.

FRANK OBERMEYER'S HOUSE SAT ON A HALF-ACRE LOT ON North Park Boulevard, halfway between Broadway and Flower, a two-story colonial-style box built of red brick and white-painted wood. There were three pillars holding up the porch, a sort of solarium with broad windows with diamond-shaped panes. The house was shaded by big sycamores standing leafless in the winter afternoon.

Argyle didn't like Obermeyer. Argyle didn't like anything that he was afraid of, and he was afraid of Obermeyer. There was something wrong with him, not to mention the fact that he was a facetious son-of-a-bitch. He was too placid, too, as if he understood something that Argyle couldn't understand, and so Argyle could never be quite sure of him. It was like being afraid of a misfiring gun; sooner or later, without warning, it could blow your hand off. It was better to keep your distance, if you could.

He brushed his hair back and looked in the mirror, deep breathing a few times before getting out of the car and walking toward the porch, past a painted jockey in a flowerbed thick with pansies. It was entirely possible, he thought as he rang the bell, that he was the world's premier sucker. Obermeyer answered at once, as if he'd been waiting. He looked surprised and slightly amused.

"Bob!" he said, holding out his hand. He was short, his hair nearly white. There was something too cheerful about his eyes, as if he were always about to laugh.

"Hello, Frank," Argyle said, stepping into the foyer. A staircase wound away toward a second level. There was a silk carpet on the floor and a landscape painting on the wall. From somewhere nearby came the sound of water running.

Obermeyer shut the door. "Drink?"

"No," Argyle said.

"That's right. You don't touch the stuff, do you?"

"Only on special occasions."

"Good policy," Obermeyer said. He led Argyle into an adjacent room and gestured at a chair. "Have a seat. What brings you all the way out from the hinterlands of Orange? It must be ten years since you were here last."

"I guess it has been," Argyle said. "Here I am again."

"You look a little peaked, if you don't mind my saying so. Flanagan hounding you for money again?"

"I put a stop to that back in '86. Probably I was a fool to do business with him. What did I gain from it?"

"You gained the world, I guess. What were you looking to gain?"

"Nothing that I couldn't have gotten on my own, probably."

Obermeyer shrugged. "Who can say? But that's hindsight, isn't it? That's the joke. In the end we sell our souls for a pocketful of trash. Here's the question: did you sell your regrets along with it? I ran into George Nelson just yesterday afternoon. George told me that he had no regrets. He told me all about how you and he were—how did he put it?—accumulating personas, I think he said. All that business about the vice presidents." Obermeyer laughed and shook his head. "I love that kind of thing. What were all those vice presidents worth in trade to the Devil, do you think?''

"I'm afraid I don't know what the hell you're talking about, Frank. All I know is that Flanagan and I are doing a little business again, despite my better judgment.''

Obermeyer sat back in his chair and shook his head, as if the whole thing mystified him. "Funny, isn't it? Flanagan was never anything more than a voice over the phone.''

"He's still a voice over the phone," Argyle agreed tiredly. "Same voice, same telephone number. Direct line to Hell. It's not even long distance.''

"That's *good*," Obermeyer said, breaking into a grin. He sat forward, as if he were suddenly excited. "Yes, sir, I like that. Imagine being a switchboard operator in Hell. What a fiasco! Machinery's hot as a pistol barrel, supervisor won't give you any peace, air conditioning's worthless, plenty of vacation time but none of the resorts are any damned good.'' He sat back, folded his hands across his stomach, and widened his eyes, as if he were just getting started. "They make you wear some kind of humiliating uniform with . . .''

"I'm not in the mood, Frank.''

"No, I guess not. Neither was poor George when I talked to him. And Murray LeRoy . . . Did you ever make a study of spontaneous human combustion?''

Argyle stared at him.

"Here's a scientific fact. Do you know what all those people had in common? No sense of humor. That's God's truth. Real laughter's not combustible.''

"The sooner I write out a check, the sooner you get your ten percent, Frank.''

Obermeyer shrugged. "I've got the receipt already made out," he said, and he picked up a slip of paper that was lying on the table next to his chair. There was a crack of thunder just then, like a sign from the heavens, and the rain let loose with a sudden fury, beating in under the overhang of the porch so that rainwater ran in rivulets down the windows.

Argyle pulled the check out of his pocket and handed it across, taking the receipt from Obermeyer. It was torn from a three-by-five-inch dime-store receipt booklet. "For Services Rendered," it said, and it struck him suddenly as the single most worthless-looking thing he had ever seen.

Obermeyer looked hard at the check, squinting at the sum. Then he looked at Argyle as if seeing him for the first time. And then, shaking like a pudding, he started to laugh.

❧ 19 ❧

WALT LOOKED UP AT THE SOUND OF SHOE SOLES SCRAPING
on the driveway, thinking it was Henry, back from his
"walk," which had kept him away for almost two hours now.
But it wasn't Henry coming up the driveway; it was apparently
a postman, a large one—six-five or -six and with a face like
a pudding, his immense bulk stuffed into a uniform that must
have been bought down at Eagleman's Big and Tall, but was
still too small. Walt put down the cellophane tape gun and
walked to the gate to meet him. There was no use letting him
into the backyard.

"Mr. . . . Stebbins?" The man looked at a clipboard to get
the name right. He had a voice like a gravel pit, and a big,
pie-eating smile on his face. Despite the cool afternoon, he
was sweating to beat the band, probably out of sheer bulk. He
wasn't carrying any packages, and Walt could see his vehicle
parked out at the curb, the tail end visible past the motor
home—not a FedEx truck, but some kind of general-issue government Chevy or Ford.

"What can I do for you?" Walt asked.

"Postal Service. Investigations." He pulled a leather wallet
out from under his blue cardigan and flipped it open so that
Walt could see his picture I.D., which was clearly him, his
face so broad that his ears weren't included in the photo.

"How can I help?" Walt asked, knowing straight off how
he could help. This was bad—if the man *was* a postal investigator and not some kind of fraud. The uniform, though, what
the hell was that? He was dressed like a mail carrier, not an
investigator. He looked familiar, too. Walt had seen him
around town.

"Mr. Stebbins, we're looking for a carton. Overseas mail,

small, contents unspecified but apparently highly valuable.''

Walt nodded. "Unspecified?"

"That's correct. It was insured in Hong Kong, and the hand-writing on the documentation is illegible. Got rained on, ink ran. It's a mess. Utterly unreadable. We've got a signature from a postal clerk at the P.O.E. in Los Angeles.'' He gestured with the clipboard.

"P.O.E.?"

"Port of Entry. Signature means it arrived, you see, and that's enough to establish our insurance liability.''

Walt snapped his fingers. "Weren't you eating doughnuts this morning down at Boyd's All-Niter?"

The man squinted at him sharply, as if the question were a trick of some sort. Then he nodded.

"Me, too," Walt said. This seemed vaguely suspicious, although why it should Walt couldn't say. Mail carriers and cops were both legendary for their doughnut consumption.

"It's a large claim, Mr. Stebbins. That's why we're investigating."

"So somebody *did* file an insurance claim?" That was interesting, if it was true—Argyle couldn't have made any legitimate claim against the loss of the box, unless that half-rotted bird corpse was worth something after all.

"Claim's been filed. That's why I'm here, Mr. Stebbins.''

"What I mean is that he could probably tell you what's in the box.''

"He who?"

"*I* don't know, for Pete's sake. Whoever filed the claim. I'm still waiting to hear what this has to do with me."

"*Does* it have anything to do with you? You seem to be under the impression that the claimee is male. Anything to explain that?''

"No," Walt said. "As far as I know the claimee is an ape. And don't you mean *claimant*?''

He shook his head. "What you're suggesting is not that simple. We didn't actually talk to the party that instituted the claim. It was filed by number, apparently, before the party left town on business. Entirely routine, except for the size of the claim itself.''

"Well if I was the Postal Service," Walt said, "I wouldn't pay him a penny. The box was probably loaded up with rocks.

My guess is that your man conspired with this postal clerk, who put his signature on . . . what was it? Some kind of bill of lading?''

The man nodded heavily. "Like that."

"Okay, and then he threw the box into the ocean. That's where you'll find your box—at the bottom of the harbor. For my money this is some kind of insurance fraud.''

"Mr. Stebbins," he said, "we don't see it quite that way. We don't think fraud's an issue here. We're pretty sure that the box was delivered—*to the wrong house*. Just a simple mistake. And either the mistake hasn't been discovered yet, or else the homeowner *simply kept it*.'' He inclined his head and squinted in order to underscore this utterance.

Walt nearly laughed out loud. No postal investigator on earth would come up to a man's gate in the middle of the afternoon and outright accuse him of theft. That kind of thing was probably actionable. Thunder sounded just then, way off over the mountains, and Walt heard the first big raindrops hit the roof of the carport.

"More rain," the investigator said, easing off now. "I guess the drought's over."

"Laid to rest," Walt said. He wondered suddenly about Uncle Henry, out in the neighborhood on foot. Probably he should drive around in the Suburban and try to find him to give him a lift home. Except that the old man was almost certainly down at the All-Niter. . . . Walt was suddenly impatient. Life was too short to fritter it away hobnobbing over the gate with a man in a costume. "So what *does* all this have to do with me?''

"Nothing," the man said, holding up his hands. "Don't get me wrong. For God's sake, we don't want that.'' He gestured, dismissing whatever it was that Walt might have been thinking. "What happened is that the delivery address is right here in the downtown, and it's close to the same as yours, you see. That's all. I've got . . . six more possibles.'' He looked at his clipboard again, as if he wanted to be sure of himself. "I'm just running down leads. I don't guess you've found any box, then?''

"No." Walt shook his head, lying outright.

"Well that's good," the investigator said. "That's what I like to find. The last thing in the world I want is to find out that something's been . . . what the hell can I call it? *Stolen*, I guess. You know what I mean? A man's life thrown away over a thing like this. Family embarrassed. Jail time. It's a minimum sentence now, too, mail theft is.''

The rain was pounding down now, gurgling through the downspout that drained the carport roof. ''You've got a job to do,'' Walt said. ''Somebody's got to bring these people to justice.''

''Then we see it the same way. But it pains me to have to do it. It truly does. Half the time it's what they call a crime of passion. A man makes the mistake in a bad moment, you know. He finds something in a box addressed to someone else, and it's too much for him. He wants it. And he's a good man, too—a good man who's made a mistake. But the judge doesn't care. The judge throws the book at him. Why? *Because the man ought to know better.* Postal theft is worth ten years of a man's life, but I'll be doggoned if he thinks of that. No, sir, he keeps the article, whatever it is.''

''I guess they call that temptation,'' Walt said, shaking his head as if it were a pity.

''Let me tell you a sad story—one of my cases a couple of years ago. There was a man up in Bell Gardens who kept a little bitty crystal dog, meant for his neighbor. It came in from Czechoslovakia, cut by hand, you see. Worth a good deal. Well, he took one look at it and he coveted that dog. He thought, what the hell. Who'll know? And like I say, he kept it. I talked to that man just like I'm talking to you.'' The inspector nodded soberly, letting this sink in. ''I suppose you can guess what happened.''

''They didn't let him keep the dog?''

''That man's doing time now, out in Norco.''

''That's a tragedy,'' Walt said.

''Yes it is. And what I'm telling you is that it's my job to find the guilty party, if there is one, but it doesn't make me happy.''

Just then Walt heard whistling, a carefree rendition of ''Sophisticated Hula.'' It was Uncle Henry, coming down the sidewalk, sheltered under his umbrella, which he was spinning in his hand, with the air of a man who had zeal enough to spare. He spotted Walt and headed up the driveway, shaking out the umbrella when he came in under the roof.

"Thanks for your help, Mr. Stebbins," the investigator said. "Keep an eye peeled." He turned and headed down the driveway, nodding at Henry.

"Rain, sleet, or snow, eh?" Henry said to him.

"That's right," he grunted. "One or the other." He hesitated, looking out at the curtain of rain for a moment, then moved ponderously toward the street in what was meant to be a hurry.

When he heard the car engine start up, Walt went out through the gate and peered through the front porch hibiscus, keeping out of sight. It was a government car all right, E plates and all.

He wandered back up the driveway, thinking things over. Putting the rifled box on Argyle's front porch looked like a monstrously stupid prank to him now—especially scribbling on it with a marker like that. Maybe Argyle *could* press charges for mail tampering or theft or whatever they'd call it. If Walt wanted to, he could throw the bluebird of happiness into the Dumpster behind the medical center right now, ditch the evidence, just walk down there and get the damned thing out of his life. They'd never prove anything. . . .

But at the same time he thought this, he knew that he wouldn't. Right now he was going to keep the bird, and to hell with Argyle and the inspector both.

"Post office man, eh?" Henry said to him.

"Yeah," Walt said. "Routine investigation. Missing package, apparently."

"They should have insured it," Henry said, shaking his head. "A stitch in time . . ." He shrugged.

"Sounds like Dr. Hefernin," Walt said.

"You can bank on it." Henry winked broadly. He was worked up, full of vinegar. "Look," he said, "I met a man this afternoon whom I think you'll find fairly interesting." He nodded slowly, unblinking, meaning what he said.

Walt braced himself.

"Man name of Vest. Have you heard of him?"

"*Vest?*"

"Sidney Vest. He's a financial advisor. What they call a lone wolf in the business. Used to work out of Merrill Lynch, but it was too crowded for him. He needed room to move, if you follow me—a bigger canvas. He's got *vision*." Henry inclined his head, coming down hard on the word.

"Name is unfamiliar."

"Well, it won't be for long."

Walt waited to find out why.

"I let him in on the popes," Henry said.

"Was that wise?" Walt asked. "Can we trust him?"

Henry waved his hand. "I know I should have asked you first, since we've pretty much gone in partners on this. But I think he might be willing to underwrite the whole megillah, lock, stock, and barrel. He's got a couple of other ideas, too. He's a go-getter."

"Maybe we should do some checking around," Walt said. "Something as important as this . . ."

Henry shrugged, as if to say that checking around wasn't out of the question. "Well, to tell you the truth, it smells like capital to me. What I did was set up a meeting—tomorrow for lunch, over at Coco's. I think you'll be surprised. The man drives a Lincoln Town Car, late model. He bought it for cash on the proceeds of a little sales venture he's got going. We can get in on that, too, if we want to. This man's the gift horse, Walter, and I mean to climb aboard."

"Yeah," Walt said. "Sure. What the heck. Doesn't hurt to hear the man out, does it?" He listened to the words issue from his mouth and nearly hated himself. His first impulse was to tell Ivy about it, to try to work something out. But of course the news would get straight back to Jinx, who would put the kibosh on it, and forever after he'd have to live with having betrayed Henry, with being the man who scuttled the popes. He'd never be able to look the old man in the face again.

A horn honked, and Ivy's Toyota pulled up. The doors opened and two children got out—Eddie and Nora, Darla's kids. What the hell was this . . . ?

Walt waved at Ivy, who stepped out of the car and walked around to the trunk, yanking out two suitcases. Nora, who was four, looked like some kind of orphan child with her stick-skinny arms and gypsy eyes. She turned her face to the sky and opened her mouth, trying to catch a raindrop.

"Hi, Eddie!" Walt called to the boy, who waved back at him, then took one of the suitcases from Ivy, holding it with both hands. He was clearly wearing last year's pants, which were flood-quality now, and he needed a haircut. He had a

long face, and even at five there was something in him that
reminded Walt of an undertaker. Maybe it was his interminable
seriousness. He let go of the suitcase with one hand and
grabbed his sister's wrist, hauling her along toward the house,
following Ivy.

"Looks like company," Walt said to Henry. "You remember Miss Nora, don't you?"

"Indeed I do," Henry said, shaking Nora's hand. She
looked at the ground, swiveling on the balls of her feet, and
shoved her thumb into her mouth.

"And here's Eddie," Walt said. "What's up, Eddie?"

Eddie shrugged. "The sky," he said.

"That's pretty funny. What's in the suitcase?"

"Clothes and stuff."

Together they stepped up onto the front porch. Jinx opened
the door of the house just then and threw her hands to her
mouth theatrically. *"My,"* she said. "This *can't* be Nora and
Eddie."

"It sure is," Walt said.

"Well, come in out of the rain." She held the screen door
open. The children went in timidly, as if stepping into the great
unknown. Through the open door came the smell of something
cooking on the stove—something awful, like a smoldering
dust bin hosed down with vinegar. Walt couldn't place the
smell for a moment, but then with a shock he realized it was
beets.

Ivy came up onto the porch and handed Jinx the suitcase.
"Spare room, I guess."

"All right," Jinx said. "And maybe we can find a snack.
Bread and butter and sugar—how does that sound?"

Walt heard Eddie mutter something. "There's more in the
trunk," Ivy said to him. "Some toys mainly."

"Okay," Walt said.

"And can you take them down to the preschool on Prospect
tomorrow and sign them up? It would save one of us driving
out to Irvine every day. Unless you want to look after them
at home." She widened her eyes, as if this just might appeal
to him.

"Look after them? What gives?"

"Jack's gone. Drunk. Darla thinks he's shacking up with
someone. She's going back east."

"Back *east*?"

"To Ann Arbor. She needs some space."

"*She* needs some space? For how long?" This was unbelievable. Space? The house was turning into some kind of castaway's retreat. Had Ivy done this on purpose, to teach him some kind of obscure lesson?

She shrugged. "I don't have any earthly idea how long. What could I say to her? To hand the kids over to social services? They're our niece and nephew, and I think they deserve better than that, better than what they've got."

"Of course they do," Walt said. "I was just . . . It's just that it's Christmas and all. . . ."

"And there's no room at the inn?"

That clobbered him. "Of *course* there's room at the inn. That's not what I meant. What the heck, eh? The more the merrier. But really, Darla's just up and gone?"

"She's probably somewhere over Kansas right now."

"And Jack just . . ."

"Jack's a shitbird." She opened the door and went in, letting the screen slam. The discussion was over.

Uncle Henry stood with his hands in his pockets, watching the rain come down, lost in thought. "We work the western angle," he said at long last, nodding at Walt.

Walt waited, wondering what this meant: "the western angle."

"Pope-along Cassidy," Henry said. "On a horse."

⊰ 20 ⊱

THE RUINS OF THE HOUSE THAT HAD BELONGED TO MURRAY LeRoy sat a hundred feet off the cul-de-sac at the end of Water Street. It was a two-acre lot that occupied most of the street front and stretched north nearly to Chapman Avenue, where it was separated from the offices of lawyers and chiropractors and real estate agents by a brush-tangled wire fence and a row of immense eucalyptus trees.

The Reverend Bentley parked a block away, left his car beneath a streetlamp, and set out carrying an umbrella and a flashlight. A car rolled past, its tires throwing a sheet of water over the curb, and Bentley skipped back out of the way. He shook his umbrella at the driver. "Damned pretzelhead," he said under his breath. There was a light on in the office of St. Anthony's Church up the street, but otherwise the night was lonesome and empty; rush hour was long over.

LeRoy's acreage had once been a walnut grove but was overgrown now with old grape arbors and unpruned fruit trees and fenced by an ancient windbreak built of weathered timbers and age-darkened redwood lath, all of it tangled with rusted chicken wire and vines. The blackened remains of the burned-down farmhouse lay deep within the grove, and during its ninety years it had been more visible at night than in the day, its curtained windows glowing through the wild shrubbery and the heavy trunks of the walnut trees. Now there was nothing but darkness through the trees, and Bentley couldn't see that there was a house there at all.

LeRoy had bought the two acres years ago, after a success-ful career in real estate and insurance sales. It was an R-4 zone, a prime spot for apartments or condominiums, but LeRoy hadn't ever sold it or built on it. He had lived there alone in the old house like a vampire, rarely seen, only rarely going out into the neighborhood—at least during the day.

Bentley angled across the cul-de-sac, took a quick look around, and slipped in through a garden gate in the fence, picking his way along a litter-covered path that led to the house. There was just enough moonlight to see by, and he had no intention of switching on his flashlight if he could help it, not until he was out of sight of the street. He didn't know quite what he was after, but he was certain that he would know it when he saw it, whatever it was. Somebody had sabotaged the bells at St. Anthony's. Probably it was Murray LeRoy, who had obviously gone stark raving crazy there at the end. But maybe it wasn't; maybe it was someone else.

The remains of the house sat crooked on its foundation, pushed apart by the partially collapsed roof. The windows were broken out, the doors smashed open. There was the smell of burnt, water-soaked wood in the air, and something that stank—a broken sewer line, perhaps. He wondered if someone had set the place on fire—to cover something up?—or whether the house had simply caught on fire spontaneously, with no earthly help, just as LeRoy himself had.

Bentley looked around guardedly, trying to see into the dense shadows cast by the vines and brush and broken down outbuildings that sat behind the house, an old chicken coop and garden shed. Everything was deathly still. He could hear water dripping somewhere close by and the sound of small animals rustling through the dark carpet of leaves beneath the walnut trees. The wind moved through the palms out on the avenue, and from somewhere in the west there was the lonesome sound of a train whistle. The house and the overgrown grove seemed to generate its own atmosphere, something oppressive and dusky that curtained the acreage off from the cheerful old neighborhoods that surrounded it. Bentley was filled with the uncanny certainty that evil things had come to pass here, and the darkness of the nearly leafless, deserted grove was vaguely repellent to him.

He stopped himself from simply turning around and going back. This was nonsense, he told himself. It was the shadows that did it, the nighttime, the heavy vegetation, the terrible smell of the burnt, water-soaked wood. He closed his eyes for a moment to summon strength, then opened them again. He would see this through. He had no choice in the matter.

The front door was a blackened slab that lay on the boards of the porch, its twisted hinges still screwed to the jamb. Charred curtains hung in the empty windows, and inside sat the dark hulks of furniture. The beam over the door had fallen, and hung at an angle across the opening, as if to bar the door. Bentley walked around to the rear of the house, where a wide section of roof had caved in around the chimney. The rear door stood open, its white paint streaked with black. He shone his light inside, illuminating an outmoded old refrigerator and a green-enameled stove and oven that stood on legs.

He forced himself to go inside, stepping carefully up the wooden stoop, covering his nose and mouth with his jacket. The kitchen reeked of burned things, and the floor was heaped with blackened plaster, the ceiling crossed with charred lath, old wire hanging through it with the insulation burned off. There was something hellish about it—about the smell, about the waiting silence. . . . Five minutes, he thought, then he would leave.

He moved into what had been the living room, shining the flashlight across the sofa and chairs. A wooden bookcase had fallen over, and the floor was strewn with burned books, swollen with water. He kicked through them, trying to make out titles, but there was nothing that signified. Among the books lay fallen pictures, their frames half consumed by the fire, glass broken. He pointed the flashlight at one of them—a painting of a man and a woman in a bedroom nearly empty of furniture. There was something off-key about the scene, peculiar. . . .

The woman sat in a wooden chair, and the man's hand was entangled in her dark hair, as if he were removing the white ribbon that tied it back. Her eyes were haunted with shame and defeat; his burned with an almost lunatic brilliance that Bentley realized was meant to be lust. The bed in the painting was disheveled, and on the wall behind the bed hung a painting identical in miniature to the larger one, and even in this tiny painting within a painting, the look in the man's eyes was unmistakable. Meticulous care had gone into painting that face.

Bentley very calmly leaned his umbrella against the wall, then bent down and picked up a shard of window glass. Using the edge of the glass like a cabinet scraper, he eradicated both renderings of the man's face, rasping through the paint and then through the canvas itself, bearing down with more and more force until he realized that he was scraping a hole in the wooden floor. He stood up and shivered from a sudden chill, dropping the piece of glass. It dawned on him then that if the house hadn't been already burned, he would set it on fire himself.

There were two bedrooms at the rear of the house, one of them so choked with fallen roof timbers that he couldn't get through the door. The other was clear of debris, utterly bare, not even a carpet on the floor. He started toward the door, but at the threshold he was seized with a terror so profound that he stepped backward, bumping into the wall behind him.

Cautiously, he played his light around the empty room, trying to make out what it was that had affected him. The plaster walls were streaked with soot that rose flamelike toward the ceiling, and the wooden floor was broken open, as if firemen had pried it to pieces in order to get at the subfloor. He saw then that there were two eye hooks screwed into the back wall about a foot from the top—heavy hooks, the iron shafts nearly the circumference of his little finger. There were two more in the ceiling; one had a couple of inches of burned rope shoved through it. He stared at them, his mind flitting around them, wondering what they might be, what uses they might have been put to. . . .

He turned away, glancing quickly into the bathroom, which was a wreck of broken tiles, the toilet torn away from the wall and hammered to pieces, the old claw-foot tub choked with plaster and glass and roof shingles, the wooden medicine cabinet yanked down. It seemed utterly unlikely to him that the fire would have made such a wreck of the place. The firemen, perhaps, had—what?—torn out the medicine cabinet and broken the toilet to pieces in order to put out the fire?

Still, there was nothing apparent, no single piece of evidence that told him anything certain. Convinced of that, he went out through the kitchen and down the stoop, into the clean night air. It had started to rain again, and he hoisted his umbrella, walking down toward the shed and the chicken coop. He spit into the weeds to clear the burned taste from his mouth. There were a couple of rusted old tools in the garden shed, but nothing else. It was just a lean-to shell sitting on the dirt. A wire fence ran out from the corner of it, caging the chicken coop, its roosts long ago fallen apart. The place had clearly been used as a dump for years, and was a litter of broken bottles and rusted cans, old eggshells and rotted garbage. Bentley stood beneath his umbrella and shoved at the debris with his foot, shining his flashlight on it.

He had the uncanny feeling that he had suddenly drawn closer to something, or as if something unnameable had suddenly drawn closer to him. Beneath the sound of the rain and the night wind there was a slow whispering, almost a breathing, that slipped into his consciousness as if through an open window. He looked up sharply, abruptly certain that he wasn't alone, that someone, something, stood close by, observing him. He saw that something was painted on the wooden slats directly in front of him. The paint was faded, obscured by darkness and weather. He shined his light on it, illuminating what appeared to be two crosses, except that the horizontal member was too low. He realized abruptly that they were upside-down crosses, and that beneath them was painted a five-pointed star, the points connected in a pentagram, all of it enclosed in a circle.

A broad wooden platform sat at the base of the wall, the legs wrapped in rusty chicken wire as if the thing was a cage, and sitting on the ground within the cage was a small iron kettle containing animal bones, as if it had been left behind from a cannibal feast. Beside it stood a rough chalice made out of pewter or some other lead-colored metal. A few feet away, hidden in the deep shadows, sat an open sack of quicklime, the white powder congealed by rain. Bentley stared at the bones in the kettle, suddenly and utterly convinced that whatever the empty room in the house meant, this meant the same thing. And he knew almost instinctively that the wooden platform hung on the wall was meant to be an altar.

He turned and fled, down the path between the white trunks of walnut trees and a long tangle of clumped vines. Rain flew in under the umbrella, and the cold water braced him. He stopped, panting in the middle of the path, realizing that he had panicked badly. The chicken coop and its diabolic scrawls couldn't harm him. "I shall fear no evil," he said out loud, but he was full of fear anyway.

Ahead of him, beneath the bare, overhanging boughs of a walnut tree, sat a wooden outhouse, apparently long disused.

Ignore it, he thought. Surely there was nothing hidden in the outhouse. He had seen enough—more than enough. How this damned satanic foulness had remained hidden in this couple of acres of downtown land could be explained in only one way: LeRoy was protected. Whatever forces hovered in the air of the abandoned chicken coop somehow conspired to veil what had gone on here.

He stepped toward the outhouse cautiously. He would take a quick look at it and go, making a clean sweep of the place. He grasped the wooden door handle and yanked on it, but the door was jammed shut, and the entire outhouse wobbled on its foundation. He pushed on it to loosen it, then yanked again. Apparently the wooden door had swelled in the wet weather. Rain began to beat down hard now, soaking his shoes and pants, running down the collar of his shirt.

Suddenly filled with anger, with the shame of having been chased by fear from the burned house and then down this muddy path, he stepped back and kicked the door hard with the bottom of his foot, damning it to Hell. The entire outhouse tipped backward, hung there for a moment like the Tower of Pisa, then toppled over, slamming to the ground, the vent pipe breaking off when it hit the trunk of the walnut tree behind it. Bentley stood there breathing hard, half surprised at what he'd done, gaping at the fallen outhouse, at the sawn-out circle in the upended plank seat.

Then he saw that there in the dirt lay a heavy slab of wood, worm-eaten and rotted, lying where there should simply have been a hole dug in the ground. Collapsing his umbrella now, he poked the tip under the edge of the wood, reached under with both hands, and levered the slab over onto its back, revealing a dark rectangular pit in the earth. He hoisted the umbrella again, got the flashlight out of his pocket, and shined it into the hole.

The light reflected off a sheet of painted metal, a dirty ivory white with faded red hearts and curlicues painted on it. The paint was chipped away at the corners, and the metal was rusted and dented. It was the top of an old bread box. Bentley knelt in the mud, trying to keep the rain off with the umbrella while he reached down into the hole. He grabbed the rolled metal handle on top of the box and lifted it out of its shallow grave, clinging lumps of mud falling away into the hole. Whatever was inside clanked together like glass jars.

❧ 21 ❧

THERE WAS SOMETHING UNFAIR IN THE DINNER ARRANGE-
ments that night, although clearly Walt couldn't say so,
couldn't let on that he was jealous of the children's food. Nora
and Eddie both had grilled cheese sandwiches that had been
fried in margarine, for God's sake, and the rest of them—the
adults, who ought to have more sense, and ought to eat what
they damned well pleased—were sharing Jinx's "sailor's
meatloaf," a casserole made out of albacore and broccoli and
egg whites, stiffened with bran so that it cut like a pâté. Walt
salted his plate for the third time and then passed the salt to
Henry, who took it without a word. Everyone had boiled beets,
too, which was probably unfair to the children, but Jinx hadn't
really known about Nora and Eddie's arrival either, and the
beets had already been boiling on the stove.

Nora, whose bobbed hair made her look like a character out
of an old silent movie about street children, nibbled on the
corner of her sandwich like a hamster. The freckles on her
cheeks might have been dabbed on in ink. Walt winked at her,
and she hid her face behind her sandwich and didn't move.

Eddie called the sandwiches "cheesers." Apparently they
were the only thing he would eat aside from pizza, and he
would only eat the sandwiches if they were made on white
bread with a single slice of American cheese that was melted
but not "burnt." Nora apparently ate nothing at all. Despite
all her hamster nibbling, her sandwich was still nearly whole.
Probably neither of them had ever tasted real food, since Darla
couldn't cook. The one time that Walt and Ivy had eaten at
Darla and Jack's, Darla had microwaved raw chicken slathered
in ketchup, which had turned out to be both gray and inedible.
In the embarrassed silence, Jack had called her a "goddamn

idiot'' in a voice that was absolutely flat, no humor at all, and she had burst into tears and run into the other room.

Walt looked at Nora and Eddie and wondered how many of those scenes, or worse, they'd witnessed over the few short years of their lives. That creep Jack! Christ, the son-of-a-bitch needed a fist in the face. They were all living in Babylon or some damned place, and it was no small miracle that any of them survived, especially the children. The world was toxic to them. Walt was suddenly full of fear and affection for every-body at the dinner table, for Henry and Jinx tooling around the country in their portable home, sleeping under the mercury vapor lamps in grocery-store parking lots and eating noodles out of Styrofoam cups, for Nora and Eddie already cast adrift in a world that betrayed its children. . . .

Nora's face was set in a glad-eyed smile, her cheeks pushing her eyes nearly shut, looking curiously at Walt as if he were the most comical thing she'd seen all day. He wiped his mouth and chin, thinking that maybe something was stuck there, a fragment of tuna fish or something. Nora set the sandwich on her plate with elaborate care and took a long drink of milk, still looking at him, and then held her empty glass out. Walt filled it out of the carton, and Nora squished up her eyes farther shut and made a rabbit nose. She'd been in the house now for nearly three hours and still hadn't spoken. Walt winked at her, turned his head sideways, and pretended to swallow his butter knife. She put her hand to her mouth, as if to stop herself from laughing out loud, and right then Eddie leaned across toward her plate, and with the palm of his hand he calmly flattened her sandwich so that it looked like something that had been pressed in a dictionary.

''Whoa!'' Walt said to him. ''Cut that out. That's *Nora's* sandwich. Squash your own doggone sandwich.'' But imme-diately he felt like a creep.

Eddie shrugged and shook his head, as if to say that it couldn't be helped. ''It's *'sposed* to be flat,'' he said, finishing off his own milk. Then, as if to illustrate, he mashed his sand-wich into his plate with the bottom of the empty glass. Rub-bery-looking cheese pushed out from between the slices of cold toast. ''See,'' he said. He held it up to show everyone. ''My mom puts it under a pan. On the stove thing.''

''I'm familiar with that,'' Uncle Henry said helpfully.

"Same idea as a bacon press." He blew his nose heavily into his napkin, which was shredded by the blast. Nora giggled through her fingers. Eddie looked very serious. The bacon press comment had vindicated him, although he couldn't have had any more idea about a bacon press than about a nuclear reactor.

"Edward," Jinx said, nodding in the boy's direction, "I'm happy to see that you've eaten your beets." There were no beets left on his plate, only a pool of red juice.

Eddie nodded. "I ate a turnip once," he announced. "They taste like sour dirt."

At the mention of dirt, Nora giggled again and made her rabbit face at Walt.

"I nearly took a bus to work this morning," Walt said, "but I took my lunch instead." He winked big at Nora, who hid her eyes with her hands and slid straight down out of her chair, very slowly, entirely disappearing under the table. Walt could hear her giggling under there, mostly through her nose. Ivy gave Walt a look that implied she couldn't understand why he had to talk like that, giving Nora fits. Eddie sat there stone-faced, acting incredibly grown-up and dependable.

Walt shook his head in wonderment, then lifted the edge of the tablecloth and peered at the floor under the table. Nora was crouched there, still with the cheeky smile, but with her thumb in her mouth now. He nodded toward her empty chair, suddenly afraid that this was going to turn into some kind of crisis.

"*I'll* get her," Eddie said, starting to push his chair back.

Walt shook his head. "It's all right," he said. "Here she comes now." He widened his eyes at her, and she shook her head. Then he held his hand out, and to his surprise she pulled her thumb out of her mouth and latched onto his fingers, climbing out from under the table, back up into her chair. Walt picked up his napkin and, holding it out of sight, wiped the spit off his hand.

"Well, *I'm* through," Uncle Henry said suddenly, standing up. Jinx looked hard at him and then nodded at his seat. "What?" he asked.

"It's better to ask to be excused," she said. "Let's set an example."

"Oh, yes. Of course." He sat back down. Then, as if forgetting that he'd already quit eating, he forked up a cube of beet and started in on his plate again, making no move to excuse himself.

Aunt Jinx waited, looking vaguely astonished. "Why, this is remarkable," she said, speaking mainly to Ivy. "What are they good for? Why did God bother?"

Henry was oblivious to the comment. With elaborate care he pushed together a piece of beet and a wad of casserole, salted it, and shoved it into his mouth. "You can use an old flatiron as a bacon press," he said, looking at his empty fork. "Works as well as anything."

There was a certain tension in the air now, a hovering cloud of uncertainty that made conversation impossible, and it struck Walt that like some baffling oriental tea ritual, the business of six people eating together was a deep and very nearly senseless mystery.

"May I be excused, please?" Eddie asked, looking at Walt.

"Certainly," Jinx said, nodding deeply. "And please clear your place. Put your plate in the sink. There's a good boy."

Eddie stood up out of his chair, holding his plate in one hand and clutching his crumpled napkin in the other. Walt looked at him in astonishment: the entire crotch of his khaki pants was stained blood red in a blotch the size of a plate.

For a long moment the room was dead silent, and then Nora, wide-eyed and no longer smiling, pointed at her brother and said, "Eddie blew up."

WALT GOT UP FROM THE FLOOR OF THE DINING ROOM, AND put down his rag and spray bottle. The beet stain wouldn't come out of the rug any easier than it would come out of Eddie's pants. He had to laugh, though. He had barely stopped Ivy from calling an ambulance. When the wad of beet cubes had fallen to the carpet, Jinx and Ivy still hadn't gotten it—that out of politeness Eddie had shoveled all the beets onto the napkin in his lap, intending to sneak the whole mess into the trash.

Walt remembered that one, a typical childhood ruse, way more effective than the usual business of shifting vegetables around your plate as if you'd eaten big healthful holes in them. When he was a kid he'd been a master of making food disappear in just that same way, but he had usually thrown the uneaten food onto the roof of his house, napkin and all. His father had found evidence of it once, when they were all out working in the yard on a Sunday afternoon—dried food in wadded up napkins lying among the dead leaves in the rain gutters. His mother, planting bulbs in the flowerbed below, had been utterly baffled. Walt's father had looked down at him from the top of his ladder, shook his head just slightly, and said, "I bet it's from that meteor shower." And that had become a sort of code for them later on, especially when they were served alien foodstuffs. He smiled now, thinking about it, how hard they'd worked that line over the years. . . .

Then he thought about poor Eddie, mortified over the beet incident. It was no good saying anything to cheer him up for a couple of hours yet; it was better to let the mortification ease up. Later on Walt could say something to make things right, before the boy went to bed. He picked up the remains of Nora's flattened sandwich and took a bite out of it. Even cold the sandwich had a pleasant, salty taste. In a few minutes Ivy and Jinx and the kids would be back from their walk; despite their coats and umbrellas, they wouldn't be out long in the threatening weather. Henry had retired to the motor home, where he was probably polishing off a box of vanilla wafers and sketching out potential popes.

Walt sat down to finish the sandwich. The sad remains of the sailor's meatloaf sat in the serving dish, and he wondered vaguely if there was some way he could use it to terrorize Argyle. Nothing came to him. He poked at it. Somehow the loaf was setting up, like a hybrid of rubber and plaster of Paris—probably because of the gluten in the oat bran. He pressed it with his fingers, fashioning a head out of it, pinching out ears and a hook nose, surprised to find that it kept its shape like modeling clay. He gave it a long neck and a thrust-out chin and deep-set eyes under a heavy brow, then picked up scraps of cooked broccoli and shoved the little flowerets into the top of the sculpture, over its ears, but leaving it mostly bald on top. It looked like the bust of some kind of German nobleman, very dignified and proud, but with a terrible case of chlorophyll poisoning.

Hurriedly he cleared the rest of the table, tossed the tablecloth into the dirty clothes, and then put the head back onto the table as a sort of centerpiece.

The door burst open and Nora and Eddie tumbled in, drip-

ping with rainwater. Walt could see that it was pouring, and
a gust of rain-laden wind blew into the room. Nora stopped
abruptly, as if she was caught on something, then gave her
still-open umbrella a tug, yanking it through the door, which
was about six inches too narrow to accommodate it. The umbrella turned itself inside out, and Nora happily dragged it
dripping into the room.

Walt took it from her and tried to invert it again by pressing
it upside down into the carpet and leaning into it. "Wind got
to it," he said to Ivy as she came in out of the rain. There
was a popping noise as the wobbly little ribs snapped, and
when he picked it up, half the umbrella simply hung there
limp, like a victim of gravity. Ivy pulled her coat off and hung
it on the coat rack. Then she took the umbrella from him and
stared at it, nodding her head ponderously, as if to say that
he'd done a tidy bit of work.

"You see?" Jinx asked her.

Ivy pushed open the screen door and tossed the umbrella
out onto the porch.

"See what?" Walt asked.

"Men," Jinx said. "Never you mind. We were having a
conversation. I really don't mean you, Walter. I needed an
example and you obliged, that's all."

"I was trying to fix the umbrella." He looked at Ivy for
support, and she squished up her face, making one of Nora's
rabbit-noses at him.

"And while we were out you cleaned up the dinner dishes,"
Jinx said. "I wasn't being fair. I'm sorry." She patted him on
the forearm.

"That's all right," Walt said. "I don't mean to be touchy."

"Did you put the rest of the loaf in the fridge? Henry loves
to make a nice sandwich out of the leftovers."

"Sure," Walt started to say, already turning toward the table. If he was quick he could hammer it flat before Jinx or Ivy
saw what had happened to it, no harm done. . . .

But there was a hoot of laughter then, from Eddie, followed
by Nora giggling insanely. They'd already found it. "Such a
funny!" Nora said, picking up the bust from where it sat on
the table. She held it out by the neck so that everyone could
see it. At that moment it broke in half, just below the chin,
and the head fell heavily to the carpet where it lay staring up

at the ceiling like a dead man, its features considerably flattened out by the impact.

"What in God's name?" Jinx asked, looking down at it in
apparent disbelief.

"I . . . bet it's from that meteor shower," Walt said. He bent
over to pick it up along with the bits of cooked broccoli scattered on the carpet.

Nora took it out of his hands, and she and Eddie hauled it
into the kitchen together, Eddie trying to snatch it away from
her.

"In the *sink*!" Jinx shouted. She fixed Walt with a stare,
then waved her hand tiredly and moved toward the door. "I'll
turn in with Henry," she said.

Walt chanced a look at Ivy, who eyed him sternly. But then
she clearly couldn't stand it any longer and burst into laughter
that she turned into a coughing fit before rushing away up the
stairs. The front door swung shut, cutting off the sound of the
rain, and Walt headed toward the stairs himself, glancing into
the kitchen where Eddie stood at the counter now, beating the
living hell out of the remains of the head with a big wooden
spoon while Nora stood next to him on a chair, holding the
egg beater and waiting for her turn.

⊰ 22 ⊱

Bᴇɴᴛʟᴇʏ ᴛʜᴏᴜɢʜᴛ ꜱᴜᴅᴅᴇɴʟʏ ᴏꜰ ᴍᴏɴᴇʏ, ᴏꜰ ᴛʀᴇᴀꜱᴜʀᴇ: ɴᴏᴛ gold coins—this wasn't heavy enough for coins—but maybe rolled-up wads of twenty-dollar bills stuffed into jars and hidden in a hole beneath a privy!

He set the bread box on the dirt next to the hole, covering it with the umbrella. His hands trembling, he twisted the latch. The front of the box fell open. It was full of glass jars, all right—pint-size Mason jars, all of them lidded, all apparently empty, and certainly empty of money.

He picked one up and looked closely at it. Something lay in the bottom. He illuminated it with the flashlight. It was a tooth, a human molar with a silver filling. He set the jar down and picked up another, this one containing a lock of hair, curled together and bound with a single strand. He shone the light into the tin box now. All the jars were the same: each apparently contained nothing but a single small remnant of a human being—a fingernail paring, eyelash hairs, a tooth, a leathery little patch of skin.

Shutting the front of the bread box, he carried two of the jars toward the shed and ducked in out of the rain. He dropped the umbrella, shoved a couple of rusted trowels off onto the ground, and set the jars on a wooden shelf. He laid down the flashlight and picked up the first of the jars again. The ring twisted off easily, but the lid was tight. He pushed at the rim of the lid with the edge of his thumb but couldn't move it. Someone had done a fair job of canning. . . .

The idea of these things having been canned horrified him and he set the jar down, his mind returning to the empty room in the burned house, to the iron hooks in the ceiling, to the foul picture on the floor in the living room. He laid the edge of the jar lid over a protruding nail head and pried at it. There was a slight pop, followed by an exhalation of escaping air and what sounded unmistakably like a human cry, small and immeasurably distant.

And just then, out of the corner of his eye, Bentley saw a light moving through the trees. He switched off his flashlight, then hurriedly screwed the lid back onto the opened jar. It was raining hard enough now so that the house and the trees beyond were obscured by a gray veil of drops. The moving light swung in a misty arc, two barely visible shadows hunching along behind it.

Making up his mind, Bentley moved away from the shed, pocketing his flashlight and carrying the two jars and his closed umbrella. He looked behind him. Whoever it was had stopped near the house. Their light swung his way, illuminating the path. He hurried the few feet to the bread box, picking it up and darting away again, crouching behind the fallen outhouse. Opening the front of the bread box, he tilted it back and replaced the two jars inside. The light was moving again, darting out along the little path toward the garden shed.

Bentley crept backward through the mud on his hands and knees, dragging the box and the umbrella along with him. His foot kicked the trunk of the big walnut tree, and he scuttled around behind it, peering out past the trunk. The two men had stopped to look over the shed. They'd see the trowels knocked down, rainwater on the wooden shelf, footprints in the mud. . . .

Sure enough, here they came, bent over and casting the flashlight beam in front of them, looking for him. They both wore hats pulled low over their eyes. One was big, heavy, but Bentley couldn't make out his features in the darkness.

"What the hell's this?" the smaller one asked. He played the light along the edge of the outhouse, then shone it on the hole in the dirt. Bentley looked behind him. The shadows of eucalyptus trees loomed overhead, and the wire fence, choked with oleander, blocked his retreat that way. Wait them out, he thought, bending over and grasping the handle at the top of the box. If he had to, he'd run for it. He was in plenty good enough shape to get away—from the big one, at least.

"Empty," the small man said, looking into the hole. "Full of shit, just like you."

"That's right," the other one said tiredly. "This hasn't been used for years, and it wasn't knocked over last night, either. This is what we're looking for, but someone got here first."

"Yeah, well, I think we're chumps, out here looking around for something nobody don't even know what it is. Let's just bring him a goddamn bag of walnuts."

"That's a *good* idea," the big man said. He swung the flashlight slowly, aiming it into the trees. "I think he's still here, whoever it is. The snoop. Look at this."

He shone the light on the ground now, the two of them bending down to have a look at something—footprints probably, or the depression made by the bread box in the mud. Bentley nearly got up and ran for it, but he held on. What lengths would they go to in order to stop him? He thought of poor Simms, dead, and he knew the answer.

The thought of Simms galvanized him, and something stirred within him—a wild gladness, a righteous fire kindled out of nowhere. This was *it*. This was what he was *paid* for. Push had come to shove. He'd spent countless Sundays warning people about the Dragon; now it was damn well time to skewer the bastard!

He stepped out from behind the tree, waving his umbrella in the air. "That's right!" he shouted. "Here I am!" His voice was pitched high, from the excitement. He was giddy. Out of his mind. He shook his umbrella in the air like a Zulu, rainwater blowing into his face.

The two men looked at him, apparently mystified by his behavior, the small one shining the flashlight beam into his eyes and then down to the painted bread box. The big one said something to the small one, who nodded, and immediately the big one set out around the opposite side of the outhouse, clearly thinking to cut off Bentley's escape. The other one stepped forward, holding out his hand, palm up.

"Hand it over, pops," he said.

"Absolutely," Bentley shouted. And then, without another thought, he raised the closed umbrella like a lance and charged at the man, holding it stiff-armed in front of him. The big man turned around and lumbered back toward his partner, who threw both hands into the air in surprise, taking a wild swipe at the umbrella but missing it entirely. The blunt tip struck him in the chest, and the umbrella itself crumpled, its hollow stem bending in half as the ribs flew open, the thin fabric pushing into the man's face like bat wings as he staggered backward, slipping in the mud.

The fat man lunged toward Bentley, grabbing him by the arm, and the preacher flailed at his face with the open, broken umbrella, yanking backward and shouting scripture into the man's face, wild verses out of Ezekiel. The man let go of him, treading backward and stepping on the fallen vent pipe from the outhouse, tripping and sitting down heavily across the outhouse door, which crumpled inward so that he sat in it like a drunken man sprawled over the sides of a canoe.

Bentley turned and slapped the destroyed umbrella at the small man again, dancing toward him and stamping at him as if the man were a bug that he could crush underfoot, and the man rolled away into a clump of bare vines, holding his hands over his head and yelling, "Whoa, whoa, whoa!"

Just then the door of the bread box dropped open. Bentley felt the contents shift, felt the weight of the door banging down on its flimsy hinge. He snatched at the box, trying to right it, but the whole passel of jars flew out, into the mud, into the bushes, raining down on the small man, who sat up now, grabbing at the jars. Jars broke against rocks, against each other, and the night was full of the soft sounds of escaping human cries, audible even in the rain and the banging around. The fat man struggled up out of the outhouse, his arms swimming, lurching to his feet and bending forward in a crouch, hands out in front of him now as if he meant to squeeze Bentley in half.

Bentley flung the empty bread box at him, lashed the umbrella at his partner, then bent over and snatched up two of the jars. He turned to run, heading in among the ghostly trees. He didn't look back, but high-stepped it down the path, squinting against the rain.

They were following! Footsteps pounded along behind him as he wove through the trees, kicking through leaves, heading for the street with a jar in either hand. In school he'd been a sprinter, and although he hadn't run in thirty years, he poured it on now, putting his heart into it, sucking air into his lungs, half expecting the snap of a groin muscle or the sudden tightening of his heart seizing up. But the sounds of pursuit trailed away behind him. They were giving up.

And then he was out of the gate, into the street and loping down toward his car, running easily now, into his stride. Knowing he was safe, he looked back over his shoulder. No one was following. Why should they? They apparently had what they were after. Thank God he hadn't recognized either of them; that way they wouldn't have recognized him either. There was no way Argyle could suspect him.

He flung the car door open and slumped onto the seat, hauling in his legs, turning the key, and throwing the Toyota into reverse, careening backward toward the intersection at Almond, where he shifted into forward again and gunned away toward the Plaza. Then, on impulse, he turned up Shaffer Street, slowing down and switching on the heater, trying to catch his breath. He felt pretty doggone good, considering. . . . He hooted out loud and slapped the wheel. By heaven he'd given the Devil hell, hadn't he? Grabbed him by the shirtfront and slapped his silly face for him!

He felt *real* good, was how he felt—better than he had for years. He glanced down at the two jars on the seat beside him, their contents visible in the glow of the streetlamps. In one lay what looked like a severed eyelid, lashes and all. His smile faded, and on impulse he pulled into the parking lot of the Holy Spirit Catholic Church. The light was on in the sacristy.

❧ 23 ❧

"NOT UNTIL THE CHILDREN ARE ASLEEP," IVY SAID, DODGING away from Walt. She headed into the bathroom, where she stood at the sink, putting her hair up with a couple of silver clips.

"They're in bed," he said. "Snug as bugs." He put his arm around her waist and wiggled his eyebrows at her.

"They're not asleep. They're wound up like tops." She pushed him out and shut the door in his face.

"They're beat," he said, talking at the door. "In a few minutes they'll be asleep. We have some important business to discuss."

"You mean monkey business, I think." She opened the door and stepped out of the bathroom, wrapped in her kimono now. "Listen," she said.

From downstairs came the sound of a giggle, then the creaking of floorboards—someone walking in the dining room, probably heading for the kitchen.

"*I'll* handle this," Walt said, nodding seriously.

"Thanks," Ivy told him. "I'm about dead. I might wait up for you, though—if I don't fall asleep." She winked at him and sat down on the bed, switching on the table lamp and picking up her glasses and her book.

Full of anticipation, Walt headed down the stairs. He'd take care of this lickety-split. Sometimes kids just needed to be *told* what to do—no messing around, no choices. Raising children wasn't any kind of democracy. . . .

There was a light in the kitchen. He looked in through the doorway. Eddie stood on a chair at the sink, trying to twist the chrome plug into the drain. The water was running full blast. Nora had clambered up onto the counter, where she was squirting a heavy stream of dish soap into the slowly filling sink.

"Hi," Walt said, stepping up to the sink. "What's up?"

"We're soaping," Nora said, smiling big. She showed him the squeeze bottle of Ivory Liquid.

Eddie pushed his pajama sleeves up and dipped his hands into the water, swishing it around to make bubbles.

"Soaping what?" Walt looked around. The dishes were done, the counter entirely cleared off.

"Soap," Nora said. "See?" She picked up a double handful of bubbles and put her face into them. Bubbles clung to her nose and cheeks.

"That's good enough," Eddie said, shutting off the water.

"I think maybe it's time for bed," Walt told him. "Why don't you start on this in the morning?"

Nora's face fell, and she slumped into a sort of rag doll position, as if most of her muscles had quit on her.

"Let's go," Walt said. "Let's hop into bed."

Apparently they heard nothing. Eddie swirled his hands in the soapy water, piling the bubbles up into towers. Nora reached into the sink and flattened the towers with her hands. Eddie built them back up again, edging his sister out of the way and blocking the sink.

"Let *me*," Nora said, trying to elbow her way in again.

Eddie stood there immovable, saying nothing but clearly determined now to keep her out.

Nora pushed him on the shoulder, but he set his feet and pushed back. Nora slapped him hard on the arm.

"Hey!" Walt said. "That's enough now. . . ."

Eddie dipped his hands into the sink and very calmly flung soapy water at his sister, who froze there on the countertop, her face suddenly full of a cold fury. She slid to the floor, her fists balled up, her pajama shirt soaked. She drew her hand back to slug him, but Walt caught her by the wrist.

"I don't *care*," Eddie said, pulling the plug out of the sink. The soapy water swirled away down the drain.

"You *fuck*head," Nora shouted at him, trying to jerk her wrist out of Walt's grasp.

"Whoa! Whoa!" Walt said. "Haile Selassie! You can't talk like that! Not in *this* house." He turned her around and marched her out into the dining room. Ivy stood on the bottom landing, a look of surprise on her face. He shrugged at her.

Nora burst into tears, pulled away from him, and ran into the bedroom, slamming the door. He could hear her sobbing in there.

"Need help?" Ivy asked, widening her eyes.

Walt shook his head. "I'm all right," he said. "They're just tired. This isn't easy on them."

Eddie stood in the kitchen, drying his hands on a towel. Walt walked in and leaned against the counter. He folded his arms. "Do me a favor, will you, man?"

"What?" Eddie asked, folding his own arms and leaning against the counter beside Walt.

"Apologize to your sister."

"She wrecked my tower."

"She just wanted her turn at the sink."

"She said . . . You heard."

"She didn't mean it."

"Yeah-huh," Eddie said. "She talks like that."

"Well, I think she's kind of scared, staying here and all. You've got to help me take care of her. She's little, you know? Don't tell her I said that."

Eddie shrugged. "I guess," he said.

"Good man," Walt said. "Let's go cheer her up."

Walt opened the door and they went into the spare bedroom. Nora lay on her bed, facedown, as if she intended to smother herself in the pillow.

"I'm sorry," Eddie said. "About the water and all . . ."

She didn't move, but her body shuddered from a quiet sob. Walt patted her head, wondering what to do. "It's all right," he said. "No big deal."

She put her fingers in her ears, closing out the world. He realized that she was still crying. What next? Pick her up? Roll her over? Threaten her? Where were her goddamn father and mother? That was the ten-cent question. One of them was pounding down another Budweiser and the other one was out looking for space. Shit. What a world.

"I'll be right back," he said to Eddie, who climbed into his own bed. Walt headed upstairs.

"How's it going?" Ivy asked when he had gotten back to the bedroom.

"You better give it a shot," he said. "I'm a dead loss."

"I bet you're not." She got out of bed and kissed him on

the lips. He had the brief feeling that he was being taken somehow, that Ivy had set him up in some complicated and devious way, and was playing him like a fiddle. She disappeared down the stairs, and he sat down on the edge of the bed to wait. Five minutes later he heard her coming back up.

"What's happening?" he asked.

"They're settled down. I promised them you'd tell them a story."

Walt gaped at her. "About what?"

"I don't know. Read them something out of that fairy-tale book in the living-room bookcase."

"All right. But you're still waiting up for me, right?"

"Why, are you going to read me a story, too?"

"Shucks, yes," he said, heading for the stairs. "Just you wait."

" 'THERE WAS ONCE A MAN WHO HAD THREE SONS,' " WALT read, trying another story. The first two he started had apparently been incomprehensible to the modern child. " 'The youngest of the sons was named Dummling, and on that account was despised and slighted and put back on every occasion.' "

"What?" Nora asked. She wasn't crying any more, but was sitting up in bed, wearing a pair of dry pajamas.

"What what?" Walt asked, smiling at her.

"What did that mean?"

"What I read?"

She nodded at him.

"Well, there's these three kids," Walt said.

"Name of Dumbhead," Eddie said, snickering.

Nora covered her mouth with her hand, giggling through it, happy again.

" 'It happened,' " Walt read, " 'that the eldest . . .' "

"The what?" Nora asked.

"The . . . oldest," Walt said.

"The dummy one?" She looked confused, like she'd lost the thread of the story.

"He wasn't *dumb*," Walt said. "That was his name."

"Why did they name him that?"

"Dumm*ling*. They named him Dumm*ling*."

"Oh," she said. She settled down in bed, waiting. Eddie

picked at the flowers on the chenille bedspread. He looked tired, his eyes half shut.

" 'It happened that the eldest wished to go into the forest to hew wood, and . . .' "

"Didn't he know he was the oldest?" Nora asked.

Walt nodded, unable to puzzle her out. There was something amazing about the question, some element of it that reminded him of the kind of special lunacy you run across in a Zen koan. Nora was apparently a sort of cosmic mystery. "Sure he did," Walt told her, closing the book. "He just wanted to cut some wood, you know?"

"For his house?"

"For a fire and all."

"It was cold," she said.

Walt nodded. "It was terribly cold. There was snow everywhere. So he got his axe and . . ."

"How do you know?" Nora looked at him, frowning. "It's not in the book," she said. "It's not in the picture. You're making stuff up."

"That's right," he said. "Don't you want snow in it?"

"Okay," she said.

Walt winked at her. "So anyway, he got this axe and went into the forest. And his friend, this guy named . . . I forget. Gooberhead, I think . . ."

Nora snickered.

" . . . showed up with a bag full of rocks. And Dummling says, 'What's in the bag?' And Gooberhead says, 'Smart pills.' "

"Was it?" Nora asked.

Walt shook his head. "It was a *trick*." Eddie was asleep now, still sitting up in bed, but with his head slumped to the side. "So Dummling says, 'Let me have some,' but Gooberhead wouldn't give him any."

"He was *mean*," Nora said.

"Wait. They were *rocks*, remember? So Dummling says, 'C'mon, Gooberhead, give me some smart pills.' And so Gooberhead opens the bag, and Dummling takes out a handful of the rocks and puts them in his mouth and tries to chew them up."

"Mmm," Nora said. "Were they candy?"

Walt blinked at her. "No, they were rocks, like I said. They broke his teeth out."

"Oh!" Nora said.

"And Dummling says, 'Hey! These taste like *rocks*.' And Boogerhead . . .'"

Nora burst into laughter, pointing her finger at Walt. "You said *booger*."

"I meant Gooberhead. . . ."

"*Booger!*"

"Okay, but just never mind that. When Dummling says, 'Hey, these taste like rocks,' Gooberhead says, 'See, you're getting smarter already.' " Walt laughed a little bit. "Pretty funny, eh?"

Nora gaped at him. "Where's Uncle Henry?" she asked suddenly.

"Why, he's outside, in the motor home."

"Is he old?"

"Sort of. I mean . . ."

"He's funny. He looks like that head."

"What head?"

"That cabbage head."

"*What* cabbage head?" Walt asked.

"That *one*. That fell on the floor."

Walt nodded. "But did you like the story?"

"Yes." She pulled the covers up to her chin. Eddie was sound asleep. "But I don't like that Gooberhead man."

"I don't either," Walt said. "He's a dirty pig. Go to sleep now."

"G'night," she said, turning over and snuggling down into the blankets.

He kissed her on the cheek, then eased Eddie down into bed, covered him up, and tiptoed out through the door, leaving the dining-room light on as a night light.

Upstairs, Ivy lay in bed. She still wore her glasses, but her book had fallen out of her hand, and she was clearly asleep. Walt set the book on the nightstand and eased her glasses off. She murmured something and slid down under the covers. He kissed her on the cheek, wondering vaguely whether it was still a husband's right to wake his wife up under circumstances like this, or if the politics of marriage had changed along with everything else. He decided to cut his losses. There would be other nights.

Somehow he wasn't sleepy yet, and he turned around and went back downstairs, where he switched on the Christmas tree lights. The room smelled strongly of pine. He sat down on the couch, watching the bubblers and the whirligigs come to life. Ivy had started buying old-fashioned-looking painted glass ornaments—Santa Clauses, grinning moons, clowns, comical dogs. There was a silver baby's head as big as his fist, with three different faces on it, each of the faces vaguely astonished, as if all of them had just that moment seen something wonderful and unlikely. He searched the baby head out now, finding it finally among a cluster of glass icicles, and it occurred to him that it was his favorite ornament because it was ridiculous, because it made the least sense.

He loved all of it, though, the whole thing together—the blinking lights shining through the icicles, the bubbles rising in their glass tubes, the colored balls glowing like tiny planets, the gaudily painted figures—and it seemed to him now, late in the evening, as if the tree signified all the light and color and magic in creation.

He laid his head back against the cushion. I'll just shut my eyes for a moment, he thought, and then get up and go to bed. And for a brief time, he could see the colored lights winking on and off even though his eyes were closed, and he wished Ivy were downstairs, too, sitting with him on the couch.

PART TWO

❧ ❧

Doubt and Decision

A man was meant to be doubtful about himself, but undoubting about the truth.

G. K. CHESTERTON
ORTHODOXY

The wood was green, and at first showed no disposition to blaze. It smoked furiously. Smoke, thought I, always goes before blaze; and so does doubt go before decision.

ANDREW MARVELL
REVERIES OF A BACHELOR

❧ 24 ❧

"WHAT DO YOU MAKE OF THEM?"

Father Mahoney held one of the jars in his hand. It was the jar with the eyelid. He shook his head. "I don't know. You say you heard something when you took the lid off?"

"A human cry. Just as sure as I'm standing here now."

"Could have been the wind?"

"Could have been. I don't happen to think so."

"What's your take on it, then?"

"I surely don't know. I don't mean to be morbid, but I wonder if when they take to digging up LeRoy's acreage they might not find worse things."

Mahoney was silent.

"I don't mean to dump these on your doorstep like a couple of orphan babies, but to my mind there's no denying that we're both involved in something here." He gestured around—at the boarded-up, stained-glass windows, the washed-down walls with the ghosts of filthy words still visible, waiting for a second coat of paint. "LeRoy came after your church. Another one of them got the bells at St. Anthony's and killed Simms. They aren't going away. Push is coming to shove. Now, we've had our differences in the past, you being a Catholic and all, but I've always known you were the real McCoy, and I hope I never let on any different about myself."

"No, sir," Mahoney said. "I've admired your work here, Protestant or no Protestant." Mahoney winked at him.

Bentley stood silently for a moment, as if he were working something out in his head. "I'm going to tell you a few things, then. And afterward you can decide whether you want to stand by what you just said, or amend it."

The priest nodded. Then very seriously he said, "Would you prefer the confessional?"

"Damn it!" Bentley shouted. "This isn't funny. I'm not con*fess*ing something. I'm telling you what happened."

"Sorry," Mahoney said. "Honestly, I *am* sorry. I couldn't help myself. Go on with your story."

"All right," Bentley said. "I'll make it plain. For a long time I led what you'd call a double life, and what I did in that other life was shameful."

"All of us have done shameful . . ."

"I'm not talking about that. What I did was worse. Murray LeRoy knew me, or thought he did, as a diabolical priest named Flanagan."

"Priest?"

"Minister, then. It doesn't matter which. Anyway, I introduced LeRoy and another man, George Nelson, to the notion of selling their immortal souls, literally speaking. You know who Nelson is—the lawyer down on the Plaza who found LeRoy burning to death in the alley. Together they conscripted another man, Robert Argyle, who had fallen on hard times after some kind of trouble with the authorities. Argyle had certain . . . business connections, let us say, in the East. There were certain things he could acquire for them. Anyway, with my help, the three of them sold their souls to the Devil." He paused, waiting for Mahoney to respond.

"*Sold* them?"

"That's right. For a price. A good one, too. I didn't really believe it myself at the time, just as you don't quite believe it now. I can see that much in your face."

"You're telling me they thought they'd *sold* their souls? Like Faust? Was there a piece of paper? Something signed?"

"Well, no, not signed exactly. As a signature they bit down hard on a bar napkin and rubbed the indentation with charcoal. Along with that they gave me . . . tokens. I didn't ask for them, mind you. This was arranged by a third party, so to speak, a man named Obermeyer, who lives out in Santa Ana. Nelson's token was a lock of hair. From Murray LeRoy it was a severed fingertip. He was a sadomasochist of the worst type. Utter degenerate. Argyle offered a little vial of blood. These objects arrived in common household canning jars. And now you know why I don't like the look of these things here.'' He pointed at the jars on the table.

"I don't like them much myself," Mahoney said.

"I can see that you don't. And quit looking at me over the top of your spectacles like that. You don't know the half of it yet. Nelson and Leroy were already involved in spiritualism, dabbling in the occult, some of it pretty nasty. I had known LeRoy for years, and I didn't like him. His conscience, if he ever had one, had rotted. George Nelson was a complete idiot. The only thing he had going for him twenty years ago was that he knew he was a small-timer. He had a pitiful little divorce practice. He had come to know his own prospects, and he didn't like them a bit. As for Argyle, heaven knows what he would have come to without stumbling into this pit these other two dug for him. And me, too, I guess. That's what I'm trying to say here. I worked on it myself, like a steamshovel.

"Anyway, the whole thing was simple. This man Obermeyer hinted around that he could set up this contract business for a fee, a commission. None of these men were wealthy at the time, but then the initial fee wasn't all that high, either. It was later, if they were satisfied, that they would pay me the real money. Of course I never expected to see it. This whole thing was a joke. I was going to pick the Devil's pocket and make a few dollars for the Church.''

"Well, pardon me if I'm a little skeptical about that last part," Mahoney said.

"What *should* I have done with the money, bought a Cadillac?''

"Perhaps you shouldn't have taken it at all.''

"Then someone else would have. That's capitalism, isn't it? Somebody pays money out, somebody else gathers it in. I did the gathering that day.''

"I think I see. What you're telling me is that you sold your own soul to gain . . . what? Not the world. You were above that. What you wanted was to do good works—Christian charity. You saw yourself as a sort of Robin Hood of the Church.''

"Well," Bentley said. "That gets close to it. I suppose I did. It's vanity, I know. But if I *did* sell my soul, by God I didn't sell it for my *own* gain.''

"I believe you. But you don't sound happy with it anyway.''

"Of *course* I don't sound happy with it."

"Then what's eating you?"

"Well, it didn't end there. The three of them prospered, and I didn't, so I squeezed them a little bit, now and then, and kept the con alive. I always meant to quit, but then the lunch van would break down or the plumbing would back up, and I'd have my man call up Argyle or LeRoy and ask for an 'offering.' Heaven help me, that's how I phrased it. Argyle got richest, of course, so I squeezed him the hardest. And it worked, mind you, because they believed in me. And worse than that, they were *afraid* of me. How do you like that? Shameful, isn't it?"

"I suppose it is," the priest said.

"Here's the bad thing: all three of these men got what they wanted. I conned them, you see, and yet it never *looked* like a con. To the contrary, they were satisfied customers. A few years pass, and what happens? George Nelson carves out a legal empire. He goes out to D.C. to lobby senators and does who-knows-what kind of damage. His law firm opens branch offices all across the country. There's even a law school named after him. After eighteen years he comes back home to take it easy, and he buys a big house in Panorama Heights. And Argyle? He's got the Midas touch. Whatever he sets his hand to, it returns to him tenfold. Half of it's fraudulent, outright criminal, but no one pays any attention any more, despite his past. It's as if he's got *protection* of some kind. LeRoy? Utterly debased. Real estate millions spent on filthy pursuits, right here in the middle of town. Life going on roundabout him like he's invisible."

"Take some comfort in the fact that you *didn't* know," Mahoney said. "What did you *think* you were doing? Ask yourself that. I haven't got any grievance against guilt, but I insist that it be applied accurately."

"No, there's no comfort in it, I assure you. You know why? Because I saw the truth. Here's the clincher: *There hadn't been any con.* They *intended* to give themselves up to the Devil, and I walked in and paved the way. I pretended to be some kind of satanic . . . minister, and by heaven I *was that thing*. There is no king's X when you're dealing in souls. That's what I found out. I did the *wrong* thing, and I did it laughing and smiling. I saw something pretty clearly then. I saw that all of us, LeRoy and Nelson and Argyle and me, too, all of us had the same ally—the Father of Lies. I cut it off then. I prayed that was the end of it.''

"Then now's the time to face the Devil down.''

"That's what I'm telling you. That's why I came here. I've botched it. I can't do it alone. I'm not strong enough. A few days ago Argyle called me on the phone, looking to talk to Flanagan again. He wanted to buy his way free, just like he'd bought his way in all those years ago.''

"And what did you tell him? The truth?''

Bentley shook his head. "It didn't do any good. He offered me a hundred thousand dollars.''

Mahoney slumped backward in his chair, looked down his spectacles, and whistled softly.

"Just like that. Easy money. I told myself that the bastard was a dead man anyway. The Devil doesn't care how many checks Argyle writes out, or who he writes them to. Take the money and run before the man goes down the well, I thought—the damage is already done.''

"You didn't cash the check?''

"No, I didn't. But I took the money in weakness, and I'm a little afraid that . . .'' He shrugged.

"Well,'' Mahoney said, picking up one of the jars. "You've got my help. I'm in. And with the help of God we'll prevail, too.'' He picked up one of the jars and peered into it. "You've already opened one of these things. Now I will. Excuse me if I'm a little doubtful, but I want to know what we're up against.''

Before Bentley could protest he twisted the lid off the jar. There was the sound of a human cry, and then a fluttering sound, as if a bird had gotten into the church and lost itself among the rafters. Bentley felt a lightness in his throat that made him want to swallow. And, as if a wind were blowing straight through him, he was suffused with remorse and fear and regret and a dozen unnameable sensations that filled him utterly, then evaporated on the instant. Abruptly the fluttering was gone, the church was quiet, and he could hear the sound of the rain out on the street.

"Sorry,'' Mahoney whispered.

"Well, now you know.''

Although what either of them knew, Bentley still couldn't say.

⊰25⊱

IT WAS NEARLY MIDNIGHT WHEN THE PHONE RANG. WALT woke up instantly, lurching across the bed and snatching up the receiver before Ivy could get to it. He was certain it was Argyle, upping the stakes, maybe the enormous postal inspector. . . .

But the voice on the other end didn't belong to Argyle, or to the inspector either. It was vaguely familiar. "*Who* is this?" Walt asked.

"This is *Jack*, Walt. Your brother-in-law."

"Jack!" Walt sat up in bed, motioning at Ivy, who was awake now, looking at him curiously. "How the hell are you?"

"What in God's name is going on with Darla and the kids? She say anything to Ivy about taking off or something? I've been trying to get hold of her since this afternoon. The pre-school tells me Ivy picked up the kids."

Walt could hear noises in the background—someone talking, laughter, what sounded like glasses or bottles clinking. Jack was in a bar. He didn't sound drunk, not toasted anyway. Walt covered the phone and whispered the question to Ivy.

"Tell him the truth about Darla," she said. "We can't hide it from him. No use starting out with lies. Tell him to relax about the kids. We'll think of something."

"Here's the deal," Walt said, into the phone now. "Ivy tells me that Darla flew back east, to Ann Arbor. You know, to stay with the folks for a little while."

"Why the hell didn't she tell me?"

"She didn't *tell* you?"

"Not a goddamned word. When the hell was this?"

"Today, I guess. She called up Ivy to take over the kids for a few days. She didn't leave you any kind of note, maybe?''

"Not word one. And what are you talking about here? Nora and Eddie didn't go with her? They're over at your place?''

"No. Yeah. They're downstairs, asleep. Hell, I thought you knew all about this. Ivy told Darla that the kids could stay here for a few days, until Darla got herself together—whatever she's up to. I think she misses her folks, to tell you the truth, what with Christmas coming up and all. They aren't getting any younger.''

There was a muffled silence, and Walt could hear Jack mumbling to someone. A woman giggled, and then Jack snickered and said something else to her. Walt nearly hung up the phone.

"So what about the kids?'' Jack said. "What the hell am I supposed to do with the kids while she's back east? I've got a damned job. She apparently didn't think about that.''

Walt took a deep breath. Starting something now was the worst thing he could do. He'd have Jack over here in a drunken rage, pounding on the door. "That's just it,'' Walt said to him cheerfully. "That's what I'm saying. We invited the kids for a visit. It's fine by us, Jack. We've been talking about having the kids over for what?—a year? Now's just about perfect. I'm working out of the house. Jinx and Henry are here for the winter. And you know Jinx, she's crazy about both of them.''

"I don't know,'' Jack said. "What did . . . ? Shit. Darla told me *nothing* about this.''

"Well . . . heck. I don't know what to tell you about that. But we were looking forward to having the kids around for a week or so. Two weeks if we can talk you out of them. Just between you and me, man, I think Ivy's got some kind of female thing about this, you know what I mean? She's been riding the kid bandwagon these days. It's some kind of maternal thing—like a nesting instinct.'' He grinned at Ivy, who scowled at him and narrowed her eyes. "Anyway, she had this all worked out with Darla.''

"Yeah, okay,'' Jack said. "Everybody had the whole thing worked out except their damned father.''

Stepfather, Walt thought. The man who's down at the Dewdrop Inn with his part-time squeeze. "Well, just don't worry about the kids, Jack. Jinx has got them both doing the damned dishes. And she's got some idea of taking them out to Prentice

Park tomorrow, to the zoo, if this rain lets up.''

"Well, hell," Jack said. "I guess there's no harm. You sure you *want* the two of them?"

"*Hell*, yes. Like I said, Ivy's made all kinds of plans."

"Okay, then. I guess so. Sounds like everything's copacetic. Tell the kids I'll give them a call tomorrow—tomorrow night, I guess. Busy day tomorrow."

"I'll tell them," Walt said. "You want me to wake 'em up right now and . . ."

"No," Jack said hastily. "No need for that. I'll get back with you after I talk to Darla."

"Good. You take it easy."

"I will," Jack said. "You, too."

He hung up then, and Walt did, too, breathing a heavy sigh of relief.

"Drunk?" Ivy asked.

"Not stinking. He's ticked off about Darla going back east without his permission, but I don't think he gives a damn about the kids being over here. It gives him a clear week or two."

"That won't last. Once he talks to Darla, he'll be calling back."

❧ 26 ❧

AT THREE IN THE MORNING, CENTER STREET WAS NEARLY
dark. The streetlamps were off for some reason, and only a
couple of houses had front porch lights on. Argyle nearly
turned up the alley toward Grand, but then he noticed that
Christmas lights were shining on a house near the end of the
block, and instead of turning he killed the headlights, eased
the car into the curb, and put the shift lever in park, letting
the motor idle. He was tired, worn out, and he sat there for a
moment undecided. He shivered in the dark. There was a hint
of sulphur in the air, and his head was full of insects. He saw
his own face reflected in the glass circle over the speedometer
along with the foggy colors of the Christmas lights. It was the
face of a corpse, milky-white, the eyes dead and staring. He
licked his lips and looked away, hearing something now, above
the droning noise that rose in his ears—a sound like iron doors
slamming shut and distant human voices.

Fear prodded him into movement, and he turned and
reached behind the seat. From the floor he picked up a broomstick with a coat hanger hook on the end, then took a quick
look up and down the street before he opened the door and
stepped out onto the curb. He trotted silently across the lawn,
stopping beneath the lowest point of the eaves. Swiftly he
slipped the hook over the string of lights and yanked on it,
pulling the entire length down onto the bushes without a
sound. The falling lights filled him with a sudden glee, and he
grasped the cord between the hot bulbs and yanked on it. There
was a snapping sound and the pop of a bulb breaking, and
then the lights went dark. He dropped the cord, stomped on
three or four bulbs, turned around, and trotted back to the car,
climbing in and pulling away.

Thirty seconds! For a moment he felt invigorated, drunk with success as he turned the corner and gunned away up Palm Avenue. Then, as if a switch had been thrown, his stomach abruptly churned with fear again, and he looked into the rear-view mirror half expecting to see an outraged homeowner running after him down the street, shaking his fist.

Nine houses that night; surely that was enough! Nine houses full of potential witnesses; nine times that he might have been caught; nine paths to utter ruination. . . .

Would he kill to avoid it?

"Murder." He mouthed the word, feeling the shape of it with his lips.

It had a ring to it, a certain . . . thrill. On the instant he was gleeful again, full of desire. The noises in his head were gone. One more house. He would make it an even ten, tonight. He thought of the lighted Christmas star that he'd pulled down at the first house he'd visited, and he laughed out loud, turning up past the Holy Spirit Catholic Church for the third time that night. He fought the urge to pull over, to pay the bells a small visit, but instead he drove on up the quiet street, making aimless right and left turns, letting his mind run until he found himself on Oak Street, drifting to a quiet stop in front of the Stebbinses' house.

Coming to himself again he was filled with a sudden panic, and he sped away. This was too much. They'd left their Christmas lights on! The fools! It was like an invitation to a dance. He turned left at the corner and circled the block, driving slowly past again. One last time. An even ten houses. Whatever power had been leading him around tonight, sniffing out lights, had led him here at last!

He wavered, caught between desire and fear. What an incredible blunder to be caught pulling down Christmas decorations at the Stebbinses' house! It would end it all—everything. Ivy would despise him. If he were accused of murder, of treason, of nearly anything, he could look her in the eye and imply that he'd had his reasons. But this—lurking in the neighborhood after midnight, committing the sins of a monster like Murray LeRoy—it would fill her with horror and loathing.

His hands shook on the steering wheel. His mouth was dry. His mind spun in an idiot whirl, empty now of argument. He turned up an alley and pulled into the deserted parking lot of a medical center, parking where he'd be invisible from the street. He got out of the car, carrying the pole, feeling the wind through his black wool sweater. Abruptly he realized that his mouth was working, as if he were talking to someone, to himself, and the idea of it terrified him.

And then, an instant later, he stood among the shadows at the edge of the Stebbinses' front porch. He scarcely knew how he'd gotten there. Hadn't he turned back to the car? For a moment he looked around blankly, horrified. His car was gone, the street empty.

He had parked in the alley! Of course. His teeth chattered, and he clamped them shut, fighting to control himself. The bushes and trees and front-porch furniture were charged with secret meaning, with some kind of horrible, mocking vitality. Across the street a rooftop Santa Claus stood like a sentinel, watching him through eyes painted on plywood. The Christmas lights on the eaves overhead shone like little pools of warmth and color on the lawn and on the concrete porch.

His mind lurched, suddenly rioting with ideas—what a man could do with a pruning saw, a can of paint, a hedge clippers, a can opener, something nasty to smear across stucco walls! The neighborhood was a vast canvas, a block of marble. Defilement! He tasted the word. And inside the houses—families asleep, children in their beds. Why not give them a face at the window, a sudden shriek and then away like a highwayman? Who would suspect *him*? If only he had a mask! They said that Murray LeRoy wore a goat's mask when he terrorized the old priest. . . .

He had a vision of himself wearing such a mask, the chin and ears tufted with stiff hair, the tongue lolling out. Perhaps a costume out of stiff goatskin, something he could be sewn into. . . . Full of a murky passion, he reached into his pocket and found a piece of a fat brown crayon that he'd taken from one of his own classrooms. Holding it in his fist, he scrawled an obscenity on the wall of the house, careful not to click the crayon against the wooden siding. Then he stepped up onto the porch and peered in through the front window, at the old furniture, the bits and pieces of their hateful, pitiful lives.

At that moment, like the tip of a knife blade, it occurred to him that Ivy lay somewhere inside, sound asleep. His head spun, and he staggered from the porch, still clutching the crayon. The pole lay on the lawn in the moonlight. Had he dropped it? His mind was murky again, and he realized that he was drooling. He wiped his mouth with his sleeve, and then, in obedience to whatever dark urges filled him like black water in a well, he picked up the pole and raised the hook toward the strand of lights.

Yank them down and get out! He leaped, hooking the strand, his weight tearing it loose from the eaves. He ran farther along the side of the house and yanked again. The lights swung, clattering against the siding, and he pulled again, throwing his weight into it. The cord snapped, and he sprawled backward, the lights blacking out.

He crouched on his hands and knees in the wet grass, panting like a dog. A light blinked on in the motor home parked in the driveway. He scuttled forward, out of view, crouching behind an overgrown camellia. There was the creak of the motor home door opening and the shuffling of bedroom slippers on concrete. Carefully, he parted the limbs and looked through the camellia. An old man stood on the sidewalk, wearing a bathrobe, looking around warily. He came along a few steps, then started up the neighbor's driveway, adjacent to the row of shrubbery. Argyle stood very still. He was deep in the shadows, dressed in dark clothing, well hidden. The old man wouldn't see him. He licked his lips, reaching slowly into his coat and putting his hand on the can of pepper spray in the inside pocket.

The old man looked straight at him—at the camellia, at the string of lights lying along the ground, draped across the shrubbery. He stepped gingerly across the wet lawn, toward the fallen pole. Argyle held his breath, slowly removing the can of spray from his coat. He licked his lips, anticipating the old man's reaction, the doubling up, the wheezing, the grunt of surprise when it blinded him. . . .

The old man stood looking down at the pole, then nudged it with his foot, as if it were a snake. He looked again at the torn-down lights, figuring things out. Argyle carefully slid his hand through the branches, leaning forward and holding onto the trunk as the old man bent over to pick up the pole. There was a clear shot with the spray, straight into his eyes.

But just then the old man noticed the crayon writing on the

wall. He stood up and stepped back, then turned around and hurried out to the sidewalk, disappearing past the corner of the house. Argyle stepped out of the bushes and peered toward the driveway, watching as the old man headed toward the backyard—toward an unlocked back door! He was going to waken the house!

Argyle grabbed the pole and ran, as quietly as he could, glancing back at the windows of the motor home for the tell-tale movement of curtains. He felt exposed, as if the dark windows of the houses were eyes watching him lope away, and again he was swept with the knowledge that he had risked everything, chanced Hell itself. He was suddenly nauseated, and he turned his head, twisting over, unable to prevent himself from being sick on his own pants and shoe. He dodged past the hedge, into the mouth of the alley, out of sight now, sick again—wildly, uncontrollably sick.

He ripped the car door open, falling onto the seat and starting the engine, backing wildly out of the parking stall and looking hard back toward the Stebbinses' house. A light was on in an upstairs room. They were awake. Were they calling the police?

He shifted into drive and moved away up the alley, turning right onto the first street, finally calming down, taking possession of himself again. Abruptly he recalled that he had nearly hosed the old man down with pepper spray. Why? Purely for pleasure, he thought. For fun. An unaccountable urge.

He passed slowly across the end of the block where the Stebbins house lay. The old man stood looking at the crayon mark, gesturing at the fallen lights. Stebbins stood next to him, his hands on his hips. Argyle's mood shifted again, and he smiled. At that instant Stebbins swiveled around and looked toward the corner, straight at him. Stebbins pointed, cocking his head. Argyle half expected him to take off running, to pursue him on foot, in which case . . .

He'd knock him down and run over his head!

He burst into laughter, unable to contain himself. Stebbins just stood there, wearing an idiotic nightshirt, his mouth open in disbelief. Argyle swung around onto his own street. Still laughing, he pushed the switch on his garage door opener and pulled into the dark garage, the door swishing closed behind the car.

❧ 27 ❧

THE REVEREND BENTLEY DROVE SLOWLY PAST ST. ANthony's Church, where the bell tower was still cordoned off. They would apparently have to get a crane to hoist the fallen bell back up into place, and that would require pulling the top of the tower apart. And none of it could be done until after probes by police and insurance investigators, who couldn't have the slightest idea who or what to look for. The bells might be out of commission for months, which left the single bell over at Holy Spirit to chase out all the demons in Old Towne. At least Mahoney knew what he was up against. Desecrating Mahoney's sacristy had been one thing—almost infantile, really, the work of a madman. But this business at St. Anthony's, the murder of poor Simms—and now the damned jars—all that was something else entirely.

"You might as well have murdered Simms yourself," he said out loud.

This time he didn't contradict himself. It didn't do any good anyway. He'd gone round and round with it for years. He'd rationalized it. He'd wrestled with guilt, trying to deny that what was coming to pass was his fault. And now he had Argyle's check in the church safe. What would he do if Argyle combusted tonight, was simply gone out of the world? Would his money be too dirty to use? He had already committed a sin by taking it; how, exactly, would it compound things to spend it once Argyle had gone to Hell? It occurred to him that he might have held out for twice what he'd asked, but he pushed the idea out of his mind.

He turned left at the light on Cambridge, driving slowly, watching the houses along the east side of the street, looking for signs of anybody out and about. It was just past four in the morning—nearly the same hour that the bastards had gotten to Father Mahoney.

He pulled up to the curb and cut the engine, then sat in the dark car and waited, watching clouds boil across the sky. In the light of the streetlamp, raindrops swooped down toward the windshield. Bentley had spent the last two hours loading sandwiches into Ziploc bags for the church's Backdoor Lunch—one hundred and thirty-four of them, made out of bread donated by the local day-old shop. Each bagged sandwich went into a paper sack along with an apple and a foil packet of pretzels—lunch for the homeless. It was nearly the end of the pretzels. He'd have to go around to the Elks on Friday night and ask them to ante up another couple of cases. The sliced deli ham had come out of pitiful cash, as he liked to call it, and so had the apples. Usually Mrs. Hepplewhite made the sandwiches, but she'd spent the night with Mrs. Simms. . . .

Argyle's front porch light was on. Bentley decided to sit there for a few moments and scope things out. He that hasteth with his feet sinneth, he told himself, but actually he simply felt monumentally tired, and it seemed to him that he could easily lie down in bed and simply never get up again.

Last night, after his chat with Mahoney, he had spent two hours going over the books at the church. Doing good works wasn't cheap. Mahoney had understood that part of it. He was locked into a mortgage that had looked pretty reasonable just a few years ago, but now it was a buyer's market again, and you could find comparable buildings all over town for two-thirds the money. And besides that, the place was falling apart. It needed paint, plumbing; the electrical wiring was like an illustration out of a fire-prevention manual.

The rain came down in a deluge, and he switched off the wipers, listening to it beat against the roof of the car. That did it. Between the rain and the porch light and very nearly no sleep at all last night, it just wasn't a good morning for the business of spying on Argyle. Bentley was too damned tired to get wet. He reached for the ignition key, but just then, as if it were a message, a light blinked on inside the house.

Argyle was up before dawn again, like a man who had desperately important work to do. Bentley slid across the seat, eased the passenger door open, and slid out, shutting the door

as silently as he could before jogging toward the side of the
house in a crouch. He ducked in among the hibiscus and tree
ferns, pushing his way through them until he was well hidden
from the street.

Rain dripped from the brim of his hat as he crept forward,
edging past a gas meter, pushing in among the rain-heavy
fronds of a fern. The window shade was up a good inch, and
the window itself was open. He could see the entirety of the
room inside: books, stuffed chairs, an old table scattered with
junk. On the floor lay what looked for all the world like a
cross between a packing crate and a coffin. It was empty. Argyle was sitting in a chair, dressed in a pair of red pajamas,
his back toward the window. He was utterly still, as if he'd
just gotten out of bed to fall asleep in the chair. But there was
something rigid and grotesque about his posture, as if he was
a lifelike wooden puppet.

The moments passed. Bentley turned up his collar against
the rain. This was worthless. He would catch pneumonia
watching Argyle asleep in a chair. . . .

Argyle moved. His arm jerked upward spastically, like the
arm of a man snatching at a fly, then flopped down again, the
palm slapping against the arm of the chair with a sort of limp-
wristed determination. He repeated the movement, started to
rise, then slumped back down, his head lolling forward now
so that his chin pressed against his chest. His neck was a grotesque, almost larval white against the red of the pajamas, and
his hair, mussed up with sleep, seemed to sprout from the
white scalp in tufts. The head bobbed, as if he were listening
to inaudible music.

He's *drunk*, Bentley thought—and at four in the morning!
Argyle's head swiveled from side to side then, unnaturally
again, as if he had a crick in his neck that he was trying to
work out, but couldn't. No, he wasn't drunk. He was in the
grip of some kind of fit. A grand mal seizure? He tried to
stand, but sat back down hard, and Bentley could hear the
sound of gibbering now. A rush of laughter followed the gibbering, and then a low moaning, almost like a foghorn.

In a frightful rush, Bentley understood the truth. What he
had feared had finally come to pass: like Murray LeRoy had
been, Argyle was possessed, inhabited, manipulated by demons. "Lord have mercy," Bentley whispered.

Argyle stood up now, swaying on his feet like a marionette. Shakily, slowly, he reached up and jerked out a fistful of his own hair. Clutching it in his hand, he shuffled across the carpet, making a noise like flies buzzing against a window, one hesitant step at a time, until he slammed his foot into the wooden box on the floor and pitched forward across it like a stuffed dummy, where he lay heaving, his face mashed into the carpet, ghastly noises wheezing out of him. Then abruptly he fell still, apparently dead or comatose.

Bentley crouched there speechless, nearly unable to move. Rain swept in under the house eaves, thudding against his shoulders. He shivered in the chill air, certain that he had just witnessed a man's damnation, that Argyle had quite simply gone to Hell.

What did this require of Bentley? He was a minister, a man of God. Had he been led to this window merely to witness Argyle's descent into damnation? He felt tiny, exposed to the wind and rain and cold, and the darkness settled around him pitilessly, like an accusation.

He saw something then, dimly through the nearly closed door at the opposite side of the room—a shadow approaching, as if along a hallway. Someone else was in the house! He ducked out of sight, then peered up over the sill at the very corner of the window, keeping well back out of the way. His hands shook against the wooden sill as the door to the room swung open slowly, as if the intruder were doubtful, wondering what he might find. Whoever it was paused there in the shadows, then stepped forward into the room. Light from the ceiling lamp fell across his face. . . .

Bentley croaked out a hoarse cry and fell over backward, tearing fronds off the trunk of the tree fern and scrabbling in the muddy flowerbed on his hands and knees as the rain pummeled his back and shoulders. He crawled along the side of the house, blinking the water out of his eyes. A hibiscus limb snatched off his hat, and he groped for it blindly, clutching it in his hand now and reeling forward, suddenly free of the shrubbery and staggering through the rain toward his car. He tore the car door open, slid in behind the wheel, and started the engine, glancing backward as he accelerated up the rain-swept street, half expecting Argyle's corpse-pale face to peer out through the lighted window.

For it had been Argyle himself who had come out of the shadowed hallway and into the room, carrying two glasses of orange juice and dressed in red pajamas identical to the pair worn by the dead man on the floor.

❧ 28 ❧

THE NEWSPAPER LAY IN THE BUSHES THAT MORNING, HIDDEN from view, just like he'd asked. It was early. The paperboy must have set the alarm for three A.M.! Not bad for a dead bird in a jar, he thought. He smiled uneasily. Of course it was just coincidence. . . .

But what if it wasn't? He stood on the sidewalk and thought about it, looking down the empty street toward the church. First the tomatoes, now the newspaper. The bluebird of happiness was apparently granting his wishes. The idea was lunatic, and he chuckled now, thinking about it. A man runs across a magical charm, Aladdin's lamp, and he gives its genie full rein, casting spells and calling down wishes. Does the man conquer kingdoms, attain vast power, amass a fortune? No, he makes the genie work out on newspapers and tomato vines, uses it to control the ant problem in the kitchen.

So give it back to Argyle, he told himself suddenly, and his smile faded. This idea had slipped into his mind as if out of nowhere: essentially he had *stolen* it, hadn't he? And normally he didn't *steal* things. And he didn't lie, either. And now he was up to his ears in both these crimes.

But hell, there wasn't anything *normal* about this. Here he was confronted by liars and cheats, with Argyle's baloney and the giant grinning postal inspector with eyes like a sand hog. Whose rules was he supposed to play by? What if a man found a grocery sack full of money in the bushes, and he *knew*, say, that it was dirty money, drug money—a lot of wrinkled fifties and hundreds, utterly untraceable. What would he do with it? Advertise? ''Attn. scum, found yr. money in a shrub. . . .'' How *could* that be the right thing to do, in any way you could explain in under an hour? And anyway, this wasn't a bag full of money, it was just a dead bird pickled by some Third-World trinket company with an arcane sense of humor.

Unless of course it wasn't.

The door to the motor home swung open and Henry looked out, fumbling with his eyeglasses and dressed in a pair of pajamas and floppy-looking slippers. He spotted Walt out on the sidewalk and gave him the high sign.

"Paper?" Walt asked him. He stepped toward him across the wet lawn, pulling off the plastic wrapper and handing it over. *There,* he thought, abruptly relieved of his burden. *It's out of my hands now. Like giving the sack of dirty money to the church, it expiates the living daylights out of the sin.*

Henry looked at the paper, then tried to hand it back. He was too much of a gentleman to take it. "Go ahead," he whispered, clearly not wanting to wake up Jinx. "You first. I can work a crossword or something."

"No, heck," Walt said. "I've got work to do anyway."

"Well, here. Take the sports or something. What do you read first? Financial page?"

"Not a thing," Walt lied. "I'm just going to stuff boxes with it. You might as well take a look at it first."

"If you're sure . . ."

"Sure I'm sure."

"Thanks," Henry said. He nodded and then shut the door, and Walt found himself standing in a fresh drizzle, his newspaper gone. Well, this took care of it. He could quit agonizing over the damned bluebird. Apparently the creature didn't work after all; he hadn't gotten his wish, had he?

He headed for the garage and cranked up the space heater, then climbed up the ladder and had a look in the rafters. Spotting the tin box, he reached in among the fishing tackle and pulled it out, opening the lid and sniffing the ginlike aroma that wafted out of it. The bird itself wasn't nearly as deteriorated as he remembered it. Its feathers were almost glossy now, a bright, clear blue, and its eyes were open and alert. Well, not alert, for heaven's sake. There was no use getting nutty about it.

He thought suddenly of the demons hightailing it out of Pandora's box, and he replaced the jar and shut the lid again, shoving it back in among the salmon eggs and the fishing lures, then stuffed the tackle box back into the rafters. Maybe later he would find an even safer place for it.

He climbed down and poured a cup of coffee, then sorted through the half dozen mail-order catalogues that had arrived in yesterday's junk mail—the competition. Walt was on every address list in the country by now. It fascinated him to think of it: his name and address reproducing itself like a slow virus along with thousands and millions of other addresses—long lists of them sold back and forth as if they were eggs in a basket instead of words and numbers. Somewhere, right now, enterprising people were pulling down a staggering fortune buying and selling names. The concept was almost mystical, sublunar capitalism in the information age.

Two months ago he himself had paid good money for three lists of a thousand addresses each—seven cents per address— which was about all the catalogue production and mailing he could afford to do right now. There was forty pages of offset printing along with darkroom work, collating, stapling, addressing, and bulk-rate postage, which added up to more than two thousand dollars per catalogue, and the cold truth was that within three weeks of the catalogue's coming out, orders dwindled nearly to nothing, and it was time to put out another one that was in some clear way different from the last, and him wondering all the time whether he ought to hustle another thousand addresses in order to expand things generally. But he had no real idea how much was too much—how many catalogues, how much inventory. It wasn't like planting corn; in the business of catalogue sales, the relationship between sowing and reaping was in no way clear. Probably Dr. Hefernin could sell him a pamphlet on the subject.

He found the current Archie McPhee catalogue, one of his favorites, and the American Science and Surplus catalogue, which was offering overstock Water Weenies right there on the first page along with dental burs, radiation gloves, and something called a "Toilet Seat Alarm," the purpose of which wasn't made clear. There were sixty-five pages crammed with this kind of stuff, half of it electronic. Walt envied the hell out of that kind of inventory. His little collection of rubber skeletons and palm-tree hats was pitiful in comparison. Now that the tin shed was up, though, he could expand a little bit, make fewer trips out to the wholesale warehouses in Bellflower.

One of the catalogues was new to him—something called *The Captain Grose Collection.* It was expensively done, full color, offering ''antiquities and religious relics and reproductions of all natures, direct from the East.''

Walt sipped his coffee, fingering through the catalogue with idle interest at first, then with growing disbelief. It offered hundreds of sacred and sanctified relics: fragments of the true cross, vials of tears from a dozen different sources including the Savior himself, links of the chain that bound St. Peter, droplets of blood from an inventory of martyrs two pages long, wine from the marriage at Cana, toenail parings from the apostles, Tubalcain's fire fender, the brass-shod broomstick of the Witch of Endor, one of the seven golden lampstands, a tooth from Balaam's ass, the preserved ears and snout of one of the Gadarene swine, a chip of the stone that the builder refused. . . .

He burst into laughter and shut the catalogue. This *had* to be a joke, an impossibly elaborate, lowball prank. But who on earth . . . ? He looked at the cover again, trying to estimate how much it had cost to print—the slick, full-color cover, the high-quality paper. It was put out by something called ''Millennialist Products, Ltd.'' He checked the address—Santa Ana! It was a local company. Immediately he thought of Dr. Hefernin, but this wasn't in his line. In fact, this had a family resemblance to the stuff in Argyle's misdelivered box. Maybe it wasn't a prank after all.

Suddenly suspicious, he opened the catalogue again. A number of the items had no price—apparently you had to call an 800 number to inquire. The priced items were classified as ''reproductions'' that were ''strict copies'' of originals in the Captain Grose Collection, with which these replicas were ''kept in close association.''

About halfway through the catalogue the listings changed, and instead of sacred relics and reproductions there was a list, much shorter, of ''profane'' relics, ''offered strictly in the spirit of scientific inquiry.''

This clearly *was* the stuff in Argyle's box: the ''dead mans grease,'' the twigs from the ''tree of living flesh,'' figures of saints carved out of their own finger bones and preserved in oil, vials of blood. . . .

Walt dialed the number on the back of the catalogue. It was

impossibly early, not even seven. Obviously no one would be there, although possibly they'd have a voice-mail ordering system. . . .

A man answered. "Dilworth Catalogue Sales. Twenty-four-hour service."

Walt was bowled over. *Dilworth!* Argyle after all! Nothing in the catalogue had . . . "Hello," he said, scrambling to find something more to say, to keep the man on the line.

"What can I do for you?"

"I'm calling about the catalogue," Walt said. "The relics catalogue."

"Mastercard, Visa, or American Express? There's a fourteen-dollar minimum. Any order over thirty dollars receives the 'Get Out of Hell Free' card at absolutely no cost whatsoever." The man's voice was perfunctory, as if he had reeled this nonsense off a hundred times that morning already. "Are you interested in the card? I'll mark the appropriate box on the order form."

Walt laughed out loud. "I'll take ten," he said.

"No can do," the man said to him. "One per customer. Nobody needs more than one anyway, do they?"

"Of course not," Walt said. The man was serious! "Just a little joke. Not very funny."

"Mastercard, Visa, or American Express?"

"Visa," Walt said hurriedly. Apparently the man wasn't in a joking mood. He thought about hanging up but he held on instead, thumbing through the catalogue, looking through the reproductions for something cheap. Hell, he could write it off. It was business. And it was only thirty bucks, after all, give or take. No way he was going to miss out on the free card. He reeled off his Visa number and expiration date.

"Delivery address?"

He gave the man his address.

"I need the description, catalogue number, quantity, and price, in that order," the man said.

"All right. Let's see. Send me the 'Ever-burning Brimstone,' number S-883, quantity one, $8.95, and the 'Reproduction Golden Lampstand,' Q-452, quantity one, $26.50. Now what is that exactly?—the lampstand?"

"Revelations 1, verse 12."

"Ah," Walt said. "From Revelations. Somehow I remem-

ber that those were *candlesticks*, but what you've got is lampstands?''

"The catalogue number you gave me is lampstands. That's
Revised Standard Version. King James is candlesticks. Now,
if you want the candlesticks instead of the lampstand, we offer
those, too, but they're a little more pricey, although they do
come with good candles—aromatic.''

"No," Walt said. "That sounds nice, but I think I prefer
the lampstand. I just can't . . . *Surely* it must be one or the
other?''

"It's our policy to please the customer.''

Walt nearly hung up again. This was blatantly fraudulent.
Fraud with its mask torn off. A moment ago the whole thing
was funny; now he felt like a credulous fool. "Look," Walt
said, "what's the deal here? Seriously.''

After a moment the man said, "What do you *think* the deal
is?''

"To tell you the truth," Walt said, "I think I'm getting
hosed.''

"Well, then that's the truth. You're getting hosed.''

"That's it?''

"Let's put it this way—sometimes you get what you *think*
you pay for. It's like that here. All I can tell you is that we've
had a *lot* of satisfied customers. You might be one of them,
or you might be one of the other. The choice is yours. The
choice is always yours.''

There was something about this speech that took the wind
out of Walt's sails. Whatever else was true about Dilworth
Catalogue Sales, this man clearly believed in it on some fun-
damental level. He was a salesman, not a shyster.

"Shall I enter this?" the man asked.

"Yeah," Walt said. "I guess so. What's the total?''

"That's $35.45 plus tax plus two dollars shipping . . . that's
$40.10.''

"Great," Walt said. "Don't forget the card.''

"It's already on the order form—no extra charge.''

Walt hung up. He had just paid forty dollars for junk. It
was a damned good thing that Ivy was going to work for
Argyle. Lord knows how they'd get the bills paid otherwise.

He razored open a box and pulled out the contents, plastic
bags full of dollhouse furniture—not the usual plastic trash,

but high-toned wooden furniture, mouse-size. There were even little rolled-up rag rugs. He sold the heck out of these to doll-house fanatics, usually adults crazy for little bitty things.

The motor home door slammed shut, and he looked out in time to see Jinx cutting across toward the front porch. The world was waking up.

"Bluebird," Walt said, glancing toward the rafters just in case it was necessary, "fetch me my golden lampstand this very day, a quarter hour before the sun reacheth the zenith." He chuckled a little bit, as if to imply that what he'd said was a sort of joke.

29

"AND WHAT ABOUT THE TESTIMONIALS FOR THE SENSIBLE Investor? I don't want the same crowd we ran through the Start-up America meetings last year. They'll be all right up in San Jose in the spring, but we'd be in bad shape if one of them was recognized as a ringer. We need some new faces. And tone it down, too. This is the nineties. A couple of years ago the public believed any damned thing. Now they don't want risk."

Argyle studied himself in the mirror. He hadn't gotten a good night's sleep in weeks now. And he had a splitting head-ache. His late-night forays into the neighborhood inevitably made his head ache as if he'd been hit with a club. And the voices—the satanic gibbering and muttering in his nightmares, like someone had opened a door onto Hell . . .

"The testimonial crowd is entirely new," the man on the other end of the line said tiredly. "New faces, new stories. Don Little over at the temp agency worked that out along with the gimmick. You'd have to look hard to spot any kind of pyramid element. I'm surprised nobody got back to you with the prospectus."

"I am, too," Argyle said flatly. But then he remembered. In fact someone *had* gotten back to him—weeks ago. He'd forgotten it, put the paperwork away in a drawer. His mind just wasn't with it somehow. Business kept getting shunted aside by this damned . . .

Abruptly he had the uncanny feeling that someone was look-ing at him, a feeling so profound that he swiveled around in his chair and looked behind him, although it was impossible: the wall was windowless, only three or four feet away, There was a sound in his ears like the rushing of wind and a creaking like a heavy body swinging slowly on a wooden gallows. Sweat ran into his collar as he sat staring, tensed, his head pounding, waiting for something to happen. Slowly he opened the bottom desk drawer. There were four jars in it, from LeRoy's collection. He untwisted one of the lids, releasing the sigh of breath, the last exhalation of life trapped within.

The sounds faded and disappeared. The presence in the room evaporated. There was nothing behind him but framed diplomas and thank-you trophies from Little League and from kids' soccer teams.

"Are you there?"

"Yeah," he said into the phone. He looked at his list, trying to concentrate. "What about the orphans?"

"They're gangbusters. We got IRS approval last week. The photo layouts are perfect—Filipino girl about four years old, crying at the edge of this vast dump, scrounging for garbage. She's got enormous eyes, like a kid in one of those paintings. Big crocodile tears."

"Where'd you find her?"

"The girl? Pasadena. The photo shoot was at some kind of landfill out in Whittier. We trucked in a lot of crap to set it up right—rags and bottles and rotten fruit, that kind of thing. Big mountain of it. Looks like a typical third-world dump. Anyway, the girl's got this little busted-up basket with—get this—an old brown banana and a stuffed doggy in it. We took a rock and beat the hell out of the doggy, yanked its eye out, really made it look loved. It's purely pitiful. Girl's mother's a maid for Benson up there. You remember Jim Benson?"

"Benson?" Argyle groped through his mind, trying to remember the name. The words "yanked its eye out" echoed in his head, going around like a nursery-rhyme refrain. "Didn't Benson threaten to go to the press over the coupon giveaway? I thought he met with a couple of broken legs."

"That was *Benton*, with a *T*. He's up in Camarillo now, state hospital, completely mental. This is the guy who did that great PR package for 'Get Rich Yesterday.' "

"How about the maid and the girl? Are they all right?"

"We put them on a plane back to Manila. No chance the mother will ever see the ads."

"I didn't mean all right that way. I mean *happy*. The kid. The little girl."

"Happy?"

"Yeah. Did you take care of her? I don't *use* children, not unless they're imaginary children."

"Sure, we took care of her. Absolutely. We gave the mother two one-way tickets and a thousand bucks—a choice between that and deportation."

"Send her another thousand. Five thousand. And the same in trust for the girl. And call George Mifflin in Manila. Tell him to keep an eye on both of them."

"Whatever you say."

"That's what I say. What kind of ads have we got?"

"Twenty-four so far, all in slick magazines. Save the starving orphans—the usual deal. Pathetic enough to make you cry. It'll draw like rotten meat. Beats the hell out of the legitimate ads, I can tell you that."

"Good. That's it?" He could hear the creaking again, as if there were ghost children on the swings outside, and he realized that it was far hotter in the room than it should be. There was rain pattering against the windows now. He loosened his tie and unbuttoned his shirt, looking around uneasily. He could swear something was *here*, in the room, now.

Three more jars in the drawer.

"One more thing quick," the man said. "Benson's got a dynamite idea for an estate liquidation ploy. He wants me to run it past you."

"Shoot." Argyle looked at the desktop, working hard to listen. There was static on the phone, and the voice seemed to come from a long way away, as if the man were speaking on a string-and-can phone from some other room.

"Basically you donate your dead parents' estate," he was saying, "especially properties. The money goes—get this—*to buy wilderness land.* We run up a color brochure showing 'holdings in trust'—so many million acres of northwest wilderness. Pictures of moose, buffalo, long article about the threat to the national parks system, mining, grazing, sale of public lands. . . . "

Argyle lost track of what the man was saying. His mouth was dry and his scalp itched, and he felt a vast pressure rising up within him, as if in another forty seconds he would simply explode. He tried to ignore it.

"We punch all the rich liberal buttons," the man said, "tap all the eco-fears, if you follow me. Guarantee your children's natural birthright into perpetuity and get a hell of a big tax write-off, too. We do the whole scam Ponzi-style. Keep enough liquid income to cover ourselves in case we actually need to buy a little property. How fast can these people die, anyway? And we can show the inheritors the same piece of land over and over. It's foolproof. You got anything to add?"

"Add? I'd work Indians into it. That's always good. Picture of some old dead chief."

"Of course. We might risk the life insurance angle, too. That works like crazy for nursing homes and mausoleums; there's no reason it won't work for us. . . ."

"Right," Argyle said hurriedly. The room seemed to shake now, as if from heavy footfalls. The phone receiver thrummed in his hand. "That's fine. Save the details for some other time."

"All right. Now, on the 900 numbers. The crystal readings never got off the blocks. Standard psychic stuff is still the bread and butter. Soft porn's holding its own. That kind of thing's established, you know, but this fad stuff . . . What I'm saying is if it's current, then we've got to get on top of it quicker, get the product out there. . . ." The man's voice droned on, running down accounts. ". . . Breakfast cereal," he said. ". . . Computerized fortune cookie messages, gardening tips, dating service, Zantar the Psychic . . ."

"What?" Argyle was lost, baffled. His mind spun. He was hot, feverish. Was the man talking gibberish? "Wait." He croaked the word out, laying the phone down without punching the hold button. He put his hands to his ears, trying to press out the rushing and creaking, which had sprung up again as if someone had put a cassette tape in the stereo. The sensation of being on view increased by the moment, and he looked around wildly, at the windows, at the lamp-lit playground equipment beyond, at the murky, shadowed corners of the office. He felt shrunken, tiny, like a specimen insect in a glass jar. The very air vibrated, and he was seized with panic, with the wild desire to run. Did he hear a bell tolling?

The windows ran with rainwater, and what had sounded like the rush of wind had evened into the unmistakable exhalation of heavy breathing. He felt a stirring against the back of his neck, as if someone stood very close behind him now, whispering softly.

He didn't dare turn around, but reached into the drawer again, turning the lid from one of the jars. There was a fleeting cry, swallowed immediately in the noise and the shaking. He opened another, and the spirit fled, the presence in the room undiminished, ravenous.

He was hot, burning up inside, his very cells on fire. Slowly he stood up, desperate simply to leave, to get out into the rain and the wind. He took a careful step toward the door. His shoulders hunched forward, retracting from the presence at his back. He knew damned well who it was. *What* it was. There was a stench of something burning, something sulphurous, and tendrils of smoke curled up from the carpet beneath his feet. With a wild shriek he lurched forward and grabbed the door-knob, which throbbed like a live thing. He slammed against the door with his shoulder, whimpering and shaking with terror. The door held. He was trapped!

Something wet slithered against his neck like the tongue of a lizard, and he screamed out loud, taking the knob in both hands and twisting it, falling to his knees on the carpet, his eyes screwed shut. . . .

And the door swung inward, bumping gently against his knee. He opened his eyes. Abruptly the noises ceased, the presence in the room evaporated like steam. He heard the sound of rain against the window again. God almighty! He'd been out of his mind with fear, *pushing* on the door instead of pulling!

He realized then that the hallway outside the office door was full of children and their mothers, and he quickly pushed the door shut again. He took a long, shuddering breath and stood up, and right then he felt the wet fabric of his pants against the skin of his legs. He looked down, horrified. He'd wet himself in his terror.

The phone receiver still lay on the table, where he'd dropped it. His hands shook so badly that he could barely pick it up. "You still there?"

"Yeah," the man said. "Everything all right over there?"

"Fine," Argyle said, his voice husky. "There's nothing wrong here. The storm's apparently got the phones all screwed up. Listen, you keep up the good work. I've got a meeting."

"Good enough. I'll have Don send over a copy of the Sensible Investor prospectus. Anything else?"

The window lit up just then, and almost at the same time there was a crack of thunder that shook the walls.

"No," Argyle said. He hung up the telephone and picked up his coat from the back of the chair. Holding it in front of his crotch, he stepped out of the door and into the hallway, where, for some unholy reason, Walt Stebbins sat in a chair by the receptionist's desk, filling out papers.

⇥ 30 ⇤

IVY AND JINX LEFT AT SEVEN-THIRTY, HEADING DOWN TO Watson's for breakfast, and Henry sneaked away down the sidewalk not five minutes later without saying a word to Walt, who felt as if he were surrounded by plots. Everybody had some kind of iron in the fire this morning—capitalism, hula-hula women, crayon graffiti—and he was left with the mundane chores. At eight he had to haul the kids over to the preschool and get them signed up, whatever that entailed, then stop at the grocery store on the way to the Old Hill Mailbox, where he'd ship the morning's UPS packages.

It had been a mistake to tell Ivy about having seen Argyle out driving around the neighborhood at the time of the vandalism. She had accused him outright of jealousy. Jealousy! Argyle's vandalizing the house had been beyond her understanding, but it wasn't beyond Walt's—although, clearly, what he understood he couldn't tell her.

The television was going in the house, and he could hear the sound of a rinky-dink cartoon jingle. The melody was vaguely familiar—from ages ago. A wave of nostalgia struck him, and he stopped to listen, laying the tape dispenser on the bench. It was Spunky and Tadpole! Great God almighty, he thought, in *this* day and age? Full of a sudden curious joy, he went out through the garage door and looked in at the window. Nora and Eddie sprawled on the floor in that weird rubber-legged way kids have, half sitting and half kneeling. They stared fixedly at the screen, Nora's head bobbing time to the music. Walt heard her laugh out loud and point; it was Tadpole, all right, just then coming along the road, carrying a fishing pole with a big-headed fish on it. The fish was apparently dead, because his eyes were X'd out.

Walt abruptly recalled last night's adventure in the kitchen—
Nora and Eddie setting out to make bubble castles in the sink.
Why the hell had he broken it up so quickly and sent them to
bed? Only one damned reason: monkey business; that's what
Ivy had called it. Well, fat lot of good it had done anybody.
He wished now that he had let the kids have a few minutes
with the bubbles. Ten minutes would have seemed an eternity
to them, nothing to him.

He could remember the long cartoon mornings when he was
that age: the cold cereal, television programs stacked end to
end like books on a shelf, the clock on the wall nearly falling
asleep. . . . It was one of the wild, doomed luxuries of childhood. Say what you want, but Spunky and Tadpole were vital
in a way that was as huge as the sky, and so were bubbles in
the sink.

He realized now that Nora was watching him through the
window, making her rabbit face, and he waved at her before
turning around and hurrying back into the garage, where he
grabbed one of the plastic bags full of miniature furniture, and
headed out toward the avocado tree, the sun shining in the
east. The air was sharp and clear, and he sucked in a big
lungful as he peeked under the flowerpot. The daddy longlegs
was crouched against the roof. There was a ragged web spun
against the back wall with a couple of tiny flies already wound
up in it, waiting to be sucked dry. One of the trapped flies
wiggled a little bit, but struggling was useless.

"Hello, Mr. Argyle," Walt said to the spider. "Top o' the
morning to you." The spider seemed to retract at the sound
of his voice, flattening itself into the corner. Walt wondered if
he had a duty to the fly that was still alive; but probably there
was no practical purpose in trying to do anything for it. And
whatever moral value there would be in such a kindness was
vague. Holding the pot carefully so as not to disturb the spider
any more than necessary, he set two tiny chairs and a table
onto the shelf and spread the little woven rug on the floor.
Then he swiveled the pot around so that the broken-out section
faced outward before he lowered the thing down over the furniture.

He returned to the garage, where he slipped a flashlight into
his pocket. Then he looked in through the window again. The
cartoon was just ending. Walt opened the back door and ges-

tured to Nora and Eddie. "Put your shoes on," he said. "I want to show you something."

"Oh!" Nora said breathlessly, leaping up. Desperately she searched the floor with her eyes, holding one hand to her mouth. What she was looking for wasn't at all clear. "What kind is it?" She looked wide-eyed at Walt.

"No kind," Walt said. "Just something. Out under the tree."

Eddie leaned out and picked up Nora's shoes, which were in plain sight, and calmly handed them to her. She seemed relieved, as if a mystery had been cleared up. Eddie put on his own shoes without a word, carefully double-knotting the laces.

They followed Walt out through the door, across the wet grass. In the bright sunlight, rainwater steamed off the lawn in a mist. "It'll be summer by noon," Walt said, patting Nora's shoulder. She smiled big at him and nodded. "Look here." Walt pointed at a snail, heading for the dead herb garden. "This is Mr. Binion."

"He has a name?" Nora asked. Eddie didn't look at the snail, but studied the palm of his hand.

"Oh, yes," Walt said. "There are many animals that live in these old neighborhoods." He suddenly remembered his success with last night's story, and he cast his voice low and serious, waving his hand, taking it all in. "At night," he said, "possums and raccoons use these fences as roads, going from one house to another in search of food. In the spring, toads appear from out of ditches, and families of salamanders come to live under fallen logs."

"*What* kind?" Nora asked, squishing up her face. Eddie picked up a bent stick that had fallen from the avocado tree and swung it like a baseball bat. He looked away, deadpan, staring at some spot in the sky now.

"What kind of what?" Walt asked.

"Those things."

"Salamanders?"

Nora nodded.

"Do you know what a salamander is?" Walt asked.

Nora shook her head.

"It's a sort of newt."

"Oh."

"Like a lizard," Eddie said helpfully.

"And like toads?" Nora asked.

"Kind of," Walt said. "A toad is its cousin. And do you know what?"

"What?" Nora whispered now.

Walt squinted at her. "There was a toad out here last week that was wearing a hat and coat."

"Oh!" Nora cried.

"And a mouse with a vest on. And spectacles."

She covered her mouth with her hand, as if to keep from shouting out loud. Eddie rolled his eyes.

"What?" Walt said to Eddie. "You don't believe me?"

Eddie shook his head, grinning faintly.

"I'll bet you a plug nickel," Walt said. "Try me."

"Bet him!" Nora shouted. "Bet him, Eddie!"

Eddie shook his head, still grinning.

"Well, let's just see, then." Walt led the way into the garden shed, pretending to search around among the shovels and rakes. Nora followed him, taking exaggerated steps and biting her bottom lip. Eddie swung his stick with one hand, as if it were a sword now.

"What's this?" Walt said. He stopped in his tracks, double-taking at the overturned flower pot. "What have we here?"

"What is it?" Nora said. "The snail?"

"It's a *pot*," Eddie said.

Walt pulled the flashlight out of his pocket and switched it on, then shined it in through the jagged door in the side of the pot. He could see the doll furniture in there. "What on earth? Nora, take a closer look."

Nora stepped forward, glancing at him wide-eyed, then stood on tiptoe and peered into the hole in the pot. Her breath caught. She'd seen it. Very slowly she turned toward Walt. "Something's house," she whispered.

Walt nodded. "It's the house of the amazing Mr. Argyle." He motioned to Eddie. "Have a look-see." He held the light on the hole.

Eddie looked in, and Nora clutched his arm, trying to get in close enough to take another look herself. "Don't pig up," she whispered. And then, with his free hand, Eddie reached up and grasped the top of the pot, upending it, exposing the doll furniture, the quivering web, the buzzing little fly wound in gauze. The spider, big around as a silver dollar with its legs fully extended, rushed down the side of the pot and out onto Eddie's wrist. Nora screamed, leaping backward into Walt, and Eddie hooted with wild surprise, flinging the flowerpot into the fence and raking the stick down his arm to dislodge the spider. It fell into the dirt, and Eddie drew the stick back and slammed it down, yelling, "Shit! Shit! Shit!" and flailing at the spider until the stick broke off short in his hand.

Nora shook with spasms of fear and shock, and Walt hugged her, trying to calm her down. Eddie stomped on the spider, or where the spider had been, grinding it into the dirt until he worked all the wild terror out of himself. Then he stood there breathing heavily, looking at the ground as if for signs of movement.

"I think you got him," Walt said after a moment.

"What *was* he?" Nora asked, calming down now that the threat was passed.

"Daddy longlegs," Walt said.

"A daddy?"

"A *spider*," Eddie said.

"Is he Mr. Argyle?" Nora asked. "Like you said?"

"No," Walt lied. "I don't know what he's done with Mr. Argyle."

"He killed him," Nora said.

"Oh, I don't think so," Walt said.

"He killed Mr. Argyle." Nora started to giggle, finally covering her mouth with her hands.

Walt was relieved. She was apparently coming out of it. "What's funny?" he asked her.

"Eddie said 'shit,' " Nora said. "Shit, shit, shit."

"Yes, indeed," Walt said. "He had a reason to. You don't have a reason to, so don't say it."

"I'm telling you."

"I already know."

"Poor Mr. Argyle," Nora said, and together they walked back toward the house.

Walt heard the sound of a distant church bell tolling eight o'clock. For a moment he thought it was the bells of St. Anthony's, miraculously restored—but it couldn't be. These were tolling somewhere across Old Towne, beyond the Plaza, probably the bells in the tower at Holy Spirit Catholic Church. He couldn't remember that they tolled the hours, but then maybe he'd never been listening for them, having always had bells closer to home. They took up the first notes of a Christmas carol, and carols were still ringing fifteen minutes later as he and Nora and Eddie drove east on Chapman Avenue, toward the Oak Lawn Preschool, the rain coming down hard again.

Walt ushered the children in through the door, past a half dozen mothers dropping off kids. One child stood in the hallway and sobbed out loud, and two others, apparently sisters, slugged and pinched each other, kicking like fiends on the carpeted floor of a classroom, or whatever they called it. There was a scream from down the hall, muffled by a closed door.

"I guess it's just another day in paradise," Walt said to the receptionist. He introduced Nora and Eddie to her, and the woman handed him a couple of forms to fill out and then started chatting with the kids.

A door swung open off the hall just then, and through it, looking like a hammered mannequin, strode Robert Argyle, heading toward the open front door, and carrying his coat over his arm. He spotted Walt and seemed to go brain-dead for a moment, his face losing all powers of expression. Slowly he recovered, forcing a smile as he stepped forward, holding out his hand. Walt shook it for an instant and dropped it.

"You're surprised to see me," Argyle said.

"Slightly."

"This is one of my schools. I'm the director."

Walt nodded, noticing suddenly that there was the rank smell of sulphur and piss on the air of the hallway. He squinted at Argyle, who still held his coat carefully in front of him. Forget it, he thought; this wasn't something he wanted to know.

"Who are these, then?" Argyle asked, gesturing at Nora and Eddie. The preschool was quiet now, the hallway emptied out, the door to the classroom closed. The bells from across town were still playing carols, although it was too distant to make out the melody.

"This is Nora," Walt said, "and this is Eddie, my niece and nephew. Kids, this is Mr. Argyle."

Instantly, Nora covered her mouth with both hands, her eyes shooting open. She began to giggle. "The one the spider ate?" she asked.

"That's right," Walt said to her. "He's not dead after all. Just like I told you."

Argyle blinked his eyes hard, several times in succession, staring at Nora. Then he cocked his head, suddenly hearing something, his face white. Clearly it was the bells. They fell silent for a moment, and Argyle turned toward the door without saying another word, and right then they started up again, clanging away as if they'd ring right through until Christmas.

❧ 31 ❧

ROBERT ARGYLE HAD A BUSINESS OFFICE IN A BIG OLD FLAT-roofed Spanish-style house on Chapman Avenue. Probably he owned the house itself, which had been renovated and converted to office space, and which he shared with two law firms and some kind of consultant. His own office was subdued and unassuming—a couple of leather easy chairs, mahogany desk and file, Tiffany-style lamps, and a Berber carpet. There was no receptionist. Clearly it was more a hideaway than an office. Ivy had no real idea how much wealth he had managed to accumulate over the years; Argyle had never shown it off. It would have been nice to think a little better of him because of this, that despite his money he was a simple man, down to earth. And maybe he was.

She stood alone in the office, looking out the back window, down onto the old walnut grove where the house had burned. There was something horrible about a burned house. She saw now that there were police cars parked on the property. Men with shovels dug among the walnut trees in the grove, and others milled around, waiting.

"This morning's paper said it might be arson," Argyle said, coming into the office behind her.

She turned around. "Frightening when it's right next door, isn't it?"

He nodded grimly. "Especially with this latest news." He gestured at the work going on down below. "I understand they've found what might be human remains buried out there."

"Like a grave?"

"Not an old one, from what I hear. Maybe someone murdered—fairly recently."

She shuddered. "Not here—not in town?"

"That's the kind of world we seem to be living in, isn't it? There's not a lot of decency left."

"Oh, I think there is, really," Ivy said. "The decency hasn't gone anyplace; it's just that a lot of the other is always in the news."

"Of course you're right. This kind of thing is an aberration, isn't it?" He sat down, gesturing at a chair. Ivy sat down, too, facing away from the window. Robert didn't look as bad this morning, as tired and bedraggled, as he had in Watson's a couple of days ago. Then it struck her that he was covering it up—wearing an undereye concealer and a foundation. She glanced away, vaguely embarrassed for him. He smiled at her wanly. "I get a little pessimistic sometimes," he said. "A little lonely. I don't mind telling you the truth. I've always wanted children, but . . ." He shrugged, opening the desk drawer and bringing out a bottle of aspirin. He shook out a couple of the pills and swallowed them dry.

"Well, what about this property?" Ivy asked, steering the subject to business. There was no way she was going to discuss children with Argyle. "It's commercial?"

"Industrial, really—out on Batavia. There's two of them, adjacent lots. I've been sitting on them for years. The whole neighborhood is concrete tilt-ups now, and a big self-storage yard. *Very* profitable area. Not much square footage left to rent. The lots, conservatively, are worth a half million dollars apiece. You'd be the sole agent." He opened a drawer in the desk and took out a manila envelope, which he set in front of her. Her name was written across the top.

She sat for a moment, stunned even though she'd expected something like this. The commission would be somewhere in the neighborhood of sixty thousand dollars. "Why don't you build on them yourself?"

He waved the suggestion aside. "I'm lightening the load a little. Throwing the ballast overboard. How about you? Ship running smoothly?" He leaned back in his desk chair and appraised her with a look that was probably meant to be heartfelt. He looked goofy, somehow, like a nervous teenager.

"Ship's running very smoothly," she said. "Walt's got big plans for his catalogue sales business. Real estate market's turning around."

"That's *good*," he said, sitting up and smacking his palm against the desktop. He laughed, shaking his head. "Big plans!" He paused for a moment, looking wistfully out the window now, as if something had just drifted into his mind. "You know," he said, "after all these years, I still don't know what happened to the three of us. We were quite a team once."

"It's all water under the bridge, Robert."

"I don't think I ever had a chance to explain myself, my ambitions for . . . us."

"There's no need to explain ambition to me. I'm acquainted with it."

"No," he said. "Wait a moment. Hear me out. What I mean has something to do with big plans, with what you said. Walt and I have different ideas about that, about . . . size. Walt wouldn't have wanted what I wanted."

"That's probably true," she said, letting him talk. After all these years, an apology was overdue. He had behaved like a creep, even though essentially he was right. Walt didn't have his kind of ambition. Walt saw the world from a different point of view, from somewhere in outer space, usually, and the idea of the two of them as partners seemed impossible now.

"I knew we'd reached the end of things, of the partnership. But I didn't know that it would mean reaching the end of things with you. Even now, if I could change that, I would. Especially now."

She shrugged. "Things happen. There's no use carrying them around with you, is there?"

"If a man could change the past . . ."

"But he can't. Best just to let it go."

"I could have made you happy, Ivy. Instead, I'm afraid I made all of us miserable."

"Well, it's good of you to clear the air."

He nodded and shrugged. "Look at this." He took a photograph out of the desk and laid it atop the envelope. It was he and Ivy, taken back when he was in his early twenties, not long after he'd gotten out of school. She was nineteen. The photo had been taken during the time of Argyle's first big success independent of Walt. He had promoted a vitamin supplement sales organization, which licensed salespeople who would pay a fee for the right to license further salespeople. All of them took a graduated percentage of profits, mainly from fees, and almost nobody sold any vitamins, which were largely worthless in the first place: "natural vitamins" that were mainly gelled infusions of alfalfa and carrots. What it had amounted to, according to Walt, was money changing hands, shifting upward, filling the pockets of someone who was selling greed and lies. Half of Argyle's working capital had been Walt's money, which Argyle had eventually returned—tainted, according to Walt, who knew the difference between clean money and dirty money.

Walt wasn't in the photo. Ivy wore a sequined evening dress that Argyle had bought for her, simply to go out to dinner. It must have been a five-hundred-dollar dress even back then. . . . It occurred to her suddenly that she'd made the right choice. Walt was the one, not that she had any doubts.

Argyle picked up the photo and stared at it. "I wonder sometimes what would have become of us if things had gone differently. We would have made a formidable pair, you and I."

"I guess it just wasn't destined to be."

"Destiny," he said. "Sometimes destiny fools you, especially if you have too much respect for it. We can make our own destinies. That's one of the things I've found out. Who would have thought you'd be destined to sit across from me now, the two of us doing business together? Sometimes you have to *make* things happen. It's possible I can make things happen for Walt, too. It's no secret that my own companies have been successful. There's no limit to that commodity, you know, to success."

"That'll be encouraging to Walt," she said, imagining the conversation. Walt would have to take a pill to calm down.

"Mention to him that I'll help in any way I can, won't you?"

"Gladly."

"And, Ivy . . . Let's start out fresh. The two of us." He held out his hand.

WELL, HE HADN'T EXACTLY MADE A PASS AT HER. SHE glanced down at the envelope on the seat of the Toyota as she drove up Chapman Avenue toward Batavia, and she imagined that it was stuffed with hundred-dollar bills instead of papers. Then she whooped out loud and slapped the steering wheel. Would she take the man's money? Yes, she would.

There was no use inventing motives for him. Maybe he didn't have any. He was lonely; anybody could see that. But that didn't mean that his apologies, or whatever they were, weren't real. Probably he meant what he said. And until she knew otherwise, there was no use assuming that he meant *more* than he said. Of course if she was certain that he had, that he was pulling something, then she'd have no choice but to hand him the envelope back and explain that they'd both made a mistake—again.

And she could do that as easily tomorrow as today.

❧ 32 ❧

EVEN THOUGH THE WHITE DELIVERY VAN THAT ARRIVED JUST before noon had the words "Dilworth Catalogue Sales—We Deliver" painted on the side in red block letters, Walt stood for a moment wondering what it was.

A man in a khaki uniform got out carrying two boxes—a big one apparently containing the lampstand and a small one containing the brimstone. "Membership card's in with the . . . brimstone," he said, looking at the packing slip, which he handed to Walt along with a pen. Walt signed it and handed it back, and the man gave Walt a copy along with the two cartons, climbed into his van, and sped away. The box with the lamp in it was heavy as hell.

"Membership card?" Walt wondered out loud, watching the van roll away from the stop sign at the corner.

He looked at his watch even though he knew what time it was. The curious thing, he told himself, wasn't just that the packages arrived today; it was that they arrived *exactly when he'd asked*: before the sun rose to its zenith. He had thought he was being funny. If they had arrived a half hour from now, at quarter past, he could have dismissed the bird as a fake, a toy, but as it was . . .

As it was, what? What did this prove? Only that Dilworth Catalogue Sales was on the ball. Maybe there was a lesson in it—the virtues of lightning-fast delivery. Hefernin would recommend it. It was worth a twenty-dollar, illustrated pamphlet.

Ask for something more.

The thought occurred to him like a voice in his head, more a command than a suggestion, as he turned up the driveway toward the garage. Money?

He imagined wishing for a million dollars in small bills—

just for starters; later he could raise the stakes. How would it come to him? Out of the sky, floating like flower petals? Maybe he should complicate the issue in order to *really* test the thing—ask to find the money in a suitcase guarded by toads in a drainage ditch in Oz.

He chuckled, letting the thought slide away as he swung open the gate. Just then a voice sounded behind him: "Mr. Stebbins!"

It was the postman—not the "inspector" from yesterday, but Phil, their real postman. Walt retraced his steps down the driveway and took the mail from him after setting down the two cartons.

"I don't know what happened to it," Phil said, gesturing at the envelopes.

There were a dozen envelopes, already torn open—torn apart, rather—most of them containing checks. About half of them were so shredded and dirty that Walt couldn't even read the names and addresses imprinted on them. Obviously they'd been dropped in a puddle and run over. The tread marks were clearly visible, as if a car had rolled onto them and spun its tires. "Hell," Walt said. "Wouldn't you know it, the damn junk mail's fine."

"That's the way I found them this morning," Phil said. "I can't explain it, and neither can anyone else. Some kind of accident that nobody will admit to, I guess. I'm sorry. Looks like maybe they were dropped in the parking lot coming in from the truck or something."

"Just *my* mail?"

He nodded. "Far as I know. I'll keep on it. Maybe we can find out what happened."

"Forget it," Walt said. What good would it do? What he'd have to do is figure out where each of the checks had come from and ask for another, which would hold up payment for heaven knew how long, if he ever got paid again at all.

It dawned on him suddenly that Argyle was somehow to blame for this—either him or his man, the postal inspector. "Say, Phil," Walt said. "Is there a *big* guy that's a postal inspector, works locally?"

"How big?"

"Size of a bus. Six-five, maybe. Fat, but big—call it three hundred and fifty pounds. Giant head."

Phil shook his head. "Nobody like that, unless he's new. Why?"

"Nothing," Walt said. "A friend of mine wanted to know. They went to the same high school or something."

"Well, anyway, I'm sorry about the mail."

"Not your fault," Walt said.

"I can give you an affidavit from the post office acknowledging the damage."

"Sure," Walt said. "I guess so. Thanks."

Phil walked away across the lawn, sorting the mail for the next house. Obviously this was the long arm of Argyle again, playing petty pranks. The guy was a mental case—writing dirty words in crayon, yanking down lights, trashing a man's mail. How he had gotten to it was a mystery, but dollars to doughnuts it involved the inspector. Well, this was it—an open declaration of war. Argyle was throwing it into Walt's face.

Back in the garage he razored open the small box, the ever-burning brimstone, which, Walt noted, wasn't even hot. Inside the cardboard was what looked exactly like a tiny cigar box, built out of cut-rate Asian mahogany with finger-jointed sides. The word "Brimstone" was stamped in gold on the top of the box along with two little stylized flames containing ghostly faces that bore a family resemblance to the masks of comedy and tragedy. The eyes of one seemed to be suffering the tortures of the damned; the eyes of the other were almost insanely glad. Walt opened the box, half expecting a spring-snake to fly out at him. Instead, an inch-high flame rose slowly from the interior. The box was lined inside with metal the dull gray color of lead, and lying in the center of it was what looked like a chunk of lava rock. The flame smelled of sulphur, and he was reminded of Argyle standing in the hallway of the preschool this morning, stinking the place up.

He closed the box, wondering if the flame had gone out. When he reopened it, the flame rose from the box again, as if drawn upward by the hinged lid. He put his hand into the fire: it was hot, all right. He closed it and opened it—same thing: the flame sprang to life without even a whisper. The damned thing was like a refrigerator light that came on the instant the door opened, but you could only speculate that it went out again when the door was shut.

Walt noticed a folded paper in the bottom of the cardboard

carton, along with a flat plastic-wrapped package. He unfolded the paper, which turned out to be a paragraph of information on the brimstone, printed in a smeary sort of ink, as if in someone's basement. "Brought back from the everlasting fires of Hell," the paper read, "by intrepid explorers. Lights fireplaces, barbecues, cigars. Perfect for heating fondue. Useful as a night light. . . ."

He put the paper down and picked up the plastic package. Inside was his "Get Out of Hell Free" card, a stiff, wallet-sized bit of paper with a place to sign his name. Along the edge were printed the words "Dilworth Catalogue Sales, Member in Good Standing," and the card was signed by Denton Dilworth above a couple of lines guaranteeing the card's authenticity. Beneath that were the words "not to be sold or reproduced." On the back of the card was a drawing of the faces in the flame, the same as the ones on the top of the brimstone box, like souls going up in smoke. Walt slipped it into his wallet, then opened the big box.

The golden lampstand, he was surprised to find, was wired for electricity. Somehow he hadn't counted on that kind of modern innovation. He screwed the several parts together, nicking the gilt paint when his screwdriver slipped. There was pot metal underneath, and the base, which was the heavy part, was a thin metal shell that hid a saucer-shaped lump of plaster of Paris. All in all the lamp resembled a tall, dietetic candelabra, and it required three candle-flame-shaped bulbs, not to exceed fifteen watts. The bulbs weren't included in the price.

"What a haul," Walt said out loud, stepping back to look at what he'd paid nearly forty dollars for. He tried to see something biblical in the lampstand, something apocalyptic, but the thing defeated him. Maybe he could give the brimstone to Uncle Henry as a Christmas gift.

Thirty minutes to go until the meeting with the man Vest at Coco's, and Henry wasn't home yet. He'd been gone all morning. Walt walked down toward the front yard, noticing just then that a car was pulling up at the curb—another government car, for heaven's sake. It was apparently the post office again, hounding him. A woman got out, small and gray-haired, like someone's old granny. She smiled brightly at him as she came up the driveway.

⊰33⊱

WALT AND HENRY SAT IN A WINDOW BOOTH AT COCO'S,
waiting for Sidney Vest, who would probably turn out to be
another postal inspector. Unlike the big man, the woman this
afternoon had been pleasant and undemanding—no threats, no
jail talk. Her name, she'd told him, was Hepplewhite. When
Walt had referred to the other inspector, she hadn't stumbled.
"Probably another operative," she'd said, and then she'd
given him her name and a phone number and left.

He glanced at Henry over the top of his water glass. Henry
had the popes in a manila envelope. He was sparked up, looking over the menu like a trencherman, squinting his eyes and
nodding, as if everything he saw looked first-rate. Something
had given him an appetite. It was probably time to ask him
outright about the Biggs woman, before he did anything re-
grettable.

"I might try the chicken fried steak," Henry said, winking
at Walt and inclining his head toward the waitress, who was
helping the people at the next booth. Henry leaned over and
whispered, "Nice gams," and darted his eyes a couple of
times.

Walt nodded, although the word meant nothing to him.
Gams?

Henry leaned back and picked his teeth with a wooden
toothpick he'd pulled from the dispenser on the way in. He
had the relaxed air of someone who was in for the long haul,
who had the afternoon off and was going to do some real
eating.

"Women," Henry said, heaving a sigh.

"Yes, indeed," Walt said. He watched the street, looking
out for a Lincoln Town Car.

"Who was that Italian woman, that blonde who ran for the senate or parliament or whatever the hell they've got over there? Reminded you of a couple of mush melons in a sack."

Walt shook his head helplessly. "Italian woman?"

"She took off her clothes and climbed into a public fountain. It was all over the newspapers."

"Oh, sure," Walt said, remembering. "That was a few years ago. I think they call that a photo opportunity. What was her name?—something like Chicolina. I *think* that was it. I guess that was pretty much why they elected her, that prank with the fountain."

"I've always liked the Italians," Uncle Henry said. "They understand beauty, the female form."

"Did you know it's against the law to lie about a cheese over there?" Walt asked. "A Parmesan cheese *has* to be made in Parma. Over here you can make a Parmesan cheese in Iowa."

"Now, the blonde women are from the north," Henry said, "up around Switzerland . . . It's the cooler climate that fleshes them out." He gestured with both hands, winking heavily. "*Bella, bella,*" he said.

Walt grinned weakly. "Good pasta in the north." Henry was full of beans. What was this, his hula-hula woman? Success? Anticipation? Certainly it was trouble with a capital T.

"I met a woman from Varese once. . . ." Henry shook his head, as if the words had suddenly failed him, and Walt would have to imagine her.

"I wonder where your man Vest is," Walt asked, still trying to shift the subject. He checked his watch.

"He'll show," Henry said. He put his arm across the top of the Naugahyde booth and stared out the window at the afternoon traffic. "Varese." He rolled the word out of his mouth, stretching the second syllable.

Walt nodded.

"It was on a train." Henry paused again, remembering. "We were riding down to Rome. Crowded as hell, and *hot*. It was the first of August, and every Frenchman in creation was on the train heading south, speaking out of their noses like they do." He inclined his head at Walt. "Now, there's nothing wrong with a Parisian woman, although they're a little too thin." He paused, looking as if he expected an argument on this one.

Walt widened his eyes. "I was only in Paris once—with Ivy, of course. We found a bed and breakfast on a little street called the Rue Serpente—fresh bread and jam in the morning. And the coffee!" He clucked in appreciation. "Good coffee in Italy, too."

"Well, Jinx was in the first-class compartment, and I was out in the aisle getting some air, and here was this . . . this vision, absolute vision. Blonde like you wouldn't believe. Biggest . . ." He gestured with both hands, nearly knocking over the water glasses, indicating something that flew in the face of gravity. "She was wearing her grandmother's nightgown."

Walt glanced over at the waitress, hoping that . . . She was staring at Henry with a fixed grin. Walt smiled and shook his head, wishing he could make the pinwheel sign around his ear. He'd have to leave her a hell of a tip.

"This woman Chicoletta reminded me of her," Uncle Henry said. "She's an Italian *type*. Now, in the south, there's a touch of the Mediterranean in the women, a swarthiness. But in the north . . ."

Walt waited for the conclusion of the story, for what happened on the train full of Frenchmen, the woman in the nightgown, but Henry had abruptly fallen silent, perhaps lost in thought. "Did you meet this woman?" Walt asked.

"What woman?"

"On board the train. The woman from Varese."

"Oh, no. No. Not really. She got out in Milan, and the train went on to Rome. We stayed on it."

"And you never saw her again?"

"Never. I wouldn't expect to, though. Never got back to Milan."

"Then how did you know anything about her nightgown?"

"Well, she was *wearing* it. Here he comes!" Henry sat up straight and pointed out the window. An old green Torino was just angling into the parking lot. The paint was sun-faded, and the rear fender was banged up, with a taillight made out of duct tape and red cellophane. When the car hit the dip in the gutter, the entire rear end slammed down, as if the springs were shot, and a plume of black smoke exhaled from the tailpipe.

"I thought he was driving a Lincoln Town Car," Walt said doubtfully. "Are you *sure* this is the guy?"

"One and the same," Henry said. "I imagine that a man of his talents owns more than one vehicle. This is what you might call the practical art of understatement."

Walt nodded. "Hefernin?"

Henry winked and nodded.

Vest rounded the corner of the building on foot and headed up the sidewalk, carrying a briefcase. Henry waved at him through the window. He was short and stocky and looked a little too much like a well-fed chipmunk. He moved ahead with a will, like a man with places to go and people to meet, a man who was running a half hour behind. He came in and sat down in the booth, next to Henry, who introduced him to Walt. Vest gestured immediately at the waitress, who came around now to take their order. Walt studied his menu, not quite wanting to meet her eye.

As soon as the waitress was gone, Henry hauled out the popes. He had an even dozen renditions—side views, front views, measurements and notes in the margins. Vest looked through them for about thirty seconds and handed them back.

"What do you think?" Henry asked.

"I think I know a man who can help you out," Vest said. He drained his water glass with a noise that sounded like he was sucking the water through his teeth.

"Henry rather thought that you yourself were interested," Walt said.

"Oh, I *am*, but I've got a few things hanging fire right now. Don't count me out, though. Do you have a financial advisor, Mr. Stebbins?"

"I hardly have any finances," Walt said. "About a nickel's worth of advice would cover it."

"All the more reason to take care of business," Vest said. "Let me give you my card." Vest handed over a business card, and Walt took out his wallet in order to put it inside. The little flip-flop plastic slipcase fell out, exposing his new Get-Out-of-Hell card.

"I can get you a twenty-six-percent return," Vest said. "What are you making now, bank interest?"

Walt nodded, and just then Vest noticed the card. "Are you a current member?" he asked, tapping it with his finger.

"Well, yeah," Walt said. "So it says here, anyway. It's got the Dilworth signature." He took the card out of its slip so Vest could see it more clearly.

"V.P.?"

"What? I'm sorry . . . ?"

"Are you a vice president?"

"No, I guess not. I just got the card, actually. I ordered a couple of items through a catalogue. . . ."

Vest nodded broadly, then drew his own card from his wallet, tossing it onto the table. "I can get you started on the lamination process. There's a twenty-dollar fee, but it's worth its weight in gold. The connections are fabulous."

"Connections?" Walt asked.

"Business connections. It's the best twenty dollars you'll ever spend."

"*I'm* in," Henry said, inspecting the card himself. He turned it over and stared at the faces.

"Actually," Walt said, "I didn't pay anything for this. It came free."

"That's what I'm telling you. Yours isn't laminated. Take a look at mine. Take a look at this lamination." He clicked it against the table. "It's a chemically impregnated space-age plastic. It's actually impervious to gamma rays. Won't burn. Floats. What I'm talking about is having your card *activated*, cleared for takeoff."

"Takeoff? What *is* it actually?"

Vest sat thinking for a moment. "It's like . . . what? Like the Catholic thing—the scapular. They wear it around their necks, you know, for salvation. Now, this card, *I* call it insurance. You're welcome to wear it around your neck, like the Catholics. I don't know how a hole punch would affect the lamination, though. . . . You better hold off on that."

"Why does all this sound preposterous to me?" Walt asked.

"I don't know," Vest said. "Do you own life insurance?" Walt nodded.

"Nothing preposterous about that, is there?"

"I'm not sure," Walt said. "There might be."

"There's where you're wrong," Vest told him. "A man can't have too much insurance, not a family man like you. Take my word for it."

Their lunches arrived. After Jinx's meatloaf last night,

Walt's burger looked like heaven. Vest had ordered a top sir-
loin, fries, and a salad—the seven-ninety-five lunch. "Put
aside a piece of that Harvest Pie for me, will you?" he asked
the waitress.

"Anyone else for pie?" she asked.

Henry shrugged. "I'm about famished."

"Looks like pie all around," Vest said cheerfully. He
picked up his water glass and peered into it for a moment.
"Look," he said seriously, setting down the glass. "Thursday
night after Christmas there's a meeting up on Batavia, at the
union hall. I'm going to recommend it to you. It's a business
venture put together by three of the most successful men you
or I will ever meet. It's called the Plan for the Sensible Investor."

"Now you're talking," Henry said, nodding hard at Walt.
"This is the kind of thing I was telling you about."

"There's a short testimonial first," Vest said. "Then they'll
tap out the men who'll be cleared for takeoff. I think you'll
be impressed with the ceremony. There'll be a general discussion about selling distributorships and about the officer hier-
archy. If you're interested, you'll get a supply of coupon
booklets right then and there. You're on your way."

"Is this a sales organization?" Walt asked. Something was
odd here—all this business about the card, the connection between Vest's nonsense and Dilworth Catalogue Sales. Argyle
again, like the many-armed octopus, tightening his grip.

"Indirectly. The real object is *service*. That's the point of
the coupon booklets." He opened his briefcase and drew out
a booklet the size of his palm. He flipped through it, showing
Walt and Henry examples of the hundred-odd coupons—
brake-job discounts, offers for free sodas at fast-food joints,
two-for-one dinners, motel travel packages, cut-rate Vegas
shows. "These will save you a buck every time you go to the
movies," Vest said, indicating a discount card for a local chain
of theaters. "And look at this." The back of the booklet was
a Get-Out-of-Hell card, just like Walt's, but without the Dilworth affidavit and signature. This one was imprinted with the
Sensible Investor logo instead, and had little squares around
the perimeter that apparently could be punched out by mer-
chants when you redeemed coupons. "You can accumulate as
many of these as you want," Vest said.

"Why would you want more than one?" Walt asked, echoing the sentiment of the Dilworth man.

"For your children."

"I don't have any children," Walt said, heating up a little. Henry was clearly roused by this baloney.

"Then put a few aside for your grandchildren. Think about the future. *Look*, what I'm saying is that you can hold activated cards for *anybody you please*—dead relatives, what have you. The cards are *entirely* retroactive. And five percent of coupon sales are put into a fund for locating the missing children. This is a *service*-oriented organization, but it's got nothing against making a profit."

"The missing children?" Walt asked, letting the "retroactive" part go.

"That would be the children depicted on the milk cartons?" Henry said helpfully.

Vest nodded in Henry's direction. "Like that except different, if you follow me. But the *real* money is in distributorships. I don't mind telling you that. None of us will make a dime by playing games here. When you buy the first program packet you're a distributor, and *five percent of your sales come to me*. That's right. You heard me right. *Straight* into my wallet. If I can pull in twenty distributors I'm what they call a 'Hundred Percenter.' That's the end of the rainbow. The pot of gold. Just four distributors and you're a vice president. That's what I was asking about when I saw your card. That's the Lamination Level. I myself was *four* vice presidents, and I've only been in the organization for two months." He hit the table with his fist, to underscore things. "Do you have a pen?"

Walt took his pen out of his pocket and handed it over. Vest tore a coupon out of the booklet and wrote an address in the margin. He handed the slip of paper to Walt, who tucked it into his shirt pocket.

"You're *four* vice presidents?" Walt asked. "All by yourself?"

"I was. George Nelson is thirty-eight vice presidents. You know George?"

Walt shook his head.

"Law office up on the Plaza? Well, he's a charter member. Inner Circle. One of the First Captains. The sky's the limit here. No ceiling. There's only one question to ask: *how rich do you want to be?*"

Their pies arrived, and Vest started forking his down in a hurry.

"How many vice presidents are you now?" Walt asked.

"That's not the point," Vest said. "The point is, I *sold* my vice presidencies back to the Sensible Investor. That's how it works. It happens that mine were bought by one of the Captains, and for *ten times their face value*. I made a couple of bucks on that one, and, listen to this, I receive two percent of the off-the-top profits into *perpetuity*. This is capitalism, gentlemen; there's no part of this that you can't sell at a profit. Surefire gain. What I'm thinking of doing is cashing out entirely. I'm from North Carolina, out around Raleigh. I'm going to take my nest egg and go home, buy a little place of my own."

"Good for you," Walt said. "But this whole thing sounds a little like a pyramid scheme, doesn't it? Excuse me for saying so."

"Perfectly reasonable question," Vest said. "But I can assure you this is no pyramid. This is *circular*, with levels. Look, don't take my word for it. Come around on Thursday and you'll hear the real McCoy, the horse's mouth, from men and women who are already making money. And I mean *money*."

He stood up to leave. "Thanks for the lunch," he said, shaking Walt's hand.

"About the drawings . . ." Henry said, picking up the envelope.

"Why don't you bring those around on Thursday night when you come?" Vest said. "We'll see if we can't put something together."

"Now you're talking," Henry said.

"And what about the sales club?" Vest asked. "Have you thought that over?"

"I certainly have," Henry said. "I'm ready."

"Can you take delivery tomorrow? Betty's got a party set up already, gratis. You don't pay any percentage on your first party—profit's all yours, so you can't lose. It's a house right over here on Harwood, ten women so far and a couple more possibles."

"Ten . . ." Henry said, nodding.

"We're talking a *three-figure party*. That's not chump change. I'd jump in with both feet on this one."

"By heaven, I will. Tomorrow's fine. Jinx is going out to see Gladys," he said, turning to Walt, "in Costa Mesa."

Vest nodded and turned to leave, heading toward the door without a backward glance.

"I told you he was a go-getter," Henry said.

"He's a ball of fire," Walt said. "What's this 'delivery' he was talking about?"

"I mentioned that yesterday, I believe."

"You said something about a business venture that Vest was going to let you in on. That wasn't this 'Sensible Investor' scheme?"

"No," Henry said. "This is something else—*immediate* money. He's already shown me the ropes." Henry paused, looking shrewdly at Walt. "What do you think? Partners? It's ready money. I'll put up the three hundred to cover Vest's stock."

"Sure," Walt said weakly. "I guess so."

"Don't worry about me. The three hundred's entirely refundable if we can't sell the product. But that's not the issue. We'll sell it. You heard what Sidney said about that. He represents a surefire line of clothing articles. He books what they call 'parties.'"

"I've heard of that," Walt said uneasily. "So this isn't crystal or Tupperware or potted plants or something?"

"Women's lingerie," Henry said, scraping his pie plate clean with his fork.

Sidney Vest bumped out of the parking lot just then, the old Torino boiling away up Chapman Avenue toward the Plaza. The waitress arrived, and Walt found himself paying for the lunch, for Vest's steak, for "pie all around."

Rain swept against the window in a sudden gust of wind, and Walt heard the bells start up again, over at the church. It was the top of the hour—two o'clock. If they rang true to form, they wouldn't let up for twenty minutes, which was perhaps getting to be too much of a good thing. Probably it was in the memory of poor Simms. Walt picked up his card from the tabletop and slipped it back into his wallet, noting for the first time that he hadn't signed it yet.

Maybe he'd wait. . . .

And anyway, he didn't have a pen—Vest had taken it.

⇛ 34 ⇚

ON THE WALK IN FRONT OF THE SPROUSE REITZ STORE ON
Chapman Avenue stood several dozen Christmas trees nailed
onto the crossed sections of bisected two-by-fours. A scattering of over-the-hill trees had been piled off to one side, and a
boy in a T-shirt was just then dragging two of them around
the side of the building toward a big trash bin, leaving a wide
trail of fallen needles on the wet asphalt behind him. Walt
parked the Suburban near the trash bins and rolled down the
window. "Throwing them out?" he asked.

An idea had come to him, an inspiration; why shouldn't he
take a few trees home, for the kids—maybe set up some kind
of Black Forest under the avocado tree?

"They're not really any good," the boy said. His T-shirt
had a picture of a trout on it, along with the words, "Fish
worship, is it wrong?"

An eccentric, Walt thought, immediately liking him. He was
right about the trees, too; they *were* pretty clearly shot—not
dried out, but mangled, with lots of broken limbs and twigs.

"What will you sell them for?" Walt asked.

"They're not really for sale. They just came in, but most
of them are broken up like this because they fell off the truck
or something. The supplier is going to refund our money for
the wrecked ones. So . . . I don't know."

"So you're throwing them away?"

He nodded toward the trash bin. "They compost them."

"Well, I'll take a few off your hands," Walt said. "Say,
ten bucks? I'll compost the heck out of them later."

"I don't think I'm supposed to sell them. . . ."

"You're not really selling them, are you? I need a few for
a sort of . . . theatrical production, for my niece and nephew.

It's hard to explain. I want to make a . . . a Christmas forest, I guess, in the backyard, around this garden shed, which would be the woodcutter's cottage.''

The boy nodded, as if finally Walt was making sense. ''How many do you want?'' he asked.

''Let's see . . . we can load a few on the rack here and then shove a couple more inside the truck. Whatever I can fit.'' He dug his wallet out of his back pocket then and pulled out a ten-dollar bill. ''Just drag a few more around here. If there's any trouble I'll say I was digging them out of the bin, and that you tried to stop me but I wouldn't listen.''

He handed the money to the boy, who dropped the two trees he'd been holding onto, took the bill, and stuffed it into his pocket. Walt got out of the Suburban, picked up a tree, and lifted it onto the rack, swiveling the two parts of the wooden base together. He loaded the second tree back-to-front with the first, then took a roll of twine from the back of the truck and tied the trees down, yanking them flat so that he could fit more on top. Finally he opened the tailgate and crammed two more inside. Even tied down, the trees added about six feet to the top of the truck, which looked like some kind of specially camouflaged alpine vehicle.

''Thanks,'' he said, handing the twine back and putting away his pocketknife. ''Can I give you a hand with the rest of them? I really appreciate this.''

''I guess not,'' the boy said. ''Thanks for the ten dollars.''

Walt headed into the store, feeling lucky. He wasn't sure exactly what he was going to do with the trees, other than that it involved Nora and Eddie. There was too much rain to set up the trees outside, now that he thought about it. And there was no way Ivy would let him drag them all into the house. What was that play, he wondered, in which the old man ended up living in an attic full of Christmas trees? It involved ducks, Walt seemed to remember—ducks and garden elves. Walt admired that kind of who-cares-what-you-think lunacy, but it seemed to him to be the special province of either the very young or the very old. A man his age had to watch out.

He looked over the Christmas ornaments on the way into the store, picking out a couple of strings of illuminated candy canes suitable for hanging outdoors. He could decorate the porch with them. Then Argyle could come around and smash them to pieces with a stick. It would be an Argyle trap, a sort of monkey-and-coconut effect. Walt could watch through the upstairs window, and when Argyle really got going, Walt could point him out to Ivy: "Look, isn't that poor old Bob Argyle dancing on the candy canes . . . ?"

"Aren't those fun?" a woman asked him.

He looked up and nodded. She stood near one of the registers, an open bag of popcorn sitting on the Formica counter in front of her. Her wispy hair was blue-gray, and she wore a frilly kind of calico apron. The smell of popcorn was heavy in the store, and Walt noticed a big popping machine near the candy counter. "I'm taking two strings," Walt said.

"Good for you," she said, full of good cheer. Walt was apparently the only customer in the store.

"Tell me," he said to her, wishing that she didn't look quite so much like somebody's nice old granny. "I notice that you sell parakeets."

"That's right," she said. "They're at the back of the store, in the corner, past yardage. Pick one out and we'll get Andrew in here to catch it."

"Well, what I need," Walt said, "and this is going to sound weird, is a dead one."

The idea had come to him after he and Henry had gotten home from Coco's: he would give Argyle the dead bird after all, or at least *a* dead bird. He'd give it to him in a jar, too, filled with gin. "I'd be happy to pay full price," Walt told the woman. "This involves—what do you call it?—a science fair project. Dissection. One of these eighth-grade science projects . . ."

. . . and it occurred to him that he might simply have asked the bluebird itself, up in the rafters, to supply him with another bluebird, a facsimile.

The idea simply leaped into his mind, like a suddenly appearing ghost. Almost at once he wondered if he could make a request like that at a distance, if the bird would grant it anyway, even though it was locked in a fishing tackle box in the rafters of a garage two miles away.

Abruptly he cast the idea out. *I don't want your help,* he thought forcibly.

"Well," the woman said, "it happens that I *do* have a dead

parakeet. We sell a good number of birds, and once in a while we lose one.''

He winced. Success, just like that. *Had* the bluebird granted his wish? Did the mere *thought* command the thing's obedience? ''Parakeets can be delicate,'' he said to the woman, trying to smile, to show his appreciation.

''Well, this one had some kind of cold. We separated him from the others and then dosed all of them with vitamins and antibiotics, but the poor thing died just this afternoon. I didn't know quite what to do with him. It didn't seem right just to toss him into the trash.''

Walt nodded sympathetically, following her toward the back of the store, past yardage displays and racks of notions and gizmos. She brought the bird out of the storeroom in a shoebox, lying in a little bed of tissue paper. It was blue, all right— bluebird blue.

''So it's been dead for a while?'' Walt asked.

''A couple of hours. I didn't want to just throw it in the bin.''

''Of course not.'' Two hours ago! That settled it. The bluebird couldn't have *anticipated* his wish. Could it? The idea was absurd, no matter how much the parakeet looked like the bird in the jar. Which it did, Walt realized, looking closely at it. No, it was impossible. This was outright coincidence.

''How much can I pay you for him?'' he asked, getting out his wallet.

She waved the suggestion aside and rang up the two strings of candy-cane lights.

''If you're sure,'' he said. Somehow he had counted on being able to pay for it. There was something almost immoral about it otherwise, what with the lie and all.

''Tell your son that I hope he gets an A on his project,'' she said.

''I will.'' Walt felt like a criminal. He took his package and the shoebox and went out into the rain. Somehow the act of lying to the woman had taken all the wind out of his sails, and the prank he intended to play on Argyle wasn't nearly as funny to him any more. The boy in the parking lot was tossing out the last of the trees when Walt came out, and he waved as Walt fired up the Suburban and drove slowly out toward the street.

After stopping at the liquor store for a pint of gin, he drove home and unloaded the trees into the new tin shed, intending to turn it into Nora and Eddie's own private forest. He rolled out a piece of green indoor-outdoor carpet and then stood the trees up in two rows so that their branches interlaced. Somehow the whole process wasn't as much fun as he had anticipated. He felt a little weary, as if weighted down by the idea of dead birds and by the tangle of lies that was like a net dropped over his head.

With a pruning clippers he removed the bottom limbs and the worst of the broken twigs. By now the shed smelled like a pine woods. He stood for a moment simply breathing it in, listening to the freshening rain beat down on the roof, then slid shut the shed door and went into the house. Jinx and Ivy were out, and apparently hadn't been home all day, since the mail still lay on the coffee table where Walt had tossed it earlier.

He noticed then that a folded sheet of paper lay on the living-room floor beneath the mail slot. He picked it up and pried out the staple. It was a Xeroxed flyer, hand done, offering a reward for a "lost carton" possibly dropped from a mail truck in the neighborhood. . . .

A thousand dollars would be paid for the carton's return, no questions asked.

❧ 35 ❧

ON THE FLYER THERE WAS A DESCRIPTION OF THE THING IN the jar, which—the flyer claimed—was the corpse of a now-extinct sort of Chinese sparrow bound ultimately for the Natural History Museum in Los Angeles.

Walt laughed out loud. A thousand dollars! At that rate he would hand the thing over after all and hoot in Argyle's face.

Except, of course, that handing it over would establish his guilt. And there was no way on earth Argyle would pay him the money anyway, not now.

The more he thought about it, the more it smelled like a plot—probably something set up by the inspector. The extinct sparrow talk was obviously a lie. The bird was something else altogether, something that was clearly worth a *lot* more than a thousand dollars. Suddenly a thought occurred to him and he went outside again, heading next door, carrying the flyer with him. He checked with three of his neighbors before he was satisfied that nobody else on the block had gotten one—only him.

So this was a sting operation. They expected him to come panting along with the jar after having lied to a postal inspector. Probably that constituted some kind of vicious fraud.

Except of course that the postal inspector was himself a vicious fraud. Walt went up the driveway to lock up the garage, wondering idly whether two frauds canceled each other out. He crumpled the flyer and tossed it into the tin bucket, then stepped back and looked into the rafters. The tackle box sat up there as ever, gathering dust. The bird was in it. Somehow Walt knew that without having to check, as if the thing had a *presence*—exactly as if something were *living* up there in the dusty shadows beneath the roof beam, something small but with immense mass, so terribly heavy that the rafters groaned beneath its weight, and at any moment it would come smashing down. The idea of it gave him the willies.

A few hours earlier he had been on the verge of asking the thing for money. But he knew it was better to throw it into the ocean. His sudden fear of it in Sprouse Reitz had been healthy—sanity itself. He walked down the driveway to the motor home and knocked. Henry opened the door, saw who it was, and waved him in. Walt slid behind the table, looking out through the window at the rain. Henry's little space heater whirred away on the sink, and the trailer was close and warm.

"Coffee?" Henry asked, shutting off the television.

"Thanks," Walt said, taking the cup from him. "Rain won't quit."

"It gives people something to talk about," Henry said.

"Weather. That's the king of small talk."

Henry shrugged. "Everyone's interested in it. It's common ground."

"It's safe, I guess."

"Nothing safe about the weather. On the television they were just showing some homes out near Portuguese Bend—slid right into the ocean."

"I meant as a topic of conversation. You don't get into trouble talking about the weather. It's not like politics and religion."

"That's so," Henry said. "It's one of the only subjects people still give a damn for after ten thousand years of civilization. And it doesn't matter where you find yourself, Egypt, Peru, hell—*China*, for God's sake. People all over the world talk the same talk when they talk about the weather. It's the great leveler, the only thing time won't change in people. It's the same with food and drink. There's nothing small about any of that kind of talk."

Walt blinked at the old man, who dumped several spoonfuls of sugar into his coffee and stirred it up. Somehow this all sounded tremendously sane, a side of Henry that Walt wasn't familiar with. The old man was apparently in a philosophical mood. He had come down off the wild buzz he'd been on at Coco's.

"Let me ask you something," Walt said, suddenly deciding to confide in Henry. "This is going to sound a little nuts, but did you ever have any interest in . . . what do you want to call it? Magic, let's say. Ouija boards, Tarot cards, that sort of thing?''

He nodded. "Gladys used to read cards."

"Really, Aunt Gladys?"

"Terrible bore. She was always showing you the horoscope, too, warning you about things, giving you advice."

"You believe in any of it?"

"Believe in it?" Henry shook his head. "I don't know about *believe*. I know I don't like it much."

"Neither do I," Walt said. "What would happen, though, if Aunt Gladys was reading your cards, and you started to think there was something to it after all, as if the cards weren't just *pictures* any more, but really were . . . *windows*, say. That Gladys was actually communicating with something?"

"I'd walk right out of there." Henry nodded for emphasis, setting his jaw. "I'd say, 'Gladys, you've gone crazy.' "

"Well, this is interesting," Walt said, "because the damnedest thing has happened. I wonder what you'll think about it. I got this shipment, from Asia. . . .''

Walt explained the bluebird, leaving Argyle out of the picture entirely and saying nothing about newspaper delivery or tomatoes or anything else that would make him seem certifiable. The details of the story seemed almost trivial now that he was recounting them, and he realized that the fear he had felt in the garage a few minutes ago had evaporated. "The thing is," Walt said at last, "what if it *can* grant your wishes?"

"Then you've got to get it out of here. And I mean *now*. Otherwise I've got to tell you the same thing I'd tell Gladys. I'd say, Walter, you've gone crazy."

"But what if there's a million dollars in it?"

"What if there's *ten* million dollars? It'll buy you the same thing—ruination. A ticket straight to Hell in an upholstered sedan chair. Bank on it. You'll ride to the Devil in comfort. Anyway, I've never pegged you as the kind of man who had his price."

"Well, thanks," Walt said. "You want to have a look at it?"

"I'd be glad to," Henry said. "I'm happy to help." He set down his coffee cup and took his sweater from a hook on the trailer wall. Together they went into the garage, and Walt climbed up into the rafters and pulled down the tackle box, setting it down on the bench and unclipping the lid.

"This is it," Walt said. He took the jar out of its painted tin box and held it up to the light. The milky gin-water inside swirled around the corpse of the bird, and the surface of the liquid was agitated, as if the jar held a miniature, white-capped sea.

"It's apparently a dead bird," Henry said. "Nasty-looking fellow."

Walt nodded, suppressing the urge to argue with him. The bird was actually a fairly beautiful specimen, the blue as bright as an afternoon sky. Abruptly he wished that he'd never brought the subject up to Henry at all. This was something he could handle on his own. He didn't need help. He set the jar on the bench and said offhandedly, "Like I said, it's supposed to grant wishes. It's some kind of charm, like a rabbit's foot. I don't know why I brought it up, really."

Henry looked at him over the top of his glasses. "Throw it straight into the trash," he said. "That's no rabbit's foot."

"You're right, of course."

"There's something not right about it, some kind of juju. Get it the hell out of here. You don't want something like this around."

"No," Walt said. "That's right. That's why I wanted to show it to you, to get your opinion on it."

"Does Ivy know about it?"

"*Know* about it? No, I guess not."

"Take my word for it. Don't show it to her. Get rid of it, somewhere off the property. If I showed Jinx a thing like this . . ." He shook his head and reached into the open tackle box, pulling out a bottle of salmon eggs. "What is this supposed to be, fish bait?"

Walt took it from him. Something was wrong with the eggs in the bottle. They were moving, as if swimming sluggishly in the gelatinous pink liquid. Walt looked closely at them, horrified to see that they were looking back out at him through round black eyes the size of flyspecks, and that each had a tail and fins, almost transparent. The jar pulsed in his hands, and he had the odd feeling that the sides of the jar bulged, that at any moment it would burst, spewing larvae through the air of the garage like a pod spewing out seeds.

"Damn thing's full of maggots," he said, rolling the jar into several sheets of newspaper and twisting the ends before putting it in the trash bucket. He saw that the old bottle of cheese bait had turned a purple-black, like the color of a bruise, and he threw that into the trash, too, without looking at it closely. "I'll toss it all into the Dumpster down behind the medical center on the corner." He nodded seriously at Henry and picked up the bluebird, started to put it into the bucket, too, but then stopped and set it on the bench again. "What's tomorrow—Thursday? The bin doesn't get emptied till late in the afternoon, so I can toss it out in the morning."

"Do it now," Henry said. "You wanted my opinion? Well, that's it. Get it out of here. Posthaste."

"Sure," Walt said. He put the jar back into its tin and laid the tin carefully in the bucket, picking the whole works up by the handle. Henry walked down the street with him, to the alley adjacent to the medical center. The bin was about half full. Walt dropped the tin in among tied-off plastic bags and jumbled papers and office trash.

"Good riddance to bad rubbish," Henry said.

Walt reached in and yanked a trash bag over it so that no one would find it and fall prey to it as he had. He upended the tin bucket, dumping the rest of it in. By noon tomorrow the whole works would be landfill.

❧ 36 ❧

"THE KIDS ARE TIRED OUT TONIGHT," WALT SAID HOPE-fully, watching Ivy move around the bedroom, hanging clothes and straightening up. She looked at him, seeing through him immediately.

It was past ten, and things were blessedly quiet downstairs. Apparently the kids had finally settled in. Walt was a little disappointed that they hadn't given much of a damn for the Christmas trees in the shed. They'd gone inside and looked, but stepped right out again, as if they thought this was another spider prank or something. "Why are there trees?" Nora had asked.

"You can play in there, if you want," Walt had answered, and right then Eddie had suddenly remembered that there was something on television, and he had run back into the house without saying a word, not coming back out again. Nora had gone into the front yard and drawn hopscotch squares on the sidewalk with pink chalk and spent fifteen minutes hopping up and down on one foot. Then, over dinner, Nora had told Aunt Jinx that Walt had tried to make them "go into the shed," and Walt had found himself explaining about the forest of trees while Jinx regarded him with a look of astonishment and doubt.

"You and the kids . . ." Ivy said now, shaking her head and closing the wardrobe door. "You've gone head over heels."

"Well . . ." Walt said, trying to get to the bottom of the statement, which sounded loaded to him, like an attractive piece of fish bait. "It's fun having the two of them as house-guests. You can spoil them, whatever you want, and then give them back to their parents and go on your way."

Ivy was silent. "I hope so . . . Wherever their parents are at the moment. I guess I ought to call Mom and Dad and see how Darla's doing." She sat down on her side of the bed. "What I meant, though, is that I think you've got a knack for it, for parenthood."

"It's a lot of work," Walt said. "There's a lot you give up."

"There's more that you gain. They both think you're a peach."

He shrugged. She nudged him in the ribs and winked at him, and he knew that this was her round; she'd outscored him. There was no need to accuse him of fear or of being self-centered tonight. It was enough that the kids thought he was a peach. She'd caught him in a vanity trap.

"You didn't tell me that it was one of Argyle's preschools," he said to her, changing the subject.

"It was the only one nearby that allowed for drop-ins and temporaries in the kindergarten class." She shut off the lamp now, so that the room was dim, the only illumination coming from the light in the downstairs landing. "Did you speak to Robert?"

"Robert?" he asked. "Oh, you mean Argyle. Only for a second. To tell you the truth, he looked like hell, like he'd been worked over by midgets. I'm not just making this up to give him a hard time. I'd have to guess that he'd been drinking hard. He stank, too, like he had some kind of bladder disease."

"He didn't look like that when I saw him at ten."

"Obviously he'd been at it all night," Walt said. "Probably put away a couple of fifths. He went home and cleaned himself up for his meeting with you."

"He said to give you his best. He was full of nostalgia, I think, for old times."

"His best," Walt said flatly. "How good is that, exactly?"

"Maybe it's better than you think it is."

Walt kept silent, thinking of Argyle out navigating the late-night streets, vandalizing houses. There was no use arguing about him, though. He wasn't worth it, especially if it meant exposing any of this business with the bluebird, which, happily, was a thing of the past, now that the bird was in the Dumpster.

"He even talked about how he missed having children, never getting married."

"You talked to him about personal matters?" Walt asked. "About having children?" This was astonishing. "I don't suppose you discussed me? Us?"

"No. And don't get riled up. This was a business meeting. How much do you think the commission is?"

"Never mind the commission. I can't believe you talked about something like that. What business is it of his?"

"We didn't *talk* about it. He mentioned it in passing." She slid farther under the covers, turning toward him and leaning her head on her elbow. Her kimono fell open, and she casually straightened it, but when it fell partly open again, she left it alone. "I couldn't be a creep to him, could I?"

"It wouldn't be all that hard."

"Well, maybe you're right. Maybe I should have been. Never mind about the commission, like you said. Money, who needs it? Filthy lucre." She ran her finger down the sleeve of his nightshirt and off the tip of his finger. "I like a man in a nightshirt," she said. "Especially a big roomy one."

"I don't know where you'll find a big roomy man this time of night," Walt said, brushing a strand of hair away from her face. "But maybe I can be of service."

"Maybe."

"How much *is* the commission?" he asked, kissing her on the nose.

"It's nothing, really. Let's pretend I didn't even bring it up. I'll throw it back in his face tomorrow. I'll call him names, too. What shall I call him? A skunk?" She raised her eyebrows, then pushed herself up on her elbow and kissed him on the lips. "I'll call him a *damned* skunk, and then I'll tweak his nose for him and box his ears. I always wanted to box a man's ears."

"*Tell* me."

"Maybe I'll tweak your nose, too."

"You won't have me unless you tell," Walt said. But he slid his hand into her kimono and let it drift across her belly.

She lay down again, batting her eyes at him. "I bet I will," she said, and pulled his head down, kissing him again. "I bet I'll have you right now."

He had suddenly run out of things to say. He kissed her, slipping his hand down and loosening the tie on the kimono.

She ran her fingers down his spine, putting her other arm across his shoulders.

And right then she sat up, clutching shut the kimono and pulling up the covers. He started to speak, but she put her finger to her lips.

"Listen," she said.

He heard it then, the sound of movement downstairs. There was the patter of feet coming across the dining-room floor, heading toward the landing. It sounded like both of them. Soft footsteps sounded on the stair runner, and Nora and Eddie burst into the bedroom. Nora was breathless and wide-eyed, sobbing with fear.

"What's wrong?" Walt asked. Was someone downstairs? A prowler—the inspector! This had gone too damned far! He'd kill anyone who scared Nora and Eddie. Argyle! The dirty son-of-a-bitch . . . Walt was full of adrenaline, worked up, wild with it.

"A b-bug," Nora said, her voice shaking.

"A b-bug?" Walt asked.

"It was *big*," Eddie said. He held up his hand, illustrating with his thumb and forefinger. "Like this."

Apparently the bug was several inches long. "Where was it?" Walt asked, calming down now.

"On the floor," Eddie said. "It ran under Nora's bed. It's under there now."

"Cockroach." Ivy whispered the word in Walt's ear.

"Was it black?" Walt asked. "Like a beetle, sort of?"

Eddie nodded.

"What *is* it?" Nora asked. "This house has *bugs*."

"Every house has bugs," Walt said. "Bugs have to have a place to live, too. Many of them are involved in fertilization. They're part of God's great plan."

"I'd kill it," Eddie said, "if I had a stick or something."

"Uncle Walt will kill it," Ivy said. "Won't you, Uncle Walt? I bet it won't take a minute. Bring a shoe along to smack it with. We don't want it in the house."

"Well, I *would* kill it," Walt said, "except that I think I know this bug. It's an Egyptian waterbug named . . . Smith. E. Hopkinson Smith. He's very friendly. He was probably on his way to a party—to the ugly bug ball. You know, to find his friends. Was he carrying a bag of . . ."

Nora burst into tears again, gasping out a sob that emptied her lungs.

"Oh, *I* don't think so," Ivy said, giving him a look. "Not under Nora's bed. I don't think this could have been Smith."

"Of course not," Walt said. "This must be some other bug." He could see he was defeated. Going on about bugs in trousers and top hats wouldn't do him any good, not now. "I'll go mash him," he said, climbing out of bed.

Nora suddenly began giggling. Like that the sobbing was gone, evaporated.

"What?" Walt said.

"You have a dress," she said, pointing.

"It's a nightshirt," Walt told her. "Aunt Jinx made it for me. It's the family's plaid, from Scotland."

"It's like a *dress*," she said, climbing into his spot in bed and pulling the covers up to her chin so that only her head and her fingers showed. She made her rabbit face at him, crinkling up her eyes. Her bug fear was forgotten, just like that. Eddie sat down at the foot of the bed and yawned.

"Bring back the corpse," Ivy said to him. "I'll keep the children entertained."

"No falling asleep?"

"Me?"

He gave her a hard look and descended the stairs, carrying a tennis shoe. Going into the service porch, he grabbed a flashlight and a broom, then headed for the kids' room, where the light was on. Of course there was nothing under the bed. The roach, if that's what it had been, had slipped away through a gap in the floor moldings or gone into the closet. There was no way it would show itself. He was damned if he was going to spend all night on this quest. Laying the broom down, he raised the tennis shoe over his head and slammed it against the floor a half dozen times, then went out into the living room and opened the front door, shutting it hard. He put back the broom and the light and went up the stairs again.

"Got it," he said. The children lay side by side on the bed, looking at pictures in a magazine.

"Let's see," Nora said anxiously, sitting up.

"I pitched it out the front door," Walt lied. "Didn't you hear the door shut? I smashed him flatter than a molecule."

Nora looked at him in silence, her mouth half open. "You said he'd show us," she said to Ivy.

"He will," Ivy said to her. She looked hard at Walt, seeing straight through him. "I think that Nora and Eddie will sleep better if they know the bug's really, *really* dead," she told him.

"I'm sleeping up here," Nora said.

"No, you're not," Walt told her. "Everyone in their own beds."

"What if *it's* in my bed?" Nora asked. "What if it's the bug again?"

"It is," Eddie said. "I think it was a kind of bedbug."

"I don't think so," Walt said.

"Maybe you could get its corpse," Ivy said, "from wherever you threw it. That would settle things, wouldn't it?"

"Sure," Walt said. "Of course it would." He turned around and headed for the stairs again, still carrying his shoe, an idea suddenly coming to him. There were ten million roaches out on the streets at night, especially in the water meter box. He should have thought of that in the first place—not wasted his time looking for the actual bug. Any dead roach would do.

⅜ 37 ⅜

IT WAS CLOSE TO ELEVEN O'CLOCK. BENTLEY AND MAHONEY had been out walking the empty streets of Old Towne for over an hour, ringing bells. It had rained off and on, but now the rain was off, and Bentley tapped the wet sidewalk with his umbrella as if it were a walking stick. The Benedictus bell that he held in his other hand kept up a constant ringing that should have set off half the dogs in the neighborhood, but for some curious reason it didn't, as if the dogs understood.

Probably they should have split up, he and Mahoney, in order to cover more ground, except that alone they would be more open to attack. He looked behind him down the street, but it was deserted.

He relaxed and took in a lungful of the wet evening air. He liked to walk in the evening, especially in stormy weather, when he could see into softly lighted living rooms through open curtains: families sitting around warm and dry, watching television or reading, surrounded by the comfortable clutter of their lives. There were lighted Christmas trees in windows and cats on front porches and dogs looking out through screen doors, and it was easy to imagine that people were happy with simple things.

It wasn't all that long ago that bell-ringing was a common enough evening ritual, and in past centuries no one would have questioned the power of church bells to drive off evil. In the old days the sound of consecrated bells would have been as comforting to good people as it was intolerable to monsters like Argyle and LeRoy. Things had changed.

But here was the pot calling the kettle black, Bentley thought: it was only in the last few weeks that he himself had come to suspect that the vandalizing of neighborhood church bells *meant* anything. In fact, until this past week he had never given a second thought to the ringing of church bells. The history of bells was Catholic history for the most part, which, at least to his way of thinking, meant that it was nearly as hard to separate it from superstition as it was to chew the wrinkles out of a piece of gum. And look at him now: here he was, hand in glove with a priest, out in the rainy night, ringing a Benedictus bell and with more bells tied to his belt like wind chimes.

"Look at that," Mahoney said, pointing his umbrella at the shadows alongside a front porch. A big plastic snowman, meant to be illuminated, lay on the grass, its face smashed in as if someone had yanked it off the porch and jumped up and down on it. Its electrical cord was wrapped around its neck in a sort of noose.

"Another one," Mahoney said. "Do you think it's him again?"

"Either it's him or . . ."

And just then, a car rolled slowly past the end of the block, heading east on Palm Street. It was the third time that evening that they'd seen it. The driver was a shadow, but it seemed to Bentley that the shadow was observing the two of them, and the preacher raised his umbrella as a greeting. The car sped up and was gone. Bentley didn't recognize the car, but he was almost certain it wasn't Argyle. The driver appeared to be a short man, maybe heavyset. Probably it was George Nelson, halfway to Hell in a handbasket.

Bentley wondered again if he should have cashed the check that Argyle had given Obermeyer. Making the deal final— actually taking the money—might have stopped whatever it was that was coming to pass. . . .

But that was nuts. Whatever was going on with Argyle had nothing to do with money, and it never had. A man could as easily sell his soul for a nickel as for five billion dollars, and you couldn't put a price on salvation—or on damnation, either, he reminded himself.

"What makes you think this thing in a jar is a demon?" Father Mahoney asked.

"What else would it be?"

"Do you mean a demon out of Hell? Beelzebub or Belial or one of them? Something with a name?"

"Well, there's no point in getting too specific about it. We don't care about the thing's credentials."

"Why not something else?"

"What, exactly?"

"A bottle imp. A monkey's paw. A genie."

"I don't believe in imps and genies. A demon's a demon the world around, as far as I'm concerned. What I know is that something has come into the country from the China coast, something Argyle has been waiting for. It was part of a shipment that included the golem, which I saw with my own eyes through the window. My sources believe this thing to be a demon, and *I* believe it to be a demon, and I believe that Argyle intends for this demon to ride his golem into Hell in order to give the Devil his due, which is to say, a soul. In a nutshell that's what I think."

"And it's packaged as a toy?"

"Insidious, isn't it? Looks fairly innocent, apparently—some kind of good-luck item. You make a wish on it like you'd wish on a rabbit's foot or a star. Then it's got you. Pulls you in by appealing to your desires. What it means is damnation, which is nothing to Argyle—he thinks he's already damned."

They turned the corner and headed up toward Cambridge. "It's Stebbins that I'm worried about. I'm certain he's got it, and that he's lying when he says he doesn't. Looting his garage won't do us any good any more. He'll have the thing hidden by now. There's nothing left to do but confront him about it. We've got to appeal to his decency, and we've got to appeal to his fear."

"Do you think he'll listen?"

"No," Bentley said. "I don't suppose he will."

⊰ 38 ⊱

THE MOTOR HOME WAS DARK, THANK GOODNESS, AND IT wasn't raining, although it smelled like rain, and the sky was heavy with clouds. Walt walked out to the curb and looked out into the street, where, on any other night of the year, there would have been a dozen roaches going about their senseless business. Tonight there was nothing; the streets were empty except for a few earthworms in the gutter. Somewhere in the distance there was the ringing of bells, small bells.

The wind billowed out the hem of his nightshirt, and he clapped his hands down against it, looking around him for the first time and thankful that he was wearing his shorts under the nightshirt. If a police cruiser were to appear . . .

Hurrying now, he tucked his finger into the hole in the concrete lid of the water meter box and pulled it off, laying it on the grass. The streetlamp barely illuminated the inside of the box, which was about a foot deep, the meter itself casting a shadow across the bottom of it. He knelt against the curb, wishing he had brought the flashlight. There was movement down there, all right, small dark things creeping through the tangled roots of the Bermuda grass that had grown up through the bottom of the box. Of course there could as easily be black widows down there as roaches.

He shuddered and straightened up, looking out at the street again. *Surely* there was a lonely roach out and about, happy to sacrifice itself for something like this. The ringing of bells grew louder suddenly, accompanied by a random jingling, as if a Christmas-decorated horse and carriage had just then rounded the corner. Two men, he saw now, *had* rounded the corner and were approaching from up the street, coming along hurriedly, jingling as they came. One of them strode along a little in front of the other, and passed just then beneath a street-light. He was heavyset and balding and wore dark clothing and spectacles—the image of Mr. Pickwick. Walt realized with a shock of recognition that the man was a priest. The other man, for God's sake, was the Reverend Bentley, the two of them out on some kind of joint mission, probably ferreting out sinners.

Walt was seized with the sudden desire to run. Here he was in the street, barefoot, wearing a nightshirt, hunting roaches with a tennis shoe. What would he tell them? That this had something to do with sex?

Bentley spotted him and waved, and just then, as they drew near to the driveway, the priest set into a sort of dance, a fantastic, one-legged caper, waving his umbrella in the air as if he were casting out demons and hopping toward Walt with a look of wild glee on his face, his spectacles leaping on the bridge of his nose. Walt stood dumbfounded. Of all the late-night lunacy, this took the cake.

Nora's hopscotch! The old priest was simply hopscotching. Relieved, Walt shook Bentley's hand. Bentley was as sober-looking as Mahoney was gleeful.

"This is Walt Stebbins," Bentley said to the priest. "The man I've been telling you about. Stebbins, this is Father Mahoney, from the Holy Spirit."

"My pleasure," the priest said. He had a firm grip. Walt saw now that there were little clutches of bells clipped to both men's belts.

"Mr. Stebbins once donated heavily to the lunch program," Bentley said to Mahoney. "I think we can use him if we can get him off his high horse."

Walt grinned at him. *Use* him? What the *hell* was the man talking about?

"I haven't hopscotched in sixty years," the priest said, breathing heavily. He took off his spectacles and wiped them on his shirt, then put them back on.

"We must look like a couple of crazy men to you." Bentley squinted at Walt and jingled the bells.

"No," Walt said, "not at all." He held onto his nightshirt, fighting the wind. "I'm hardly in a position to . . ." He gestured with the shoe.

"We're ringing bells," Bentley said. "In the middle of the night. Do you know why?"

Walt shook his head. "I guess I don't, really."

"Because the bells at St. Anthony's were sabotaged and Mr. Simms was murdered. That's right, I said *murdered*. Does this come as any surprise to you?"

"Well, I had no idea. . . . " Walt said. "I haven't read anything . . . "

"Of course you haven't read anything. And you won't, either. Do you know why he was murdered?"

Walt shrugged.

"To silence the bells." Bentley nodded hard at him. "Church bells, Mr. Stebbins, are abhorrent to the ears of fiends and demons. Drives them mad. The streets of European cities used to be patrolled by bellmen throughout the night. Back me up here, Mahoney."

"The Reverend Bentley is correct," the priest said. "These bells we carry are Benedictus bells, and with them we mean to drive the demons out of Old Towne. It's an old tradition, really, very old. 'Mercy secure you all, and keep the goblin from you while you sleep.' That was the chant of the bellman."

Just then a cockroach came up out of the water meter hole and sprinted out onto the curb. Walt lunged at it, slamming it flat with the sole of the tennis shoe. He felt the cold wind on his rear end, and so he pinned down the hem of the nightshirt with his free hand again. "Got him," Walt said weakly, noticing that Bentley was frowning at him.

A light came on in the motor home, and the curtains were pushed aside. Aunt Jinx looked out at them, and Walt waved the tennis shoe at her as naturally as he could, as if he were just going about the usual business. Father Mahoney nodded politely. She shut the curtain again and the light went off.

"I don't suppose we'd better wake up Henry?" Bentley said to Walt.

"Better not to," Walt said. "He turns in early." He nudged the smashed roach with his foot in order to loosen it from the concrete. The light was still on upstairs, and he could see a shadow move in front of the window, so it was good odds that Ivy was still awake.

"We'll tackle him tomorrow," Bentley said.

"Good," Walt said. "It's getting pretty late."

"What about you?" Bentley asked. "Are you willing to do your part?"

"Sure," Walt told him. "I guess so. What part?"

"We're going to run the Devil out of town. Can we count you in?"

"I could contribute something, I guess."

"Oh, we're not asking for money," Mahoney said. "We're looking for recruits."

Walt blinked at them. He had gone through this once before with Bentley. "I don't know . . ." he said.

"Of course you don't know," Bentley told him. "Why should you know? I'm going to tell you something now. Can you stand to hear it?"

Walt nodded, feeling a drop of rain hit the top of his head. He was damned if he'd drown to hear it.

"It was me that burglarized your garage."

"You?" Walt asked. And of course it was true. Everything was clear to him. Obviously Bentley had gone over the fence, then circled back around the block to where Walt had run into him.

"That's right. And by golly I'd burglarize it again if I had to. And I might, too, unless you make up your mind to come in on our side."

"Why?" Walt asked. He knew the answer to his question even as he asked it. Of course Bentley wanted the jar. Everyone wanted the jar. Well, it belonged to Walt now, and everyone could go whistle for it.

And then he remembered—Uncle Henry had made him pitch it into the Dumpster.

"I was looking for something," Bentley said. "I have certain . . . certain *sources*. There's a thing that's come into the country, into the neighborhood, encased in a jar, boxed up in painted tin. Do you know what I'm talking about?"

"I don't deal in jars very much," Walt said evasively. "I got a case of snow globes—flamingo globes, actually, filled with water. You know the kind of thing—glitter, a palm tree."

Bentley waved the idea away. "Don't meddle with me, son. There's no time for it now."

"Why didn't you just *ask* me about this jar?" Walt said. "Why break in?"

"Do you believe in the Devil?"

"I'm not sure what you . . ."

"Of course you're not sure. That's why I didn't ask you about it."

He was serious! Well, so was Walt. It was his garage, and by heaven it was his jar, too. *Like* to call it . . . "Who killed Mr. Simms?" Walt asked abruptly. "Do you know?"

Bentley looked at him for a moment, as if calculating, then said, "We think we do. We believe it to be Robert Argyle, the financeer."

"Well, that's hasty," Mahoney said. "We don't know any such thing."

"He was an old friend of yours, wasn't he?" Bentley asked.

"Years ago," Walt said, turning this whole thing over in his mind.

"Well let me give you a tip, straight from the horse," Bentley said. "*He'll kill you, too.* Don't think he won't."

Walt realized that the shoulders of his nightshirt were wet. The rain was coming down in a mist, but harder by the moment.

"Keep a weather eye out," Bentley said. "We've got work to do. We can't stand here talking. If you find this jar, be *very* careful with it. Treat it like an unexploded bomb."

"Take these," the priest said, disconnecting the bells from his belt and handing them to Walt. "Hang them up on the porch, like wind chimes."

Walt took them. What the hell—it couldn't hurt.

A car turned the corner just then, from the Chapman Avenue end of the street, two hundred feet away. Its high beams were on, and Walt automatically turned his eyes away. The car accelerated suddenly, angling in toward the curb, straight at them, and Walt could see nothing but the blinding glow of its headlamps. He backpedaled, up onto the curb, felt a hand clutch the back of his nightshirt and yank him sideways. He sprawled onto his hands and knees, throwing the tennis shoe, and at the same time heard a heavy thud and squeal as the car sideswiped the curbside palm tree, then bounced down onto the road again and sped away.

Walt scrambled to his feet and helped Mahoney up. "Thanks," he said breathlessly.

The priest nodded. "Which of them was it?" he asked Bentley.

The preacher shook his head. "I couldn't see. Car's probably stolen. Anyway, it didn't have any plates. It's the same one we saw earlier, though—I know that much. I don't think it's Argyle. I think it's Nelson."

"What on earth was that?" Aunt Jinx asked, coming around the back of the motor home now, dressed in a robe and wearing a pair of fuzzy bedroom slippers. She held a newspaper over her head to block the rain.

"Drunk driver," Bentley said. "Looked like he fell asleep at the wheel." He winked at Walt and then widened his eyes, as if this attempted murder were a nice illustration of what he'd just been talking about.

"Is everyone all right, then?" Jinx asked.

"We're fine," Walt said. "No harm done."

"Then go to bed," she said. "It's too late for all this pow-wow, drunks or no drunks." She turned around and hurried away then, and Walt heard the motor home door click shut.

"I'll stop by tomorrow," Bentley said meaningfully to Walt.

"Hang those bells up on the porch," Mahoney said. "Let the wind work on them."

The two men turned and hurried away, jingling toward the corner, and Walt grabbed the tennis shoe, then pinched up the flattened roach and dumped it into the shoe. On his way back into the house he hung the bells on a loop of bare wisteria vine. Right now he would take all this lunacy at face value. Whatever else Bentley might be, he wasn't a liar. He believed, at least, that Argyle had murdered Simms for some kind of diabolical purpose. And with this car business . . . *Some*thing was going on—perhaps something deeper and darker than Walt had thought.

On a sudden impulse he laid the shoe on the porch, turned around, and stepped down onto the driveway, tiptoeing past the motor home as quickly and silently as he could and then cutting across the street fast. Bentley and the priest were nowhere to be seen in the opposite direction; they'd turned the corner, maybe heading up toward Argyle's in order to use the bells against him. Walt shaded his face from the rain, ducking into the alley and opening the chain-link gate that cordoned off the Dumpster. He yanked a couple of trashbags out of the way, leaning over the edge of the bin, balancing there, the sodden nightshirt clinging to his legs, the scent of gin rising up around him like spilled perfume.

❧ 39 ❧

WALT RAKED LEAVES ON THE FRONT LAWN. IT WAS JUST PAST noon, and the weather had cleared up some, although there was more rain forecast. It was going to be a wet Christmas. And a strange one.

It seemed to Walt that last night's adventure out on the sidewalk might have been a fabulous dream: the streetlight under a black sky, Father Mahoney hopscotching toward him down the dark sidewalk, Bentley with all his wild talk about murder and demons, the mysterious car with the license plates removed. The little cluster of bells that he'd hung from the wisteria was gone, vanished in the night, as if all of it, bells included, were a figment—all of it except the return of the thing in the jar, which was in his possession once again.

Throwing it away had clearly been a bad idea after all. Argyle wanted it. Bentley and Mahoney wanted it. So who was Walt Stebbins to be hasty with the thing? And right now it looked to him as if throwing it out was every bit as hasty as . . . what? *Using* it, maybe. Whatever that really consisted of. He wasn't entirely sure yet, not authentically so.

The bluebird was buried in the ground now, beneath one of the stepping-stones that led back to the garden shed. Henry knew about the tackle box, and that compromised it as a hiding place. Not that Walt didn't trust Henry, who, after all, thought that the jar was still in the Dumpster, but there were too many strange forces at work in the neighborhood to be careless. As an extra precaution, he had dropped the Sprouse Reitz parakeet into a pint-size Mason jar, filled the bottle with gin, and put it into the bluebird's tin box, then put the fake into the tackle box. If anyone broke in and stole it now—Argyle or Bentley—they could have it with his compliments.

He raked a pile of sodden leaves into an oversized plastic dustpan and dumped them into the barrel, and just then a horn tooted. It was the Reverend Bentley himself, just like he'd promised, pulling in at the curb, his face full of the same determination and urgency that Walt remembered from last night.

Walt waved at Bentley, who climbed out of the car and gestured at the motor home. Walt nodded. Henry was in. He had been out for a couple of hours that morning, but had come home an hour ago looking a little under the weather and had gone into the motor home and pulled the curtains. Whatever fires had been burning in him yesterday afternoon had dimmed considerably. Jinx was home, too, inside the house now, washing dishes.

The telephone rang, and Walt dropped the rake and went in through the screen door just as Uncle Henry appeared on the driveway, apparently having come out of the backyard. Jinx had already answered the phone. She handed Walt the receiver and went back to scrubbing dishes at the sink.

"Hello," he said into the receiver.

For a moment there was no answer, and then a voice said, "Walt? Is that you?"

"Yeah," Walt said, "who's . . ." But then he recognized the voice. It was Jack, liquored up. "Jack! How the hell you doing? I figured you might call yesterday, like you said. The kids aren't here now."

"*I'll* be the goddamn judge of that," Jack said.

"What's wrong?" Walt said. "Something up?"

"Don't give me any goddamn *talk*," Jack said to him. "I got through to Darla this morning. No more happy crap, man. That was all bullshit the other night. Shinola. *No one* does me like this."

"Like what?" Walt asked.

"Like you know goddamn well what. What I call this is kidnapping, plain and simple. You took a man's children."

"What I call this is drunk on your ass, Jack. Nora and Eddie are Darla's children, and she asked us to look after them."

"I *raised* those kids, damn it. I paid their bills, and I know my rights."

"You don't have any rights, Jack, except the right to sober up. It's just past noon, for God's sake. Put the bottle down.

Give it a rest. You'll talk more sense when you're sober."

"There's a few people I'm going to talk a *hell* of a lot of sense to," Jack said. "Or else my lawyer will. What I want you to do is have Eddie and Nora ready to go. Whatever crap they brought along, have that ready, too. I'll be around to pick 'em up."

"Don't waste your time, Jack. You can't have them."

"Look, fuck you and fuck whatever game you're playing. They're *my* kids. *I'm* the only father they ever had."

"Then that's a hell of a dirty shame."

"What the hell do you know about it? You don't have any kids. It takes a *man* to raise kids. I don't know what the hell *you* are, living off your wife, out in the garage all day yanking the goddamn crank, but you don't have *any* right to keep a man away from his kids. I want 'em now. If I have to bring a cop along I'll do it."

"Bring a cop, Jack. You're drunk as a pig. I wouldn't trust you with a box full of tin bugs."

"You listen . . ." Jack started to say.

"Shut the hell up," Walt said, his voice perfectly even. "I want to ask you something about being a *man*. Where the hell were you all day yesterday? You call up night before last worried about Nora and Eddie, but you don't want to talk to them—you'll call them tomorrow. But where the hell are you tomorrow? Sloshed. Isn't that right? You've been living on pretzels and salted peanuts? Vitamin C out of the lime slice? I didn't even bother to tell the kids you called, because I *knew* you wouldn't call back. You're a king-hell asshole, Jack. Maybe you get it naturally. Maybe it comes out of a bottle. I don't give a damn either way. But you better get a handle on it. Because until you do, I swear to God I won't let you near these children. What you'll get if you come around here is a fist in the face."

"You can't . . ."

"And fuck you, too."

He hung up the phone without listening to another word. His hand was shaking and he could barely breathe. He'd lost it, gone right over the top. And now what had he done? Kidnapped the kids? Maybe Jack *did* have some kind of rights. You pay property taxes long enough on a house, and you *own*

the house; did Jack *own* the kids in that same way? He realized
that Jinx was looking at him wide-eyed.

"I'm sorry about the language," he said, shaking his head.
"That was Jack. He's been drinking for a week now. Darla's
gone back east to get away from him. That's why Ivy and I
have the kids. I've got a real attitude about all of it."

"Lord have mercy," Jinx said, putting her hand to her
mouth. "Ivy told me something about that. And now Jack
wants to take them back? He's just figured all this out?"

"That's about it."

"Does he know which school they're at? Because if he does
we ought to call and warn them."

"No," Walt said. "And I don't think he can find out, either,
unless he calls every preschool in the area. Even then they
might not tell him anything. Security's pretty tight these days.
I just don't want him coming around the house when the kids
are here, not when he's drunk. I'd have to call the cops myself.
Nora and Eddie don't need that kind of scene."

"You watch out for him, Walter. Don't push him. Nora and
Eddie don't need that, either."

Walt nodded. She was right. Whatever else he was, Jack
was telling the truth about raising Nora and Eddie, and that
was probably worth something. "It'll work out," he said.
"Once he sobers up he'll calm down." Unconvinced, he went
back outside, where Bentley and Uncle Henry were sitting on
the clamshell chairs on the front porch.

"Here he is," Henry said, motioning toward the front porch
swing.

Walt sat down, his mind racing.

"Lorimer was asking about the jar," Henry said, keeping
his voice low.

"Lorimer?" Walt looked at him.

Henry nodded at Bentley, and Walt caught on. "Oh, of
course," he said. "I guess we haven't really been on a first-
name basis, have we?"

"I told him we threw it in the bin," Henry said.

Walt looked from one to the other of them. "I'm afraid
that's true," he said to Bentley. "In the alley. I didn't want
to tell you last night. Frankly, I was a little miffed about the
break-in. Anyway, Orange Disposal hauled it away this morn-

ing. It's landfill now.'' Actually, this was a lie, but Bentley couldn't know anything about trash schedules.

Bentley continued to stare at him, as if he were doubtful about all this. Henry watched Bentley uneasily.

"I'm afraid *I* made him toss it out,'' Henry said. "It looked . . . evil. Something about it . . . Anyway, we got rid of it.''

Bentley nodded finally, then sat back in his chair. "You were absolutely right,'' he said. "You did the right thing. It's what I would have done with it.''

"Good,'' Henry said. The old man looked nervous, somehow, like he was in trouble.

"Something wrong?'' Walt asked him.

"No, no, no,'' Henry said, wiping his forehead. His hand was trembling.

"You're not a stupid man,'' Bentley said, looking Walt in the eye.

Walt waited.

"What did you do with the bells?''

"Hung them up,'' Walt said, surprised at this turn.

"Where? They're still hung up?''

"No. I hung them right here on the porch. They disap- peared. Someone stole them, I guess. The wind was still blowing them around at midnight, so it must have been early this morning.''

"Why would they do that—steal a few brass bells in the middle of a rainy night?''

"I . . .'' Walt shrugged. "What were you saying last night?'' Somehow Bentley reminded him of his fourth-grade teacher, Mrs. Bender, drilling him for information, being as subtle as an ice pick.

"What I said last night was true. You can bet your immortal soul on it.'' He leaned forward. "What do you know about the connection between Robert Argyle and Murray LeRoy?''

"I wouldn't have connected them at all,'' Walt said. "I read about LeRoy in the paper, about his going nuts.''

"He didn't go *nuts*,'' Bentley said. "It's closer to the truth to say that he went diabolical, although maybe that's the same thing sometimes.''

Walt nodded, widening his eyes. *Diabolical*, here it came again. . . .

"Don't play the fool," Bentley said. "If you mean to say something, say it."

"It's just that all this diabolical talk . . ."

"Is what? You don't like it, do you? You don't want to think about damnation, do you? Not like that. It's too unpleasant. It's too *sharp*. It makes certain things too *clear*, and it's an easier world when you can keep those kinds of things a little bit out of focus. 'Don't tell me too much,' people say. 'Let me believe the easy thing.' Well, gentlemen, what I'm about to tell you isn't easy."

❧ 40 ❧

"Go on," Walt said to Bentley. "We're listening."

"I'll put it to you straight," Bentley said. "Robert Argyle *sold his soul to the Devil.*"

"Then the Devil got stiffed," Walt said, "because Argyle's soul wasn't worth a glass of milk, even back then when it was fresh."

Bentley looked hard at him.

"Sorry," Walt said. "I didn't mean to make a joke out of it."

"I'm not philosophizing here," Bentley said. "I'm talking about *what happened*—as if I said that Argyle signed papers to buy a house. I mean to say he made a bargain with Satan. Money, power, what have you."

"I get it," Walt said, picturing the transaction—the Devil in natty clothes, snazzy hat, probably driving a Lincoln Town Car and offering Argyle a twenty-six-percent return. . . .

"Murray LeRoy sold his soul, too, at the same time."

"Then you're right," Walt said. "It's not very funny."

"And if you're with me this far, then I'll tell you something worse. Simms is dead on account of it. You can take that to the bank. All of this is my fault."

"I don't see how," Henry said, leaning forward in his chair. "So far you're in the clear. Let these other men *go* to the Devil. That's their choice. That avenue's always open to a man, buyer beware."

Bentley waved him silent. "What I'm telling you is that I'm the man who brokered the deal, paper contract and all. Signature in gold ink."

"What do you mean, 'brokered'?" Walt asked.

"Middle man. I set it up—the mumbo jumbo. I made a few

dollars, too; I can tell you that, although I won't tell you how much. I was even fool enough to think that some good could come of it—taking their dirty money. Maybe it did, too. I used it hard enough. It bought more lunches than you'd believe, and it paid a few bills, too. Both of those scoundrels worked for the Church. It's a good joke, eh? Don't you think? Their money was a means to an end, never mind where it came from. To this day they don't know who I really am. They don't know who they did business with."

"Actually," Walt said, "if I understand what you're telling me, it was a *hell* of a good joke. Let me get this straight. You set up this phony soul-selling scam and made them *pay* for it?"

"Oh, they paid for it," Bentley said. "But paying *me* was the least of it. Now they're paying the piper. It's come full circle. Murray LeRoy was consumed by the fires of Hell— spontaneous human combustion!"

Walt nodded. Bentley was apparently off his chump after all, and just when it was looking like he had a first-rate sense of humor. "I wouldn't worry about it. You conned a couple of monsters out of a few bucks over the years. They can afford it."

"And so I thought. I had the best intentions. That much I'll claim. But the road to Hell is paved with that commodity, friend."

"I guess," Walt said skeptically.

"You don't grasp this," Bentley said. "I *used* them, didn't I? I played a hoax, a joke. And now I discover that the joke is on me. I was just larking around, slipping the wallets out of the pockets of a couple of prize idiots. But what I found out is something I already should have known: *the Devil doesn't kid around.* He's *got* no sense of humor. He's in *deadly* earnest." He looked at Walt, letting this sink in.

"Still . . ." Walt started to say.

"Still nothing. You're with me about halfway. You want to think that all this talk is some kind of tomfoolery. You're a good man, so you don't laugh at it, but you don't *believe* it either. You're thinking, what's this got to do with me?"

"Okay," Walt said. "What's this got to do with me? If you want to know the truth, I don't care if Robert Argyle goes straight to Hell. He can take the express. I'll pay to upgrade his ticket."

"You make sure you don't go with him," Bentley said. "That's what I'm trying to tell you. This thing in the jar that I asked you about, that you and Henry threw in the bin?"

Walt nodded.

"Robert Argyle must not have it."

"I tossed it out," Walt said, feeling himself flush with shame at the lie. And to a minister, too . . .

"Because if . . ."

A car was pulling up at the curb just then, moving way too fast. Hell, it was Jack's T-bird! Jack banked the tires off the curb and shut the engine down, leaving the car angled into the street. The door flew open and he heaved himself out, coming around the back of the car, taking big steps, loaded for bear. He cut it too close, though, and his hip bumped the fender hard. He staggered, caught himself, and stepped up onto the curb with exaggerated care. He was drunk, all right, but he was trying hard not to look drunk.

"Hey, brother," Jack said, nodding at Walt as he came up the walk.

"Hello, Jack."

"You got the kids ready to go?"

Walt shook his head. "They aren't here. I told you that over the phone."

"Hi, folks," Jack said, nodding to Henry and Bentley. "This man's stolen my children, and I'm here to get them back."

"Jack, the kids aren't here," Walt said. "You might as well run along."

"*You* run the hell along," Jack said, getting mad suddenly. "I told you I wanted my kids. So you get my kids."

"And I told you the kids aren't here. As long as you're drunk, they *won't* be here, either."

"I'll by God *see* who's here," Jack shouted, lunging suddenly at the door.

Walt stepped into his way, and Jack swung hard at him with the back of his hand. Walt ducked away from it sideways, and Jack's forearm slammed into his shoulder, knocking him into the Reverend Bentley, who was just then trying to stand up. Jack grabbed the handle of the screen door and swung it open, and just then the end of a broom thrust through the open door, the corn bristles shoving hard into Jack's chest and neck.

"Ow!" he shouted, stumbling backward, and Jinx stepped out onto the porch, carrying the broom with both hands like a rifle with a bayonet, her face set like a stone mask. She swung the broom sideways, hitting him in the chest with the flat of it, and he turned around and stepped off the porch, missing the second step entirely and sprawling down onto the lawn, knocking down Walt's trash can full of leaves. Jinx followed him, getting clear of the porch roof so that she could use the broom more effectively. She said nothing, just raised the broom straight into the air and pounded it down onto Jack's head as he scuttled toward the sidewalk yelling, "Hey! Hey! Hey! Watch it!" He stood up, covering his head and angling around behind the T-bird, keeping it between them.

Jinx waited at the edge of the lawn now that she'd driven him off, ready for him if he made a move toward the house. Walt turned away so that Jack wouldn't see him smile. There was no use humiliating him any more than he'd already been humiliated. The man would come back with a gun and kill them all.

The phone rang inside, and Henry stood up and made for the door. "I'll grab it," he said. "Watch out for Jinx."

Jack shook his fist, breathing in big gasps. "I'll be back!" he shouted. He looked as if he wanted to say more, but couldn't find anything good enough.

"That's right," Walt said, coming down to where Jinx stood with the broom. "We'll see you when you're sober, Jack." He put his arm around Jinx's shoulder. "You okay?" he asked her.

She nodded.

"Who *was* that man?" The Reverend Bentley came down off the porch just as Jack tore away in his car, running straight through the stop sign at the corner of the street.

"That man is a *husk*," Jinx said, breathing heavily. "He isn't fit to be those children's father. Thank God he's *not* their father."

"He's the weak brother," Walt said.

Bentley nodded. "He's been drinking."

"Indeed he has," Walt said.

Finished with her task, Jinx headed for the house again, just as the screen swung open and Henry stepped out. Somehow Henry looked hammered, worse off than Jack, as if he'd just been given some kind of terminal news. He smiled weakly at Jinx and patted her on the shoulder, but she pushed on into the house, not really looking at him, still fired up from the confrontation.

Henry glanced at Walt and shook his head.

"Bad news on the phone?" Walt asked.

"Lord, lord, lord," the old man said, sitting down heavily. He craned his neck, looking back in through the window as if to make sure Jinx wasn't lurking by the open door.

"What is it?" Bentley asked. "What's wrong?"

"It's the Biggs woman." He gestured feebly, putting his hand to his face. "It's very bad. The only good thing is that I answered the phone and not Jinx."

"Biggs?" Walt asked. "Who . . . ?"

"From the All-Niter," Henry said, gesturing up the street. "Maggie Biggs."

Walt sat down. This was it, just as he'd feared—the hula-hula woman. Trouble, and quicker than he would have thought possible. She was sixty-five years old if she was a day, so at least there wouldn't be any paternity suit.

"Talk to us, Henry," Bentley said, forgetting for the moment about himself. Walt found that he liked Bentley suddenly, just like that. There was something okay about him, something that Walt hadn't seen before, probably because he'd never been able to get past the tracts and the preachery.

"I'm in trouble," Henry said. "Jinx deserves better than me."

"Nonsense," Bentley said. "Let's have it. Whatever you've done, it can be fixed."

"Not this time." He shook his head, denying it. "It's broken this time. I . . . I've been seeing too much of this . . . this Biggs woman. I guess you knew that, Walt. You tried to warn me. Well, she got her *mitts* on me. I guess you could say that and you wouldn't be far wrong."

Bentley scowled, as if he didn't quite buy the mitts business.

"She claims I . . . had my way with her," Henry said, "and she's threatened to go to Jinx with it."

"Had your way?" Walt asked. "You've only known her for what?—two or three days?"

Henry shrugged. "It's a dirty lie. It was *harm*less, I swear it. But Jinx won't see it that way, not anymore. She'll go to Goldfarb, and that'll be the end of it."

"There's no need to swear," Bentley said. "We both believe you. My advice is to go to Jinx yourself. We'll stand behind you, by golly. Let's do it now!" He stood up.

"Good heavens, no!" Henry said. "Sit down. And keep your voice down, for heaven's sake. After last winter . . ." He shook his head. "I've been a damned fool. Why *should* she believe me?"

"Just tell her it's over with this Biggs woman," Walt said in a low voice. "It won't be easy, but you've got to come clean with her. Stop the trolley right here and get off."

"That's the ticket," Bentley said. "If you've made a mistake, own up to it. As for this Biggs, do the manly thing—tell her it's over, it's all been a mistake."

"That's what I did," Henry told them. "That's the whole trouble. Maggie Biggs lives out past Satellite Market, out on Olive. I went over there this morning and called it off, told her this whole thing was a mistake. But she wouldn't take no. She wouldn't listen. Now she's tracked me down. She'll tell Jinx some kind of lie just as sure as . . ." His voice trailed off.

"Did you . . . did you have your way with her?" Bentley asked.

Henry shook his head. "I don't claim to be innocent in this," he said, "but by God I didn't touch her."

"Then I think we can talk to her," Walt said. "She'll see reason." This struck him as the empty-headedest thing he'd ever said. Clearly she wouldn't see any such thing. Maggie Biggs was doom in a muumuu.

"I'd be happy to go along," Bentley said. "I can be a persuasive prick when I want to be."

"Thank you, boys," Henry said. "I'm on thin ice."

Walt looked at his watch. It was still early. "She called from home?"

Henry nodded.

"Will you take a look at that?" Bentley said suddenly. He pointed at the sky. Off to the west a plume of black smoke rose into the sky. There was the sound of sirens just then.

"Looks like the Plaza," Walt said.

Bentley stood up. "Let's go," he said. Suddenly his voice

was full of urgency, as if this smoke in the sky had something to do with what he'd been talking about, with what he feared.

Jinx came to the door just then, carrying her purse. "Gladys is coming by to pick me up," she said to Henry and Walt. "We won't be late, but remember that I won't be cooking dinner."

Henry nodded vaguely, and Jinx disappeared back into the house.

Bentley headed down the steps and made for the car without another word, as if he were going right now, with or without them.

❧ 41 ❧

THE FIRE IN THE PLAZA WAS OUT BY THE TIME BENTLEY pulled into a parking space near the Continental Cafe. There was smoke in the air, but only a thin blue-black haze blowing eastward in the wind. A fire truck and a paramedics unit sat at the mouth of the alley adjacent to Nelson and Whidley, and behind a barrier of yellow police tape a crowd of onlookers stood around silently, their arms crossed, a couple of them breathing through handkerchiefs.

Bentley climbed out of the car and hurried away, leaving the door open, his face stricken with fear and doubt.

"I'll wait in the car," Henry said, dismissing the entire scene with a wave of his hand. "I'm a little tired right now."

Walt climbed out and shut Bentley's door, then edged along behind the crowd, standing on tiptoe on the curb in order to see up the dead-end alley. Bentley elbowed his way to the front, apologizing left and right, until he stood among the press of firemen and paramedics that hid the scene from the street. There was the awful and unmistakable smell of burnt bone on the air, along with something more—a smell like an electrical short, like charred wire and insulation mixed up with burnt sulphur.

"What happened?" Walt asked, glancing at the man next to him.

"They tell me somebody burned up," he said, shrugging. "I got here at the end of it. Lawyer, apparently. From the offices right here on the corner. Chemical fire, I guess. Burned him to a cinder just like the fire the other day. Same damned thing, except this didn't touch his clothes. Don't ask me how."

Bentley turned around just then and surveyed the onlookers hastily, spotting Walt and waving him forward. "Excuse me,"

Walt said to two women in front of him. "Investigation Division." They smiled and stepped aside for him, and he said the same thing to the man in front of them, who scooted out of the way in order to let him pass.

Bentley stepped forward and took his elbow, shaking his head darkly. "Take a look," he said. "This is what I've been talking about."

Walt bent forward, looking past the shoulder of a fireman, down past the edge of the brick building. Immediately he wished he hadn't, and he looked away again, thinking suddenly of Simms's body at the base of the bell tower. A human skeleton lay huddled against the wall of the alley, its skull tilted downward so that its eye sockets stared at the asphalt, its fingers splayed out as if the dying man had tried to push himself to his feet.

The skeleton was fully clothed. It was wearing a three-piece suit, light blue.

Walt looked again, despite the horror of it. From what he could see—the hand and wrist bones, the skull and first vertebra—the man's flesh had been almost entirely consumed by the fire, and yet, except for the charred collar, the suit itself was unburned.

And draped across the back of the coat, just below the collar, as if it had been flung around by the force of the body falling, was a laminated card on a chain, the plastic lamination clean and smooth, as if to illustrate Sidney Vest's promise that the card was fireproof, "ready for takeoff."

A man in a tie and shirtsleeves snapped a picture of the corpse, and firemen moved in around it again, hiding it from Walt's view.

He realized that Bentley was staring at him. "Now that you've seen, you believe, eh? No more doubting Thomas?"

"Believe what?" Walt asked.

"This was no chemical fire."

Walt shrugged. "That's what they're saying."

"Who the hell are *they*? The police? What *they're* saying doesn't matter. *They* might as well say he was burned up by his own cigar. As for me, I know this man." Bentley moved off now, angling through the crowd toward where Henry still sat in the car, staring straight ahead, lost in thought.

"Let me guess," Walt said, following along. "This was another of your men, your diabolists?"

"George Nelson."

"Nelson?" Walt said. "Well, I'll be damned. It's a small world."

"You knew him?"

Walt nearly laughed out loud, suddenly recalling Sidney Vest's nonsense yesterday at Coco's. He could picture the newspaper headline: "Thirty-eight Vice Presidents Broiled in Alley."

"He was one of the First Captains, wasn't he?" Walt asked, repeating Vest's ridiculous phrase.

Bentley stopped dead, his face pale. "What do you know about the Captains?" he asked.

"Nothing. A man named Sidney Vest used the phrase yesterday. I bought him lunch over at Coco's, and he tried to rope Henry and me into going to some kind of investment meeting."

"Vest," Bentley said, nearly spitting out the name. "Don't have anything to do with the man."

"No, I won't. I don't believe in getting rich quick."

Bentley looked at him. "This is no damned joke," he said. "Get that into your head." He set out toward the car again, his face suddenly angry. But he hadn't taken two steps when, casting a glance at the Plaza, he suddenly darted forward, straight through the open door of the Continental Cafe, where he disappeared among the tables.

What the hell . . . ? Walt wondered, stepping to the door and glancing inside. Bentley sat at a table at the rear of the cafe, pretending to read a menu. His back was to the door, and he watched the street in one of the big mirrors on the wall. He caught Walt's eye and gestured emphatically, shaking his head.

Walt turned away, heading for the car again, just as Robert Argyle's Mercedes Benz pulled into an adjacent stall. Bentley must have seen the car coming round the other side of the Plaza. Argyle looked hard at Walt, squinting his eyes, clearly full of doubt, seeing him downtown at a time like this. He climbed out and nodded. Walt nodded back, leaning against one of the pine trees at the curb.

"Looks like another fire," Argyle said to him, locking up the Mercedes with some kind of remote device.

"Another case of spontaneous human combustion, apparently," Walt said, just for effect. The words hit Argyle like a blow. He licked his lips, as if he wanted to say something but the effort was too much. Seeing the reaction, Walt said, "Whoever it was went up like a torch, just like Murray LeRoy." He shook his head sadly. "I've got a hunch I know what's going on, too."

"What are you talking about?" Argyle said now, looking at him incredulously. His voice was creaky with strain.

"Devil worship," Walt whispered, winking at him. "I hear that George Nelson, this dead lawyer, *made a pact with the Devil*. The news is all over town. Now he's been burned up by the eternal fires. The Devil came for him and took him straight to Hell—nothing left but calcinated bones and a three-piece suit, the poor sap. Must have hurt like nobody's business, burning up like that. . . ."

He quit talking, suddenly afraid that Argyle was having a stroke. Or worse, that he was set to burst into flame right there on the spot. Argyle's face was red as a crab leg, and the tendons in his neck stuck out like ropes. His eyes stared at Walt, jumping in their sockets. His mouth twitched, and he made a noise, but no words came out, so he clamped his teeth shut with what was apparently a tremendous effort. Slowly he turned around and walked away toward the alley, saying nothing. There was a clearing through the crowd now, and Walt could see that they had the corpse on a stretcher. Argyle stopped and stared at it, standing ramrod straight, like a wooden dummy.

Walt was aware suddenly that Bentley was gesturing at him from the doorway of the cafe, jerking his thumb toward the corner. Walt nodded, hurrying away, rounding the corner without looking back. He waited in front of an antiques shop, and in a moment Bentley's car pulled around and whipped into the red zone. Walt climbed in, and Bentley motored away up Glassell Street, turning the corner and heading west toward Olive.

"I thought Argyle didn't know you," Walt said. "Why all this secrecy?"

"He *doesn't* know me. Not in that capacity. But I had a little run-in with a couple of friends of his night before last, out at Murray LeRoy's. I don't want to be turning up too often—not yet, anyway. Did he speak to you?"

"Not really," Walt said. "Just small talk."

⊰ 42 ⊱

MRS. BIGGS LIVED IN A SPANISH-STYLE RENTAL, A SMALL, flat-roofed house with a big garage and an unkempt lawn that clearly hadn't been mowed or raked since summer. There was an old Buick sitting in the driveway. The curtains were pulled across the windows, and Walt found himself hoping that she wouldn't be home, that she had walked down to Satellite Market or to the Spic 'n' Span Cleaners and they'd have to come back tomorrow.

They sat at the curb for a moment, none of them making a move to get out. "We're petrified, aren't we?" Walt asked finally. "Mrs. Biggs is going to work us over."

"I'm afraid you're right," Henry said. "I didn't offer her money, exactly. . . ."

"Money!" Bentley said. "Not a penny of it! We'll go straight to the police!"

"Good Lord, no!" Henry said. "I don't mean *real* money. Just a little something . . . to make amends."

"Like a gift," Walt said, taking out his wallet.

"I'm afraid I'm a little short right at the moment," Henry said. "Jinx is the banker these days, and she's a little tight with it. I'll cover any losses, though."

Walt had four twenties in his wallet along with a couple of ones. That ought to about cover it. He opened the door and got out.

"Maybe I'd better stay here for the moment," Henry said. "What do you think?"

"I think that's a good idea," Walt said through the window. "Let us run interference for you. You don't have a twenty, do you?" he asked Bentley. "That would give us an even hundred, just in case we need it."

Bentley scowled at him and shook his head. "It's *wrong*," he said, hitching up his pants.

Walt saw the window curtains move. Mrs. Biggs had been watching them. She opened the door when he and Bentley were halfway up the walk. She was wearing a muumuu and an orange wig with a flip like an ocean wave on the side of it. Somehow the wig made her head look small. She was pretty clearly assessing them, wondering whether she should parlay with them or send them packing. Suddenly she stepped aside and swung the door wide open.

"Step right in, boys," she said, dusting off her hands. She shut the door. And then, making a show of it, she yanked the curtains open, revealing the interior of the house to the street, as if to warn them against trying anything fancy. "Which one of you is the lawyer?" she asked.

"Neither of us is a lawyer," Bentley said. "I'm a minister, Lorimer Bentley." He put his hand out.

"A reverend?" She gaped at him, taking his hand for a moment and then letting it fall. "Well, he needs one, the old fraud. You know that he took unfair advantage of me?"

"He fell for you pretty hard," Walt said, deciding to play the vanity angle. "That morning when he saw you at the All-Niter—that brought back a lot of memories. He told me that you hadn't changed in . . . How long had it been? Forty years? That threw him for a loop, seeing you there, an attractive woman from his past. He was like a teenager."

"Well . . ." She smiled at Walt. "Still, he's a married man, isn't he? He ought to know better than to give a poor old woman the business. And a lie is a lie, isn't it?"

Walt shrugged. There was no use arguing with her. It was better to jolly her along, to give her what she wanted—up to a point, anyway.

She gazed at the rug for a moment, as if gathering her thoughts. "Something happened to a friend of mine once," she said, sitting down on the couch. She gestured at a couple of doily-draped armchairs, and Walt and Bentley sat down, too. "Her name was Velma Krane—with a K. She lived in Waikiki. This was in the days when there was nothing on the beach but the Royal Hawaiian and a few palm trees, not the tourist mess it is today. Today it's too much noise and buses and cheap T-shirts."

"I hear it was beautiful back then," Walt said.

"Nothing on the wind but plumeria blossoms and the smell of the ocean." She gazed at the street, remembering. "It was truly paradise." She seemed to have lost the thread.

"Look here," Bentley said, looking at his wristwatch. "Let's get down to brass tacks. What you've threatened Henry with is simply not . . ."

"Hold on, Reverend," Walt said, waving him silent. "Mrs. Biggs has a story to tell, and I think we ought to listen. What about your friend Velma Krane? You were illustrating your point, I think."

"Thank you," she said to Walt. "It's rare to find simple politeness these days. I appreciate a man who can listen— really *listen*." She looked at Bentley pretty hard for a moment before going on. "I guess you could say that Velma was just too . . . *kind* for her own good. She befriended a man, took him in, fed him. And purely out of the kindness of her heart, too. He wasn't a rich man."

Bentley sighed heavily and drummed his fingers on the arm of the couch. He looked at his watch again.

"I'm afraid your friend is impatient," Mrs. Biggs said to Walt.

"Oh, no," Bentley said. "I just fail to see how . . ."

"I think that if we listen we'll discover how," Walt said to him. "Go on, ma'am."

"Well, to make a long story short, a romance developed, and I'm afraid that she, that Velma . . ." Mrs. Biggs shook her head and looked at the carpet again. "She was taken advantage of. Against my advice. Make no mistake about that—I warned her against him. I saw him for what he was. I said, 'Velma, that man is a no-good Lothario.' But she didn't listen. How could she? *She was listening to her heart.*" Mrs. Biggs wiped her eye.

"And he left her cold?" Walt asked. "This Lothario?"

She nodded. "He was gone in the morning. He didn't take her money, but he took something more valuable by far. . . ." She paused, looking from Bentley to Walt.

"What was that?" Bentley asked.

"Her *dignity*," she said to him, squinting hard to make it hit home.

Bentley had a fixed expression on his face now. His head

swiveled slightly, and he glanced at Walt. Walt winked at him.

"And do you know what I told Velma?"

Walt shook his head.

"I said, 'Velma, you've got to be compensated.' That's just what I said. Those were my very words. Compensated."

"I fully agree," Walt said.

"Somehow I knew you would. I could see it in your face." She stood up and patted him on the hand. "I'll just put on the teakettle," she said, and stepped across the living room, through the arched doorway that led to the kitchen.

"This is an outrage!" Bentley hissed at him. "She means to take us straight to the cleaners."

"I'll mollify her," Walt said. "It won't be much of a cleaners." He went into the kitchen, drawing two of the twenties out of his wallet. Mrs. Biggs fussed at the stove, an old O'Keefe and Merritt. There was the formaldehyde smell of gas on the air, and she waved a lit match at the burner, dropping it suddenly on the stovetop and shaking her hand.

"Pilot won't work?"

"It hasn't worked in ages."

"Let me take a look." He lifted the griddle in the center of the stovetop. The pilot was burning fine. It was probably the pipes clogged with grease or dust. "I think I can finagle this if you have a rat-tail brush—like for cleaning out a turkey baster."

"I have just the thing," she said, opening a drawer.

"Henry said something about owing you a few dollars," Walt said to her. "I don't know what for—something he borrowed, I guess. He likes to pay his debts. Will this cover it?" He held out the two twenties. She took them out of his hand without answering and folded them into the pocket of her muumuu.

"When you're living on a fixed income . . ." She shook her head sadly. "Velma had a little one-bedroom walkup. I guess I should feel lucky."

She found the brush and handed it to Walt, who pulled apart the pipes in the stove. There was nothing very complicated about the plumbing in an old gas stove. A couple of minutes of sweeping out the dust was all it usually took, just to get the crumbs out. . . .

⇥ 43 ⇤

BENTLEY CAME IN AND STOOD IN THE DOORWAY. "HENRY'S still in the car," he said to Walt, nodding back over his shoulder.

"This won't take a second." Walt laid the tube that ran to the pilot back into its slot and cranked the knob. Nothing happened. He fiddled with it, but after a moment there was the smell of gas again, and he twisted the knob back off. Something else was wrong. "Let me check one more thing," he said.

"You might as well make yourself useful, too, Reverend," Mrs. Biggs said to Bentley. "Have you ever emptied a trash bucket before, or do you just do the soul's work?"

"Of *course* I've emptied a trash bucket. Emptying trash buckets *is* the soul's work."

"Then you're in luck," she said, and she swung open the cupboard beneath the sink and gestured at the red plastic trash bucket. "The cans are out behind the garage. Separate the recycle!"

Bentley hesitated for a moment, then moved into the room and pulled the bucket out from its cupboard. She opened the back door for him, and he went out. Walt took the stovetop apart, piece by piece, setting it around on the floor, only then noticing that the undersides of the chrome top pieces were slick with dirty grease. "Any newspaper?" he asked.

"Might as well wash it all up, now that you've gone and pulled it apart." She put a stopper in the drain, cranked on the hot water, and found a box of Brillo Pads under the sink. Walt picked up the cast-iron burner grills and put them into the hot water.

Bentley came back in just then, carrying the empty bucket. He didn't look happy.

"Look there," Mrs. Biggs said, pointing at the linoleum floor. There was a litter of muddy dirt on the tiles. Bentley looked at the sole of one of his shoes, which was caked with mud from the backyard. "*Now* your work's cut out for you," she said. "Broom and dustpan's in the pantry. And take your shoes off first! Put them out on the stoop."

Bentley stood staring at her. "Henry's in . . ." he started to say.

"In the car," she said. "We all know he's in the car. Let him sit there. It's the best place for him. As long as he's in the car he's not out wrecking the lives of half the women in the neighborhood. He won't get heatstroke, not on a day like this."

Bentley set the trash bucket down, turned around slowly, and went back out through the door, where he slipped his shoes off.

"These preachers," Mrs. Biggs whispered to Walt. "Too heavy for light work and too light for heavy work." She shook her head.

"He's just out of practice," Walt said. "Do you have any kind of degreaser? Something in a spray bottle?"

"Just the thing," she said, reaching under the sink again. "You might as well do the job right."

Bentley came back in.

"In the pantry," she said to him, pointing toward a big cupboard near the door.

He opened it and got out a broom, then poked at the dirt on the floor. The dirt was too wet, though, and simply smeared across the linoleum.

"Mop's in there, too," she said. "Hot water's in the sink. Use the right tool for the right job. I'm surprised I have to tell you that, a man your age. Maybe you'd better fetch Henry out of the car after all at this rate, the kind of job you do."

She took a flyswatter from a peg on the wall and slammed the hell out of a fly that was just then buzzing against the window, then settled herself on a stool by the sink.

"He wouldn't have lasted a week at the Paradise, my place in Honolulu. Any of those little Filipino girls could clean circles around him." She squinted at Bentley, who clearly kept his silence for Henry's sake. He edged past her, dipping the mop into the sink and then twisting some of the water out of it.

"That's still too wet," she said to him, pointing at the mop with the swatter. "It'll take a week for the floor to dry. You're not bathing a poodle here, you're just picking up a little dirt."

He wrung it out again, leaning into it, nearly tearing the head off the mop, then he moved off across the kitchen again and slapped it around on the muddy floor.

"Watch out with that mop! For heaven's sake!" she said. "Mind the cream pitchers!"

On a shelf above the back door stood a half dozen ceramic pitchers—cow and moose heads, a pig with a corkscrew tail, a Cheshire cat. All of them had holes in their mouths or noses where the cream could pour out. Bentley looked at them for a moment as if he didn't quite understand them, then went back to mopping.

"That's right," she said, "back away from it, don't walk through it or you'll get your socks wet and track it all over the rest of the floor. There, you missed some—along the base-board." She gestured with the swatter again. Walt sprayed the degreaser on the last of the stove pieces and wiped them down with a rag. The least he could do was leave it clean, since, he knew by now, there was no way he was going to fix it. He didn't have the foggiest idea what was wrong with it.

Bentley rinsed the mop again, then took one last swipe at the remnants of the mud. Turning toward the sink, he clipped the cream pitcher shelf with the mop handle, and the cow head pitched off the shelf onto the floor, breaking into three or four pieces.

⇥ 44 ⇤

BENTLEY STARED AT THE BROKEN COW HEAD IN DISBELIEF.
Mrs. Biggs slumped, putting her face in her hands as if this
had finally defeated her utterly.

"I'm *terribly* sorry," Bentley said, dropping to his hands
and knees. He picked up the fragments and tried to fit them
together. "Here we go, here's its eye . . ." He groped under
the edge of the clothes dryer.

"That was a *priceless* antique."

"Let me pay you for it," Bentley said. "Honestly. . . . How
stupid of me . . ." He held his hands out, shaking his head
helplessly at Walt.

"Maybe some Super Glue?" Walt said helpfully.

"That's kind of you," Mrs. Biggs said to Walt, "but I'm
afraid your friend has ruined it. I won't say that he did it on
purpose, but . . ."

"I most certainly did *not* do any such thing!" Bentley said,
his face suddenly red. "I'll be *happy* to take your word for it
being valuable." He hauled his wallet out, fingering the bills
inside and drawing out a ten. She stared at it, as if it were
some kind of Chinese phoney-dough.

"Don't in*sult* me," she said coldly.

"All right. Fair enough." Bentley took out a twenty and
started to put the ten back, but Mrs. Biggs pulled them both
out of his hand.

"Fifty dollars should just about do it," she said. "*If* I can
replace the creamer at all. That object was made in *Germany*—
prewar."

Bentley looked at Walt again. "That's it," he said. "I'm
tapped out."

"What do you need?" Walt asked, settling the chrome top

back onto the stove. "Another twenty?" He got his wallet out and handed over a twenty. Mrs. Biggs took it politely.

Uncle Henry appeared right then, out on the driveway, standing next to the Buick and looking like a lost child. He waved at them.

"You might as well get the old goat in here," Mrs. Biggs said to Walt. "He can at least lend a hand. He's got to be good for something."

"Now look here," Bentley said, starting up again. "This has gone just about far enough. We've mopped your floor and repaired your stove . . ."

"And broke my priceless heirloom, you might as well say."

Walt opened the back door and gestured at Uncle Henry. "Watch the mud," he said as the old man came around the back side of the house.

"Is she still on the warpath?" Henry whispered.

"She's had it with Bentley. He's not much of a diplomat."

"Roll up your sleeves, Henry, and scrub up this mess in the sink." She shouted past Bentley and waved Henry in through the door. "And you, Reverend, why don't you see what you can do with a tube of glue, unless you've got the shakes. You don't look too steady. Not a secret toper, are you? Or is that what your big rush is all about? Too long away from the sauce?" She grinned at him for a moment before opening a drawer and pulling out a little green tube of Super Glue. Bentley sat down at the table without a word and went to work on the cow.

"That stove looks *fine*," she said to Walt. "Good as new. Now, how about that tea?"

"I'd like a cup of tea," Henry said.

"Maybe not," Walt put in, glancing at his wristwatch. "It's nearly time to get the kids from school." The stove *looked* first-rate, but there was no telling . . .

"Oh, just one cup," she said. "Just to celebrate a job well done."

Henry hauled one of the cast-iron grills out of the sink, dried it off, and set it over its burner. Mrs. Biggs put the teakettle on top of it and twisted the knob. There was a faint hiss, but nothing happened beyond that.

"Takes a moment to run the gas back in through the pipes," Walt said, knowing what he said was nonsense. The stove was

completely buggered up. There was the smell of gas in the air,
heavy now, so something was working, anyway. Walt picked
up the matchbook on the counter and struck a match, slipping
it under the edge of the grill. The burner ignited in a whoosh
of blue flame, a fireball the size of the stovetop that singed all
the hair off both of his arms. Walt danced backward, fanning
at the stove with his hand, but there was no point; the flames
were already out. He moved forward and twisted the knob,
shutting down the burner.

"I guess this is a job for the gas company," he said, shaking
his head. "Sorry. I gave it a try."

"No harm done," she said. She looked wistfully out the
window. "I don't suppose the gas company can come out
today, though. Not this late. And I can't use the stove in this
condition—it's like to blow up the house, isn't it?" She
sighed. "Lord knows I can't afford to eat out, though, not
these days. I'll eat cold food, I guess, out of the fridge. I've
got the rest of a box of frozen day-olds from the All-Niter.
That'll do for the likes of me."

"You've got fifty dollars," Bentley said, trying to glue the
cow's eye back into its head.

"That's pitcher money," she said. "You ought to know that
much, unless that bourbon's ate up all your brain cells, too."

"Maybe we could treat Maggie to a meal," Henry said. "I
didn't bring any money, but . . ."

"I've got another twenty in here someplace," Walt said,
dipping into his wallet again. Hell, he thought, looking at the
two singles that were left. There was no use putting it off.
Obviously she'd have those too, before they left; might as well
burn it all down right now. "Here you go, dinner on us." He
handed her the whole works, tipping his wallet toward her to
make it clear it was empty of anything but moths.

"*There* we go," Bentley said heartily, setting the repaired
cow pitcher down on the table. "Darned well good as new."

Even from halfway across the room Walt could see that
there was something wrong with it. A chip was apparently
missing, and Bentley had tried to compromise by gluing the
eye in a quarter inch too far down the nose. The effect was
startling, almost demented, as if the cow were trying to look
up its own nostril. Mrs. Biggs picked up the creamer, flinching
when she got a good look at it. "Now it's ruined good and

proper," she said. "It's trash now, isn't it? You've finished me off, Reverend."

She began to cry, and set the pitcher on the counter. "Never mind me," she said, waving her hand. "An hour ago I had a stove, a cream pitcher. I had my d-d-dignity." She bleated out a sob, and Henry moved to her side, putting his arm around her shoulders.

Bentley closed his eyes, and Walt got the idea that he was counting, that maybe he would have to count several times.

"I was wondering," Henry said softly to Walt. "Maggie's Buick has been acting up, and she hates to take it over to Pinky's Garage again, not after what they soaked her for last time. Maybe you've got some idea . . . ?"

"Acting up how?" Walt asked. Bentley turned away, cutting the air with little slashes of his hand, as if he were reading his congregation a hellfire sermon.

"Overheating," Henry said. "Isn't that it?"

She nodded, sniffling a little and fingering the cream pitcher again.

"She can't drive it ten blocks," Henry said. "She's lucky to make it to the All-Niter."

"Probably just the thermostat," Walt said. "Nothing to it. We'll pull the hose and pop it out. We can run the thermostat down to Chief and swap it for a new one. Won't take a second, won't cost a cent." He winked at Mrs. Biggs, who had gotten her composure back.

"I'd be obliged," she said. "And I wonder if you'd pop into the Satellite for a few groceries, too? I know it's only a block down, but my sciatica . . ." She grimaced, and straightened her back with what was apparently a monumental pain and effort. "Here." She offered Walt one of his twenties back, but Henry stopped her.

"*We'll* take care of it," he said. "You buy yourself another one of these vessels." He pointed at the cow.

Bentley stepped to the door, opened it, and went straight out without saying a word.

"Pissant," Mrs. Biggs said. "That's the only name for a creature like that. And he calls himself a man of God." She shook her head sadly, as if it were a shame. "I'll make out the grocery list while you look to the car. There's some tools in the garage, but not many." She inclined her head at Walt.

"Leave 'em as clean as you find 'em. That's what I always told the help at the Paradise."

"Good policy," Walt said. "Leave it to us."

He followed Henry out the door again. It only took a few minutes to get the top hose off the radiator and pull out the thermostat. But the hose had gone mushy, so Walt took it, too, and then pulled the bottom hose just to be safe, letting the green radiator water run down the driveway and into the gutter while Henry diluted it with hose water. They'd have to buy clamps before it was over, and a gallon of antifreeze. Still, unless the radiator itself was shot, the whole thing wouldn't cost more than twenty-five bucks, and maybe another twenty for groceries, give or take, and if that was the end of Maggie Biggs, they'd have gotten off cheap.

Bentley had sat in his car the whole time, staring out through the windshield while Walt worked on the Buick. He popped the trunk from inside when Walt rapped on the window, and Walt dropped the hoses and thermostat inside.

"How much?" Bentley asked when Walt and Henry climbed in.

"How much what?" Walt asked.

"How much more of this damnation extortion till we're out of the woods? I tell you I've seen a few hard cases in my day, but she takes the cake, every blessed crumb of it." He pulled away from the curb, shaking his head darkly. "And I'll tell you what—you give these people an inch of rope, and they'll hang you. Velma Krane and her dignity! I'll bet you a shiny new dime there never was a Velma Krane. And that cow pitcher! Prewar Germany! That was a piece of plaster of Paris she bought down at Pic 'n Save, and she soaked us for fifty bucks! What did she take you for, altogether?"

"Pull in here at the bank," Walt said, digging out his automatic teller card. "It's your call, Henry. Shall we see this through?"

"Absolutely," Henry said. "Damn the expense. If she calls Jinx . . ."

Walt hopped out of the car and drew five twenties from the machine, then handed three of them to Bentley when he got back in. "There's grocery money and enough left over to cover the thirty you put out for the cow pitcher. Drop me off at home, will you? I'm late already to get the kids, and I don't want to get in dutch with Ivy.''

"Well . . . heck," Bentley said. "Never mind the thirty for the cow pitcher. *I* broke it." He tried to hand two of the twenties back, reaching his hand over the top of the seat.

"It's not your fight," Walt said, waving them away. "Thanks for going along. If you can see this grocery list through to the end, you've done a day's work. Keep your money.''

"Maybe it *is* my fight," Bentley said. "I came around this afternoon looking to enlist the two of you in this little affair of mine, didn't I? I thought I was up against a pretty formidable dragon, but now I'm inclined to believe that Maggie Biggs gets the brass ring." He stopped at a red light at Shaffer Street, in front of Coco's, and tucked the two twenties into Walt's shirt pocket. "In for a penny, in for thirty bucks, as they say. Keep your money. It'll all come out even in the end.''

"That's the truth," Henry put in. "And by heaven I'll reimburse both of you after the sales party. That lingerie will *sell*. You've got nothing to worry about there. Vest will have delivered it by now.''

"*That's* good news," Walt said, imagining the lingerie party for the first time, actually picturing it in his mind—he and Henry hauling foundation garments and knickers and brassieres out of a cardboard box, a dozen neighborhood women grinning at them, going into the other room to try these things on. . . .

The picture was absolutely insupportable; he saw that clearly now. There would be no recovering from such an ordeal. If he was lucky he would merely be a laughingstock. More likely he'd be considered a world-class pervert. Bentley braked to a stop in front of the house. There was no box on the porch yet; Vest apparently hadn't arrived. Bentley was talking to Henry like a Dutch uncle, giving him advice, waving his finger. Walt tuned them out, his mind consumed by his sudden horror of the lingerie, of the party over on Harwood. God bless Henry, but sometimes he was like a doomful prophecy in an old Greek myth. Oedipus is humiliated at a lingerie party. What else *can* he do but gouge his eyes out?

The popes, Maggie Biggs, Sidney Vest—it was all too

much. And it was his own fault, wasn't it?—letting things go on too long, full of futile hope. Well, this was it. Push had come to shove. Something had to be done right now. There was no more putting it off.

Then the answer came to him, like a radio signal from a distant planet. Out of nowhere he recollected Vest's chatter at Coco's, the talk about selling the vice presidencies, cashing out, moving back to North Carolina. It was all suddenly easy: Walt could put one over on fate and do Vest a favor at the same time. He made the wish right there and then: send Vest home now, he thought, talking to the bluebird. Kill the lingerie deal right this instant and send Vest back to Raleigh.

❧ 45 ❧

IVY TURNED LEFT FROM PALM ONTO BATAVIA AND HEADED north, on her way to check out Argyle's lots. Within a couple of blocks the neighborhood changed from residential to industrial. There was almost no open land at all throughout the downtown area, and the few lots still available had gotten expensive during the boom years in the eighties when the price of real estate had quadrupled. For a couple of years it just hadn't been prudent to buy, and prices drifted downward. Now, with diminished interest rates, things were starting to come back around, but very slowly. Argyle might have moved his two properties quick five years ago and done pretty well, but now prospective buyers would be looking hard for a bargain, and the money he wanted for the parcels didn't look like a bargain to Ivy. Selling them would be a long haul.

She turned into the driveway of an auto parts warehouse and pulled into a stall at the lonesome end of the parking lot, adjacent to one of the parcels, and then sat for a minute looking over the paperwork in the manila envelope, glancing up now and then to get some idea of the place. The dirt lots had turned into mud holes with all the rain, and there was a lake covering half the acreage.

She got out of the car and stood in the cool breeze, leaning back against the hood. This whole thing was baffling: suddenly she was at the edge of making real money, as if a door had opened for her. It was hard not to think of all the what-ifs, to start spending the money in her mind—and not just this commission, but those that might follow. It occurred to her suddenly that she had been treating Argyle a little hard, probably because she didn't want to fight with Walt about him. It was easier to let Walt have his way sometimes, although if she was going to do the kind of serious business with Argyle that it looked like she might do . . .

At the back of one of the lots were a couple of heavy old eucalyptus trees, the loose bark peeling off and littering the ground along with broken-off limbs. Kids had nailed boards to the trunks of the trees, and there were planks up in the lower limbs, half hidden by leafy branches. Somebody, anyway, would be disappointed if the lots sold and the trees had to come down. Such was progress. Out near the street, someone had dumped an old washing machine and some other trash—that would all have to be cleaned up. And she'd have to get a sign, too, which would be covered with graffiti in under a week.

A black pickup truck nearly as long as a limousine pulled off the road right then, onto the muddy shoulder in front of the farther lot. A man got out and stood looking, maybe fifty yards from Ivy. He was a big man—tall and heavy, like an enormous football player way over the hill. He was dressed nicely, in a coat and tie, and had curly hair cut like Nero.

He reached into the rear of the pickup and pulled out one of those bicycle-wheel measuring devices and walked out onto the lot, pushing the wheel along, avoiding the worst of the mud and heading past the edge of the lake toward the eucalyptus trees. When he hit the fence, he scribbled something into a little notebook and then traversed both lots in the other direction, ending up at the northwest corner. He scribbled again and then headed back out toward the street, along the back side of the auto parts warehouse in a route that would take him right past Ivy.

For a moment she was tempted to get back into the car, start it up, and drive away. There was something forbidding about him, out here in the lonesome afternoon. She felt conspicuous, as if she were standing on a street corner.

She stopped herself. It was simply his size, probably, that intimidated her. And whatever he was doing here, surveying the property like this, she really ought to know about it. It was possible he worked for Argyle.

He saw her and nodded. He was sweating despite the wind, and up close he looked even larger, easily six-five. His shirt, either good rayon or some very nice combed cotton, couldn't be off the rack; it must have been three or four yards of material. There was a monogram on the pocket, too.

"Beautiful day," he said. His voice was husky, like a smoker's voice.

"Isn't it?" she said. "The rain's kind of made a mess of these lots, though."

"They'll dry out. Nice couple of lots." He looked back at the ground he'd just covered and nodded his head.

"What's up with all the measuring?" Ivy said. "I don't mean to be nosy, but it happens that I represent the owner of the lots. I'm just out here looking things over now that he's decided to sell them. I've got to get a sign up, get things moving."

"Well, I'll be," he said, holding out his hand. "My name's George Peet. Short for Peetenpaul."

"I'm Ivy Stebbins—Old Orange Realty." He had almost no handshake for a big man—all fingers.

"This is a heck of a coincidence. Saves me tracking down the owner myself."

"Are you interested in the properties?"

"That's right," he said. "So don't bother with the sign. I'll take 'em to go, if the price is right."

"I'm sure we can make it right," she said. She realized then that she must have been smiling like a drunk, but there was no way she could get rid of the smile; that would take some time.

❧ 46 ❧

NORA AND EDDIE CAME OUT OF THE PRESCHOOL CARRYING notebooks covered in red and green foil. The other kids had them, too—catalogues of some kind, very ornate and costly looking.

"What's this?" Walt asked, taking one from Nora as they sat in the parking lot.

"Christmas paper and stuff."

He opened it up. Inside were two dozen four-inch-square samples of Christmas wrapping paper—embossed foil, printed paper, paper stamped with religious messages. There were photos of Christmas craft pieces, too—wreaths and candles and tree ornaments and garlands. At the back of the catalogue was a price list and a three-page order form with blanks for names and addresses and telephone numbers. "One Day Delivery Guaranteed," the order form read.

"What's it for?" Walt asked, spotting the Dilworth logo on the samples page.

"Selling," Nora said.

"You and Eddie both have one?"

"It's a fund-raiser," Eddie said. "To earn money for the school. Last Christmas they bought the dinosaur slide."

Out on the playground stood a desolate-looking fiberglass Tyrannosaurus, six or seven feet tall, in a sand pit. The thing had little bitty worthless arms like a begging poodle, and sun-faded Orphan Annie eyes. Its back and tail were apparently a slide.

"That costed a million dollars," Nora said.

"And they bought it with money from a fund drive?" Walt handed the catalogue back to her and started the car.

"At the Easter one they bought a computer," Eddie said.

"Good for them." Walt headed up Chapman Avenue, wondering what Ivy would say about this, whether she'd find it as contemptible as he did. "What are you supposed to do, go around the neighborhood selling this stuff?"

"And on the telephone," Eddie said. "They have a list of what people we can call, like our dentist and our grandma. If we can sell ten things we get a prize. Ten things is a hundred dollars."

"One of the prizes is a giant bubble thing," Nora said. "You can make these big big bubbles with it." She held her hands out, indicating a bubble four feet across. "It's a string on a stick."

"Really?" Walt said. "You earn a hundred dollars and they give you a string on a stick?"

"And soap," Eddie said. "And this kind of plate thing you put the soap in."

"A kind of plate thing . . ." Walt said. He nearly turned the Suburban around and headed back to the preschool. This was unbelievable, like something out of Charles Dickens—a hundred small children peddling Argyle's pinecone wreaths door to door in the rain, patriotically hustling funds so that the dirty bastard didn't have to spend his own money on a million-dollar fiberglass dinosaur. This was capitalism gone rancid—inbred money-mongering. Maybe the commies had been right after all. What had Ivy told him?—that Argyle owned something like seven preschools? So that was seven hundred kids at a hundred dollars a head! And how many times a year?

"Can you take us around, Unca Walter?" Nora asked him.

"Yeah," Walt said. "I guess I can. Except I've got a better idea. Why don't I buy all of it myself? Then you don't have to sell anything."

"Really?" Eddie asked. *"All of it?"*

"Sure," Walt said. "I'll take the whole pile." Tomorrow he could take the catalogues back down to the school and make Argyle eat them.

"But I wanted to do a fund raisin," Nora said.

"You *can* do a fund raisin," Walt said. "A better one. This one will help someone who really needs help bad right now. What do you think? Are you in?"

"Who needs help?" Eddie asked.

"This woman named Mrs. Simms. Her husband, old Mr.

Simms, just died. He used to ring the bells at the church, but he died, and Mrs. Simms was left all alone.''

"Then she's a widow," Eddie said. "A widow woman."

"That's right. We've got to help her out. What we'll sell is . . . cookies. People give you as much funds as they want, and they get two dozen cowboy cookies wrapped up in Christmas foil.''

"But I want a bubble wand," Nora said. "I don't want cowboys.''

"Cowboy *cookies*," Walt said. "With raisins. That's what *they* get, the people who fork over money."

"Fund raisin cookies!" Eddie said.

"Right!" Walt shouted happily. "Eddie, you're a genius. We'll make Mrs. Simms happy after all.''

"But what's our prize?" Nora asked sadly. "We were going to have a prize.''

"You get a bubble wand for sure."

"No matter what?" Eddie asked.

"No matter what," Walt said, pulling into the driveway and cutting the engine. "And for every ten dollars you earn you get another prize. Let's see. If you make a thousand dollars that's . . . a hundred prizes!''

"I'm going to start right now!" Eddie said, climbing out.

"You'll need a brochure," Walt said. "We'll run that up on the computer. And you'll need a pencil, too, and an affidavit of authenticity. I'll sign that. And order forms. Here, we'll use the order forms you got from school. They won't mind.''

He tore the forms out of the back of Argyle's Christmas catalogues, then tossed the notebooks into the rear of the Suburban. Later he could come out and soak them in the gutter for a half hour, then throw them onto the roof of the house to dry.

☆ 47 ☆

"THAT'S THE TICKET," MAGGIE BIGGS SAID. "A BLUEBIRD in a jar full of some kind of liquid—I don't know what kind. And what difference does that make anyway? Apparently there's only this one bird. You don't have to pick and choose."

They stood in the alley behind the library. The high brick wall sheltered them from the rain, which angled in from the west, and out on the street the cars had their wipers on. Rainwater trickled out of a metal downspout. Henry stared at the bumper of a car parked in the library lot. "Practice safe government," the sticker read, "use kingdoms."

"I'm telling you this bird's been thrown away." Henry forced himself to concentrate on what she was telling him. His mind was tired, and he wished to hell he was back in the motor home, taking a nap.

"What do you mean, 'thrown away'?"

"He threw it into the bin yesterday afternoon."

"Don't lie to me, you old fool. Why would he throw it away when there's people willing to pay for it?"

"Because it's an evil damned thing in a jar," Henry said, suddenly angered that he'd been called down here in the rain, and after she'd promised not to call the house at all. Thank God Jinx had been out! "I took one look at this bird and I *told* him to throw it away, and by golly he did the right thing."

"That's where you're wrong. You'd better dig it out of the bin lickety-split."

"Don't bully me," he said, taking a stand.

"I'll do worse than that, and you know it."

"You might as well save your breath. I suppose the bird's gone by now anyway."

"*Gone!* How would you know? Did you look?"

"Well, no. It's just that . . ."

"It's just that you'll have to look now, that's what it is. And quit being such a bag of pudding. For God's sake, Henry, give your infernal conscience a rest. If he threw it in the bin, then it's trash now, isn't it? There's no crime in taking it back out. And your precious nephew *stole* it from my party in the first place."

"Walter wouldn't do that."

"Did he tell you how he got it?"

"Why, in a shipment, from China. He imports . . ."

"I *know* what he imports. What I'm asking is did he *order* this bird in a jar?"

"He apparently found it in this shipment. There was just the one, and . . ."

"And hold your tongue for a second. It was delivered to his house *by mistake*, and you know it's true, don't you?"

This was the same thing Bentley had told him! It *had* all been a mistake. Maggie Biggs was right about that much: it hadn't been Walt's to throw away, and that's why he'd been so damned guilty about it. Well, that part was too bad, and he himself had aided and abetted the whole thing. He had nearly *forced* Walt to do it. "I guess it was my fault," he said.

"Well, I don't doubt it. But if that's true, then it's up to you to make it right," she told him. "You hand it over to me and I'll return it to its rightful owner. If you want a signed affidavit, I'll give you one."

"I don't guess . . ."

"And let me tell you something else. This party I represent *wants this object*, and he wants it now. I can't be blamed for what he might do if he finds out it's been destroyed. I *like* your nephew. He's treated me pretty well. He buggered up my stove, but I don't hold that against him."

"What do you mean?" Henry asked. "What will this man do?"

"For goodness sake, *I* don't know. *I* can't be expected to think like a murderer, can I? That's not my province."

"Murder!" Henry gasped.

Mrs. Biggs shrugged. "You didn't hear it from me. I'm not saying anything. Look, let's just say your nephew climbed in over his head. This is the big leagues he's playing in, and the poor fool thinks he's out on the sandlot with the kids. Now if someone were to put through a call to your wife, say, and tell her about us . . .''

"*Us!* This is rubbish. Extortion, that's what Bentley called it.''

She snorted out a laugh. "Bentley!'' she said. "I guess the Reverend's familiar with the likes of *that.* I won't dispute with the Reverend when it comes to the subject of pernicious activity. But I won't be threatened by the man, either. He comes into my home and breaks things up, vandalizes the place . . .'' She shook her head. "So you watch your words. You wave the Reverend at me and by God I'll run the whole lot of you into the sheriff.''

"What I meant to say is that you were going to leave Jinx out of this. That was our agreement.''

"Oh, *I'm* willing to leave her out. She's got enough grief, I suppose. What I was saying is that to this party who's been cheated out of his bluebird, a phone call to your wife would be a warm-up. He'd *start* with that.''

"You've simply *got* to call him off.''

"Only one thing that'll call him off, Henry, and that's this bird.''

There was the sound of a trash truck then, Orange Disposal Company making its twice-weekly rounds of commercial bins. Mrs. Biggs cocked her head, listening. "Sounds like they're out behind the bank, don't it?'' She clucked her tongue, as if it were a dirty shame. "A couple of minutes and they'll be scooping that bird, won't they?''

They *were* behind the bank. Henry watched the bin rising in the air, upending into the open mouth of the truck. Without saying another word he turned around and started across the library parking lot toward Coco's. If he cut through a couple of lots and up the alley, he could make it to the bins at the medical center ahead of the truck. There was too much at risk to hesitate now.

"Bring it over to the All-Niter,'' Mrs. Biggs shouted at him.

He waved in agreement and then put up his umbrella. Shaffer Street was running ankle-deep in water, and he was forced to slog through it. The rain fell harder, pounding down now, beating through the pine trees that shaded the restaurant. He heard the trash truck again, and looked back just as the thing rounded the corner, pulling in behind Coco's kitchen. Henry stepped up his pace, racing with the truck now, angling his umbrella back into the wind, letting it shove him along. He had gotten Walt into terribly deep water, carrying on about damnation like that, nearly *forcing* him to throw the damned jar away. "You'll ride to the Devil in comfort," he had told Walt, and now by God he had apparently delivered his poor nephew straight into the Devil's hands! Good intentions! Bentley was right; sometimes they weren't worth a handful of chicken scratch.

The brick enclosure around the trash bins loomed up ahead of him in the rain. The truck was nearly two blocks behind now. He had plenty of time. He would save Walt yet.

He rooted through the trash, yanking aside empty cartons and stuffed plastic sacks. Immediately he saw the salmon eggs that had gone bad, wrapped up in wet newspaper like a party popper. The bin was about half full, nearly the same as it had been yesterday. It was too deep, though, for him to reach to the bottom of it. He looked around the alley, spotting a couple of cinderblocks against the wall of the medical building, and he hurried across and dragged them over to the bin, one for each foot.

He was *sure* that Walt had stuffed the bird under a sack of trash at the left-hand corner, but by golly it wasn't there now. He yanked a sack out, dropping it onto the wet concrete, then heaved out three cardboard boxes and another sack. The damned thing was simply gone! There was the noise of the truck gearing up again, and he looked up the alley. The truck was bearing down on him. He pitched his umbrella into the hedge behind him and rooted around with both hands, through wet computer paper and old magazines and coffee grounds. Nothing. It simply wasn't there.

Puzzled, he stepped down off the blocks, realizing the truth. The bird was gone. Someone had taken it. The trash truck heaved to a stop, and a man stepped down off the running board and said something to him in Spanish, gesturing at the boxes and bags on the ground. Henry shook his head, having no idea what the man had said.

The man shrugged and started picking up the boxes on the ground, chucking them back into the bin. Henry bent over to help, but the man waved him away. "Is okay," he said. "No problema."

"No problema," Henry said to him, stepping back a couple of feet and watching for a moment, as if that were his duty. The man waved the truck forward, and Henry fetched his umbrella out of the hedge and headed up the street toward home, mulling the entire situation over in his mind.

So who had taken the jar out of the bin? A stranger? That didn't wash. The bird wasn't the kind of thing anybody would want.

It had to have been Walt.

Walt coveted the thing. He was under its spell. That had been evident yesterday, when he was going on about it, talking about bags full of money, trying to rationalize keeping the damned thing. This was what Bentley had tried to warn them about, and now the truth was crystal clear: Henry hadn't done *enough* to talk Walt out of it.

Maybe the best thing he could do now was to steal it back and give it to Maggie Biggs just like she said—let her murdering friends go to the Devil instead of poor Walter. Dollars to doughnuts it was back in the tackle box in the rafters—easy enough to take it back out again.

At home he climbed into the motor home. He was soaked, and before he caught his death he . . .

There was an envelope on the table. It was torn open, the contents gone. The return address paralyzed him with fear: it was from Myron Goldfarb, Jinx's lawyer friend. So Jinx had gone to Goldfarb! She intended to serve him with papers. She'd had enough of him at last.

Henry turned straight around and went back out into the rain. The least he could do was to save Walt before these monsters got to him, too. . . .

He heard the front door of the house bang shut. Nora, Eddie, and Walt came out and headed up the street. Henry watched them from behind the shrubbery at the edge of the porch, and when they were gone, he headed up the driveway toward the garage.

⊱ 48 ⊰

WALT LET THE KIDS GO FROM DOOR-TO-DOOR ALONE. IT WAS
nearly dusk, only fifteen or twenty minutes left till dark, but
he couldn't stop them from setting out on the fund drive for
Mrs. Simms. There was something endearing about them going
at it alone, like two guardian angels. He'd only be a fly in the
ointment if he went along. With any luck, he and Jinx could
kill the day tomorrow baking cookies for the neighbors.

He wondered suddenly if he were trying to salve his conscience with this thing. Well, so what if he was? It was good
for the kids, and good for Mrs. Simms, too. In fact, it was
probably good for Argyle—some kind of object lesson. Nora
and Eddie stepped down off the porch of the last house now,
turning to wave at old Mrs. Bord, who stood with her arms
folded, beaming at them. Eddie waved the order form at Walt.
By golly, they were doing it!

They headed up Maple Street, and Walt strolled down to
the corner to keep an eye on them. There were only a couple
of houses on Maple, and after that, if the day held up, they
could hit a couple more on Cambridge. . . .

An idea struck him just then, and he walked on down toward
the next corner, watching the kids knock on the door of the
Fillpots' house. No one would be home. Fillpot's Stationers,
down on Glassell, didn't close till six. "How's it going?" Walt
hollered at them.

Nora and Eddie stood on the sidewalk, looking uncertain
where to go next. "Three," Eddie said. He held up the order
form for Walt to take a look at—thirty bucks; that was ten
dollars a house! There were two checks and a ten-dollar bill.
Eddie gave Walt the money to hold. "I told the lady that
everybody was giving ten," he said.

"Good," Walt told him. "Keep it up. That's called sales-manship."

"I get three prizes," Nora said, making the rabbit face.

"Well, not quite," Walt said. "Not three prizes for each *kid*. What I meant was three prizes for each ten dollars. And if there's one extra prize, you'll have to share it."

"Oh," Nora said.

Walt pointed up the street, toward Argyle's house. "See that big house down there?"

"The *really* big one?" Eddie asked.

"That's right—with the big porch. That's where the millionaire lives, the rich man. It's getting late, but you've got time for one more house. Why don't you try that one?"

"*I'll* talk this time," Nora said, setting out up the sidewalk and trying to pull the order form out of Eddie's hand. He took off running, holding the form close to his chest where she couldn't get at it. She caught up to him at Argyle's porch and slugged him hard on the shoulder, then turned around and looked back at Walt, who shook his head at her. She and Eddie climbed the stairs and rang the bell.

Argyle's car was in the driveway, so he was probably home. If Bentley was right about him, then his reaction to the kids' homegrown "fund-raiser" would be interesting in about ten different ways. . . .

His door swung open and Walt stepped back away from the corner, moving out of sight behind the corner house. There was no use letting Argyle see him there; this shouldn't seem like a put-up job. After a moment he walked forward again and peeked down the street. They were just coming out through the door, and Nora was saying something to Argyle. She stopped suddenly, ran back to the open door, and he bent over so she could kiss him on the cheek. Then she ran off again, down the stairs and out to the sidewalk where both of them ran wildly toward the corner, Eddie carrying a check in his hand. Spotting Walt, Argyle waved cheerfully from the doorway, then disappeared back inside.

What the hell did *that* mean? That Argyle was being *gracious* about it? Walt nearly laughed out loud. The man had to be seething inside, confounded, wondering what this was all about. The best he could do was to put on a good face. His smile was some kind of terrible rictus. Maybe Walt could slip some arsenic into his raisin cookies tomorrow and just do away with him completely.

"It was Mr. Argyle!" Eddie shouted, out of breath from running.

"Really?" Walt said. "*The* Mr. Argyle?"

"From school!" Nora said. "He gave us *money*! Show him, Eddie! Oh, he's . . . !" She jigged with excitement, bouncing from one foot to the other. "He's such a good one!"

Eddie handed over Argyle's check, and Walt stared at it for a moment, unable to make immediate sense of it. He looked back down toward the house, but Argyle had gone back inside.

The check was for twenty thousand dollars, made out to Walt Stebbins.

"How many prizes is it?" Nora asked.

WALT SENT THE KIDS INSIDE AND HEADED STRAIGHT INTO THE garage where he tore the check to pieces, then threw the pieces into the tin pail, resisting the urge to spit on them. Argyle wasn't going to get away with it, whatever it was he was trying to get away with, him and his dirty money.

Walt packed boxes, crumpling newspaper and slamming the tape dispenser onto the box tops, zipping them shut, and slapping on mail labels. The afternoon had been a dead loss—first Maggie Biggs and then this damned encounter with Argyle. And that reminded him—tomorrow morning he had to fix the Biggsmobile! He ripped open a carton hard enough to tear half the flap loose. Inside lay a gross of bug catapults along with bags of rubber beetles. He shoved the box toward the garage door, separating it from the rest. Tomorrow he'd by God take it down to the preschool and hand a bug flinger out to every kid there. Every doggone one of them would get a prize. And not because they were day laborers, either, scraping together hatfuls of money for stinking creeps like Argyle, but because they were kids, damn it, and they *deserved* a prize.

Shit! The dirty son-of-a-bitch! Walt threw down the tape dispenser and kicked the leg of the bench. Argyle had done this on *purpose*, to throw it into their faces! First he murders Simms; then he turns the murder into a sort of monstrous joke, hosing everyone down with money. Well, it wouldn't wash. Twenty thousand bucks was *nothing* to Argyle. Argyle blew his nose on twenty thousand bucks. That's what this meant, wasn't it? The finger. Up yours.

He kicked the bench again, and his coffee mug fell over, spilling out a pool of cold coffee. And of *course* the check won't be any damn good anyway. The damned thing would have bounced over the moon, and Walt would have looked like some kind of criminal idiot.

The door swung open and Walt jumped. It was Ivy, smiling and happy, full of pep.

"What's this about a fund-raiser?" she asked. "Nora and Eddie are out of their minds with it." She came in and kissed him on the cheek.

Walt decided not to mention the Christmas wrap fund-raiser at all. "Just an idea I had. I wanted to put together a little something for Mrs. Simms."

"Well, I think that's wonderful. The kids are all full of talk about Robert Argyle. Nora tells me he gave them a million dollars."

"Not quite," Walt said. "Everything's a million dollars to Nora. You know how she is."

"How much, then?"

"Well, he wrote out a check, which I guess was a kind of joke. It pisses me off, too, because he obviously did it to needle me, and now the kids are all excited. I guess he didn't consider their feelings at all."

"What are you talking about?" The smile disappeared from her face.

"See for yourself." He gestured at the bucket, which was empty except for the torn-up check.

Ivy bent over and picked out the pieces, getting them about half arranged on the bench top before she made out the amount. She looked at him in disbelief.

"Obviously it's a joke," Walt said.

"A joke? Why would it be a joke?"

"Of *course* it's a joke. You don't know the whole story. Argyle's running this bogus fund-raiser at school. Get this, he drags in *thousands* of dollars with these scams, putting children to work selling worthless crap door to door. Then he spends the money on computer equipment and Lord knows what-all. I'm sorry, but I just wouldn't stand for it. I won't play the man's games."

"So you tore up a twenty-thousand-dollar check?"

"You're damned right I tore it up!"

"Don't cuss at me. Maybe you don't know this, but *every* school does fund-raisers."

"Non-profit schools, maybe. That makes sense. And that's what pisses me off. That's how he takes people, sending kids around. People trust the kids, and so they don't think anything through. Money for a good cause, they think, and they fork it over. They don't know that Argyle's a filthy rich hoser who's charging six prices already at his so-called school. He's making a *mint*. But he can't buy his own computer? The kids can't have a slide, for God's sake, unless they earn it themselves?" Walt shook his head. "What a stinking pig." He picked up the tape dispenser again, looking for another box to go after, but there was nothing more packed.

"I think we've drifted from the point," Ivy said evenly. "I don't know anything about Robert's so-called fund-raiser. What I *do* know is that you tore up Mrs. Simms's twenty thousand dollars and threw it in the trash."

"It isn't that easy."

"It isn't easy being Mrs. Simms right now, either."

"I've had a bad day, all right?"

"How bad was it?"

He gestured, unable to answer. He knew he'd been talking like a lunatic.

"Let me tell you about my day."

"Go ahead."

"I sold the property."

"Which one? I thought she already bought it."

"Who?"

"Mrs. Fabulous. I don't remember her name."

"You mean Linda Marvel. I don't mean that one. I mean the two commercial properties that Robert let me represent. Remember? I *must* have told you about it."

"All right, all right. Don't get sarcastic. Of course you told me about it."

"Because of Robert Argyle I—*we*—made something like *sixty thousand dollars* today."

"Bring it in here," Walt said, "I'll tear it up for you."

She stood there staring at him, as if for two cents she'd knock his teeth loose. After a moment she turned around and walked out.

❧ 49 ❧

"I'M SORRY," WALT SAID, SITTING DOWN AT THE FOOT OF the bed. "I was worked up. I lost my mind."

She didn't look up from her book. "Sorry is as sorry does."

"Yeah," he said. "I guess so." Clearly she was still pissed, saying insane things to avoid saying anything at all. "Anyway, I don't know why I tore up the check. I honestly thought it was some kind of . . . ploy, I guess."

"Ploy to accomplish *what*?" she asked after a long silence. "Do you really think he'd go to that length to humiliate you in some weird way that nobody but you can figure out? The truth is, he's not half as bad as you say he is."

"You don't know what you're saying."

"Do you?"

"I'm pretty sure."

"You're pretty sure. You're so pretty sure that you tore up Mrs. Simms's check?"

"What can I do about it now, tape it back together?"

"Take it back to Robert and ask for another check. It's easy."

"*Easy?*"

"Okay, *I'll* take it over there. *I'll* ask Robert to replace it."

"No," Walt said hastily. "I'll do it. I'll see him tomorrow morning anyway, at the preschool."

"I'd do it now."

"You're right. I'll do it now."

Walt walked out, down the stairs and into the family room, where Nora and Eddie sat on the floor playing "Uncle Wiggly."

"The Pipsawa nearly got me," Nora said.

"Pipsisewa," Eddie told her.

"Nuh-*uh*, Pipsawa."

"He nearly got me, too," Walt said. "I think he *did* get me."

Out in the garage he gathered up the pieces of the check, and, forcing himself not to think too much about where he was going, he set out down the driveway.

Then an idea came to him, and he turned around, heading back into the garage and climbing up into the rafters in order to yank out the tackle box. Argyle could have the phony parakeet after all, as payola for his generosity. He grinned at the thought of it. Climbing down, he set the box on the bench and opened the latch. The parakeet was gone.

He looked around. Nothing else in the garage was touched. There was no ransacking, no opened boxes. Whoever had taken it had known right where to look.

Bentley? Of course there was no way Bentley believed that Walt had thrown it away. He was too canny for that. Had he gotten the information out of Henry, the old man having revealed the bird's hiding place thinking it didn't matter anyway? Of course he had. Walt's anger drained away. Bentley was on a mission. And it was a *good* mission, too, even if it did involve stealing another man's bluebird.

He went outside, angling around into the backyard where he pried up the corner of the stepping-stone. The real bird was still under there, snug and happy. It occurred to him then that the dead parakeet scam had turned out to be genius after all: even if he wouldn't have a chance of working it on Argyle, he'd at least got to work it on Bentley.

He walked down the driveway now, and headed up the sidewalk toward the corner. When he got down to Cambridge Street he could see that the lights were on in Argyle's house, and his car was still in the driveway. He walked boldly up to the house and stepped up onto the porch, where he rang the bell. There was no use being timid about this whole thing. Argyle opened the door, blinked as if in puzzlement, and then smiled at him.

"I think this fund-raiser of yours is something else," he said immediately. "I wish I'd have thought of it myself."

"I bet you do," Walt said. "Actually, there's been a slight accident with the check that you wrote for the kids."

"I beg your pardon?"

"The check," Walt said. "It got torn up." He handed Argyle the pieces.

"This is astonishing," Argyle said. He shook his head, dumbfounded. "Enlighten me."

"Well, the truth is, it got put in with the junk mail by mistake. We've gotten a lot of crap, flyers and like that, shoved through the slot recently. And so it got torn up by mistake."

"I see." There was the hint of a leer on his face, and he nodded broadly.

"I wonder if you could write out another one," Walt said. "That is, if you're still in such a generous mood."

"Of course, of course." Argyle gestured toward the interior of the house. "Step inside?"

"I'll wait out here," Walt said.

"Good enough. Checkbook's still sitting here by the door." He turned away to pick up the checkbook, opened it up, and started scribbling in it with a pen.

"Why don't you make it out directly to Mrs. Simms?" Walt said.

"Oh, I don't want that." Argyle waved the idea away. "I don't want any mention of *me* at all. Put this in the general fund along with the rest. How much have you collected so far?"

"Quite a bit," Walt said. "The world's a generous place when you give it half a chance."

"We agree on that," Argyle said. He handed the check over to Walt. "There you go. Take better care of this one, eh?" He started to shut the door.

"Oh, oh," Walt said, looking it over. "Wait. Date's wrong. That's *last* year." He pointed at the miswritten date. "I don't know if the bank will go for that. It looks like the check's a year old."

"I'll be damned," Argyle said. "Let me have it back." He scratched at the check with his pen, then handed it over again, winking at Walt. "Good as new." He shut the door this time.

The date was corrected and initialed, but now Walt saw that the quantity was wrong. The comma was in the right place, but there were only three zeroes instead of four, so that it almost looked like twenty dollars, except with a couple of superfluous zeroes hovering off to the side. Walt was struck with the sudden notion that Argyle was doing this on purpose.

He knocked on the door, and Argyle answered immediately, as if he'd been waiting there.

"Yes?" Argyle asked, wrinkling his forehead with doubt and surprise.

"What's the amount here?" Walt asked. "The comma seems . . ."

"Why, let's see." He took the check again. "*Very* perceptive," he said. "But you always were good with numbers, eh? *Here* we go . . ." He touched up the check again and handed it back.

"And I think you forgot your last name," Walt said, blocking the door with his foot now. The signature read simply "Robert P."

"Forgotten my *name*?"

"Here on the signature."

"Well I'll be . . . *Aren't* I something!" He took the check again. "*Un*believable."

Hit him now, Walt thought—a haymaker to the belly while he messes with the check again, then work him over good while he's on his hands and knees. . . .

Argyle gave him back the check. "Everything's shipshape now, Cap'n," he said, winking again. He clicked his feet together and saluted.

Walt stared at him, leaving his foot in the door. "Looks like they'll catch the dirty little creep who sabotaged the church bells after all," he said.

"That *is* good news." Argyle furrowed up his face with concern, glancing unhappily at Walt's foot.

"Positive I.D.," Walt said. "Someone saw the bastard on the church roof, apparently. Police thought it was Murray LeRoy at first, but this new evidence changes all that. This was some other pathetic little shithead. They figure it's the same one that's been vandalizing the neighborhood, writing poo-poo words on walls with a brown crayon. Apparently he's *seriously* Freudian, if you follow me."

Argyle didn't flinch. "I'm sure it'll go hard on him if they catch him. And I believe your foot's in my door."

"I imagine they'll throw away the key," Walt said, shaking his head. "What a stinking geek, don't you think?"

"I couldn't agree with you more."

"Lowest kind of rat-eating scum, wouldn't you say?"

"Amen." Argyle's face was a mask of barely disguised loathing now.

"A man like that blows like big rats," Walt said, "if you can call him a man at all, which I can't. Personally I call him a treacherous, pig-faced, insect-brained, murdering piece of dog waste. Isn't that what you call him?"

"First chance I get," Argyle said. "And now really, Walt, I don't want to hold you up. It's been *very* nice talking to you."

"Maybe I haven't made myself clear," Walt said. "This dipshit who murdered Simms . . ."

And just then Father Mahoney's bells started to ring again. It was time for the nightly round of carols. Argyle suddenly looked as if he'd been poleaxed. Walt smiled big at him and put his hand to his ear theatrically. "Hark!" he said. "The tintinnabulation of the bells!"

Argyle thrust out his hand, pushing Walt solidly in the chest, and Walt backpedaled a step before getting his balance. In that moment the door slammed shut and there was the sound of a dead bolt striking. For a second Walt considered lifting the brass flap on the mail slot and shouting more insults into the interior of the house, but he turned around instead, walking away toward the corner. He glanced back to see if Argyle was watching him, but apparently the creature had slunk back into its den. Tolerably well satisfied, Walt headed for home.

❧ 50 ❧

IVY WAS TALKING TO DARLA ON THE TELEPHONE. WALT HAD already talked to her once that evening. She had called earlier to speak to Nora and Eddie. That had been a productive call. Afterward Nora had cried for ten minutes. Now Darla had called back to talk to Ivy again, trying hard to make sense of suddenly finding herself a couple of thousand miles from home. Flying back to Michigan ought to have clarified something, given her life direction, but so far it hadn't.

Walt couldn't puzzle Darla out. She apparently missed the kids so much she could hardly stand it, but she couldn't come home right now because she needed to "find herself." Walt imagined her fumbling through coats in a dark closet with a tiny flashlight, certain she was in there someplace. She had a duty as a *mother*, she had told Walt tearfully, but her first duty was to herself, because if she didn't love herself, then she couldn't really love anything, could she? Except of course she had loved Jack, she said, but he turned into a worthless son-of-a-bitch.

She had carried on this way for ten minutes, weeping like a faucet until Walt had wanted to tell her to shut the hell up. But then it had occurred to him, like a knock on the head, that in some terribly real sense, Darla *couldn't* shut the hell up. She couldn't help herself, not right now. That's what she was talking about, even if she didn't quite know it. He had been thinking that she was *pretending* somehow, that this was all weakness and theater, that if she wanted to she could just cut it out, straighten up and fly right. But what if she wasn't pretending at all? What if all of it was simply *true*, and that was the ghastly horror of it? The gulf between what Darla needed and what she possessed was so broad that she couldn't navigate it, not in the leaky little rowboat she'd put to sea in.

Maybe the truth was that *all* of them—himself, the kids, Uncle Henry, Mrs. Biggs, even Argyle—were bailing like sixty, trying to stay afloat in their sorry little tubs.

"Where?" he heard Ivy ask now. "A chiropractic office? Is it good money?" She nodded, looking at Walt and making a face. "He's a what? A nutritionist? Not right now, I guess. I don't think Walt would want any vitamin supplements. How much? I'll tell him. Okay, sure," she said. "Take care." She hung up. "It looks like she's got a job, but no place to live," she said to Walt. "If you want, you can subscribe to a line of vitamin supplements. This chiropractor is looking for a west coast rep. You can buy a sales kit for five hundred dollars."

"Don't let her talk to Henry."

Ivy rolled her eyes. "She sounds like she's down in the dumps."

"So we've got Nora and Eddie for Christmas?"

"I get the feeling we've got Nora and Eddie till further notice, unless we want to hand them over to Jack, which I don't think we do. Darla tells me that Jack was a little rough with Eddie a few times. That's what she said, 'a little rough.' "

"What does she mean, 'rough'? Did Jack beat him up?" Walt sat up in bed. He felt his face get hot.

"Your guess is as good as mine."

"Well, then he better not come around here anymore, because if he does I'm going to ask him about it."

"What do you mean, *ask* him?"

"Simple question before I hit him."

"Don't start fighting with Jack, for God's sake."

Walt didn't say anything. His mind had descended into a dark place, and he pictured Jack lurching up the front walk toward the house again, making demands. He half wanted the phone to ring right now. Sure, Jack, come the hell on over- . . . . Then step out of the dark with a fist full of dimes and make everything clear to him.

He realized suddenly that he'd never been this pissed off about anything in his life. Calm down, he thought, don't have a coronary. His heart was going like sixty.

"It's poison to sit there and dwell on this," Ivy said. "Lie down. We don't know anything for sure about what Jack did or didn't do. And it's not going to help Eddie for you to fly off the handle. If you want to help Eddie, there's better ways to do it."

"I know."

"Because Eddie might just depend on you in some way you can't foresee right now, and if you . . ."

"Okay, okay. I'm all right. I'm not going to hunt Jack down and kill him. But I think that if we're going to do something to fix his hash, we ought to do it. Because if it comes down to it, I'm not sure I care what's legal and what's not legal when it comes to Nora and Eddie. I think I could break the law, especially if it meant breaking that bastard's nose."

"Don't keep thinking about breaking someone's nose. You're worked up."

"Well, of course I am. It's the kids. Jack can insult me up one side and down the other and I'll laugh in his face, but he's going to damn well leave Nora and Eddie alone."

"*Listen* to you. You've gone crazy," Ivy said. "Head over heels. You're all of a sudden a sucker for kids. You've been handing me this line all this time, being rational, and it turns out you're custom-built, out-of-your-mind father material."

"Yeah, yeah, yeah. Take advantage of my better nature. Go ahead. I'm used to it."

Ivy switched the light out, and together they pulled the blankets up under their chins. Walt lay there staring at the ceiling, which was faintly illuminated by the light at the bottom of the stairs. They left the light on routinely now, just in case Nora and Eddie had to come up in the middle of the night because of bugs or something.

Routinely . . . After three days it was routine? He was already *used* to that light. How had it happened so quickly?

"Anyway, I was telling you about the lots over on Batavia?"

"That's right," Walt said. "That went okay?"

"It was amazing," Ivy said. "Actually it was pretty weird. Good weird. I was out there looking things over, and this giant man appeared and started measuring the size of the lots."

"A giant man?" Walt asked. "How many eyes did he have?"

"How many eyes? What are you talking about?"

"I thought maybe he was a cyclops."

"He had two eyes. It turned out he'd already made his mind

up. He wanted *both* of the lots. I walked straight into it.''

"You deserve a little luck," Walt said. "You work hard.''

"So do you. We both work hard. And this is *our* luck, isn't it?''

"Sure," Walt said. "But I'd like to contribute a little bit of it once in a while, too. Especially around Christmas.''

"Don't be so hard on yourself," she said. "And anyway, Mr. Peetenpaul's in charge of making Christmas green this year. We can lean on the MasterCard and take care of it later when Mr. Peentenpaul antes up the cash.''

"Pete 'n Paul?''

"The giant man who's buying the lots.''

"That *can't* be his name. He sounds like a Mounds bar.''

"He's eaten a few, I think. I guess it's a Dutch name—all one word, Peetenpaul. He says to call him Mr. Peet. He's got this voice like you wouldn't believe, like he eats sandpaper.''

"How big?" Walt asked, suddenly suspicious—the size, the voice, the impossible name. . . .

"I don't know. A couple inches taller than you, I guess.''

"Grizzly-looking guy, with a beard? He wasn't dressed like a postman, was he?''

"A postman? No. Why do you ask? Why would he be dressed like a postman, for God's sake?''

"Nothing. No reason. It sounded like someone I know, that's all.''

"You know a giant postman?''

"Met one recently.''

"Well, this was no postman. He was driving a pickup truck, but it was new and expensive. He was dressed for the office, too—very stylish for such a big man. I guess you could say he was overdressed.''

"Like he was playing a role?''

"What are you talking about?''

"Nothing.''

They lay there in the darkness. Walt listened to the rain ping against the sheet-metal chimney cap. The sound of the droplets radiated down through the flue so that it sounded like it was raining in the bedroom itself.

"What are you thinking about?" she asked him suddenly.

"I'm thinking that the Lotto's sixty million dollars tonight. I'd like to win. I'd spend the money like an idiot.''

"If our special numbers came up, and you didn't have a ticket, what would you do?"

"I dunno. Curse my fate, I guess. Then later I'd tell the story every chance I got. What it would do is turn me into a bore."

"You wouldn't jump out of a window?"

"Not over money."

"Good." She was silent for a moment. Then she asked, "What *would* make you jump out of a window?"

"Shame," he said, not having to think twice about it. "If I was Jack I'd jump out a window."

"If you were Jack, you wouldn't have any shame." For a moment she didn't say anything, then she said, "So did you buy a ticket?"

"A ticket?"

"For the Lotto."

"Sure," Walt said. "No quick-pick, just our lucky numbers. You don't want to dilute your luck when there's big money on the line."

"Good thinking," she said.

After another few minutes of silence he realized that Ivy was asleep, her breathing regular and soft. The house was quiet except for the sound of the rain. His thoughts slowly turned in his head, thoughts about winning the Lotto, about found money in a sack. Lots of money. Sixty million iron men. What was that worth, fractioned out over whatever it was—twenty years? He pictured Henry and Jinx back in Honolulu again, decked out in aloha clothes and leis and wearing go-aheads from Long's Drugs, listening to Don Ho music on a Friday night in Waikiki. Palm trees, trade winds, the scent of flowers on the air. . . .

Money: what was it but a means to an end? It was a door, wasn't it? Why treat it like a poisonous snake? You open the door and step through, into Oz or Candyland or somewhere.

He thought about the bluebird, buried out under the stepping-stone, down in the dirt with the ants and the earthworms. "Sixty bucks," he whispered. In his mind he made it a wish. It was easier than he thought, just like with the lingerie this afternoon. A thrill ran through him, a shudder.

That's all, just the sixty-dollar win. What was that?—four measly numbers in the Lotto? Sixty lousy dollars would just about pay him back for what Mrs. Biggs had taken him for. He wouldn't be greedy. And it was safe enough for a simple test. The odds against winning it without help were tremendous. The odds of *calling* your win must be nearly infinitely bad.

So if he won, he would know, absolutely, and he would resign himself . . .

. . . he would resign himself to making a decision. And you didn't make that kind of decision unless you were sure of yourself.

"You'll ride to the Devil in comfort."

He heard Henry's voice in his mind.

And then, for no reason at all, he suddenly recalled watching Nora and Eddie say their prayers before going to bed, God-blessing Mr. Argyle along with everyone else.

How long had it been since Walt had said his prayers?

He was struck with the uncanny idea that he just had—but to whom?

He pushed the idea out of his mind, then turned over to go to sleep.

PART THREE

❧ ❧

All the Bells on Earth

And all the bells on earth did ring,
on Christmas Day in the morning. . . .

"I SAW THREE SHIPS A-SAILING"
TRADITIONAL CHRISTMAS CAROL

☙ 51 ☙

MAHONEY AND BENTLEY HEADED UP SHAFFER STREET toward the Holy Spirit Catholic Church. Bentley was dog-tired.
They'd been out since eight o'clock, bell-ringing through the
neighborhoods. The wind was blowing hard, and the sky was
wild, the clouds torn to pieces by the wind, scattered stars
winking and blinking in the clear parts.

"There's Orion." Mahoney pointed his finger at the heavens.

Bentley looked, but he couldn't make anything out. "I'll
take your word for it," he said. "I never could see constell-
ations. I suspect they're a hoax. I can spot the dipper and the
Seven Sisters, which might as well be seven anything—the
Seven Santini Brothers."

"That attitude's a pity," Mahoney said. "Sometimes I
imagine they're celestial seashells arranged on a beach."

"That's real artistic," Bentley said. "I admire that kind of
talk."

Mahoney squinted one eye at him and took something out
of his pocket. "Nip?"

"Pardon me?"

The priest held out a silver pint flask. "Scotch? Little belt
after a long night's work?"

"No," Bentley said, waving it away. "Thanks, but I guess
not."

"Well, fine." Mahoney tilted a swallow down his throat
and put the flask back into his coat. "Teetotaler, eh?"

"You make it sound like a crime."

"You make it sound like a virtue."

"Well, it comes tolerably close to being a virtue. But, no,

I'm not a teetotaler. I used to take a drink now and then, in company.''

"This liquor," Mahoney said, tapping the flask with his finger, "is what they call a single malt Scotch."

"Don't patronize me," Bentley said, listening to their footfalls on the sidewalk. "I know what malt Scotch is."

The rain began to fall now, and without saying another word both of them set off jogging toward the church, cutting across the street toward a rear door. Mahoney hauled a key ring out of his pocket and unlocked the dead bolt, letting them both into the sacristy.

"Man, that's rain!" Bentley said. Father Mahoney hauled off his dripping trenchcoat and hung it on a peg in the vestibule, then unhitched the bells from around his waist and set them on the desk along with his Benedictus bell. Bentley did the same. The rain poured down outside, drumming against the plywood cutouts that filled the two window arches where the stained glass had been removed for repair. The room smelled of fresh paint.

"So you're a Scotch man?" the priest said, sitting down at the desk. He waved at a nearby chair, and Bentley dragged it across and sat down, too.

"Used to be a Scotch man. I'm descended from John Knox."

"Is that a fact?" Mahoney said. "The Presbyter himself? *Good* for you. I'll take a small drink in honor of your illustrious ancestor despite what we all know about him."

"Scourge of the Papists," Bentley said. "Maybe I'll take one little blast, in recollection of how your crowd turned a good man into a galley slave." He took the flask and poured a swallow down his throat, wishing he had something in his stomach.

Mahoney nodded and took the flask back. "The thing is," he said, "when you're using Protestants as galley slaves, you need a *lot* of them—half a dozen to an oar. Knox wasn't worth much when it came to real labor. He was mainly a talker." Mahoney put his feet on the desk and yanked at his collar, loosening it up.

"Well, he was a *good* talker," Bentley said. "He changed it all, the whole course of human destiny. The whole megillah."

"Magilla Gorilla," Mahoney said, nodding somberly and tasting the Scotch again.

Bentley took the flask from him, and for a time they sat there in silence, passing it back and forth. Bentley abruptly felt tremendously tired, worn out, and the Scotch had the effect of a hot bath on his muscles. "Here's to all the people out there," he said finally, "who are doing the best they damn well can."

"Amen," Mahoney said.

Bentley felt the whiskey in his guts now, like a living heat, and he moved his shoulders to loosen up.

"John Knox wore bobby sox," Mahoney said, giggling.

Bentley snickered, then glared at him theatrically. Then, in his best Bing Crosby impersonation, he sang, "Too-ra-loo-ra-loo-ral . . ." and then cut it off and snickered again. His teeth felt rubbery, and his head was heavy. He turned the flask over and pretended to read something on the bottom. "The Pep Boys," he said. "Well, I'll be dipped in a sack of dung, that's a high-class flask." He winked, handing it back to Mahoney.

The phone rang then—two rings, then nothing. Bentley stood blinking at it for a moment, suddenly regretting the Scotch.

"He's moving," Bentley said. He stepped across and switched off the light. The sudden darkness seemed to amplify the sound of the rain, and for a moment neither man spoke. Light from the garden lanterns filtered in through the two remaining windows, casting a dim, rainy shadow onto the linoleum floor.

"He won't come here," Father Mahoney said. "Not as early as this."

"Maybe," Bentley said. "But we ought to be ready for him anyway. He knows we're moving against him in earnest now. Edna Hepplewhite is staying with Mrs. Simms, up near Pitcher Park. If he turns up Almond, past the park, she'll . . ."

The phone rang again—one ring and then silence.

"That's Edna!" Bentley said. "That's the signal. Argyle just passed the Simms place. He's making his rounds. You're probably right about him not coming here, but we'd better get up there into the tower anyway and wait for the go-ahead." Bentley swung the sacristy door open. Through the hallway window the rainy street shone in the glow of the streetlamps.

It wasn't even midnight. Argyle would have to be a desperate man to break into the bell tower now. How desperate was he? Bentley half wished that he had a baseball bat instead of a Polaroid camera.

"Front door locked?" Bentley kept his voice low even though there was no one except Mahoney to hear him.

"Locked but not bolted. He can get in with a credit card if he wants to. We'll leave this one the same." Father Mahoney picked up the two cameras waiting on the desk along with a couple of penlights. He handed one of each to Bentley. Then the two of them set out through the darkened church, heading toward the door that led into the bell tower.

Bentley shivered. He felt a little sick to his stomach.

"Top or bottom?" Bentley asked.

"Top, I guess," Mahoney said. "Unless you want it."

"Well, I'm a younger man."

"Yeah, but you're tired," Mahoney said. "You don't eat enough fish and you drink too much."

"Yeah, but if he kills me I don't mind. I'm right with the Lord. You, on the other hand, have a lot to atone for, being Catholic."

"Probably you're right," Father Mahoney said, smiling and winking. "But if he kills you, at least there'll be a priest standing by to steer your soul toward heaven. If he kills me there won't be anybody around but a Protestant."

"That's right," Bentley said. "A *live* one. Go ahead on up. You know the drill."

"I know the drill," Mahoney said. "You hold up your end. I'll be fine."

"How long will we give him?"

"An hour?"

"An hour it is. For heaven's sake, don't fall asleep either. And if the phone rings three times, it'll be Edna calling to say Argyle's gone home. That's the all-clear."

"Good enough," Mahoney said. He turned around and opened the tower door, shining his penlight on the ladder. He stepped inside and climbed slowly up into the darkness. Bentley swung the door shut, the hinges creaking, then turned around and slipped into the little broom closet next to the tower door. He switched on the penlight and sat down in the kitchen chair that he'd put there earlier, then shined the penlight around to get his bearings before switching the light out. Even the faintest light under the door would scare Argyle off. Or worse. He put the penlight into his shirt pocket and lay the camera in his lap, wishing that the chair had a cushion on it.

Minutes passed. He strained to listen in the darkness. He could hear water gurgling through a gutter somewhere beyond the wall and a steady, slow drip every twenty seconds or so, like rain leaking through the roof onto the ceiling above his head. After what seemed a long time, he took out the penlight and shined it on his watch, counting off the moments as the second hand revolved around the watch face. It would be a long old haul sitting here in the darkness for an hour. At least up in the tower Mahoney had something to look at. . . .

He heard a footstep out in the church, and he held his breath, listening. The camera! He'd been fooling away his time when he should have been planning things out. He strained to hear something more, but now there was only silence and rain. Then there were footfalls again, closer now, and quiet—soft-soled shoes, someone creeping along. Up in the tower Mahoney wouldn't hear him, but he might easily have seen him pull in off the street.

There was silence again. Had Argyle seen something, some sign that they were there? Throw the door open and shoot, Bentley thought, before he gets spooked and runs.

He felt the front of the camera with his fingers, found the trigger, and started to stand up. The chair slid backward a half inch with a soft scraping sound, and Bentley froze, listening.

There was still movement out in the church, and then the sound of hinges creaking. The tower door! Argyle was going up the ladder!

Keeping his finger on the camera trigger, Bentley counted off ten seconds, then, fearfully slowly, he opened the door and peered around it. Sure enough, the tower door stood wide open. There was no sign of anyone inside. Bentley creeped forward, looking through the viewfinder, centering the doorway and ready to shoot. The bastard was on the ladder, all right. He could hear his shoe soles scraping on the rungs.

He waited for the flash from Mahoney's camera. Now! he thought. Take it now! Had the priest fallen asleep up there? Bentley edged closer to the open door, ready for Argyle to burst through and rush at him. A moment passed. He couldn't stand it. He stepped into the tower and looked up into the darkness.

Argyle was on the ladder, nearly to the top! Bentley aimed the Polaroid up the ladder, and just then the tower lit up in a blinding flash of light. He pressed his finger on the camera trigger, setting off his own flash. Through the viewfinder he saw something rushing down at him, and instinctively he threw his hands up, letting go of the camera just as Argyle slammed into him, crushing him to the floor. He flung his hands out, grabbing a leg, and grunted when Argyle stood up, stepping on his stomach. He held on, twisting the leg, trying to throw him, and right then he caught a glimpse of moonlight in the tower above and Mahoney's silhouette as the priest swung down onto the ladder, coming to help. Argyle's foot pressed into his cheek, grinding his head into the floor. He let go of the leg, and Argyle stepped away, kicking him once in the ribs before stepping out through the door, which slammed shut. Bentley pushed himself up onto his hands and knees just as Father Mahoney stepped down heavily onto his back in the darkness.

"What?" the priest shouted. "Is it you?"

"Of *course* it's me," Bentley said. "Don't *pul*verize me!" He stood up, breathing heavily and groping for the door handle. He found the latch and pushed. The door skidded open a quarter of an inch and then jammed. Bentley yanked it shut and threw it open again, pitching his shoulder into it. Then he yanked it shut hard again. There was the sound of something sliding, and a heavy object slammed into the door—a pew, probably. Bentley flung himself into the door, but it wouldn't budge at all now. They were trapped.

"Give me a hand here," he said to Mahoney. "Maybe together . . ."

There was the sound of guttural laughter, and Bentley put his ear to the panel. At that moment there was a flickering light from the crack beneath the door, and a burning slip of paper slid through—a couple of pages torn out of a hymnal.

Bentley stomped it out, and yelled, "Listen!" at the closed door. But there was laughter again, and now a curling tendril of smoke wisped up into the tower.

"Holy Mother of God," Bentley whispered, turning toward the priest. "He means to burn us down!"

❧ 52 ❧

"GRAB THESE PHOTOS," BENTLEY SAID, BENDING OVER AND pressing his ear to the door. Smoke drifted upward in a sheet now, and he could hear the crackling sound of the fire.

Father Mahoney retrieved the two snapshots that the cameras had spit out, along with the camera itself, which lay on the floor where Bentley had dropped it. He started awkwardly up the ladder, holding onto the camera and the rungs both, and Bentley started up behind him, hand over hand. Halfway up the camera slipped, falling ten feet to the floor where it smashed into several pieces. Mahoney stopped and looked down, and Bentley shouted, "It's junk! Leave it!" and pushed on the priest's calf, hurrying him up.

Mahoney stepped clear of the ladder, and Bentley followed him onto the little landing that encircled the single bell. The windows on the four sides of the tower were covered with angled wooden slats, and Bentley had to look down through them to see the street. At the Church of the Holy Spirit, the bell was used only to toll the hours of the day. Above, hidden in the top of the tower, were four loudspeakers, which broadcast tape-recorded hymns and Christmas carols. Apparently it didn't matter that the bells were recorded and not played live. Devils and their minions couldn't appreciate the difference. They didn't have any kind of ear for it.

"We're safe up here," Bentley said, "at least for now. Let's see those photos."

Mahoney took them out and shined the penlight onto one of them. For a moment Bentley thought that it was blank, but then he saw that it had some vague out-of-focus color to it— probably tan trousers. He had managed to snap a picture of Argyle's rear end, just about to fall on him. "Give me some light on the other one,'' Bentley said, taking the second photo from Mahoney and holding it up.

"Got him," the priest said, illuminating the face in the photo.

Bentley's breath caught in his throat. The upturned face was hideous. It was Argyle all right, although it might have easily been Argyle's animated corpse. His eyes were rolled back, like the eyes of a dead man, and there was something drawn on his forehead—something unintelligible, scrawled on as if with a soft crayon and then smeared. His mouth was wide open, and his teeth were streaked with black, as if he'd been eating burned things.

Bentley nearly dropped the photo down the well, just to get it out of his hands, and at that moment he saw that he was wrong about being safe in the brick tower: dense smoke rose around them now, and it was noticeably warmer. Mahoney coughed, breathing through his coat. He took the photo and shoved both of them into his coat. Bentley grabbed one of the slats in the window arch and jerked at it. At the bottom of the arch the ends were slid into grooves, like the panes in a louvered window. He wiggled one out of its groove and dropped it onto the floor of the tower. Now there was enough open space to get his hands in, and he yanked out four more, so that they had a ventilation and a view. The wind gusted through the opening, but somehow, just when they needed it in buckets, the rain had let up.

"Let's wake someone up," Father Mahoney said. He cupped his hands around his mouth and shouted "Help!" at the empty street, but the wind, shuddering through the tower, blew the words away as if they were leaves.

"He-elp!" Bentley yelled. "Fire!" But it was pointless, like yelling under water. He felt thick-headed and stodgy from the Scotch, as if his blood were half congealed, and he remembered now why he didn't drink. Of all the nights to throw caution to the damned wind!

The smoke was suddenly thicker, and Bentley's eyes smarted. He thrust his head out through the hole he'd made in the side of the tower, sucking in the rainy air. There was a noticeable crackling now, and smoke gusted up the well. We'll asphyxiate, Bentley thought. We're dead. Argyle has murdered us, too.

"Tear these out of here," Bentley shouted, and immediately yanked out more slats, dropping them down onto the ground. Mahoney pulled a couple out, and in a moment they were looking straight down at the lawn below. Bentley was suddenly dizzy, and he held on tight to the window frame. There was a ledge outside, a foot-wide brick frieze a couple of feet below the line of the roof. There was the yellow glow of the fire behind them now—the ladder burning, the tower door, wood paneling—and the wind through the hole they'd made seemed to feed the fire.

"Out," Bentley said. "Hold onto my hand and step out onto the ledge where you can hold onto the roof."

Mahoney squeezed his shoulder in a gesture of thanks and bent out through the arch without a word. He stood teetering there, gripping Bentley's wrist like a vise, looking down at the lawn and the street.

"Grab the roof!" Bentley yelled, but Mahoney waved his free arm wildly, trying to balance himself, knocking his spectacles off and bending forward at the waist. Bentley, holding on tight to the edge of the window, and with the toe of one shoe wedged under the sill, swung himself out into the air like a man swinging around a post. With the hand that held Mahoney's wrist, he thrust forward hard, shoving the priest backward and onto the roof.

Mahoney shouted, releasing his grip on Bentley's wrist, his arms flailing, and sat down across the curb that ran around the perimeter of the roof. His feet flew upward and his rear end landed in the dark water pooled in the rain gutter. Bentley followed him, scrambling out onto the ledge and over the curb without looking down.

"Are you all right?" he asked the priest, who pulled himself out of the water and sat down.

"I . . . Yes," Mahoney said. He put a hand on his chest and heaved a deep breath.

Smoke poured out of the open arch now and threaded out between the wooden slats. "I thought you were going down for a moment," Bentley said. "I couldn't think of anything else but to push you over backward."

"I'm fine. That was . . . that was close. Thank you."

"Is there a roof access door?"

Mahoney shook his head. "We keep it padlocked underneath."

There was a ringing sound somewhere below, and by the time Bentley realized what it was, it had stopped—three rings, the all-clear from Mrs. Hepplewhite. Argyle had gotten home safe.

At that moment there was the sound of a siren, and Bentley could see a paramedics truck and a hook and ladder pulling around a distant corner, heading toward them up Almond Street. They were saved.

Mahoney took the two Polaroid snaps out of his coat. "We've got him dead to rights," he said. "What do we do?"

"Save it," Bentley said, taking the photos. "At least until tomorrow or the day after. I want to talk to him first. It's my duty. That's the face of an insane man, and it was me who set him down that path. I'm going to pay him a visit. I'm going to shake him up."

❧ 53 ❧

WALT LOOKED AROUND FOR THE NEWSPAPER, WHICH WOULD have last night's Lotto numbers in it, but it was too late, past seven, and Henry had long since grabbed it.

He climbed into the Suburban and headed for Satellite Market, wondering what he would find. Would the bluebird pay off? Part of him wanted to throw the ticket into the trash without looking at it, and not even check the winning numbers. But it was too late to think about that now. Ivy would check the numbers herself, and then she would ask him where the ticket was.

There was something about actually knowing the results, though, that was a little like the knowledge of good and evil, biblically speaking. It was a thing better left unknown, he told himself. But there was the market, looming up on the right, and he pulled into the nearly empty parking lot, got out of the truck, and went inside. Toni, the woman who worked the liquor counter, was just opening up, and the Lotto machine wasn't switched on yet, so he browsed through the racks of liquor, idly looking at the bottles of flavored gin and oddball creme de menthes.

Then abruptly he turned around and walked outside again, where he stood on the asphalt and looked up at the cloudy sky and at the foil Christmas garland strung across Chapman Avenue between the streetlamps.

Of course Henry had been right. Walt saw it all clearly—a real insight. This was no good, this wishing on a bluebird. Once you started to develop an interest in damnable things, the interest was liable to grow like a milkweed vine until it strangled you. One day you're satisfied with sixty bucks, and the next day you're Nebuchadnezzar or somebody, King of

Babylon, and all you've bought for yourself is regret.

He went back into the store, his mind made up and made up solidly. He would look this demon in the face, size it up, and knock it down like a pot-metal milk bottle.

"Big winner?" Toni asked, taking the ticket from him.

"Just might be."

She slipped it into the slot in the machine, which sucked it in, whirred a little bit, and spit it back out.

"Sixty dollars!" she said, handing him the winning ticket so he could see for himself.

He found that he couldn't speak. He took the ticket but didn't look at it. It was all true. What he feared had been proven true. The bluebird was *exactly* what it was advertised to be. Maybe that made it a demon, like Bentley thought it was. And here he'd been playing around with it, turning it into a prank to goad Argyle.

Use it against him. The sentence drifted unbidden into his thoughts, but he pushed it away, thinking about Sidney Vest despite himself, about being cavalier with the damned bluebird, making ignorant wishes on it. . . .

And immediately that thought was replaced by another sort of knowledge—that he was rich, incalculably, infinitely rich. Once again he pictured the paper sack with a million dollars in it, but the million dollars was nothing now; it was like finding an old tuna sandwich. A billion was more like it, if they made sacks that large. His spirits soared and he nearly laughed out loud.

Toni handed him three twenties, and he nodded at her, then wandered away toward the liquor racks again, clutching his money. He stared at nothing, not daring to look at the bills in his hand just in case they wouldn't be bills at all, but would be slips of newspaper or something, and this whole thing was nothing but a dream.

He shut his eyes hard, opened them again, and looked. It was three twenties, all right. He wasn't asleep.

It dawned on him then that he was already wasting time. He could as easily already have won the sixty million as the sixty. What would he have to do to accumulate sixty million in Lotto jackpots now? The usual return was a measly three million a week, so that meant twenty weeks of winning. But of course they'd arrest him after he won the third time. He'd get away with winning twice—twice was a fluke. But the third time they'd smell a rat, and they'd round him up. What then? Would he be doomed? Why, no. He'd call in the bluebird. The thought was exhilarating and terrifying both. The world was suddenly his oyster. What would it be? Television appearances? Public speeches? Limousines? A house the size of the state of Maine? He laughed, giddy with the idea of limitless wealth.

He had no idea how to spend money! That was the truth of it. He was a piker, a lightweight, a hayseed. Could he learn fast enough? Of course the first thing was to buy Argyle out, lock, stock, and barrel, and then have him publicly humiliated in the Plaza, dressed up like an organ grinder's monkey. The bluebird would make it seem right and natural to people. They'd throw rotten fruit, eggs. . . . Hell, it *was* right and natural.

Suddenly there came into his mind a picture of Nora bringing the shackled Argyle a cup of water, a look of profound sadness on her face. Instantly he was ashamed of himself. He unclutched his hand and dropped the twenties onto the floor.

For a moment there he'd gone nearly crazy! That's what Henry had been talking about! He took a deep breath. Well, to hell with that. He would leave the bills right there on the floor, like lucky pennies, for somebody else to find. He would walk away from them, from the whole shebang. From now on he'd despise wealth like a Hindu.

And this time he wouldn't just throw the damned jar in the bin either; he'd break it to pieces, dump the gin out onto the ground, put the bluebird in a paint can and pound the lid down and haul it out to the dump where he'd pitch it under the wheels of an earth-moving vehicle.

Yes, his mind was made up for good and all, and he felt suddenly better. A minute ago he'd been drunk with anticipation, with the love of money, but now he saw the futility in it. He looked at the twenties scattered at his feet. . . .

What the hell, there was no reason not to take them after all, a pitiful little sum like that. But thank God he hadn't asked for the sixty million! Sixty dollars was different. It was simply the money he was owed from yesterday. How could there be any sin in breaking even? He didn't look for an answer.

"Well, for the love of Mike," someone said just then, "it's starting to look like the whole damn gang!"

The voice belonged unmistakably to Mrs. Biggs. Walt bent over now and picked up the twenties, then turned slowly around. It was her, all right. She stood grinning at him, holding onto the Reverend Bentley through the crook of his arm. Bentley looked like hell, unshaven, his hair a wreck, eyes bloodshot, and wearing the same clothes he'd worn yesterday. He scowled and shook his head hard at Walt, as if to deny whatever Walt was thinking.

"Look who I found in the lot," Mrs. Biggs said. "I said to myself, 'Maggie, there's the Reverend, stopping in for a fifth, and it's just coming on to eight o'clock, too.' But now I see *you've* beat him to it. Early bird gets the snort, eh? You starting a fresh bender, or finishing one up?"

"Neither," Walt said. "I stopped in to run a Lotto ticket."

She looked at the money in his hand. "Well then, hand it over," she said, "since it turns out you've pretty much wrecked my stove."

Walt gaped at her.

"That's right. I had my friend Mr. Peet in last night and he says it'll cost sixty dollars to fix it. He tells me the gas company won't touch it because it's buggered up. You apparently done something to it, which Mr. Peet explained. I misremember what, except that it was sixty dollars' worth."

"I didn't do *any*thing to it," Walt said, "except clean out the pipes. Sixty dollars!" Of course this was probably a lie. Mr. Pete was a pipe dream, a figment, pure downtown hosery. She'd seen that he was holding three twenties, so that's how much the whole thing was going to cost, to the penny. Good thing Walt *hadn't* won the sixty million; he'd be handing that over.

She nodded slowly, fixing him with a sad look, but he held out against her. And when she spoke again her voice was small, as if she had finally given up, thrown in the towel. "It's that way, is it?" she said.

"What way?" Walt asked. "What are you talking about?"

"I kind of figured you were made of stronger stuff. I thought you had some backbone. I guess I'm a bad judge of character, although I never would have thought so. . . ." She dropped Bentley's arm. "Go on Reverend, buy your hootch and skedaddle. Both of you. I'm through with the whole bunch of you."

"I suggest we take her at her word," Bentley said, gesturing toward the door. "I just stopped in after some coffee filters, actually, and then I'm on my way."

"Yessir," Mrs. Biggs said, wiping at her eyes now and turning to Toni, who was working over the bottles with a feather duster. "Do you have a tissue, dearie?"

"Oh, for . . . !" Bentley said. "A public display! This is a dis*grace*!"

Toni hauled out a tissue box from under the counter, and Mrs. Biggs took one and dabbed her eyes. "Yesterday these two went to work on my old O'Keefe and Merritt," she said to Toni, "and I said to myself, 'Now there's a couple of samaritans!' That's just what I said. And what came of it? You'd never guess." Toni shook her head. *"Rubbage."* Mrs. Biggs said, and she nodded hard, making her point. "*I* didn't mind lighting that old stove with a match, did I? I'd been lighting it that way for years. And now they've *fixed* it, as they say, and I can't light it at all, or it'll blow up. This tribe comes in for a cup of tea, and now my stove's broke, my cow pitcher's broke, my car's broke. Another hour and I suppose they'd have finished me off. Maybe it'd be better if they had." She put her face in her hands and started to cry. "Sixty dollars worth of grief!" she said.

Toni handed her another tissue.

"And the old man!" Mrs. Biggs said, looking up sharply and shaking the tissue at Walt. "That sweet-talking old devil. I guess everyone might as well know about *him*. Lord knows I *trusted* that man!" She glanced unmistakably at the money in Walt's hand again. Then she turned her head sideways so that Toni couldn't see her and winked at him—a shameless, greedy wink.

"Here," Walt said, instantly handing over the money. Clearly this was simply a matter of payola. She wasn't going to shut up otherwise. She meant to drag Henry's name through the mud right then and there.

"And what about my automobile?" she asked Walt, suddenly forgetting about Henry.

"I've got the hoses in the car. Let's get to work. We're

burning daylight standing around here.'' He headed toward the door. ''Thanks,'' he said to Toni.

Outside, he saw right off that something was wrong with the Suburban, which sat at an angle in its parking space, as if the back end had been slammed sideways a couple of feet. Walt strode across to the far side. The rear fender was caved in, and the end of the bumper, the last four inches or so, was bent all to hell. Someone had clobbered the truck and taken off. ''Hell,'' Walt said.

''You'll just have to be a little soldier about it,'' Mrs. Biggs said to him. ''There's worse things that can happen to a person.''

''*That's* the truth,'' Bentley said.

''Well,'' Mrs. Biggs said, ''another country heard from. I've got a couple of items on my list for you, too, Reverend.''

''Not this morning,'' Bentley said.

''Why?'' she asked. ''What have you got to do that's so all-fired important?''

''Sleep,'' Bentley said. ''You'll have to count me out.''

''You mean Henry'll have to count you out, don't you? *There's* friendship for you. If it involves work, the Reverend's got to sleep. I saw that yesterday, the way you handled that mop.''

''What I mean is that I was up all night long and nearly burned alive in a fire.''

''Well, get used to it,'' she said. ''That's pretty much the whole program down in perdition.''

⇒ 54 ⇐

I⟶ WAS PAST NOON WHEN WALT LOADED HIS TOOLS INTO THE
Suburban and fired up the engine, sitting there for a moment
to let it warm up. At least he had gotten the radiator fixed
before the rain started up—although he hadn't gotten a chance
to help Bentley scrub out the trash cans with bleach and a
broom; Bentley had cleaned the cans by himself after coming
back from the beauty supply store up on Main Street. The rain
had nearly drowned him before he was done.

Walt's sixty dollars was more than gone. He had gone down
to the automated teller around eleven and pulled out sixty
more. Right now Mrs. Biggs had groceries enough for a
month, a couple of rented movies for the VCR, and a new cow
pitcher that Bentley had found down at Stiffworthy's Antiques.
Tomorrow Walt was supposed to come around and look over
the garbage disposal, which had shut down and wouldn't reset.
The plumber had apparently said it was just a loose wire. . . .

Along with that, one of the garage door hinges was sprung,
the crawl space screens under the house had to be replaced
because possums were getting in, and in the bedroom there
was a leaky window that "wanted putty." And as soon as the
rain let up, according to Mrs. Biggs, someone could get on
with the work of scraping the eaves so the house could be
repainted. She had hired a Mexican to do the work nearly a
month ago, but the man had quit after half a day because he
wasn't satisfied with three dollars an hour and all the doughnuts he could eat. And, she'd told Walt, that was "under the
table," by which, Walt supposed, she meant the money.

He drummed his fingers on the steering wheel, then turned
on the defrost and pulled away from the curb, heading up
Olive and then left on Palmyra, passing a house with a life-

size Santa Claus and reindeer in the yard, the whole display vandalized—knocked down and defaced with graffiti. No doubt it was more of Argyle's high jinks. He swung a left onto Glassell, back toward home. By his calculations he was down something like two hundred dollars total. Bentley was down another thirty for the cow pitcher, and it didn't make him happy. Henry was going to pay them back with the lingerie money, except that the lingerie had never materialized, and, as of this morning anyway, Sidney Vest hadn't returned any of Henry's calls.

"Henry's going to have to work out his own problems," Bentley had told Walt after scouring out the last of the trash cans. "I *can't*. I've done what I could, but trying to pay this woman off is like pouring water through sand. It was a mistake that we ever took her on."

And of course Bentley was right. He'd been right yesterday. Walt had been the fool. What they'd done so far was the tip of the iceberg. There were worse things waiting. All morning long she'd been full of the Islands again—going back to Wai-kiki, maybe look up her old friend Velma Krane. Plane tickets were reasonable right now, during the fare war. You could fly round trip for about three hundred dollars. And who could say?—maybe once she was in Honolulu, by golly, she'd stay put. *Maybe all she needed was a one-way ticket and first month's rent on a little bungalow downtown.* Fifteen hundred would about do it, give or take. As for the house in Orange, hell, she could lease that out and make an income.

Walt hashed it over. What with Ivy's commission, it was almost easier to give Mrs. Biggs what she wanted. Except that of course she wouldn't go to Honolulu even so. She'd hang around Orange and weasel more money out of them until Walt cut her off. Then she'd rat all of them out to Jinx.

Something had to be done right now. There was no more putting it off.

Already he knew the answer. It had been circulating through his mind all morning long. Sending Vest back to North Carolina had been the work of an instant. He was probably counting his many blessings right now, along with his money, which he was spending on cheap Carolina real estate. Vest, after all, had *wanted* to go. Walt's calling on the bluebird hadn't been a matter of greed; it had been a matter of doing a man a favor, if you wanted to look at it that way.

And if that was the way you were looking at it, then why not do the same favor for Maggie Biggs, who was pining away for the Islands? And there was Uncle Henry to think of, too. Calling in the bluebird would be a blessing all the way around—everyone a winner. By golly, he'd kill two stones with one bird, he thought, laughing out loud, and he wished that he had someone to tell the joke to. Probably he'd never be able to tell it to anyone.

He made the wish quickly, just a blink of his mind, and turned up Oak Street toward home.

55

MRS. SIMMS LIVED ON WASHINGTON STREET IN A WHITE clapboard house with a wraparound porch, and when Walt and the kids pulled up at the curb, she was sitting on the porch in a wooden chair, very still, watching the rain fall, her lawn all covered with leaves. She had a shawl around her shoulders and her hands in her lap, and from the way she stared at the street, it seemed clear to Walt that all the money in the world wouldn't help her, not in the way she needed to be helped. She and Simms had been married for fifty years.

"It's *her*," Eddie said, looking out the window.

"She's *old*," Nora said. "She's a million."

"Not *that* old," Eddie said. "That's stupid."

"Yes-huh," Nora said. "Isn't she a million, Unca Walter?"

Somehow Nora had taken to calling him Walter, just like Jinx. Walt had always been a little irritated when Jinx called him that, but Nora somehow made it all right. Nora was the great leveler.

"She's *close* to a million," Walt said. "Closer than we are, anyway."

"See?" Nora said to Eddie.

"You don't get it," Eddie said.

"Do, too."

"Do not."

Walt held up the cashier's check that he'd swapped the rest of the checks for. Argyle's money had of course killed the fund-raiser. There didn't seem to be any reason to go back out after another forty or fifty bucks or whatever they might have managed to scrounge up, and then they'd have to go to all the trouble to bake more cookies.

"I'm going to let Nora carry the money," he said, and he winked at Eddie.

"That's okay," Eddie said. "I'll stay here."

"Nope. We'll all go," Walt said. "You ready?"

Without waiting for an answer, he ducked out into the rain, coming around the side of the car and opening the doors for the kids. Nora climbed out and took the check, then started out toward the porch, holding the check in front of her face with both hands as if she were hiding behind it.

"Mrs. Simms, I believe," Walt said, once they were out of the rain.

She smiled and nodded, holding out her hand. Nora shook it like a pump handle. Eddie touched it, then pulled his hand away. Walt introduced the three of them, and Mrs. Simms said she was happy to meet them. Then Nora tried explaining the check, calling it a "fund raisin," but Mrs. Simms was baffled. She took it and stared at it. "Whatever do you mean?" she asked.

"It's a collection from people in the neighborhood," Walt explained. "It's on behalf of Mr. Simms, because of the bell-ringing. People around here appreciated that. Nora and Eddie did the footwork. Every single person they talked to donated."

And that was true. There was no percentage in revealing that they'd only hit four houses before they'd quit.

Suddenly Mrs. Simms was crying. She laid the check down on a little table next to the chair, then took her spectacles off and wiped her eyes with a handkerchief that she pulled out of her sleeve.

"Why is she crying?" Nora whispered out loud.

"Shhh," Walt said.

"It's 'cause of her husband," Eddie said.

Nora put her hand on Mrs. Simms's arm, and Mrs. Simms patted Nora's hand. She picked up the check again and looked at it. "Who would have thought?" she said to Walt.

He shrugged. "Give people a chance," he said, "and they'll show their true colors." Somehow he felt like a heel, and it dawned on him just then that he himself hadn't contributed a dime to the check. He hadn't thought to.

"I'd like to know who donated," she said. "I intend to write all of them a thank-you note."

"Well, there's so *many*," Walt said. "We didn't keep any kind of record. . . ."

"There was that one lady on the corner," Eddie said. "And the other one, too, that lived next door to her."

"That's right," Walt said. "We can get you their names and addresses anyway. That's a start."

"Well, I'd be obliged," she said.

"And Mr. R-guy," Nora said. "He gave the most."

"Yes, indeed," Walt said. "That's true."

"Will you step inside?" Mrs. Simms asked. "I could put on a pot of coffee."

Walt nearly refused. He had things to do—boxes to pack for a last-ditch Christmas mailing, Christmas shopping, errands to run. He just didn't have time. . . .

Then he realized what he was thinking. This was another case of there not being any room at the inn, wasn't it? He couldn't be a good Samaritan; *he was too busy*. Someone else could do it. Charity was something you measured in dollars and cents, but you didn't go to any trouble.

"Would you like a cookie?" she asked Eddie.

Eddie nodded, and Nora held onto her hand as they went into the house. Mr. Simms had apparently owned a doily factory, because there were doilies everywhere, as if the furniture were wearing special clothes. And there were easily a hundred dolls in the living room and dining room, big ones and little ones both, with porcelain heads and glass eyes. There was a big dollhouse on a table against a wall—a three-story Victorian with tiny shingles and intricate wooden fretwork and corbels and gables. The rooms had little hand-woven rugs on the floor and Chippendale furniture, and there were tiny milk cartons and canned goods in the kitchen. Nora stood staring at the house, rocking back and forth on her heels.

"Here's a cookie from the freezer," Mrs. Simms said, coming out of the kitchen and pulling the top off a Tupperware container.

Eddie took one.

"You'd better have four, to start with," she said, and Eddie took three more, then sat down on a chair and held the four cookies in his hand.

"Oh!" Nora uttered, pointing at a doll with blonde curls.

"Do you like that one?" Mrs. Simms asked.

"Oh!" Nora said again. "She's . . . Oh!"

"Would you like to have her?"

Nora swiveled around and looked at Walt, her eyes wide open in astonishment. "Could I?" she asked. Eddie sat in the chair staring straight ahead.

"It would make me very happy," Mrs. Simms said to Walt. He shrugged. "What do you say, Nora?"

"Oh, yes!" Nora said.

Mrs. Simms picked up the doll and handed it to Nora, who held it in her arms like a baby. "I have something for you, too," Mrs. Simms said to Eddie. She led them into a den, where there was a line of books supported by two heavy brass bookends on a table. The bookends were square-rigged clipper ships tossing on ocean waves. "Do you like these?" Mrs. Simms asked.

Eddie shrugged. He was still holding onto his cookies.

"Well, I want you to have them," she said, "along with this book." She handed him an old copy of *Treasure Island* with a glued-on cover illustration of a pirate with a knife in his teeth. "Will you take them? They belonged to Mr. Simms."

Eddie shrugged again and looked at the floor.

"What do you think, Eddie?" Walt asked, smiling at Mrs. Simms. He looked at Eddie and mouthed the word "Thanks."

"Sure," Eddie mumbled. "I guess."

"Can I have a cookie?" Nora asked. "What kind are they?"

"Ginger cookies."

Nora took one out of the Tupperware, nibbled at it, and made her rabbit face at Mrs. Simms. Walt headed for the front door, and Mrs. Simms followed them out onto the porch, thanking Walt again for the check.

"Perhaps you'd like to come over some time and help me with my dollhouse?" she asked Nora, who nodded hard. "And Eddie, if you wouldn't mind looking through Mr. Simms's coins, perhaps you could help me catalogue them. I need to make a list of them."

"I could," Eddie said.

"Well, that's just fine. God bless you," she said to Walt, who nodded and stepped out into the rain.

The kids ran to the truck and clambered in, carrying their

stuff, and Nora belted the doll into the center seat belt. "She's nice," Nora said.

"Yes, indeed," Walt said. He felt like a complete fraud. Somehow he had set out to do the right thing with the fund-raiser, and Argyle had turned him into a sort of messenger boy. By remaining anonymous, Argyle had made sure that the glory would fall to Walt, who didn't deserve it, and Walt had enough conscience to feel guilty about it. And who was he kidding? He had thought up the fund-raiser to spite Argyle and the preschool's Christmas wrap fund-raiser, hadn't he? And the wild success of it had pissed him off because it wasn't *his* success. And now Mrs. Simms turns out to be some kind of saint, and he ends up driving away down Washington Street feeling like a hollow man. What a mess. Maybe Bentley had an illustrated tract to clear all this up: "Guilt as an Obstacle to Sin."

"You said we get a doughnut," Nora said.

"A doughnut? Not after all those cookies?" Walt turned up Chapman toward the All-Niter. Nora and Eddie deserved a doughnut.

"I didn't eat my cookies," Eddie said. "I'm saving them."

"I'm saving, too," Nora said, making the rabbit face. But her cookies were already gone.

The parking lot at the All-Niter was deserted. It was too late in the day for serious doughnut eating. Walt swung the Suburban into a slot and glanced into the building, through the big window in front, on the lookout for Maggie Biggs. Had she vanished? Taken the slow boat to Waikiki?

Someone was coming out to the front of the shop from behind the counter, pushing through the little Dutch door. But it wasn't Maggie Biggs; it was Uncle Henry. Henry looked up just then, apparently spotted the Suburban through the window, and stood stock-still, as if trying to decide whether to come ahead or to turn and flee. Abruptly he hurried forward, out among the tables, where he slid into one of the booths. There was an empty doughnut basket and a half-drunk cup of coffee on the table in front of him. He picked up a section of newspaper and affected an engrossed look.

Walt got out and walked to the door, pushing it open and letting Nora and Eddie squeeze in under his outstretched arm. Eddie stood looking at the doughnuts and Nora ran to Uncle

Henry, who feigned surprise at seeing them there. Walt decided to let it slide.

There was a lipstick stain on the coffee cup, so the stuff on the table wasn't Henry's; either that or he'd had company. Probably he was here for some purpose besides doughnuts. "No sign of the lingerie yet?" Walt asked hopefully.

"No," Henry said, putting the paper down. "And there won't be, either. The party's off."

"That's a dirty shame," Walt said. "Vest didn't drop the ball on us, did he?"

Henry nodded his head slowly. "Something like that. I got through to his secretary this morning. She tells me that Sidney Vest fell over dead last night at a restaurant out in Villa Park. Choked on a piece of fish. They're shipping his body back home to Raleigh for burial."

❧ 56 ❧

"DEAD?" WALT ASKED, SITTING DOWN HARD IN THE BOOTH. The word croaked out of him. His head swam, and he shut his eyes tight. "I don't believe it," he muttered.

"Apparently it's true," Henry said. "Piece of halibut got him. He sucked it down his windpipe. They worked the Heimlich on him but it didn't do any good. I guess that when it's your turn to go . . ." He shrugged philosophically.

"My God!" Walt shouted suddenly, just then remembering his other wish. "Maggie Biggs! Where is she?"

Henry looked around uneasily, his face furrowed up. "I'm not sure," he said. "What's wrong, Walter? What's the matter?" Nora and Eddie stared at him. He stood up again, looking from the counter to the door, ready to bolt for the car and drive the half mile to Olive Street.

There was a voice from among the doughnuts then, and Walt stood up and turned around. Mrs. Biggs herself looked out from the door to the back room, eyeing him suspiciously. "It's you, is it?" she said. "What's all this fuss?"

"Are you all right?" Walt shouted at her. He strode across to the counter. She took a step backward, looking uncertainly at him now, and he gestured at her and shook his head. "It's okay, it's okay," he said, grinning weakly. "Everything's all right with you, then?"

"Well, I suppose it is."

"You're feeling all right?"

"What's your game?" she asked, squinting at him. "Where's the Reverend?" She looked around suspiciously.

"He's . . ." Walt realized that he sounded like a lunatic. "The car, I mean to say." Clearly Mrs. Biggs was safe. The bluebird hadn't killed her, at least for the moment. "The car's all right? Not overheating?"

"Not so's you'd notice it, no. You look like hell, sonny, pardon my French. Why don't you go sit down? Chew on a sinker."

"That's right," Walt said. "Sure I will." He slumped into the booth again.

"Who are these, then, your children?" Mrs. Biggs waved at Eddie and Nora. Nora smiled big at her and held up her new doll. "What'll you have?" Mrs. Biggs asked, and then started piling doughnuts into one of the baskets as Nora and Eddie pointed at the racks. "On the house," she said to Walt. "Couple of glazeys for you? Cup of mud?"

Walt shook his head. "Put them in a bag," he said. "We'll take them to go."

In his mind he revised his wish to the bluebird, calling it off, half expecting Maggie Biggs to pitch over dead right then and there. Don't kill her, he commanded the bird, talking loud in his mind. Send her home happy.

But was it enough? Could he be sure that the bird was listening? "We'd better run," he said to the kids, getting up and taking the bag from Mrs. Biggs. "Look," he said to her. "For the next fifteen minutes, don't go anywhere."

"What is this?" she asked. "What's going on here?" She looked at Henry now, sizing him up. "Is this your doing?" she asked.

"I swear," he said, shaking his head. "It's a mystery."

"Because if it is . . ."

"Just stay here," Walt said to her. "Just for a few minutes. And don't eat *any*thing. Don't take any medications. For God's sake, don't do anything dangerous, like climb a ladder or something. Stay away from the windows. Just stay *put* for a few minutes." He pushed the door open and ushered the kids out, then jumped into the Suburban, fired it up, and headed for home.

"AND THAT'S ALL I WANT YOU TO DO," HE SAID OUT LOUD to the bluebird. "Get her out of here alive." It sat on the garage bench, freed from its grave under the stepping-stone. Nora and Eddie were indoors, making themselves sick with the doughnuts. He wondered if he should call the All-Niter and give Mrs. Biggs the all-clear, but that would just compound the craziness of this whole thing. She had thought something was "going on" as it was.

Was it?

The whole setup at the All-Niter was strange: Henry sneaking around behind the counter, acting furtive, pretending to have been eating doughnuts, Maggie Biggs hiding out in the back room. If Walt hadn't shouted, she'd have stayed hidden; he was pretty sure of that. Maybe Henry was just down there giving her what's what, straightening her out for good and all. But that's not the way he had acted.

❧ 57 ❧

BENTLEY LOOKED OUT THROUGH THE WALNUT TREES TOWARD the street. From where he stood he could see up and down Chapman Avenue, get a view of cars heading both east and west. It was two A.M., and there was no traffic, and except for crickets the night was still. Away across the lot he could see the shadow of a backhoe left by the men who'd been digging up LeRoy's orchard. The shell of the burned-out house shone in the moonlight, and for the first time in over a week the sky was clear and full of stars, but the ground and shrubbery and trees were soaked, and it would take them days to dry out, which was a good thing, under the circumstances.

Father Mahoney sprinkled gasoline over the low, altarlike shelf in the chicken coop and then doused the painted scrawls on the plank walls before saturating the dirt beneath, pouring the gasoline over the chicken wire and the diabolical trash behind it. He flicked the last of the gasoline out in the rough shape of a cross, mumbling in Latin. Bentley listened to him, watched him making these liturgical gestures with a gasoline can. He had thought that the church had given up Latin, but it was possible that the priest had shifted out of English simply because English couldn't quite carry the necessary weight, so to speak.

Finally Mahoney set the now-empty can on the shelf and gestured at it. "Leave it," Bentley said in a low voice. There was no use trying to hide it. Fire inspectors would know this was an arson.

They had left Bentley's car at the Holy Spirit church and walked the six blocks to Water Street carrying the gas can in a plastic sack. If they were stopped on the way back, well, so be it: the police wouldn't arrest a priest and a minister. They'd say they'd been off visiting Mrs. Hepplewhite, who was at home right now, waiting for the all-clear phone call when they got back to the church. If they made it to the church without incident, then Obermeyer would swear they'd spent the evening at his place if they needed an alibi later, which they wouldn't; who would suspect the two of them? The whole thing was Bentley's plan: as soon as the shed went up they would phone in an alarm from the pay phone on the Cambridge Street corner and then hightail it through the neighborhood on foot.

There was the reek of gasoline on the night air now, and Bentley looked around uneasily again, checking traffic, on the alert for cruising patrol cars. Mahoney stepped back and bowed his head for a moment, and Bentley did, too.

The priest nodded at him finally, and Bentley lit the wick of a Stay-Lit birthday candle and checked the street one last time. Chapman was clear of cars, from the Plaza to Tustin Avenue half a mile east. Mahoney backed away, into the shadows of the grove. Bentley let the candle burn for a couple of seconds before he tossed it into the open shed, and then he turned and ran, but even so the heat from the explosion was so intense that he panicked and threw himself forward into an arbor overgrown with unpruned grapevines, and had to scramble to free himself. Mahoney was already high-stepping it through the trees, toward the oleander-choked wire fence at the rear of the lot.

Bentley ran after him, holding onto his hat and pushing in through the oleander, yanking the stiff branches out of his way. "Go!" he shouted hoarsely, and then shoved the priest through the hole they'd cut in the fence ten minutes ago, out into the parking lot at the rear of a set of two-story office buildings. Bentley bent through behind him, careful not to snag his coat, and the two hurried across the moonlit asphalt as the glow of the fire rose up behind them.

⁂ 58 ⁂

"OH, YES, IT'S SAFE AS A BABY," MRS. BIGGS SAID OVER THE phone. "I've got it hid where nobody'll think to look."

"There's really no need for that," Argyle told her. "I'll take delivery today—as soon as possible, if that's acceptable to you. I believe I authorized Mr. Peetenpaul to offer you two thousand dollars, but I'm happy to say that I'm *so* thrilled you've been prompt and professional, that I'd like to double that figure. I don't suppose you'd argue with that?" He looked out the window. They'd started digging up LeRoy's remains again, but the rain had them stymied. Most of the grove was a mud hole now. Somehow Argyle didn't think they'd find anything much anyway. It was only at the end that LeRoy had gotten stupid.

"Four thousand dollars," she said. "Well, that's mighty generous of you, I'm sure. And like you say, I won't argue. I don't believe in it. An argument's just words, isn't it? It won't pay rent."

"There's a good philosophy," Argyle said.

"But I might just as well tell you now that there's another party has an interest in this thing. Considerably more interested than four thousand dollars, I might say."

"What are you talking about?"

"Only that there's a party who'll offer me more. And like I say, I won't argue. I let the money talk."

Argyle sat up in his chair and evened his voice. This was a new turn. Peetenpaul had grossly misjudged this woman, which wasn't at all like him. "You've misunderstood me entirely, Mrs. Biggs," he said. "I'm not offering to *buy* this item from you and never was. I offered to pay you to retrieve it. The bird itself is very rare—the only existing example of its species. The Museum of Natural History in Los Angeles commissioned me to obtain it from sources in China, and I was successful in doing so. The bird, very unfortunately, was sent to the wrong address and this entire confusion resulted. For the sake of science, Mrs. Biggs, and on the part of the taxpayer, I entreat you to allow me to send it on to its rightful owners.''

"That's not how it worked out, you see."

"What's not? What do you mean?"

"Mr. Stebbins threw the bird away."

"I don't follow you."

"He threw the thing into the Dumpster. Anybody could have took it out, couldn't they?"

"Am I mistaken, or did you say you were in possession of the item in question?" Argyle asked evenly.

"Oh, I'm in possession of it. That I am."

"Then nobody else took it out of the trash?"

"No, I've got it."

"And it wasn't carted away to the dump?"

"No, it was not. I'm telling you I've got it."

"Good! For a moment there I was lost. So, to put this in perspective, you've got the item and you're not satisfied with the remuneration despite my doubling it?"

"Well, I don't know anything about remuneration, as you call it. I was thinking more along the lines of *purchase price*. What I mean is that I don't know who *owns* this thing, do I? All I know is it was me that found it in the trash. You talk about this museum and China and all, but that smells like rubbish to me. It looks to me like *I* own it, so don't quote the by-God taxpayer to me."

"I must advise you to rethink your position, Mrs. Biggs."

"That's what I've done in regard to this other party, like I said . . ."

"*What* other party?"

"This other gentleman. I misremember the man's name, but he's *very* keen on the item."

"I don't for a moment believe in the existence of this other gentleman, Mrs. Biggs."

"That's as may be. You might just as well say you don't believe in the moon, for all the good it'll do you. What if I told you this other gentleman was the neighbor's cat and that

I'd feed this damned bird to it on a shingle as soon as give it to a cheapskate like you? What would you say then? That you don't believe in the cat? Because that's just what I'll do, and I'll do it in a cold second, too.''

"I'm getting a little tired of this entire charade, Mrs. Biggs. How much do you want?''

"Two hundred and fifty thousand dollars,'' she said. "Cash on the barrelhead.''

He heard a bang then, as if she'd pounded her fist onto a desktop. A quarter of a million dollars! The amount struck him dumb. He sat looking at the telephone receiver, as if what he held in his hand had ceased to have any meaning. After a moment he managed to laugh, but it sounded unconvincing even to him.

"You might as well laugh,'' she said. "I'm onto you and your little game. I want small bills, spending cash—nothing bigger than a fifty and not all fifties, either. Put 'em in a suitcase. Some kind of quality leather, not vinyl or cloth. Have that big Dutchman of yours bring it around. I'll give him the bird right enough. *Comprende?*''

"I'm with you so far,'' Argyle said.

"Then stay with me, because I've got one more thing to say. I've found out a thing or two about you, Mr. Swindlemeister, about some of the things you've *done*, if you take my meaning, and I think it's a crying shame. I know who your friends are, too. Your whole crowd makes me sick. I've wrote it all down, all the dirt that's fit to print, and it's a sorry thing to look at, I can tell you. What I did is I sent a copy off to my dear friend Velma, and if I don't show up at Velma's with her share of the payment PDQ, then it all goes public. Every blessed thing.''

"I think I understand.''

"I knew you would. You're a man of business. And what I hope you understand is that tomorrow, if I don't have the money in hand, I mean to dry this bird out in the oven, salt its tail, and throw it to the lions.''

She hung up the phone then, and Argyle sat there with his head in his hands. He'd managed to get the bird out of the frying pan and into the fire. And it wasn't the money that frosted him, either. He could pay her the damned money easily enough; he would have paid Flanagan as much if the man hadn't gone soft on him. What pissed him off was the idea of being hosed like this.

But what could he do, short of having the old woman tortured? Not a damn thing. She'd do what she said.

He laughed out loud. He'd been flayed! Well, to hell with it. Once he possessed the bird he'd be free, clean of the last twenty years, rid of the nightmares, rid of the black desire that drove him out into the neighborhood after dark. . . .

Last night he had come to himself outside the church, standing on the sidewalk in the midnight wind and holding a burned-down candle. Apparently he'd bitten the burning end off it, because his tongue was blistered and there was wax in his teeth. He had fled home in a blind rush, where he had found his back door open wide, water running in the kitchen sink, all the stove burners flaming. His memory of what he'd done inside the church was a heap of fragments, like an image in a broken mirror: climbing in the dim well of the bell tower, stomping on a man in a dark room, smoke curling up from torn-apart hymnals. . . .

He stood up from his desk now, picked up his umbrella, and left the office, locking the door and heading down the stairs and out onto the porch. Peetenpaul himself was just then pulling up along the curb, driving the new truck and dressed for business.

⇒ 59 ⇐

"YOU PROMISED," NORA SAID.

Walt glanced at her in the rearview mirror. She was frowning hard, looking straight ahead, her hands folded across her chest, her bangs a razor-straight line above her eyebrows.

"But I didn't know we would make that much, did I?" Walt asked. "You've got the bubble string already. Today after school we can go to the dime store and you can pick out ... let's see ... three things. We'll do that every day for ... two weeks. Three prizes a day."

"How many is that?" Nora asked.

Eddie counted on his fingers. "Kind of a lot," he said.

"Nuh-uh," Nora said unhappily.

"How many prizes did you promise the children?" Ivy asked.

Walt grinned weakly at her. "About two thousand," he muttered, "give or take." He turned left, onto Chapman, heading for the preschool.

"How many is that?" Nora asked, instantly happy again. "That two-thing?"

"It's a *lot*," Eddie said. "A *really* lot."

"But how many?"

"Count to twenty," Ivy said helpfully. "And then count to twenty again. And do it over and over *a hundred times*."

Nora immediately started to count out loud, her head bobbing back and forth.

Ivy grinned at Walt. "Old moneybags," she said. "Two thousand prizes!"

"I'll think of something," Walt said, although actually he had already tried and he couldn't think of anything at all. Through his wholesalers he could buy carnival prizes in bulk

for two or three cents apiece—plastic spiders and skulls, rhine-
stone rings, silver-painted plastic charms, window stickers—
but there was no way the children would be happy with being
handed three gross of each of these things. And even if that
would work, it would still easily cost him hundreds of dollars.

"Fourteen, fisteen, fisteen," Nora intoned, moving from
there into a realm of numbers that Walt was unfamiliar with.
She stopped suddenly. "Mr. R-Guy!" she said.

Walt looked. Argyle stood under the porch roof in front of
his downtown office, talking, for God's sake, to the inspector,
who was dressed in a coat and tie. He had gotten a haircut,
apparently, and trimmed his beard.

"Why, it's Mr. Peetenpaul," Ivy said. "That's the man who
bought the properties."

"Is it?" Walt asked broadly. "Well, I'll be damned. It's a
small world, I guess."

She looked at him. "What's wrong with you all of a sudden?"

"Well, it might be Mr. Peetenpaul," he said. "But whoever
he is, he didn't buy any properties. He happens to *work* for
Argyle." Walt widened his eyes at her, and she frowned back
at him, as if she didn't quite understand. Nora kept on counting, bouncing in her seat now.

"How do you know he works for Robert?" Ivy asked.

"Trust me. I know. I'm not sure what Argyle's up to with
this sales-commission scam, but like I told you, it's not as
simple as you think it is. Watch out he isn't playing you for
a patsy."

Ivy was silent, looking at the street now, taking it all in.
Walt felt vindicated by this, and then almost immediately
ashamed of feeling that way at Ivy's expense. But hell, it was
time that she had a glimpse of the real Argyle—Argyle the
sneak and the manipulator. Now she didn't have to take Walt's
word for it, which of course she hadn't taken anyway, to her
own peril.

"I don't mean you shouldn't take his sixty grand," he said,
suddenly thinking of the money.

"I don't want to talk about it right now."

"Okay." He glanced at Nora again, a bright idea coming
to him out of the blue. "How's this?" he asked her brightly.
"We'll consolidate."

Nora stopped counting. "Wha-a-a-t?" she asked, screwing up her face at him.

"Consolidate. It means a putting-together, a gathering into a bundle, so to speak. The many become one, the one greater than the sum of its parts."

"What's parts?" She frowned, as if she were concentrating. Eddie remained silent.

"I'll give you an example," Walt said. "Instead of twenty-five pennies, you get a quarter."

"I get a quarter?"

"No, I'm just making up an example. Look . . ."

"A zample?"

"What I mean is instead of two thousand little bitty prizes, you get a couple of *big* prizes."

"What kind?" Eddie asked now.

"I was thinking along the lines of a bicycle," Walt said, glancing at Ivy, who didn't respond. She was still in a funk. "How would you like that?"

"What did he say?" Nora asked Eddie in a loud whisper.

"He said we could have bikes."

"And maybe a swing set for the backyard . . ." Immediately Walt thought of Argyle and his fund-raiser expenditures. "Or maybe something else nice," he said.

Nora began to hop up and down in the seat now, spring-headed, counting happily again. The preschool appeared, and over the tops of the cars parked in the lot Walt could see the head of the tyrannosaur, steadfastly guarding the sandbox. Somehow it looked like an old friend this morning. "So much depends on a sad dinosaur," he said, pulling into a space, "glazed with rainwater beside the spring chickens."

He laughed out loud. "That's a poem," he said to Nora.

"Don't . . . be . . . silly," she said, rolling her eyes and opening the door. Eddie slid across the seat in order to get out on her side.

Walt climbed out into the rain and glanced at the front of the school, where someone was just then coming out the door. For a moment he didn't recognize the man, who was hunched over as if to keep the rain off his face. The man looked up, stopped, and then came on again, angling toward them now, his face full of anger and determination. It was Jack.

⇥ 60 ⇤

"Back into the car," Walt said.

Ivy turned around in her seat and grasped Nora's arm, hauling her inside again as Walt reached for the ignition key, looking back to see that the kids were safely in. Eddie slid back into his spot and slumped down in the seat, not looking at Jack, but staring at the upholstery like he'd been drugged.

Walt was suddenly full of rage. This had gone on too damned long! He wrenched on the door handle, starting to get back out of the car.

"Don't," Ivy said, grabbing his arm. "Not here. Not now."

He hesitated. The look on her face convinced him. "Right," he said, and slammed his door, shifting into reverse and backing out in a rush just as Jack started to run toward them. He changed direction then, heading toward the street, leaping over the parkway junipers in order to cut the car off when Walt pulled out of the lot. "Bad move, asshole," Walt muttered, swerving around straight at him, getting him in his sights. He punched the accelerator and Jack threw his arms up and jumped backward, stepping up onto the curb again and stumbling through the shrubs.

"Take it easy!" Ivy warned him.

"I'll knock him into the schoolyard," Walt said, but the preschool was a half a block back now, and he eased up on the accelerator, watching for Jack's T-bird to pull out onto the road, chasing them. When it didn't happen, he relaxed.

Then he saw that Ivy was giving him a look, and it came to him out of nowhere that the kids were in the car, that he'd probably scared the hell out of them. . . .

In his anger he hadn't given Nora and Eddie a second thought, but had lost his mind instead, involving them in his

own war against Jack, as if they weren't deeply enough involved in the man's creepy behavior already. Whose side are
you on? he asked himself.

"Sorry," he said to Ivy. He glanced in the mirror and saw
that Eddie was crying. Nora sat silently, her thumb in her
mouth.

He scrambled in his mind for something to say, something
to make it all right. Nothing came to him, except that there
was something terrible and hard about taking care of children,
and that no matter how good you might be with them one
moment, you were sure to screw it up another. He slapped the
wheel with the back of his fingers, making it hurt.

"Let's hit the All-Niter for doughnuts," he said, shame-
lessly deciding to buy them off. "Then we'll go down to Toy
City and pick out a couple of bicycles." He and Ivy could
Christmas shop some other time.

Nora didn't take her thumb out of her mouth, but she nodded.

Eddie sniffed, and then in a shaky voice he said, "I can't
ride a bike."

"Before the sun goes down this evening," Walt said,
"you'll know how to ride one, or by golly your Aunt Ivy will
stay up all night teaching you. She once taught an ape to ride
a bicycle, and it was a two-wheeler, too."

"An a-a-ape," Nora said, smiling again. "Nuh-uh."

"Yeah-huh," Walt said, turning into the lot in front of the
All-Niter. "After that she taught the ape to sing." There were
already several cars in the tiny lot, so he drove to the far end,
shutting off the engine.

"Look there," Ivy said, pointing. It was Peetenpaul's truck,
parked at the rear of the shop and sheltered from the rain by
a big pine tree. The man himself stood beside the open passenger door. They watched as he pulled off his black suit coat
and tossed it inside. Underneath he was wearing a garish Hawaiian shirt—big red hibiscus blossoms on a blue background.
He reached into the truck and pulled out a white linen jacket,
folding it over his arm, then reached in again and drew out a
leather suitcase. Then he took his keys out of his pocket, tossed
them into the air, caught them, and threw them onto the floor-
board of the pickup, slamming the door after them. He turned
and hurried across the lot toward a waiting vehicle, yanking

open the trunk and dropping the suitcase in on top of several others.

"I'll be damned," Walt whispered. It was the Biggsmobile, the old Buick! Maggie Biggs herself sat in the passenger seat. Peetenpaul climbed in the driver's side, backed out and swung around, straightening out and moving slowly past them, heading for Chapman Avenue.

Mrs. Biggs wore a yellow muumuu and there was a flower in her wig the size of a plate, as if she were on her way to God's own luau. She spotted Walt as the Buick rolled past, and tipped him a big wink, evidently mighty happy to see him. She picked up something off the dash—what appeared to be airplane tickets—which she waved in his direction. Peetenpaul waved, too, waggling his thick fingers and hunching over to have a look at Walt through the partly open window.

"Thanks, sweetie!" Mrs. Biggs shouted, and then the Buick was gone, bumping out onto the avenue and tearing away east toward the freeway.

"What on *earth* was that all about?" Ivy asked.

"That was my old friend Maggie Biggs," Walt said, astonished at this turn of events. "I think her ship just came in."

"She's a friend of Mr. Peetenpaul?"

"I believe she is," Walt said, "although I just now found that out myself." So Peetenpaul was the legendary Mr. Peet, the man who had taken the stove apart after Walt had screwed it up! Postal inspector, real estate entrepreneur, plumber, eater of doughnuts . . . Walt shook his head, putting it all together at last. Somehow he was unaccountably happy at this turn of affairs. "You know what I think?" he said to Ivy. "I think that sometimes what we don't see would fill a tub."

"Amen to that," Ivy said, getting out of the car. "For heaven's sake, let's eat."

Nora and Eddie and Walt got out, too, and the four of them jogged through the rain toward the All-Niter, where Lyle Boyd was just then sliding a fresh tray of glazed doughnuts onto the rack.

BENTLEY WALKED UP ONTO ARGYLE'S PORCH, THIS TIME IN broad daylight, and knocked hard on the door. He carried his Bible, and he had a half dozen appropriate verses tagged with slips of paper. That was dangerous—most people would sooner let a door-to-door salesman into the house than a man with a Bible—but it was time to come clean, all the way clean, no punches pulled.

The door opened finally, and Argyle stood there looking disheveled, as if he had woken up from an afternoon nap. He squinted, perhaps half recognizing Bentley but not quite placing him. Then he smiled. His eyes narrowed when he saw the Bible. "What can I do for you?" he asked.

"What can you do for yourself?" Bentley said, and it was instantly clear from Argyle's face that he knew him entirely now, that he recognized Bentley's voice.

"I'll be damned," he said. "It's Father Flanagan, after all these years. So you turn out to be the neighborhood bellringer, too, eh? The thorn in my side, and the man who just took a pile of my money. We meet at last. Pardon me if I don't shake hands until I know why you're here."

" 'What the wicked dreads will come upon him, but the desire of the righteous will be granted,' " Bentley quoted. There was no use opening the Bible. He knew that one by heart.

"So what?" Argyle asked.

"Well, for openers, my name's not Flanagan. That's so what. My name is Lorimer Bentley. What I pretended to be in the past isn't of interest to us any more. I've repented of that, and I suggest you do the same. That's why I've come here."

"Repented? Was this before or after you cashed the check I gave Obermeyer?"

There was a clattering noise behind him in the house, and then the sound of a heavy object knocking against the wall. Argyle turned around and looked, and Bentley caught a glimpse of something—someone—moving across the room.

He stared meaningfully at Argyle and shook his head tiredly. "As for your money," he said, "what you gave me in the past was well spent. If I had it, I'd give it back to you, but I'm afraid it's blood out of a turnip now. And I'm ashamed to admit it, too. I'm ashamed of the whole thing. I thought I was running a con for the Lord. It was pure sinful foolishness and stupidity." Bentley took Argyle's hundred-thousand-dollar check out of his coat pocket and held it up between his thumb and forefinger. "As for this . . ."

Argyle snatched it out of his hand and tucked it away in his own pocket. "Thank you," he said. "In fact, I no longer need your services. The situation has changed dramatically since I last spoke to you."

"That's true," Bentley said. "It's gotten a hell of a lot worse, hasn't it?"

"For you, maybe. You should have been quicker on the draw with that check."

"Take a look at this, if you can stand it." Bentley removed a photograph from his coat now—Father Mahoney's Polaroid photo—and showed it to Argyle, who immediately shuddered at the sight of his own idiot face.

"So what is this?" he croaked. "Some sort of extortion? The whole world's playing that game, eh? Even the Church wants in. Repentance you call it!" He took the check back out of his pocket and handed it to Bentley, who looked at it for a moment in astonishment, and then tore it to fragments, dropping them on the porch.

"You're a hard man to satisfy," Argyle said.

"Not really," Bentley said. "I want your soul."

"It's not for sale."

"It was once."

"You've got delusions of grandeur, haven't you?"

"I don't have any delusions anymore. And you didn't either when you called me the other day. You're in trouble. Take a hard look at this snapshot. That's the face of a man with one foot in Hell.'' He held the photo up again, then abruptly tore it to shreds, too, and threw the pieces onto the porch with the torn-up check. ''*There's* your extortion for you,'' he shouted, losing his temper now. ''Keep your money. I'm here to right a wrong. It's not too late for either one of us.''

''You're right about that. It's a brand-new day for me.'' Argyle smiled at him now. ''Anything else up your sleeve?''

''A new day! How? Because of that damned . . . *thing* you've got in the coffin in the back room? If *that's* your plan— trying to fool the Devil with a golem—then you're a sorry damned fool. And I mean damned, too.''

''*What* a perceptive man you are,'' Argyle said, a look of mock astonishment on his face now. ''So you're the one who's been peering through my windows! Well, you certainly are tenacious. I *like* that in a man.''

There was an immense crash now, like a drawer full of silverware hitting a linoleum floor. This was followed by the grunting of a human, or nearly human, voice.

''Destroy it,'' Bentley said.

''Would you like to meet him?'' Argyle's voice was full of enthusiasm. ''He's rather crude by some standards, but with a little help he'll do the trick. And I suppose it's true that if it weren't for you he wouldn't have any . . . life at all. I guess you'd call it life.''

''*I* wouldn't call it that, and I utterly deny having *any*thing to . . .''

''Well, come on in then and say hello.'' Argyle opened the door, stepped back, and gestured Bentley into the house.

Even though he was prepared, Bentley was struck dumb by what he saw. The thing that sat in an overstuffed chair next to the fireplace was very nearly Argyle's twin, dressed again in identical clothing. But there was something coarse about it, something blocky and unfinished. It had a vague, lobotomized look on its face, and its flesh, if it *was* flesh, was waxy and discolored. The fact that its eyes moved and its mouth twitched made it all the more horrible.

''What do you think?'' Argyle asked. He looked as if he relished the sight of Bentley's face.

''Destroy it now,'' Bentley said. ''I'll help you do it. Lord knows how, but we'll do it. Destroy it or go to Hell.''

"Don't pass Go, eh? Don't collect two hundred dollars. Don't you think it's an astonishing likeness?"

Bentley breathed slowly and steadily, trying to compose himself. "It looks like I imagine you'd look after lying dead in a ditch. Can I ask where you got it?" He glanced around the room, looking for something heavy. What would it take to kill a creature that wasn't alive?

"China. The Chinese are masters of replication. Do you know that they have carpet factories that will replicate any kind of picture onto a wool carpet?—your mother, a Picasso painting, a jet airplane, anything you want. This is the same sort of thing, after a fashion. A little more mysticism, perhaps. There's a grand, Kabbalistic tradition to it—several thousand years of mystical mumbo jumbo. . . ."

"Spare me the details. I'm not an idiot."

"All right. Let's just say that this is another case of the Chinese doing it more cheaply, that's all. Moderately cheap, anyway—at least the production end of things. Attendant expenses can creep up on you. All they need is a photo, some odds and ends of memorabilia. In my case, a ring, baby shoes, a couple of articles of clothing. It comes to you fully clothed, by the way. When it arrives it's not so . . . finely wrought, I guess you'd say, as our friend is now, but its general appearance improves as long as it's in close association with its master, shares its master's habits. It even brushes its own teeth."

"It's a filthy abomination," Bentley said, suddenly wanting to shut him up.

"Probably it is. I'll be glad to get it out of here, actually." The golem shifted in its chair, the expression on its face undergoing sudden changes as if to mimic Argyle's own phony high spirits. "Of course it's deficient intellectually," Argyle said. "I tried to teach it to play Scrabble, but it was no use. I wish I could say it cheated, but it was simply stupid. All in all it's been a tiresome houseguest: drops food out of its mouth, pisses on the toilet seat—thank heavens it doesn't smoke, eh?" He chuckled and shook his head almost fondly. "Ah well, I suppose there's no use complaining, since it's just about to leave us. It's bound for a warmer climate, and I suppose it'll serve in Hell as well as the next man."

"*Serve?*" Argyle spat the word out. "This soulless thing? The Devil wouldn't want it."

"Now, don't insult my houseguest!" Argyle said. He waggled a finger at Bentley. "And you know absolutely *nothing* about its soul, such as it is. It has one, actually. It's lying around here somewhere, locked in a jar."

"If you're talking about Walt Stebbins's demon," Bentley told him, "then I think I can assure you that you'll never get hold of it. It's beyond your grasp now."

"*What* a dirty shame," Argyle said, putting his hand to his mouth and widening his eyes. "So you've come all the way over here, full of passion, to tell me that I've failed?"

"Worse than failed," Bentley said.

"And what would you have me do? Follow George Nelson and Murray LeRoy into that damned alley myself?"

"Repent!" Bentley shouted at him, suddenly losing his temper.

The golem abruptly stood up and took a couple of halting steps forward, and Argyle reached over and pushed it solidly on the chest, propelling it backward into its chair again. "You crawling little hypocrite!" he said to Bentley. "You Johnny-come-lately. Your kind is all the same, pointing the self-righteous finger at everyone else while you go around doing what you damned well choose. By God, *listen* for once! I don't *need* your help. *I* am all the help I need!" He jabbed himself in the chest now. "*You* can damned well go to Hell, because I've got better things to do. Now get out of here." He pointed toward the door.

"All right," Bentley said evenly. "Self-righteous, is it? What about poor Simms? Was he self-righteous, too? Is that why you murdered him?"

"Get out," Argyle said evenly. "You understand *nothing*. Simms was an accident. I compensated his widow. If she needs something more . . ."

"*Compensated!*" Bentley shouted. "I'll show you compensation!" He dropped his Bible onto a tabletop, then bent over and picked up the fireplace poker, slapping it once against his palm. He took a step forward, threw his arm back, and swung the poker hard at Argyle's head.

⇥ 62 ⇤

HENRY LOOKED INTO THE MOTOR HOME, THROUGH THE closed screen door. Jinx worked at the little counter inside, putting together a couple of sandwiches. There was a jar of mayonnaise out, lettuce, sliced ham. . . . She caught sight of him, stared for a moment, then leaned toward the door and said, "Don't stand out in the drizzle, for heaven's sake. Come on in. I'm making lunch."

Henry nodded, pulling open the screen and climbing the steps. Jinx had a space heater going inside, and so keeping the door open was a waste of energy, except that both of them liked the rain, especially the sound and the smell of it. A long time ago they had come to the mutual decision to waste the damned energy when they felt like it. How many rainy days did they have left, after all?

He sat down at the table and watched the street. He was speechless, thinking about this, about how he and Jinx had come to share this attitude about the rain. They'd driven just about every highway in the western United States in their day—slept in parking lots, eaten in diners; Jinx had a thimble collection from everywhere, hundreds of thimbles, porcelain and copper and pewter. Every one of them contained a memory, too, like a little cup—that's what Jinx said; those were her own words. And now she'd been to see Goldfarb.

"You're quiet this afternoon," she said. She wasn't giving anything away. He couldn't read her face.

"Yes," he said, "I guess I am."

"What's wrong? Are you eating that bran cereal that I bought?"

"Oh, yes," he said, waving away any thought to the contrary.

"Well, here's a sandwich. Did you want sprouts on it, or lettuce?"

"I don't guess I want any sprouts."

She put the sandwich on a plate along with a couple of lettuce leaves and slid it in front of him, then sat down opposite him with her own sandwich. He took a bite and chewed on it without any interest, and then shoved the plate away.

"All right," she said, "what's eating you? You look like a lost soul."

"I saw the mail," he said. "You've been to see Goldfarb."

"Yes, I certainly have." She looked at him curiously.

He shook his head at her, trying to find the right words. "Whatever she . . . whatever they told you, it was a lie."

"Was it?" she asked, putting her own sandwich down. "How much of it was a lie?"

"All of it. I didn't *touch* that woman. You can ask Walt or Bentley; either one of them will tell you. She's a damned extortionist. She'll say anything at all, anything. I wish to God I'd never . . ."

"Who *is* she, exactly? Not one of the lunchwagon women again?"

"No, she's not one of the lunchwagon women. You know her, actually. Maggie Biggs. She used to run the Eastern Paradise restaurant out on King Street in Honolulu back when we were in the Kahala bungalow."

Jinx squinted at him. "Who?"

"Short woman? Hair . . ." Henry gestured with his hands to illustrate Maggie Biggs's hair.

"Hair?" Jinx said, nodding her head and pursing her lips. "That too . . ." Then suddenly she broke into a smile. "What *are* you talking about?" she asked.

"Don't *mock* me," Henry said, shaking his head at her. "For God's sake, don't play dumb. You've seen Goldfarb. We both know that. I'm trying to clear the air. What I'm telling you is that there was no reason for you to talk to Goldfarb. Not *any* reason. I . . . I love you like . . . like . . ." He realized that she was gaping at him. "Like I don't know," he said. "I guess I'm a damned fool." He got up and turned toward the door, taking his hat off the peg and reaching for his coat.

"Now where are you going?" she asked. Her voice didn't have any amusement in it any more.

"Walk," he said.

"Now? In the rain?"

He shrugged. "I guess I just don't know."

"Henry, I called Mr. Goldfarb about the children."

"Which children?" he asked, not grasping this.

"Why, Nora and Eddie. What other children are there?"

"You called Goldfarb about Nora and Eddie? Why? What did they do?"

"They didn't *do* anything. Sit back down, for goodness sake, and I'll tell you about it. Walt and Ivy are in a dead panic about that damned Jack, and so I took it upon myself to find out what's what. That's why I called Mr. Goldfarb. So I don't know anything about any woman with hair like you've described. You've quit seeing her, then?"

"I never *was* seeing her. That's what I've been telling you."

"Good. I never much liked her anyway. She was too brash. I remember she used to sit on a stool at the end of the counter and order the little Filipino waitresses around. So I'm glad you haven't been seeing her. Who else haven't you been seeing?" She narrowed her eyes.

"Why, I haven't been seeing anybody else," he said, puzzled.

"That's good," she said. "Neither have I. I don't want to; do you know why?"

He looked at her for a moment, trying to puzzle her out. She was apparently serious.

"Because I love you, too," she said. "Just like you love me."

He nodded at her. "Good," he said. "That's good. And I do love you, too."

"I know you do," she said. "Now sit down and eat your sandwich."

⊰ 63 ⊱

ARGYLE THREW HIS HANDS UP AND STUMBLED BACKWARD, grunting as the poker whistled past his face. Bentley whirled around and lunged at the golem, slashing at the thing's neck. The heavy iron head of the poker sank into its flesh as if into wet clay. Bentley wrenched it free and threw the weapon back for another blow, but just then Argyle slammed into his back, wrapping his arms around Bentley's shoulders and grabbing the shaft of the poker, wrenching it hard.

Bentley stumbled forward, clamping his free hand onto the heavy end of the poker, cranking it around like he was steering a bus and pulling Argyle off-balance. "No!" he shouted, but Argyle held on, falling to one knee. Bentley stomped hard on his ankle and twisted the poker again, yanking it free, then stepped back and kicked Argyle in the small of the back. "That's for Simms!" he shouted, whipping the poker behind his back with both hands now, as if he'd take Argyle's head off with it. He skipped forward and swung it hard, pulling it short again, scaring the bastard away. Argyle yelped, going over backward and knocking over a small table, scuttling away on his hands and knees, heading around behind a stuffed chair, where he stood up, waving both hands to ward off Bentley.

"Put it down!" Argyle shouted. "For God's sake . . . !"

"Burn the church down, eh?" Bentley yelled, full of a wild rage, and he smashed a potted palm, hacking it to smithereens with the poker. Dirt and leaves flew in the air, raining down on the golem, and Bentley skipped across and hammered a vase on the fireplace mantel, then pounded the hell out of a table lamp, flattening the lampshade and smashing its porcelain base. He took aim at a piece of bird statuary, knocked a flamingo's porcelain head flying, and then lunged without warning toward Argyle again, stabbing the end of the poker into the chair that stood between them, tearing a long gash in the material and yanking out a big wad of stuffing.

Argyle made a sideways move, as if to run, and Bentley drove the poker downward like a saber and lunged in at him again, swinging his weapon in a wild tumult of blows as if he were knocking down an army. Argyle retreated into a far corner, his arms in front of his face, and without an instant's hesitation Bentley spun around and rushed the golem again, intending this time to finish it off. He swung the poker savagely, catching the monster full in the face as it attempted now to stand up out of its chair, its expression an eerie mixture of idiot confusion and of Argyle's own fear and hatred.

Bentley saw the poker drive into the thing's mouth and nose, saw a piece of its waxy flesh tear loose, heard the noise that came out of the thing's throat. It jerked backward, perhaps from the force of the blow, perhaps to escape, and sat down hard on the arm of the chair, then slumped onto the seat, resting its disfigured head against the cushion. There was no expression in its face now, only vacancy, but somehow that made things even worse, and Bentley was suddenly full of horror at what he'd done.

He stood there panting, drained of energy, holding the poker loosely in his hand. It was over. He felt degraded, monstrous, and for a moment he was nearly sick. He hadn't killed it. Probably he couldn't kill it. Its eyes wandered around the room as if it didn't quite know where it was, and it made a noise, a breathy, rapid whimper. Bentley had simply worked out his anger on it. In his mind it had been Argyle himself that had taken the beating. He wondered abruptly if the golem could feel pain. Surely not.

"Get out," Argyle said to him, his voice croaking out of him like the voice of a strangled man. Bentley turned around, dropping the poker in surprise at what he saw. Blood ran out of Argyle's nose and from a cut on his lip, and there was a heavy red welt across his neck. Stigmata, Bentley realized. Mirror images of the golem's own wounds.

Full of self-loathing, Bentley groped for something to say, something to justify himself. Before whom? Argyle? God? He gestured at the golem, which lay in the chair like a dead man, its throat caved in, its face mutilated. "I didn't mean . . ."

"I don't care what you meant," Argyle told him, smearing his bloody face with his hand. He looked at the stain on his palm. His hand trembled violently. His voice was wheezy and labored, and he coughed and tilted his head back as if to open his throat. "Understand me when I say that I'm indifferent to you. Just go now. Go on. Get out. Get out. Get out." He waved both his hands, wrists turned downward, as if to sweep Bentley out of the room, out of his life. Something had come into his eyes, almost a glow, as if in the taste of his own blood he savored his victory, his imminent success.

Bentley stepped across to the door. He was deflated, utterly fatigued. Argyle hadn't defeated him—he saw that clearly— he had defeated himself. He felt sickened and ashamed. The act of hurting the golem had humanized it in some odd, back-handed way. He felt as if he'd beaten a dumb beast, a cow or a sheep.

Pushing the door open, he stepped out onto the porch. With-out looking back he descended the steps, out from under the porch roof and into a heavy drizzle. Right then something struck him hard in the small of the back, and he grunted and stumbled forward. It was his Bible. Argyle had thrown it at him.

Slowly he bent over to pick it up off the wet concrete. He steeled himself and turned around, reminding himself that the book was none the worse for wear, that Argyle couldn't hurt it. He opened his mouth to speak, to redeem . . .

But the door slammed shut, hard enough so that the entire front of the house shook on its foundation. Bentley stood look-ing at it for a moment, then turned around and walked toward the street, standing by his car for a minute before getting in, looking up at the rainy evening sky.

Mahoney wanted Bentley to go shelling with him tomorrow morning at dawn, rain or shine, and Bentley had told him that he didn't have time for it—too many duties, too much work. Well, suddenly he was ready for it. He couldn't remember how long it had been since he had gone anywhere merely for plea-sure. What he needed right now was air—ocean air, brisk enough to blow the moths out of his coat. And according to Mahoney, there was no telling what you'd find on the beach after a storm.

⇥ 64 ⇤

IVY FOUND ARGYLE AT HIS DESK IN HIS BUSINESS OFFICE. He wore a turtleneck sweater, and he sat and stared with his hands folded in front of him, apparently in a contemplative mood. She carried the manila envelope full of the Batavia property paperwork. "You've hurt yourself," she said, seeing that his lip and cheek had been cut open. The wound was held shut with three butterfly Band-Aids.

"Golfing accident." He gestured at the office chair and beamed at her, as if suddenly full of zip. "I can't tell you how happy I am that you've come to me today."

She stopped herself from pointing out how idiotic this sounded, how full of vanity, and instead she sat down and waited for him to go on.

"Everything is absolutely sailing along with the properties. They're rushing the loan papers; escrow's already moving. We could close in no time. Mr. Peetenpaul is *extremely* happy."

"I dare say he is."

"Now," Argyle went on, winking at her, "I've got a little surprise for you."

"What's that?" She kept her voice even.

"I'd like to advance you half the commission right now, if you don't mind, just to start sewing things up. How's that with you? Do you mind half the money now? No added tax burden, is there, if you get it before the first of the year?"

"No," she said, standing up and wandering over to the window. "I don't think it'll have any effect on taxes at all." She saw that Murray LeRoy's property was dug to pieces now, areas cordoned off with yellow plastic tape flipping and dancing in the wind. A generator chugged away under a plastic awning, pumping muddy rainwater out of a hole, but she couldn't see any workmen or watchmen around the premises, and there was no longer any sign of earth-moving equipment. By this time next year the place would be up in condominiums, which was a shame.

She glanced down into the rear parking lot of the office building. The black pickup truck sat in a stall. "Where is Mr. Peetenpaul?" she asked. "He seems to have become un-available."

"Oh, he's around. I can assure you of that. He's a busy man, what with his plans. I think we can depend upon him for more business in the future."

"Is he here now? In the building?"

"No," Argyle said, his smile fixed on his face. "Here? Why do you ask?"

"Well, that seems to be his truck down there in the lot, doesn't it?"

"*Is* it? Oh, of course it is. I'm having it . . . detailed for him. My man's coming around this afternoon if the weather stays clear. Mobile detailing unit."

"That's big of you," Ivy said, sitting down again. She saw that Argyle had his checkbook out. Apparently he was going to write out a great big check right then and there. She was reminded suddenly of Walt's tearing up Mrs. Simms's check in the garage the other night, and she could easily envision herself doing the same thing here, throwing the pieces in Argyle's face. She realized that she was thinking of him as Argyle again. Robert had disappeared. "I saw Mr. Peetenpaul at the doughnut shop yesterday, at the All-Niter."

He nodded, as if this fascinated him.

"He seemed to be on his way somewhere."

"To eat a doughnut, probably."

"Actually, he didn't buy any doughnuts. He apparently abandoned his truck in the parking lot and drove away with a local woman, a Mrs. Biggs. It looked for all the world like they were carrying airline tickets."

Argyle stared at her now, as if he didn't quite take this in. "A Mrs. Biggs," he said flatly.

"That's what I was told. I wonder what exactly happened to his truck after that—the way he tossed his keys onto the floor and just walked away. I wonder, did he come back after it? Maybe I was wrong about the airline tickets?"

"Well, I don't quite know," Argyle said. "I've been a little busy myself. I see that I'm not up on the details of Mr. Peetenpaul's life. Are you certain about this . . . this Mrs. Biggs? About the name, I mean? You saw the two of them leave together?" All the humor, even the false humor, had gone out of his face.

"I'm afraid I did. They seemed to be an item, actually. It almost looked as if they were taking off on their honeymoon, off to Tahiti or somewhere."

Argyle looked away, thinking hard about something, his checkbook apparently forgotten for the moment. "I'll be damned," he said finally, then abruptly barked out a laugh. "Mr. Peet! That old son of a gun . . ."

"Look," Ivy said, leaning forward. "Don't bother with the check, all right? Let's quit pretending. A little bit of honesty once in a while wouldn't hurt much. I had hoped that after all these years things would have changed with you, but apparently they haven't."

"I'm afraid I don't . . ." He shook his head helplessly.

"Walt was right, wasn't he? He said that Mr. Peetenpaul was an employee of yours, and that this entire property transaction was set up to deceive me. I wanted to think differently, but it's true, isn't it? You've had something up your sleeve all along. You've been playing some sort of game, saying one thing, doing another. This has all been a deception."

He looked steadily at her for a moment, as if he were scrambling to find something to say in his own defense. "We had a contract," he said, just a little desperately, "and I intend to honor it. Humor me, Ivy, for old times' sake. Give me another chance." He picked up a pen and reached for the checkbook. "*This* is no deception, I assure you."

"I'll tear it up, Robert. I mean it. I don't want your money. As for another chance, I don't quite know what you mean by that, and I don't think I want to."

"This commission could *make* you, Ivy. It could open doors for you. I've got powerful friends, wealthy friends. They buy and sell property for sums of money that would astonish you. And certainly this commission, as small as it is, would very nearly save Walt, wouldn't it? You were telling me about his business. Hanging on through the first year is *crucial*. This money could make Walt's dreams come true—get him out of the garage and into a commercial building, who knows where he'd end up?''

''Nobody knows,'' Ivy said. ''What I know is that you don't understand the first thing about Walt, and you never have. He wouldn't touch your money twenty years ago, and he won't touch it now. Neither would I. Don't make me say any more about it. Please. And don't pretend to have Walt's best interests in mind, because you don't, and you know it. This whole thing was a mistake. Let's end it here.''

He shrugged and slumped back into his seat. After a moment he closed the checkbook slowly, but left it on the desktop. ''I did it for you,'' he said. ''What does it matter who bought the property?''

''What matters is that *nobody* bought the property. You were trying to buy *me*. That's closer to the truth, isn't it?''

''Don't say that. I·wouldn't do that. I can't explain what I mean, exactly, but believe me when I tell you that I'm undergoing *changes* in my life. Profound changes. I don't know what you'd call them—spiritual changes, I guess. I've finally managed to square things away. There's a . . . a spiritual bankruptcy, I guess you could say, that a man can apply for when he's in the sort of debt I'm in. I mean to say that I've filed Chapter 13, Ivy. I'm getting out from under a great . . . a great debt, a great weight. I'll be free of it. By tomorrow I'll . . . I'll finally be able to feel *good* about myself.''

''I don't have any idea what you're talking about, Robert. And to tell you the truth, I don't think you do either. I think you're the most incredibly self-deceived human being I've ever known. I'd bet a shiny new dime that by tomorrow you won't have changed in any way at all, although you probably *will* feel good about yourself, heaven help you. So *please* don't mention your commission again, or whatever you want to call it. Save your breath.''

He gestured at her, holding up both hands, then slid them under the edge of the heavy checkbook and tilted it at her, letting her see his name embossed in gold on the leather cover. ''You've *got* to understand what this would mean . . .''

''I'm *really* tired of this,'' she said, interrupting him again. She stood up and leaned on the desk, looking down on him now. ''I'm going to say one last thing, and while I say it I don't want you to speak. I know that something's gone on

over the past few weeks between you and Walt. I don't know
what it is. I thought it was him making it up, out of jealousy
or something, but I don't think so any more. So listen to this:
if you so much as touch that man, if you come near our house,
if you do *anything* to damage him or his business or anything
else, I swear to God I'll find a way to hurt you.''

She laid the manila envelope on the desktop, then walked
out the door.

⇥ 65 ⇤

WALT FITTED CANDLE BULBS INTO THE DILWORTH CATA-
logue golden lampstand, then carried it out to the tin shed and
set it in among the pine trees. He stepped back to take a look
at the thing, breathing the scent of the pine and listening to
the rain on the roof. The lampstand reminded him suddenly of
the lamppost in Narnia; there was something magically incon-
gruous about it, even if it was made out of pot metal and
plaster of Paris.

It occurred to him that he was rationalizing having spent
good money on what was evidently a piece of junk, and he
turned around and went back out into the rain, heading for the
garage.

That was tough about Ivy's losing Argyle's big commission.
At first Walt had tried to talk her into taking it anyway, the
whole sixty grand, just like she'd made him take the check for
Mrs. Simms. Why not?—cash the check and then tell Argyle
to his face what kind of a stinking geek he really was. Take
his money and insult him both, so as to double the satisfaction.
Of course, that wasn't the sort of thing Ivy would do, and he
was proud of her for that. The only trouble was that he had
pretty much convinced himself that spending forty bucks on
this crap from the catalogue was no big deal, since they were
suddenly rolling in money anyway. Now it looked like a big
deal again, because suddenly they weren't rolling in money at
all; they weren't rolling in anything but visiting relatives. It
was going to be a drier Christmas than he'd thought. And by
spring, if things didn't pick up considerably, he was going to
be reading the want ads in the morning instead of the comics.

In the garage he shifted boxes out of the way and uncovered
an old chair that Ivy was making him store out there. She'd

bought it at a garage sale—too good a deal to pass by—but then they hadn't had any room for it, so it had gone into storage. He pounded on the worn tapestry seat a couple of times to knock the dust out of it, then picked it up by its wooden arms and carried it around to the shed, setting it down inside the door so that the pine boughs nearly brushed against it. Now all he needed was some kind of little table to set a drink and a book on, and the shed would be about perfect.

He wondered idly how he could hide the lamp cord, which right now snaked across the floor, ruining the effect. Maybe straight up through the roof. Or maybe a hole in the indoor-outdoor carpeting and then through the floor itself, run it into the garage through plastic conduit instead of using an extension cord.

He glanced out through the open door, at the concrete stepping-stones in the lawn. There was a patch of blackened grass around the stone that hid the bluebird, and some kind of greenish-looking puffball toadstools coming up through it, as if the ground had been poisoned. He thought about the mutated salmon eggs in the tackle box and Bentley's talk about demons.

Probably it was time to get the jar out of there, he thought idly, off the property altogether. How easy would that be? Was he tough enough? It was easy to refuse the demon when you had other options, but when the ice was getting thin, and your dreams were one by one falling through . . .

It was true that he had made a hideous error when he set the bird on Sidney Vest. Lord knows there was plenty of evidence that the thing meant trouble. It had given him tomatoes but killed his herbs. It had delivered his newspaper early and then sabotaged his mail. It had given him sixty bucks in the Lotto and then smashed up his car. He had asked it to send Sidney Vest home to Raleigh, and by golly the bird had done it. Thank God he had gotten to it before it killed Maggie Biggs, too.

And what exactly *had* happened there? The bird had apparently come through in fine style, and the result of that whole deal was that Ivy's money went down the rat hole. There seemed to be some kind of awful *cost* that went along with making a wish on the bluebird—an equal and opposite reaction that was utterly unpredictable and vicious.

He sat down in the chair and stared into the trees. Of course, he had no way of knowing that any of this was true. The herb garden, the mail, the bent fender, even Vest's death—all of that might easily be coincidence, and not even unlikely coincidence, either. The Maggie Biggs wish had certainly been successful, unless of course it *had* cost them the sixty grand.

Maybe there was a way to *phrase* things, he thought. He had gone about the first wishes haphazardly, like an amateur. It wasn't until he'd saved Maggie Biggs that he'd considered *how* to talk to the bird. Perhaps it was simply necessary to phrase the request carefully. . . .

Just then there was a loud metallic knocking, and he nearly leaped out of the chair at the sound of it. Robert Argyle stood in the doorway under a black umbrella, the rain dripping down around him. Walt blinked at him for a moment, as if Argyle were a hallucination. Someone had apparently given him a fat lip. Well, good for them, whoever it was.

"Top of the morning to you," Walt said, recovering. "What brings you out into the rain?"

"Can I step inside?"

Walt gestured, inviting him in, and Argyle closed up his umbrella and shook the rain off. "I want you to know there are no hard feelings," he said.

"About what, exactly?"

"Forgive me for saying so, but you seem to have taken all this too personally, Walt. You shouldn't let morons like Lorimer Bentley feed you full of ideas. You've always been your own man. Keep it up. The Bentleys of the world can't see past their noses, but men like us have vision."

" 'Men like us,' " Walt said flatly. "Why am I troubled by that phrase?"

"There's no need to apologize," Argyle told him.

"Apologize? That's a relief. You don't know how good that makes me feel."

"I'm happy to hear that."

"That's why you dropped by, to tell me I don't have to apologize? Or do you have something else in mind?"

"Well, in fact I do—two things. First I want you to know that the Robert Argyle you've known for the last twenty years will shortly cease to exist, in a manner of speaking."

"Well, I'll be damned," Walt said.

"I guess you could say that I'll be the phoenix that rises from the ashes. It's a long story, Walt. By now Bentley's told you most of it, so there's no need to pretend that you don't know what I'm talking about. I guess . . . I guess I want to make amends, you might say. I want you to know that I forgive you for coveting the bluebird, which you have to admit was rightfully mine. I'm sorry that I had to resort to . . . to the methods I had to resort to in order to retrieve it, but honestly, I gave you every opportunity."

"Yes, you did. No hard feelings."

"Good. One more thing. As you know, Ivy and I have had what you might call a special relationship, and . . ."

"Don't push your luck," Walt said.

"Pardon me?"

"You haven't had any sort of relationship at all with Ivy except in your pitiful imagination. If you say another word about her . . . Look, just do yourself a favor and shut the hell up."

Argyle stared at him. "I certainly didn't mean . . ."

"Then what did you mean? Say what you mean and get the hell out of here."

"I owe her a considerable sum of money, which she refuses to take for reasons that I don't at all understand. I happen to be very interested in absolving myself of debt right now; I guess that's the best way to put it. And I came here hoping that you and I might come to an understanding between ourselves."

"Let me get this straight. You figure that Ivy has too many scruples to take your dirty money, but that I don't have those scruples. You 'understand' me, is that it? Is that how you'd put it?"

"I didn't say that. I just think that as a businessman *you* understand . . ."

"Do you have the check?"

Argyle nodded. "In my pocket."

"Then you're right, I'll take it," Walt said.

Argyle took a check out of his coat pocket and handed it to Walt, who looked at the sum. It was written out for an even sixty thousand. Walt crumpled it into a ball and threw it out into the rain. "Now take a hike," he said. "I've got nothing else to say to you, except that you ought to do yourself a favor and open your damned eyes. You don't look like any kind of phoenix to me; you look like a man who's lost his mind. I seem to recall that you used to have one.''

He bent over and picked up the plug end of the lamp cord, connecting it to the extension cord running out of the garage. The candle bulbs in the golden lampstand flickered on, seeming to waver like candle flames. For one eerie moment the darkness in the shed actually deepened, as if night had fallen. The bulbs shone like fireflies and the black shadows of the trees stood out against the shed walls like etchings. Then the glow from the bulbs spread—not as if the bulbs were gaining in wattage, but as if the light emanating from them was actually moving very slowly, billowing into a cloud like the smoke rising out of a genie's lamp.

Walt glanced up at Argyle, who stood staring, his eyes wide. His face seemed fleshless in the light of the lampstand, a grinning skull. His teeth were brown, like old ivory, and he raised his hands slowly, turning them over and looking at his palms in apparent disbelief, as if he could see his bones through his flesh. A noise came out of his mouth, a groan like the creaking of a door, and he turned on his heel and staggered out onto the lawn, where he bent over and picked up the balled-up check, putting it into his pocket without looking at it. He stood staring up into the avocado tree, his hands crossed on his chest like a man laid out for burial.

''What's wrong?'' Walt asked him, getting up out of his chair. It looked as if the bastard was having a heart attack. ''You all right?''

But Argyle waved him away and lurched off in the direction of the gate, past the family room window, where Nora and Eddie sat watching the television. Argyle looked in at the children, and Walt heard him utter another groan. Then he staggered forward again, almost falling, and Walt followed, swinging open the gate to let him out. Hunched over, Argyle went away down the driveway, hurrying now, as if he were pursued by something. His car was parked at the curb. Walt watched him climb into it and drive away. Strangely, there was a passenger in the car. Someone had been waiting for him.

❧ 66 ❧

"WAS THAT MR. R-GUY?"

"Yeah," Walt said, turning around. Nora had come outside. Eddie stood in the doorway.

"He was all bent," Nora said.

"Yes, he was," Walt told her. "That's just what he was. He's one of the bent people. Come on over here, out of the rain."

"Eddie drew Mr. Binion," Nora said.

"What?" Walt looked at her, baffled. "Mr. Binion?" Eddie stepped down onto the walk and hurried across to the carport to join them, holding out a piece of paper with a crayon drawing of a snail on it. The snail was apparently wearing a hat.

"Mr. Binion," Nora said. "The snail." She waved at the lawn. "*You* know. Don't be funny."

"Oh, *that* Mr. Binion. Of course." He looked at the picture. "Yes, indeed," he said. "That's a good likeness." Eddie was very nearly smiling. "I'd like to have this," Walt said. Eddie nodded.

"Can we play in the trees?" Nora asked.

"Sure," Walt said. "Of course. I just put up a light in there." This staggered him. Mr. Binion, the trees . . . It had worked. His nonsensical plans to entertain the children had worked.

He and Eddie followed Nora over to the shed door and looked in. The shed was filled now with the glow from the lampstand. The light hung in the air like a mist, like translucent gold. The shadows beneath the trees were as deep as caves, and the green floor stretched away like a meadow. It was almost impossible to say just where the shed walls were, as if the light created the illusion of vast depth and width. The interior of the shed might have held an entire forest, and heaven knew what beyond that—a place with running streams, grass, deep skies, and moving clouds. . . .

He realized that Nora was holding onto his leg, still staring with wide wonder into the light. He put his arm around Eddie's shoulders and gave him a squeeze, and Eddie didn't draw away as he usually did, but stood still, holding the picture of Mr. Binion.

How long they had stood there Walt couldn't say, but after a while he heard the gate scrape open, and there came into his mind the idea that Argyle had returned for some desperate reason. And then abruptly he was aware of the smell of something burning—an electrical smell, like a hot wire. He shook his head to clear it. There was a low, electronic buzz, then a snap and spark from the lampstand plug. The light in the shed wavered and dimmed, and the magic evaporated on the instant.

Walt pushed Nora and Eddie out the door, away from the pine trees, which would go up like Hell if they caught fire. He stepped forward, grabbing the lampstand cord. It was hot and soft in his hand. He stepped down hard on the extension cord and jerked, yanking the two plugs apart in a shower of sparks like a waterfall.

"Whoa!" Eddie shouted, looking in through the door from the middle of the lawn.

Walt dropped the hot cord and closed his fist over the burn on his palm, touching the metal lampstand pole with his other hand. It was hot, too. The bulbs were melted in their sockets, and the molten glass had run down the sides of the sockets like a sugar glaze.

"What happened?" a voice asked behind him.

"Nothing," he said instinctively, and turned around. Ivy stood between Nora and Eddie, sheltering the three of them under her umbrella and looking into the shed skeptically.

"It's these doggone cheap extension cords," Walt said, smiling big at her. "No harm done."

"Not yet anyway." Then to the kids she said, "Go on into the house and find Aunt Jinx. I want to talk to Uncle Walt alone." She didn't look happy, but it wasn't the lamp; it was something else.

The kids ran off, and when they were out of earshot Walt asked, "What gives?"

"Jack. He's on his way over. He's apparently got a lawyer. And he's sober, too."

"A lawyer?"

"Some crook, probably, but he means business."

"That's good. I'll give him business."

"Don't start it up," she said. "Stay cool this time, will you? Jinx's lawyer friend is on the way—Mr. Goldfarb."

"Good for him," Walt said. "I'll need a lawyer when I'm done with Jack. We might as well put him on retainer as soon as he pulls in. Call in a plastic surgeon, too, and alert the trauma center down at St. Joseph's."

"Cut it out, okay? Just stop. Can you watch the kids? Get them out here with you, maybe? Keep them tied up?"

He looked at her, considering this. Moments passed. "Sure," he said finally. He was big enough to give it a try, to hold onto his temper. "Have them bring out some paper and crayons or something. I'll be the last line of defense. If I turn out to be unnecessary, then you can tell me I told you so. But look, Jack can't come into the backyard. If he does, I'll make him sorry for it. It'll be a bad thing, but I'm through talking with the man. He's poison, like a snake, and if he comes back here or into the house, if he gets pushy in any way, says or does anything out of line, then I'll feed him his head. So have Mr. Goldfarb do his job, whatever that is."

"He'll do it. Jack's history." She kissed him, turned around, and hurried away.

He stood there for a moment controlling himself, realizing that what he wanted to do was hit something hard, break something, smash something. Jack could drink himself crazy every night; who cared about that? With any luck he would drink himself to death. But his hurting Eddie, that made him an end-to-end creep, a stain on the human landscape, a blotch, a poison. A little bit of remorse would have lightened him up—any little effort to do the right thing. But there wasn't any effort. His conscience had flatlined. How he had gotten that way just didn't matter any more.

Walt caught sight just then of the stepping-stone, the black-ened grass, the toadstools. The bluebird sat buried beneath the ground like an accusation, like a cancer, like the evil filth that it was. It occurred to him right then that it was astonishingly easy to condemn another man's temptations—liquor, greed, lust, whatever they were—*because they weren't your own temptations.* And when you yourself fell, you'd find that it was your own temptations that had nailed you, and never mind anyone else's.

Suddenly seeing what he had to do, he shoved his hand under the edge of the stepping-stone and flipped it on end, then picked up the concrete slab with both hands and smashed the toadstools to mush, using the corner of the stone to reduce even the smallest of them to a pale green slime, which he beat deep into the earth. Then he threw the stone down and picked up the jar with the bird in it. Without looking at it, without listening to it, he drew his hand back and pitched it sidearm into the redwood fence, a fastball, dead center against a post. The glass shattered, spraying gin and shards in a wide arc. The bird fell straight down into the dirt of the flowerbed. He jogged into the garden shed and grabbed the shovel, then went back out and dug a hole in the wet dirt. He prodded the corpse of the bird into the hole with the tip of the shovel and buried it, packing the dirt back on top. Feeling considerably better, he threw down the shovel and went to meet Nora, who was just then coming out the door, carrying a book—the fairy-tale book he'd read from the other night.

"Read us that one story," she said. Eddie followed her, carrying the crayon box and paper.

"What story?" Walt asked, bending over to set the stone back into the hole. He stood up again, dusting his hands. "What was it about? You don't really remember, do you?"

"Yes-huh," she said. "It was that dummy, who they made him eat rocks, and it made him smart."

"I guess you *do* remember," Walt said, putting an arm around each of the kids. "I guess it's me who keeps forgetting."

⇒ 67 ⇐

JACK AND HIS LAWYER ARRIVED BEFORE GOLDFARB, PULLING in at the curb in a new BMW, clearly the lawyer's car. Jack wore a tie, and from what Ivy could see of him, he was clean and sober, just as he'd threatened. The front door opened behind her, and Henry stepped out onto the porch.

"I think I can handle this," Ivy said to him. There was no use in Henry's getting involved at all. Jinx had agreed to stay inside the house, listening through the window. She could run information out to Walt if she had to, although Ivy wondered if it wouldn't be better to avoid that kind of thing. There was no use working Walt up if it wasn't necessary. And she was determined that it wouldn't be necessary.

"I'd just as soon stay," Henry said quietly. "For moral support. Walter thinks this man is a skunk, and I trust Walter's judgment in these matters."

"So do I," Ivy said. "Thanks."

Jack and the lawyer sat talking for a moment, then opened the door and got out, hunching through the rain toward the house, and then up onto the porch. The sun was going down, and Ivy opened the door back up, reached in, and flipped on the porch light and the Christmas lights.

"All right," Jack said straight off. "I suppose you've got them ready to go this time?" There was no smiling this time, no joking around.

"Who?" Ivy asked.

"You know who, Ivy. Legally you don't have a leg to stand on. Thank me for not charging you and Walt with kidnapping. And after that stunt in the street outside the school yesterday morning, with attempted murder, too."

"I don't have any idea what you're talking about," Ivy said.
"Who tried to murder you?"

"Get off it."

"Were there witnesses?" She looked up toward the corner.
Goldfarb was only driving out from Santa Ana; surely he
ought to be here by now.

"You know damned well there weren't any . . ."

"Watch your language, young man," Henry said, interrupting him. "We don't allow profanity on the premises. And
I certainly won't let you swear at my niece. If I'd have known
what kind of creature you were, I wouldn't have let you marry
Darla, either, if I could have stopped it."

"That's rather more to the point, isn't it?" the lawyer said,
leaning in and waving the several sheets of paper in his hand.
"Since my client is in fact married to Darla Douglas, my client, Mr. Douglas, is the legal guardian to"—he looked at the
papers—"Nora and Eddie Douglas. Are the children on the
premises? I believe I called to alert you to our coming. You
haven't in fact hidden them somewhere?"

"They're not hidden anywhere," Ivy said.

"Then if you'll produce them, we'll be on our way. I assure
you that neither I nor my client wishes to file any sort of
charges against you. This is a court order," he said, showing
Ivy the papers.

"What kind of charges don't you and your client want to
file against us?" She didn't bother to look at the papers. For
all she knew, Jack had gotten a court order, in which case the
kids were gone, and there was going to be trouble with Walt,
who wasn't in a mood for court orders.

"Numerous possible charges," the lawyer said. "Take my
word for it."

"Let me ask you one thing, Jack," Ivy said.

"Shoot. Make it quick, though. I've got places to go."

"Why did you abuse Eddie? Darla tells me you like to beat
kids up. Is that only when you're drunk, or do you like to do
that when you're sober, too?" As soon as she said it she
wished she hadn't. It was the kind of thing Walt would say.

Jack's eyes seemed to glaze over, and his face turned red.
He stood there silently, maybe counting to ten. The lawyer put
a hand on his arm, and Jack shook it off.

"I'll warn you against making false accusations against my

client," the lawyer said. "Please don't attempt to provoke him.
For the record, are you suggesting that Mr. Douglas intends to
harm these children?"

"Intends? I guess I'm not suggesting that. I certainly hope
he doesn't."

"Have you filed a notice of Manifest Bad Intent in regard
to my client with Child Protective Services?"

She shook her head.

"Because this is a serious charge. I suggest you go through
proper channels and eschew public accusations."

"Let's not get involved in that kind of horsecrap," Jack
said. "We're here to pick up Nora and Eddie. That's it. Case
closed. And let me tell you something," he said to Ivy, "anyone charges me with anything, there's going to be more trouble
than anyone wants."

"Don't threaten us, young man," Henry said.

"Please," the lawyer said. "Let's avoid escalation here.
The fact remains that Mr. Douglas is the children's legal
guardian by virtue of his marriage to Darla Douglas. If you
refuse to give up the children, this will become a police matter.
I'm trying to avoid that for the good of everyone involved,
including the two children. I'm sure you understand that."

"I do," Ivy said. "Thank you. Maybe you think you're
doing the right thing, but I'm afraid that in this case you're
wrong. You might as well call the police on your car phone
right now, because we're going to be entirely uncooperative."

"You're damned right we'll call the police," Jack said.
"We're talking serious jail time here. This is a court *order*.
I've had enough. Get 'em down here," he said to the lawyer.

"Surely you . . ." the lawyer started to say to Ivy.

"Call 'em now."

"Go ahead," Ivy said. She took Henry's arm and waited.

The lawyer shrugged, turned around, and headed down the
steps toward the car. They watched as he placed the call, got
back out, and returned to the porch. "I'm sorry it has to go
this way," he said to Ivy.

"I'm not," Jack said. "And I'm not paying you to be sorry,
either."

They waited. The idea came into Ivy's head to offer them
coffee and cookies, and she almost laughed out loud. Then she

saw that there was something near hysteria in her thinking, and the thought scared the laughter out of her.

"Where are they coming from?" Henry asked her.

"The police department's down on Batavia. Call it five or ten . . ."

A Cadillac turned the corner off Chapman Avenue.

"Here's the cavalry," Henry said. "Thank God."

⅔ 68 ⅔

IT WAS GOLDFARB IN THE CADILLAC. HE PULLED UP AT THE curb and got out, unfurling an umbrella and hurrying across to the porch. He wore a dark suit and tie and was short and heavily built, evidently Henry's age, but fit-looking. He glanced at Ivy and winked, then shook Henry's hand. Right then a patrol car rounded the corner and parked behind the Cadillac, and two uniformed officers got out. Before anyone spoke, the policemen joined them on the porch.

"It'll be all right," Henry said to Ivy, who nodded at him. It looked like doom to her, despite Goldfarb's wink.

"I represent the Stebbins family," Goldfarb said to the policemen. "I'm afraid there's something wrong here that I don't quite understand. I'm here to help clear it up. Just to put things in order, let me say that my clients have been caring for the two children in question. Mr. Douglas has attempted without success to take them several times. The Stebbinses refused to relinquish the children because Mr. Douglas was both intoxicated and irrational."

"The hell if I was . . ." Jack started to say, but his lawyer shook his head to silence him.

"With all due respect," Jack's lawyer said, "that's all beside the point. We have a court order mandating the release of the children." He handed the papers to one of the policemen, who looked them over, showing them to his partner.

"Do you have anything other than a fax copy, sir?"

The lawyer shook his head. "I'm afraid not. I was out of the office, and my secretary was compelled to fax them to me."

"Court's closed by now," the second cop said, looking at his watch. "Where's your office?"

"Los Angeles, I'm afraid."

Jack looked at his attorney, who watched the officer's face as he looked over the fax again. The officer looked up at Ivy. "You've been caring for the children?"

"Yes. What Mr. Goldfarb told you is entirely true. Mr. Douglas has been drinking heavily for days. My sister left the kids in my care."

"Well," the officer said, "thank you for helping out, but Mr. Douglas doesn't appear to be intoxicated now. According to this document, he's the children's legal guardian. At least until court opens tomorrow we'll have to assume the document's legal. I'm afraid you'll have to get the children. Are they here?"

"They're here," Ivy said.

"Why do we assume the document's legal?" Goldfarb asked. "I have reason to believe it isn't."

Ivy looked at Jack's lawyer, who was stone-faced.

"That's a lie," Jack said.

"May I?" Goldfarb held his hand out, and the officer gave him the fax. "Well, this *is* odd," he said after a moment.

"What the hell's odd?" Jack tried to grab the fax, but Goldfarb snatched it away.

"The judge's name. Benjamin Meng. He retired six months ago, didn't he? I seem to recall that he moved up north, up to Oroville. The date's just right, though, isn't it? How do you explain that? Has he come out of retirement?" He looked Jack's lawyer straight in the face, but the man said nothing. The second of the two officers turned around and walked down the steps and out to the patrol car.

"What I think is this," Goldfarb said. "I think you took an old copy of a court order, whited out the inaccurate information, typed in fresh information, then had it faxed to yourself in order to obtain a clean copy. You set this appointment up late in the afternoon because you knew that court would be closed and the document's authenticity couldn't be established. Am I right so far?"

"No," Jack said. "We're out here this late because *these* people"—he gestured at Ivy and Henry—"have had the kids hidden away. I call that kidnapping. I call that taking a man's kids away, and if that's not a crime, then it's a sorry damned world we're living in."

"But then of course they're not your kids, are they, Jack?" Ivy kept her voice even.

"I as good as raised them," Jack said. "What they had, I bought them, didn't I? They'd be on the *street* if it weren't for me. Deny *that*."

"Okay," Ivy said, "I'll deny it. They never would have been on the street. They'd have been here. They *are* here, aren't they?"

Jack's lawyer still said nothing.

The second officer came back up onto the porch. "Judge Meng retired last March. The order's bogus."

Jack's lawyer shrugged. Jack shoved his jaw out, as if he were trying to bite his upper lip. "This is all crap," he said.

"Actually," Goldfarb said, "I've got a fax of my own from the San Diego County courthouse. Weren't you married to Darla Schwenk in San Diego County, Mr. Douglas?"

"Yeah. So what?"

"There's no record of any such marriage. I believe you were actually married in Tijuana."

"So what? That's legal. Isn't that legal?" He appealed to his lawyer who rolled his eyes tiredly.

"I'm afraid I've been seriously misled," Jack's lawyer said to the two officers. "I've got someplace to be by six." He looked at his watch. "So if I can't be of any more service here . . ."

"Stay where you are," the first officer said. "You're going to be late, wherever you've got to be."

"This," Goldfarb said, showing them a second paper, "is from the court of the County of Orange. There's no record of Darla Schwenk having been divorced at all from her first husband. I put through a call to a Mr. Bill Schwenk, the children's biological father, and he sent back this notarized letter stating that there had been no divorce. The papers were never filed. He's still the children's legal guardian. In the letter he gives his permission to Walt and Ivy Stebbins to care for the children until their mother returns to claim them. The letter's a fax, too, I'm afraid, but as you can see, the original was notarized." He handed all the documentation to the police, who looked it over hastily.

The front door opened then, and Walt looked out through the screen.

"Hi," he said, coming out onto the porch. "Jack! How are you? Is all this cleared up? I sure hope so." He smiled brightly at Jack. "I'm Walt Stebbins, Nora and Eddie's uncle," he said to the two officers. "If I can help . . . ?" He gestured with both hands.

"You can help by fucking off," Jack said to him.

"Now, Jack," Walt said, "that kind of language won't do. You haven't been drinking again, have you?"

"You going to let them talk to me that way?" Jack said to his lawyer. "After what I paid you? I want these people arrested. Kidnapping and assault."

"You didn't pay me half enough as it is, Jack," the lawyer said.

"Well, then, why don't you go to Hell, you shyster bastard?"

"Try to calm down, sir," the first officer said.

"I know my rights, asshole. I can say anything I want, and you can't touch me, and you know it. To hell with you, man, and your friend, too."

"*Have* you been drinking, sir?"

"Shove it up your ass."

"Oh, *no!*" Walt muttered, and Ivy elbowed him in the ribs.

"I'd like your cooperation here, sir. I believe there's reason for you to take a field sobriety test. If you're unwilling to submit to a test here, we can take you to the station and draw blood. The choice is yours."

"The hell if you'll do anything like that. You know I'm not drunk. I haven't had a drink since last night. There's no damn way you'd take me in and risk my being sober. I'd ream you both out, and you know it damn well." His voice rose, and the veins stood out in his neck. He looked furiously at Walt, who smiled like a Cheshire cat, and Jack threw his arm back to take a punch at him.

"Don't do it," the second cop said. "Don't even think about it. So far no . . ."

"*Shut* the hell up," Jack said, swiveling around toward the cop and poking him in the chest with his index finger. He tried to step past him then, to storm away, but quicker than Ivy could see exactly what happened, the second cop's arm shot out, spun Jack around, and Jack was on his knees on the porch with his arm bent around behind him. The other officer already had his handcuffs out. There was a double click of the cuff latches, and then Jack was hauled to his feet.

"Where are the kids?" Ivy asked Walt.

"With Jinx. In the shed."

The police read Jack his rights as they led him through the drizzle toward the patrol car, taking his lawyer along with them.

"Assaulting a police officer," Goldfarb said, clicking his tongue. "I'm afraid Mr. Douglas made a rather grievous mistake. He must have wanted those kids very badly."

"This doesn't have anything to do with the kids," Walt said. "Believe me, I know. This had to do with getting mad, which is pretty much the same as getting drunk, as I see it. You lose your mind either way."

"Write that down," Ivy said to Henry. "Let's post it on the refrigerator."

"Let's order a pizza," Walt said. "Drink, Mr. Goldfarb?"

"Thanks," the lawyer said. "Don't mind if I do."

They opened the door and went in. "Darla called this afternoon," Ivy said, looking at Walt.

"What'd she say?"

"She got a job working for that chiropractor. She's putting her life back together, she said, one piece at a time. I told her we were happy to keep the kids for a while, for however long she needs."

"Good," Walt said. "And good for her." He could see Nora and Eddie coming in through the back door, and he heard Nora's laughter. He was happy to see them. "I hope Darla finds herself," he said. "I honestly do."

❧ 69 ❧

IT WAS DARK WHEN ARGYLE PARKED IN FRONT OF THE ALLEY next to Nelson and Whidley and shut the car off. The unlit alley where LeRoy and Nelson had burned to death stretched away into the darkness, wet with rainwater. On the front wall of the architects' offices that formed the south wall of the alley, a long strand of pinlights spelled out the words "Merry Christmas," blinking on and off and casting a feeble light down onto the hood of his car. He was swept with the sudden urge to tear the lights down, to climb up onto the hood of his car and leap for them, to beat them to pieces against the bricks. . . .

He found that the door was open and he was standing in gutter water. A wet wind gusted out of the alley and into his face. Hurriedly he climbed back into the car. It was a week-night, so there were only a few diners at the Continental Cafe, and all of them sat inside, out of the weather. The sidewalks were deserted, the streets virtually empty. No one had seen him. He hadn't called attention to himself.

The golem sat in the seat beside him. It looked as if Bentley had knocked the living sense out of the thing with the poker—whatever sense it ever had—and it stared out the window now as if it were drugged.

Since being blinded by the weird lamplight in the Stebbinses' shed, Argyle's vision had flickered in and out, and he wondered if he were working up to have a stroke, if that's what would get him. Was the alley as black as it seemed? The dead end couldn't be more than forty feet distant, but it was hidden in a shadow as black as ink. His ears rang with a leaden clanging sound, and very faintly he could hear what sounded like voices, weak and far away.

He opened a leather satchel on the seat and took out the tin box with the bird in it. It was a hell of an unlikely basket to have put all his eggs into, so to speak, and there was a solid chance that when he sent the golem down the alley, bird or no bird, it would do nothing but bump into the wall and fall over, which is pretty much what it had been doing for the past few hours.

There was the sound of footsteps on the sidewalk, and he looked up to see a man and woman walking arm and arm, heading toward the cafe. For a quick moment the woman looked just like Ivy, and he was full of a sudden shame, of the urge to hide the golem somehow, yank a sack over its head, ditch the bird in the jar, deny who and what he was and what had brought him to the mouth of this dark alley on a rainy winter night.

But it wasn't Ivy, and the two passed on by without even seeing him there. He closed his eyes for a moment, settling himself down again, clearing his mind. Then, seeing that the sidewalks were empty again, he unscrewed the jar lid, dipped two fingers into the liquid, and pulled the bird out by the tail, letting it drip onto the floor. The car was instantly full of the juniper smell of gin. The golem twitched, swiveling its head, looking out the side window at a passing car as if the creature had suddenly woken up. Good, Argyle thought. Something was stirring in it, some sense of purpose.

"It's time," he said. It was anybody's guess whether the creature understood anything at all, but he had fallen into the habit of speaking to it, like a person might speak to a goldfish in a bowl. He reached across, grasped its chin between his thumb and forefinger, yanked its mouth open so that its ivory teeth separated, and shoved the bird's head down its mouth.

"Eat it, god*damn* it!" he said. Then he pushed the golem's head back with the palm of his hand in order to open its throat. He knelt on the seat and pried its jaws open even wider, corkscrewing the bird, pinning the golem to the upholstery where it jerked and twitched, mumbling blue feathers out of its mouth, its eyes shifting back and forth like clockwork.

THE GOLEM STOOD IN FRONT OF THE CAR NOW, ITS FACE turned half toward him, illuminated in the light of the Merry Christmas sign. Its clothes were disheveled from the tussle over the bird, its hair wild, its eyes demented. He could barely stand to look at it, standing there stupidly, like some kind of horrible alter ego, the wreck he might have become if his life had gone differently, if he hadn't managed to pull himself up by his own bootstraps, if he had allowed himself to become like Murray LeRoy. . . .

A shudder ran through him, and he forced the thought away. "Go," he said out loud. "Go now."

Its jaw hung open, unhinged in the struggle, so that it looked as if it were gagging. There was a lump in its throat where the bird had lodged. Argyle had tried to massage it down, but the flesh of the thing's neck had started to tear like soft rubber, and he'd left it, unable to go on with the process. The golem took a step down the sidewalk, heading toward the cafe. Argyle started the car, shifting into drive, and looked around wildly. He couldn't let it wander off alone. It would have to meet its fate in the alley, whatever that fate might be. If he had to, he'd run the golem down, pin it against the wall, cripple it and drag it into the alley himself. . . .

It stopped suddenly, staggered, and turned around, looking up the alley now as if it had suddenly heard something there, a whispered command. Argyle fancied that he heard it, too. The voices in his mind grew louder, and he clamped his hands over his ears. But the sound was simply magnified, rising like a chorus. He squinted, rubbing his eyes to clear them. Shapes like the shadows of bats seemed to flutter in front of the window, and he thought he could hear the sound of their rushing wings. A wind sprang up, sweeping dead sycamore leaves from the alley floor, and a sheet of newspaper tumbled out of the darkness and burst into flames, falling on the hood of the car. There was a scattering of raindrops then, and Argyle switched on the wipers, hunching forward to watch as the golem slouched away into the darkness and was swallowed up by shadow. He waited for it to turn around, to come wandering back out again, and he put both hands on the steering wheel, ready to slam forward and knock it to Hell himself if he had to.

Then, with a startling suddenness, there was a flash of dazzling yellow light and what sounded like a human cry. The golem turned in slow circles, flapping its arms slowly, caroming off either wall of the alley, engulfed in flame. The fire was white, like a chemical fire, and Argyle could feel its heat, incredibly intense. The golem fell to its knees, then straight over onto its face, curling up on the ground like burning paper. It was over. The thing was dead. The voices in Argyle's head were silenced. He looked up at the Merry Christmas sign, but he felt nothing, no dark desires, no compulsions. He climbed out of the car and hurried back to the trunk, throwing it open and hauling out a fire extinguisher.

Out of the corner of his eye he saw people coming out of the cafe, hurrying forward. "Here!" he shouted stupidly, and ran to the mouth of the alley, squeezing the lever of the extinguisher. The rain beat down now, harder by the second, and he had the incredible urge to laugh out loud, to turn around and hose everyone down with the extinguisher. The golem was a heap on the ground, like a burning pile of trash, and the flames flickered lower, running up and down like witch fire across what had been the thing's back. There was a sighing noise, like wind through a grate, and the rain whirled around the burning corpse in a wild little vortex.

Argyle forced back his laughter, his joy. By God, he had done it!—deceived the Father of Lies, swindled the master swindler and got off scot-free. The Devil had taken it, lock, stock, and barrel.

❧ 70 ❧

"SOME KIND OF WINDFALL," LYLE BOYD SAID, DIPPING CAKE doughnuts into pans of frosting. "About a quarter of a million from what I heard. Her and her boyfriend headed straight for Honolulu, booked a room at the Royal Hawaiian. I don't guess she'll *ever* be back."

"What was it," Walt asked, "inheritance?"

"Something like that."

"How about her house over on Olive? She just lock the doors and go?"

"Realtor's selling it for her." Boyd scraped frosting off the big wooden breadboard with a spatula. "She'll make a couple of bucks there too. She owned that, you know."

"She *owned* it?" Walt said incredulously. "I had the idea she was just about broke, living on macaroni and cheese."

"Hell," Boyd said. "That's what she let on. She sold that place of hers in the Islands and outright *bought* the house here in town. Then she started to regret it right off. She was always pining away for the tropics. Anyway, I imagine she'll clear another hundred thousand on it, all told. She's a rich woman, at least by my standards."

"I'll be damned," Walt said, looking out the window at the cloudy afternoon sky. "I guess you never know."

"That's the truth."

A man and four kids came in the door just then, and Walt nodded at the man, then winked at one of the boys, who had to be about Nora's age. The boy's eyes shot open and he ducked behind his father, looking out at Walt from behind the man's leg.

Walt turned around and grinned at Henry, who tried to grin back, but couldn't. His face was full of trouble.

"What's wrong?" Walt asked. "You're not thinking about Maggie Biggs, are you? It's almost funny, the way she took us to the cleaners. And now she's dancing the hula with Don Ho. Bentley's going to drop dead when he hears about it."

Henry waved his hand. "I guess so," he said.

"What I wonder is where she got the money. I'll bet you a shiny new dime that she shook somebody down, and I'll bet you it was Argyle, too. She had something on him, her and Peetenpaul."

Henry nodded weakly. "I don't . . ." He stopped, gesturing helplessly.

"What's up?" Walt asked.

"I think I know how she got the money out of Argyle."

"How? She blackmailed him?"

"I guess you could say that."

"What gives, then? She didn't involve *you* in it, did she? She didn't leave you holding the bag and skip town?"

"No, not like that. Worse, I guess. She threatened to go to Jinx again. And more. I . . . I couldn't let her. I was afraid."

"So . . . ?"

"So I stole that damned bird of yours. You look in the tackle box and it won't be there."

Walt blinked at him. So that was it. "I guess you figured out that I'd gotten it back out of the Dumpster?"

"Next day. Maggie told me all about these men who wanted the bird—what they'd do to get it. To tell you the truth, I thought it was in the can anyway, so I played along. Then when it was gone, when I knew you'd gotten it out of the bin, I figured it had this . . . this *hold* over you, and somehow that gave me the right to steal it. That was wrong. None of us has any right to another man's possessions. We can make up whys and wherefores till the cows come home, but all of it's lies we tell ourselves to justify our sins. That's what I think. Anyway, I gave the bird to Maggie, and Maggie cut a deal with these men."

Walt nodded at him, thinking about this. As usual, Henry was right. "It was the wrong bird," Walt said to him.

"I beg your pardon?"

"You gave her a fake. The bird in the tackle box was a dead parakeet in a Mason jar. It was a dummy. The real bird's . . . I took care of the real one."

Henry sat there silently for a moment, thinking this out. "It hardly matters, morally speaking," he said finally. "I thought I was stealing the real McCoy. This doesn't make it right."

"Maybe not," Walt said, "but the way I see it, you tried to do the right thing, and more than once, too. I wish you *had* stolen the real one."

There was laughter behind them, and the man with the kids was pushing out through the door again. "I'd stay out of that alley, anyway," he said over his shoulder to Boyd, "unless you've got an asbestos suit." He laughed again, and the door swung shut behind them.

Boyd shook his head and squirted Windex on the top of the glass doughnut case. "How do you like that?" he said.

"What?" Walt waited.

"That guy that burned up in the alley last night? It was an effigy."

"A Fiji?" Henry asked, picking up his coffee cup. "Well, I'll be go to Hell. That's tough on an immigrant. They come over here looking for the American dream. . . ." He shook his head sadly. "Wasn't there a Samoan family over on Harwood Street? Big people, I seem to remember. I wonder if they knew this man, poor devil."

"I said an *effi*gy," Boyd told him. "A dummy. Fire department got there and apparently this thing was made up out of dirt and sticks and melted wax and crap like that. Patrick just told me it had a goddamn *bird* in its mouth. Some kind of prank, I guess."

"Sure sounds like it," Walt said. "Heading home?" he asked Henry.

"I think I'll sit for a while. I told Jinx I'd go Christmas shopping downtown. I'll have another cup of coffee first."

"I'll drop you."

"I can use the walk."

Walt stood up and drained his coffee cup. "I guess I better roll, then. I've got some unfinished business." He couldn't help thinking about what Argyle had said about rising out of the ashes like a phoenix. There was something unlikely in the picture. They didn't let just anybody be a phoenix. You had to qualify.

❧ 71 ❧

WALT FORCED THE SPADE DOWN INTO THE WET DIRT WITH his heel, digging out a wide hole. He didn't want to cut the bluebird in half. It wasn't his to cut. He shook the heavy clods off the shovel and knocked them apart, but there was no sign of the bird, so he dug out another shovelful. Still there was nothing. Maybe the bird was so dirty it didn't look like a bird any more. . . . He moved the loose dirt around in the hole. The bird *couldn't* be deeper. He was already down into soil that hadn't been turned over in years.

He rejected the first notion that came into his mind—that Argyle had come back and stolen it after all. He had found the shovel exactly where he'd left it, and the filled-in hole had looked as he remembered, tamped down with the shovel and then stomped on. He prodded around some more, working the shovel carefully, slicing away at the edges of the hole. A patch of dirt suddenly loosened and fell outward, exposing the mouth of a neat, round tunnel. A gopher hole! Apparently a gopher had dragged the bird away.

Getting down onto his hands and knees, he peered into the little tunnel, but it was perfectly dark and he could see nothing. He dug out another shovel of dirt, and then another, following the hole until it disappeared under his neighbor's garage. He hacked away at it sideways, under the old slab floor, more determined than ever to drag it out of there. He had never intended to leave it buried, and he was damned if he was going to let it hang around and demonize the neighbor's garage.

He threw the shovel down finally and went after the flashlight, fetching it outside where he knelt in the dirt again and shined the light into the hole. It ended a foot farther on. The bird lay jammed against the back end of the tunnel, as limp and dead-looking as ever, but shiny blue, as if the dirt wouldn't stick to it. There was no gopher to be seen, no outlet to the hole. The faint smell of gin hung in the air.

He was abruptly certain that nothing had dragged the bird into the tunnel. It had somehow burrowed its way under there itself, going somewhere under its own power. . . .

Its wing twitched suddenly, and there was a papery sound, like dry corn husks in a sack. Walt jerked backward, averting his face, fearful that the bird would fly out at him, that it would escape into the evening gloom like a demon out of Pandora's box. He crammed the flashlight into the hole, stopping it up, and went into the house after the fireplace tongs. He carried the tongs into the garage, where he found a nearly empty pint-size paint can. He pried the lid off and poured the paint out, then he hurried back outside, carrying the can and a hammer, and took the flashlight out of the hole. He felt around gingerly with the tongs until he found the bird. Carefully he dragged it out into the open and peered at it in the waning light.

It seemed to vibrate in the tongs, as if it were charged with an infernal energy, and its eyes were clear and bright and focused on Walt's face, as if it were as interested in him as he was in it.

A picture slowly formed in Walt's mind, like a flower opening up. He saw Maggie Biggs sitting in her suite at the Royal Hawaiian, looking out over Waikiki and sipping a Mai Tai, watching the afternoon waves reel in over the reef. A leather valise lay open on the hotel bed, neatly filled with bills. Mr. Peetenpaul stood on the balcony in his aloha shirt. Far beyond him, the steep green sides of Diamond Head rose against a sky as blue as the feathers of the bluebird itself. The lazy strains of Polynesian music, steel guitars and soft voices, drifted on the trade wind. There was the smell of blossoms on the air, as clear and heavy as if Walt wore a lei around his own neck.

He looked across at the tin shed, empty of anything but dry Christmas trees, at the garage with its pitiful inventory of gag gifts, and suddenly he saw himself crumpling up Argyle's check, throwing it out onto the lawn, paying heavily for his principles. The bluebird peered into his face. Its eyes were full of possibility, full of suggestion. There was the sound of thunder, a rumbling echo that went on and on.

Speak any wish, he thought, remembering the promise on the little bit of folded paper that had accompanied the thing. . . .

HE WAS STARTLED OUT OF HIS REVERIE BY THE SOUND OF bells, ringing out an evening hymn. Six o'clock. It was the bells at the Holy Spirit. It was raining again, and obviously had been. Somehow he hadn't noticed. And he was surprised to see that darkness had fallen, that his arms were weary from holding the tongs, which were clamped like a vise around the bluebird's neck.

"Go to Hell," he said to it.

Then he dropped the bird like a plumb bob into the paint can, set the lid over it, and pounded it down tight. He took it back into the garage, where he crisscrossed the lid with duct tape, then headed out toward the street to where the Suburban was parked. There was a thumping noise from within the can, as if the thing were angry, and he hammered it against the steering wheel a couple of times to shut it up. He started the engine, switched on the wipers and angled away from the curb, heading toward Argyle's house in the downpour.

❧ 72 ❧

ARGYLE LOOKED OUT THE WINDOW AT THE DARK STREET. Rain was falling again, heavily now. It was going to be a hell of a stormy night. Well, let it storm! He stepped across and put Edward Elgar on the stereo. Carrying the record jacket with him, he sat down in the chair that Bentley had torn up with the poker. When it came to music he still preferred vinyl to tape or compact disc, and over the years that his records had sat in their sleeves unplayed, he had kept them organized and perfectly shelved. Now he could play them again, by God, and he aimed to work through them steadily, savoring them, starting with "Pomp and Circumstance," which seemed somehow appropriate, given his success with the golem.

He felt like a new man. He *was* a new man. It was damned good to have the golem out of the house at last, to have this whole sorry episode finished. It was a brand-new day. He picked up a glass on the table, a piece of cut crystal with an inch of bourbon in the bottom. Bourbon was his one great vice, although he never allowed himself more than a single glass. Swirling the whiskey, he held it under his nose and breathed in the vapors, then set the glass back down onto the tiled tabletop without tasting it. There was plenty of time to drink it.

The strains of the music seemed to expand and fill the room. He smiled, recalling from down the years the first phrases of the piece, and he moved his hand like a conductor and bobbed his head, listening closely, thinking how the sound of the rain lent the music a certain something.

Then, abruptly, a pain shot across his forehead, and he closed his eyes and took his face in his hands. Thunder rattled the windows, then died away. The music sounded suddenly louder to him, as if the electricity in the storm had doubled the wattage. The pain passed, and he breathed deeply and gratefully. Clearly it was nothing. He set in to listen again, but the melody was slightly discordant now, slightly off-key. Of course, he hadn't heard it in years. . . .

The music seemed to swell, compressing the atmosphere in the room like air pumped into a tire. He could almost see the walls balloon outward, vibrating with the bass. The windows rattled in their frames, the glass panes humming like an insect swarm. He felt the pain in his head again, coming on more slowly this time, a mounting pressure at the back of his eyeballs, pushing at his forehead and temples as if his brain were swelling.

He fumbled for the bourbon glass, choked on the liquor, and spat it out, standing up out of the chair and slamming the glass back down onto the table. And then, to his horror, the liquor burst into flame in the glass, and the flames slipped down the outside and ignited the whiskey puddled on the tabletop. He slapped at it, splashing the burning liquor onto the rug, knocking the glass itself over. His hand was on fire! He beat it against the back of the chair now, stamping at the rug. The music was unbearable, chaotic, raucous, like a cage full of parrots. Smoke rose from the wool rug, and Argyle fell to his hands and knees and pounded at it, the scorched wool stinking in his nostrils. He clutched his head again and stumbled to his feet, reeling across toward the stereo cabinet, a deep moan pushing up out of his open mouth. He heard secret voices in the music now, clanking machinery, howls of inarticulate pain, and a deep thumping in the very foundation of the house, as if some mechanical beast were coming for him, as if at any moment the earth would open and swallow the house, dragging him down to Hell.

He knocked the tone arm off the record, and the abrupt silence nearly took his breath away. He saw clearly that something had gone wrong. The golem hadn't worked. He had been betrayed. Everyone had betrayed him—Stebbins, Peetenpaul, the Biggs woman, that goddamn Bentley. Even Ivy had betrayed him! The whole crowd of them had conspired to ruin him!

He realized suddenly that the silence wasn't complete. In the distance, from the tower at the Holy Spirit Church, came the sound of the evening bells. For God's sake, they were still hounding him! He pressed his hands against his ears, and the whole world seemed to him to vibrate like a tuning fork, like a church bell, vibrations that would shake him to atoms. He strode away through the house, howling to drown out the noise of the bells, moving from room to room, turning on lights, every light he could find. He talked out loud, reciting old poems he'd been forced to memorize in high school. He realized with a shock of long-overdue recognition that he was utterly alone. There was nobody to call, nobody to help. That had been true of Murray LeRoy when LeRoy had been consumed. And of Nelson, too. Nobody had given a damn for George Nelson's death—not even his so-called friends. Especially not his friends! Argyle walked back into the living room now, looking behind him at the empty rooms of his house, at the lonesome shadows in the corners.

He fell silent, listening. The bells had stopped, but that wouldn't last long. There was a scuffing sound outside, on the porch, and he saw something move beyond the curtained window in the door.

"Yes!" he shouted, unable to contain himself. He didn't care who it was, as long as it was company. Even Lorimer Bentley would do. He stepped eagerly across the carpet toward the door, putting his hand on the knob and throwing the door open wide to let in the night air.

But the porch was empty when Argyle opened the door and looked out, ready to welcome the world into his house. "Who is it?" he asked, peering out into the darkness beyond the glow of the porch lamp. "Who's there?" He stepped outside onto the porch.

Something moved in the shadows, out near the sycamore tree that shaded the lawn. A human figure stood there, hunched over like a beggar out of an old illustration. It was dressed in rags, its face turned away. "Get the hell out of here!" Argyle said to it. His voice shook. "I'll call the police!"

The man's head swiveled toward him, and for a moment, when they reflected the lamplight, his eyes glowed red. Argyle's breath caught. The man's jaw was broken, unhinged. His—its—flesh was charred, its clothing ragged and blackened.

It was the golem, reanimated, returned from whatever place it had gone.

The front door slammed shut behind Argyle, hard enough to shake the house. He flung himself around and grabbed the knob. It was locked. And his pockets were empty! His house keys were inside, the back door locked, the windows bolted.

He was swept with the utter certainty that the creature had come back to fetch him. Had been *sent* back.

From beyond the Plaza, the bells at the Church of the Holy Spirit tolled the hour.

Argyle sat down in the rattan porch chair and gripped the armrests. He would stay right there. Whatever the thing wanted of him, wherever it wanted him to go, it would have to force him. By God, it would have to carry him. And it would have a fight on its hands first! He'd go kicking and screaming.

The chair burst into flames beneath him, and he threw himself out of it, smelling the stink of burned hair. He swiveled around, hooking his leg through the armrest and dragging the burning chair away from the side of the house. His shoe caught fire, and he hopped away, kicking the chair down and pulling off his sweater, whipping his shoe with it to put the fire out. The sweater itself burst into flames, and he flung it away from him, screaming out loud. The golem remained slouched in the shadows beneath the tree, as if waiting patiently for Argyle to finish up his earthly antics so that the two of them could get down to the business at hand.

❧ 73 ❧

RAIN FELL OUT OF THE SKY LIKE THE END OF THE WORLD, running in a sheet down the windshield, so that even with the wipers on high speed Walt got only small, momentary glimpses of the road ahead of him as he turned off Maple Street onto Cambridge. A river of water six feet across rose over the curb on the low side of the street, flooding out onto lawns, and above the drumming of the rain he could hear the sound of thunder and, impossibly, the weather-muted sound of the bells of the Holy Spirit rising somehow above the tumult— melody in the chaos of weather.

The paint can on the seat beside him bounced and jiggled, as if it were full of jumping beans. For a moment it levitated above the seat, hovering two inches over the upholstery and vibrating like a can in a paint shaker. He could hear a beating sound from inside it again, a thumping against the walls, and suddenly the can leaped completely off the seat and banged into the dashboard, falling to the floor and rolling against the door panel where it lay still.

He spotted Argyle's house through the blur of rain, and he angled across toward the curb. Through the gray haze of the downpour he saw that something was burning on the front lawn. Argyle danced in front of it, trying to beat out the fire, slapping at his own shoes with his sweater.

Walt cut the engine and scooped up the paint can, climbing out of the Suburban and bending back into the car to haul out his umbrella, which he hoisted against the rain. The flames that engulfed the chair dwindled in the deluge as Walt hurried across the lawn to where Argyle stood clutching his forehead, his eyes wide like the eyes of a lunatic. He fell to his knees on the wet lawn and clasped his hands in front of him as if he had suddenly decided to say his prayers.

Walt tilted the umbrella so that it sheltered Argyle's face from the rain, and he wished suddenly that he had Ivy along. He was in over his head here. Argyle was a wreck, hardly sensible. Walt grabbed him by the arm and lifted, and he reluctantly got to his feet, slouching under the umbrella. Walt turned him and navigated through the rain toward the porch, and right then lightning flashed. There was a simultaneous crack of thunder, and the night lit up like noontime.

In the flash of light, Walt saw that someone stood beneath the dripping sycamore tree, a hunched ruin of a man dressed in rags. His eyes were rolled back into his head, and his jaw hung slack so that his mouth lolled open grotesquely. Walt shouted out loud in surprise as the night plunged into darkness again. Walt squinted, his eyes adjusting. There was enough porchlight shining through the rain and tree foliage that Walt could see that the man still stood there, unmoving.

Walt dragged Argyle forward now, propelling him up the porch steps, under the eaves. "Who the hell is *he*?" Walt asked. Rain hammered the porch roof and sluiced out of the downspouts. The street was very nearly a river now, and water lapped at the porch steps of the houses across the street.

"That's my *soul*," Argyle said. He shivered, wrapping his arms around himself. Walt could hear his teeth chatter.

"Let's go inside." Walt tried the door, not waiting for Argyle to voice his opinion. "Door's locked."

"Of *course* it is."

"Where's the key?"

"Locked inside. It's no good. He won't let me in. It's over."

"Who won't let you in? *That* character?"

The paint can thumped hard, jerking in Walt's hand. He set it down on the porch and stepped on it.

"No, not *that* thing. I've sold my soul to the Devil, and now I've got to pay up. Don't tell me Bentley's kept this a secret from you."

"What about the phoenix?" Walt asked, trying to not get mad.

"What?"

"Rising out of the ashes," Walt said. "Like you were talking about yesterday."

"I got a reprieve," Argyle said. "But it didn't last."

"Well, listen," Walt said. "I've got something to confess."

"You want Bentley for that—him or the priest from the Holy Spirit. I'd suggest the priest."

"The bird that you bought from Maggie Biggs . . ." Walt said.

"What's he *doing*?" Argyle's voice was suddenly shrill. He jerked forward as if tugged by an invisible rope.

The creature under the tree had stepped out onto the sidewalk. Walt saw what it was now; it was the thing that Bentley had described to him, the golem, the effigy that Lyle Boyd said had burned in the alley last night. The creature had apparently come back from the dead, or from wherever it had been. It moved away down the sidewalk, and Argyle went down the steps as if to follow it.

"Wait!" Walt said, picking up the paint can and following him out into the rain, putting up the umbrella again. "Let it go. To hell with it."

Argyle ignored him, moving off at a pace identical to that of the golem, the two of them drawn inexorably toward the distant boulevard.

Walt hurried up behind Argyle and kept up with him, sharing the umbrella. "The bird that Biggs sold you was the wrong one," he said. "It was a dead parakeet I got from the Sprouse Reitz. Same color blue."

Argyle groaned. "I'm finished," he said. "Tell Ivy . . ."

"I've got the real one right here." Walt held up the paint can, which flew out of his grasp at that moment and clanked down onto the sidewalk, the rain beating on it as it hopped and jittered there. Walt scooped it up and tucked it under his arm, holding onto it tightly.

Argyle looked at him hard now, his mouth half open in disbelief. "That's a lie," he said, not breaking his stride. He licked his lips, and his eyes darted toward the paint can. Ten paces ahead of them the golem stepped down off the curb, into the floodwaters that flowed down Maple Street, and headed for the opposite shore.

"No it's not," Walt said. "It's the bluebird. If I told you

any lies about it before, I'm sorry. I shouldn't have. It was wrong. But you were, too, of course.''

"What do you want for it?" Argyle asked flatly. He looked ahead again, matching the golem's shambling stride. "Anything. There's no time to haggle. Name it."

"Nothing."

"Damn it!" Argyle said. "This is life and death! This is sal*vat*ion.''

"This is *not* salvation," Walt shouted. "This is the opposite of that." There was another lightning flash, and the figure of the golem was thrown into sharp clarity against the rainy night. The lightning seemed to glow straight through the thing's flesh and torn clothing, as if it were made of cheesecloth or cobweb.

"A million dollars."

"No! For God's sake, Bob, open your eyes."

"Name it. Whatever you want. Say the word and it's yours.''

"Damn it! No! Get it through your . . .''

"Do you think I'm joking, Walt? Are you a goddamn self-righteous moron?"

"Joking!" Walt realized that Argyle was weeping openly now, his face contorted with it. Here he was talking like the Devil himself, and out of fear of the Devil! There was a noise from ahead of them, as if the golem had moaned out loud, and Walt wondered what would happen if he sprinted ahead and just tackled the bastard, stuffed it down the storm drain, shoes and all. He watched it step up onto the curb at the opposite side of the intersection, and, just as it did, Argyle stepped down into ankle-deep water, following in the thing's wake, stepping where it had stepped. Walt kept pace with him, and they waded to the curb and up onto the sidewalk again. Clearly the golem was moving toward the Plaza, bound for the alley behind Nelson and Whidley.

Across Chapman Avenue the bell tower at St. Anthony's rose into the sky. Dark sheets of rain slanted across the pale stucco walls. The curved base of the fallen bell was visible through the hole it had broken in the tower. Walt saw Argyle look at it, shut his eyes, and turn his head away.

"I heard that Mrs. Simms is giving the fund-raiser money to the church," Walt said to him. "All of it. In order to restore the tower. Can you beat that?"

"I didn't mean to kill Simms."

"I didn't say you did. I was just saying that . . ."

"Give it to the children," Argyle said.

"What? Give what? What the hell are you talking about?"

"The money. Take the money I'm offering to you and give it to the children, to Nora and Eddie. Put it in a trust fund, for God's sake, and they'll never have to worry about money for the rest of their lives. Do it for them if you won't do it for yourself. You *owe* me, Walt. We go back a long way. I screwed up bad back then, and I'm paying for it now, any way I can. So just let me make amends a little bit, will you? Go ahead and do it for the kids. Or are your principles so high and mighty that you'd take the money out of their hands, too?"

Walt looked away, muddled by the thought of it. Argyle's money could make all the difference in the world to Nora and Eddie—no hardships, no sweat. Did he have any *right* to turn something like that down, just on principle?

"A million dollars?" Walt asked, calculating what that would be worth, put out at interest—enough for a private college, a big house on Easy Street.

"That's right. What's wrong, not enough? You want more? Ten million?"

They were passing the back of Walt's own house now, one street away, and over the garage roof of the nearby house he could see the enormous shadow of the avocado tree where Mr. Argyle the daddy longlegs lived. Used to live.

"No," Walt said to him. "There's not a thing that I want, not that you could give me. And there's nothing very high and mighty about my principles. They're small principles, but they're mine, and right now I'm in a mood to hang onto them."

Argyle laughed out loud, but it wasn't a convincing laugh. They were approaching the corner of the street. The golem would turn right and head downtown, where it had an appointment with destiny. Walt determined to stick it out, to see this thing through, even though by now Ivy would be wondering where he'd gone. Jinx would be cooking dinner. The kids would be goofing around, coloring or playing Uncle Wiggly. Henry was probably out in the motor home with the space heater running, eating Cheez-Its, warm and dry and listening to the rain on the roof like another man would listen to music.

"Take it," Walt said, and he handed Argyle the paint can. "It belongs to you anyway. That's why I brought it over to your house instead of throwing it into the ocean. If you want my opinion about it, though, about all your little tricks here, I'll give it to you along with the can."

For a moment Argyle was silent. Trudging along, soaked to the skin, he looked at Walt in apparent disbelief, as if being given the can had taken him utterly by surprise. Then Walt heard him mumble the word "Thanks." After a few more steps he said, "I guess I already know your opinion."

"Well, I'm going to give it to you anyway. That thing in the can there, that's not salvation. If it were *my* bluebird, I'd throw it out, just like Henry told me to do."

The street was a river of rushing water, curb to curb, and the windy rain swept across it in flurries, reminding Walt of a monsoon. They passed the last house on the block, and moved out into the wind that blew along Chapman Avenue. Away to the west, the lights of the Plaza shimmered and winked through the rainy dark, and Walt could see the enormous white bulk of the cellophane snowman next to the Plaza fountain, waving up the avenue toward them, as if it were happy to see them out and about on a night like this.

St. Anthony's Church was lit up inside, and the stained-glass windows shone in a hundred different hues, illuminating a window-shaped curtain of falling rain. From somewhere within came the sound of the choir, hushed by the weather and by the wood and plaster walls of the old church building.

Argyle's step faltered at the corner. He jerked to a stop, went on a couple paces, and stopped again. He looked around then, puzzled, like a sleepwalking man just shocked into wakefulness. The golem stood still, waiting, staring toward the Plaza. A car drove past on the street, its tires singing on the wet asphalt, and the driver looked at Walt and waved, although Walt didn't recognize him—probably it was just the season, and he was waving for no reason at all except some sudden impulse toward friendliness.

Argyle held the paint can in both hands and stood staring at it, as if he were reading the label. And just then the wind died, making an odd creaking sound like a door opening, and Argyle threw his hands into the air like Moses smashing the tablets. He stood just so for a scattering of seconds and then hurled the paint can straight down into the flooded gutter, where it sank beneath the current.

The earth shook, and Walt staggered sideways toward the curb, grabbing onto the streetlamp to keep from falling, and in the same instant a bell began to ring, so loudly that he let go of the lamppost and pressed his hands over his ears. A flock of pigeons rose from the ruined bell tower at St. Anthony's, flying straight into the sky, where the clouds parted to reveal a wash of stars and an enormous moon. Walt realized that it was the fallen bell that was ringing, perhaps reverberating from the shock of the earthquake, its impossibly clear tones soaring out over the neighborhood.

The paint can surfaced and bobbed away on the tide, swept toward the open mouth of a storm drain through which the floodwaters rushed in a cascading torrent. In a moment the demon and the can it lived in were swallowed up, delivered into the subterranean river that would carry it to the ocean, gone out of Old Towne, out of their lives.

THE TOLLING OF THE BELL FADED, AND THE NIGHT FELL SILENT. Walt watched Argyle, who had his face in his hands now and was standing still. The golem lay in a heap on the wet sidewalk, its face staring up at the moon.

"I'll be damned," Walt said finally. "I think it's dead. It'll miss its appointment now."

"I guess I will, too," Argyle said. He put out his hand, and Walt shook it.

Together they walked over to the golem. Its wreck of a face bore little resemblance to Argyle's any longer, and it lay limp and decrepit, an old mummy left out in the weather. Argyle nudged it with his foot, pushing it toward the gutter. Walt joined him, and together they slid the thing off the curb and into the torrent. It rolled away toward the storm drain, turning over in the flood before it slid headfirst beneath the sidewalk and vanished, its head compressing like a wet bag, moonlight glinting for one last moment on the soles of its worn-out shoes.

THEY STOOD IN THE SILENCE, LISTENING TO THE NIGHT, TO the palm fronds rustling in the curbside trees. The choir started up again inside the church, and the rain fell off and then stopped entirely. Walt furled the umbrella, looped the fastener around it, and buttoned it.

"I guess I'll head home," Argyle said to him at last.

"Your door's locked, isn't it?"

"I'm not sure. Maybe it's not locked at all. Not any more."

"Come on over to our place," Walt said, although he realized that he still didn't like the idea of an evening with Robert Argyle very much at all, which he knew was uncharitable. He'd have to work on that. Probably there would always be something to work on.

"I guess I won't."

"Nonsense. Come on over and have a bite to eat. Nora and Eddie would love it. You know what Nora calls you?"

He shook his head.

"Mr. R-Guy."

Argyle smiled, and Walt smiled back at him.

"She's a case, isn't she?" Walt asked. "She'd like to see you. What do you say?"

"It's . . ." He shrugged.

"Plenty of room at the inn," Walt said. "It's Christmas. It's the best time of the year to let bygones be bygones. We might as well start tonight."

"Some bygones can't be forgotten," Argyle said. "This business with Mr. Simms . . ."

"There's tomorrow for that. Tonight we both need dry clothes and something to eat."

Argyle stood looking at him for a moment, then said, "Okay, then."

They walked up toward Oak Street and turned the corner, heading home. Walt could see his house halfway down the block. Ivy had strung the candy-cane lights around the porch. The light was on in the motor home, and Henry's profile was silhouetted against the curtain. What was he doing, Walt wondered, working on the popes? Reading Hefernin?

"I guess I better warn you that Henry's got a business proposition for you," Walt said.

"For me?"

"I think you can count on hearing about it before the evening is through."

"I'm not in business like I used to be. I guess you know that. I did some things. . . ."

"Bygones, Bob. This plan of Henry's is different from the kind of thing you're talking about, whatever that is. This is some novelty items that Henry's cooked up, and he wants me to go in partners. He's convinced we'll make our fortune in Japan. What he's looking for is investors, start-up cash. You'd better be ready for him."

"This wouldn't be the popes, would it?"

"You know about the popes?"

"Sidney Vest told me about it. Surefire moneymaker, he said."

"Good old Sidney Vest," Walt said uneasily.

"I'm surprised he didn't jump on it himself. I always say that when opportunity knocks, you answer the door dressed to go out."

"If I didn't know better," Walt said, giving him a narrow look, "I'd guess you've read Aaron Hefernin."

"*Read* him?" Argyle said back to him. "I *am* Aaron Hefernin."

Walt heard a child's laughter then, unmistakably Nora's, and she and Eddie both appeared from behind the motor home, carrying open umbrellas and followed by Ivy and Jinx, just come down off the porch for the evening walk. Nora shouted and ran on ahead, and Walt tossed his own umbrella onto the lawn. Dropping to one knee on the wet sidewalk, he opened his arms to catch her.